THE SUMMONED MAGE

BOOK ONE OF CONVERGENCE

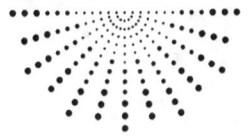

MELISSA MCSHANE

Night Harbor Publishing

Cover design by 100 Covers https://100covers.com

AUTHOR'S NOTE

The Summoned Mage begins with Book Six. This is not a mistake, and you're not missing anything; it will be explained almost immediately.

A glossary and pronunciation guide appear at the end of this book.

PART I
BOOK SIX

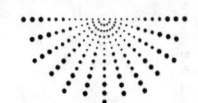

CHAPTER ONE

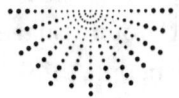

13 Senessay

I'm going to try again tonight.

If I'm wrong, this could be my first and last entry in this new book, the sixth record of my travels through Balaen and beyond. Probably will be my last entry, considering how that last test left me pissing red for a week. But I think I know what I did wrong, and I feel pretty confident. Mostly confident. Terrified. No one's ever going to read this, and I'm not sure why I keep writing, except to have someone to talk to, even if it's myself. I hope that doesn't mean I'm going mad.

I don't even know if these preparations matter. None of the ancient writers agreed on anything, and they all swore by their own methods. Fast for twelve hours. Sit by a puddle of water in which the moon is reflected and meditate. Burn three kinds of incense. Take off all your clothes—I'm definitely not doing that, even if I *am* the only one around. The best I could do was find common threads and then use my instincts. That's something they all *did* agree on, that magic comes from who you are, at the core, and all this incense and water and fasting and nudity are supposed to make you more yourself. Or something. Anyway, I need this pouvra, and I'm willing to try anything at this point.

Maybe I am mad. Any one of these pouvrin I've learned could get me executed, if I wasn't torn apart by a frenzied mob first. It's hard to believe there was ever a time when magic wasn't feared, but I've found all these stories that say there was. Maybe I should have taken up a career as a traveling tale-teller; it would be less dangerous. Though with the kind of stories I've learned, I'd probably be just as likely to get killed if I went around suggesting maybe magic isn't as evil as all that. I can see why people think it is.

The pouvrin I've learned are frightening—I can summon fire, or water, and I can see through things, and I can walk through walls, though I've only done that once and I'm afraid to try it again. Suppose I went solid in the middle of something? And if I do this new pouvra right, I'll be able to make things move without touching them. I hurt myself trying, last time, but—I'm stalling now, aren't I, writing things I already know? No sense putting it off any longer. If I can make this work, they'll never be able to trap me again.

13 Senessay (later)

It worked. I made the bunk in the corner lift off the ground and I didn't even tear my insides, though my arms hurt afterward as if I'd used them instead of the pouvra. Then I practiced working the barn door lock, which was harder because I had to picture what it feels like to use the picks on it—I still can't look inside things instead of through them, though I haven't given up on that. Eventually I could lock and unlock it with the new pouvra faster than I ever did with lock picks. Of course, the lock is probably a hundred years old, so it wasn't exactly difficult—I'll have to try again on something more finicky.

I can't help remembering being caught in Wirstan for stealing that stupid woman's purse, and how they would have shut me away for good if I hadn't found a couple of skinny iron nails to pick the lock with. No more worries about having my tools taken away!

I'm feeling low, the way I always do after I learn a new pouvra. It's as if I put so much of myself into figuring it out, then learning to bend my will to the magic, that everything else feels like a disappointment. There's still time to sleep before dawn, when I'll have to move out again. This barn smells musty, and the hay is stale and prickly, so I assume it's been abandoned for a while, but I don't want to take the chance that someone will come along and want to know what I'm doing here. People on the borders of Balaen don't trust travelers (how well I know that!) or even anyone who comes from anywhere more than half a day's walk from their home. And I've come so much farther than that.

This is also the time when I wonder if I wouldn't have been happier staying in Thalessa, working at the fishery, which was awful but at least it was steady work. But that lasts about two seconds before I remember the stench of fish guts, and the tiny hovel I could never keep clean, and Mam getting drunk all the time and then begging me to forgive her, over and over again. I couldn't have stayed, anyway, not once this magic took me over and I started doing things I couldn't keep hidden. Besides...

I was going to write "it's beautiful" but that's wrong. It's powerful and terrifying and when I use one of the pouvrin it fills me to bursting, and I wouldn't give that up for anything, however dangerous it might be. But it's not beautiful.

Sleep, now. I haven't decided where to go next. Maybe Barrekel, it's nearly harvest time and they could probably use some hands out at those big plantations. I'll need to start saving for the winter.

14 Senessay (maybe)

I've managed to keep this book hidden so far. I don't know where to start or what happened. Maybe learning the new pouvra did something, because it's too big a coincidence otherwise. Everything hurts, not just my arms but the whole rest of my body, and my stomach feels like I'm going to throw up again, though they haven't fed me since I did. The door is locked, but when I try to use the new pouvra to pick it, my body aches more. I can't focus. I need to start at the beginning.

I think it was nearly dawn when I woke feeling like I needed to take a piss. So I got up, but I felt as if I were stretching like taffy at a carnival, like part of me was still stuck to the ground and the rest of me was being pulled away from it. That made me think I was dreaming, but I've never dreamed so real before, and my arms still hurt, which I didn't think happened in dreams. And I still felt this need, though by this time I could tell it wasn't my bladder; it was just this steady pull, and it was starting to hurt.

So I let it pull me for a bit, thinking it might hurt less if I didn't fight it. The air looked thick, like heat waves only sideways to the ground, and when I turned around I saw they surrounded me and even went through me. That was when I panicked. I ran for the door, but it was like wading through the tide, only hot and dry and stronger than any tide off Thalessa ever was. I tried swimming and I tried going in other directions, but it didn't matter, it just kept pulling me away from wherever I tried to go.

That was about when the sun rose, at least that's what I thought, but the light was more blue than pinkish gold. It was as if the sun were rising backwards out of twilight, is the best I can describe it. Wherever the light touched me, coming through those tiny barn windows, it burned. I think I went a little mad, there, because I remember screaming and not much else, and the burning got worse and the tide got stronger and then it was all gone, and I was here.

Not here as in this room. Some other place in this...I don't know if it's a building or a cave, because the place I—might as well say "arrived"—in was hollowed-out stone, but this room seems to be constructed. That is, the walls are made of finished stone blocks, but the floor is the same rough stone as in the large chamber...anyway, it doesn't matter, because either way I'm locked in here. But that comes later.

I couldn't see anything at first. My eyes were blind, the way you get when you stare at a fire too long. I could tell I was lying on a cold stone floor that wasn't very smooth, and the air smelled of scented smoke, like incense, woody and sweet, and the tide was roaring in my ears. That faded quickly, and my eyes adjusted, and that's when I realized I was in a cave, an enormous cave, and there was no tide anywhere. So I'm not sure where the sound came from. Probably not important. More important was that there were people all around me, standing about twenty feet away in a rough circle, and none of them looked very friendly.

I panicked again and summoned fire in a circle surrounding me, which made them all step back fairly fast and start talking, words I couldn't understand over the sound of the fire. I stood up and tried to breathe normally, though the heat of the fire made my mouth and eyes dry. The people gradually calmed down and were watching me again, like they were waiting to see what else I would do. That made the panic rise again. The pressure of maintaining a fire with no fuel made my chest ache, worse than all the other pains, but I pushed on because I didn't know what *they* would do if it wasn't defending me.

But eventually I couldn't keep it up anymore, not to mention the heat was making me dizzy. The cave was absolutely silent when I let the fire go out. I turned in a circle, trying hopelessly to keep them all in sight, and I shouted something like "Leave me alone! Why did you bring me here?"

The people—I forgot to say they were all dressed in these knee-length pale gray wraparound robes with wide sleeves over black trousers, men and women both, and they all wore their hair shoulder length or longer, tied back from their faces. They were almost completely expressionless, and combined with how alike they were, it was damned unsettling, like looking at a ring of dolls. One of them who didn't look any different from the others took a step forward, holding out his hand like I was some kind of mad dog he was trying to calm. He said something, and it made me panic and bring up the fire again, because I didn't understand the language he was speaking. Not even enough to know which one it was.

That was when someone grabbed me from behind, and I lost control of the fire and it went out. I fought, but more people took hold of me, until I couldn't move anything but my head, and that's when I threw up, all over myself and them, which made some of them start yelling. I know I was screaming at them, but I can't remember what I said, and they were shouting at me in that unknown language, which made me fight harder, not that it mattered. Then they half-carried, half-dragged me to this room, threw me inside, and locked the door.

I don't think it's meant to be a cell. The light comes from a glass basket hanging from the ceiling by a silver chain. The basket has interesting patterns engraved in it, but I can't take a closer look because staring at the light makes me feel like I'm going blind. It's clearly not fire, because it doesn't smell like anything and it doesn't flicker or feel hot, but I have no idea what it could be instead. It has to be magic. There are a couple of chairs that are more like padded cylinders with no backs, and a woven, gritty-feeling mat on the floor, but more importantly, the walls are painted. As in, pictures directly painted on the walls. The strange thing is they're made to look like windows, showing blue sky and grassy fields dotted with flowers.

They're very realistic—so realistic I tried to open one. That was actually the third thing I did, after trying to open the door and taking off my vomit-stained jacket. I wadded it up and put it in the corner, but the room still smells of vomit. Nothing I can do about that. Then I tried seeing through the door, but that made my head feel as if someone poured molten iron into it, so I gave up on that.

So now I've explored every corner of the room, and I'm writing all of this down. I'm guessing they'd take this book away from me if they knew about it. I wonder if they can speak my language? Probably not, or they would have done by now, if only to say "stop setting things on fire."

Strange. It's only just occurred to me to wonder why they didn't try to kill me when they saw I can work magic. They were upset and surprised, yes, but nothing more. That, and the strange language, and the fact that there aren't any caves that size for a thousand miles in any direction from where I spent last night, suggests I'm a long way from where I started. It also suggests it was these people and not the pouvra that brought me here. Maybe they're not afraid of magic because they work it themselves. But I've never read about a pouvra that could move a person between places instantly. If they've figured that out...but I can't do anything about that.

What I can do is try to get out of this room and find a real window, or a door, or something that will tell me where I am. I've traveled a good many miles in the last ten years and seen a lot of places; maybe I'll recognize it. I'll try the mind-moving pouvra again, and then...I guess I'll figure that out when I come to it. That's my least favorite kind of plan.

Still 14 Senessay, probably (though without the sun, who can tell?)

Well, *that* was a waste of time. And it started so well, too.

The mind-moving pouvra worked, which was a relief. It's so new to me that after the first failure, I was afraid I'd lost the ability to use it at all, and I didn't want to be trapped in here. The lock was strange, with tumblers that moved not at all the way I'm used to, and I would've bet I knew every kind of lock there was, after all these years of opening them. If it hadn't been for the mind-moving pouvra, I might not have been able to open it at all, even with my tools, which got left behind with my pack in that old barn.

I used the see-through pouvra on the door, which makes a two-foot-wide hole in whatever I'm looking through—not really a hole, it only seems like it, and I'm the only one who can tell it's there. It's too bad it's not a real hole, or I could stick my head through it and look around, but as it was I could only see the stone of a wall opposite. So I opened the door a crack and peeked out, and saw nothing but an empty stone hall lined with metal doors, extending away from me in both directions. The doors were ordinary smooth metal, which told me wherever this country is, it's at about the same level of development as Balaen. Though the only places in Balaen where I've seen metal doors are jails, which is not a comforting thought.

I'm more and more convinced this place is underground, which I'm trying not to think about. It's not that I'm claustrophobic, just that I can't stand the idea of all those tons of stone hanging over my head, waiting to crush me. I listened, and heard some distant noises coming from the right, though nothing I could identify. I decided to go left instead. The whole place reminded me of breaking into the Sendesstal about four years ago, looking for that tome that turned out to be a collection of cooking recipes—the hall is dark, and it curves like a snake so you can't see if someone's coming until you're right on top of them. Which is what happened to me.

I don't know if it's all the gray-robes or just the one woman, but she was wearing sandals that made no noise on the stone floor, and I came around a curve of the hall and walked right into her. She dropped the wooden tablet she was carrying and staggered; it cracked in half when it hit the floor. I know I was moving near-silently myself, so she was as startled as I was. More so, actually, because she didn't expect to see me and I was prepared to see someone like her. I set the hem of her gray robe on fire and I ran.

I meant it as a distraction, but I shouldn't have started the fire— she started screaming, which meant I had to find a hiding place fast. So I ducked into the first room I passed—it wasn't locked—and then I ducked back out *fast*, because the couple in that room were mostly naked and they started shouting at me too, even before they realized I wasn't one of their kind. I ran for the next door, and that room was empty, so I shut the door behind me and stood there until my breathing and heart rate were back to normal.

People were running down the hall and shouting things in their language, but no one came in. That was no comfort. At some point they were going to start a methodical search of the rooms, and I needed to be out of this corridor trap before then. So I looked around to see if there was anything in my hidey-hole I could use.

It had window paintings like the room I'd started in, but this room was a bedchamber, with a very narrow and long bed covered with a couple of white sheets, no blankets. There was another one of those glass baskets lighting the room, and a dresser with three drawers and a wardrobe beside it. None of the furniture matched; the bed frame was made of wrought iron, the dresser was white oak, and the wardrobe looked like walnut. The floor had no rug, not even one of those gritty mats, and I couldn't help thinking what it would be like to climb out of bed barefoot onto that cold stone floor.

I rooted around in the dresser and wardrobe and immediately found the gray robe I was hoping for. Its sleeves were smudged with pale colors, pink and green and blue, with the occasional darker gray mark, and I hoped this wouldn't set me apart from the others. No black trousers, but my own trousers are dark gray and I figured they could pass for black long enough to get me outside. I tied my hair back—this is probably how he caught me, most of them have black or dark brown hair, much darker than my own muddy blonde—and slipped out of the room, then headed in the direction I'd been going before.

At first I thought it would work. There were more people in the hallway, but everyone was so agitated, they weren't really looking at one another, and I wasn't challenged or even looked at properly. I kept a concerned look on my face and moved quickly, and after only a minute or so I emerged from the hallway and found myself back in the chamber I'd arrived in.

I wish I'd had time to thoroughly examine it, because it's about three hundred feet across and maybe a hundred feet tall, and there are three levels to it, with ramps between the levels. The two higher levels have rails surrounding these ledges that go all the way around the cavern (I have to call it a cavern now, it's clear that's what it is) and there are lighted openings that lead off those ledges. But that was all I had time to observe.

I swerved left and followed the curve of the cavern, looking for a door. By now there were a lot of people running around, stopping to talk to each other in excited voices, so I kept my head down and kept moving. I saw many, many wooden workbenches and stools, most of them with those thin wooden boards lying on them as if their owners had abandoned them in a hurry, which was probably true.

The walls of the cavern were rough all the way to the ceiling, but they had been perfectly smoothed from the floor to a height of about seven feet, and there were words (I guess words) and little pictures drawn all over them in chalk. Some had been rubbed out and written over. It reminded me of Kerrek Hetessar's house, the room where his children were educated. Lucky children. I learned to read from smutty pamphlets and to write with a stick in the sand. Not that I'm bitter about that. At least I can read, which is more than most of the poor of Thalessa can say.

Anyway. I circled the room until I reached another corridor. My instinct is that it was the other end of the corridor I'd come from, and if that turns out to be wrong, I'm going to feel very stupid. But I passed the corridor, still trying to look as if I belonged, when I heard someone saying—well, I don't know what the words were, obviously, but they were clearly a command. And then someone grabbed my wrist and twisted my arm up behind my back. I fought for a bit, but the man had a grip like a clocker crab and twisted harder until I yelped and gave up.

Several other people ran up to us, and the man started talking in a more normal voice, but he sounded so...sarcastic, I suppose, and I didn't need to understand his words to know that. I suppose sarcasm sounds the same in every language. He pushed me toward two men, and I managed to get half a step away before they grabbed me, but it was enough that I could turn and look at the bastard who'd caught me.

He's got the sort of face it's easy to hate, that smooth, arrogant look that says he knows he's better than you, and I probably should have burned that look off his face, but I still can't bring myself to burn actual flesh, no matter how I'm threatened. His hair is almost black, and although he wore it pulled back like everyone else, there were strands of it falling over one shoulder, like he'd been running. That made me feel better, knowing he wasn't as unruffled as he seemed.

He kept talking in that sarcastic voice, and I could tell by the way their hands trembled that the men who were holding me, at least, were cringing under his sarcasm. Then he switched his attention to me. His eyes startled me, because they're the same strange green-gray color as mine, and I've seen that only rarely in my travels. They were also perfectly indifferent to me, enough that I felt like cringing myself. Instead I stood up straight and glared at him, and said, "I'm going to escape this place, and if I can make you look like a fool when I do it, I'll celebrate."

He kept looking at me, and then he raised one eyebrow—how do people do that?—and said something to me that of course I didn't understand, then made a dismissive gesture, and the men holding me marched me away. I didn't fight back—I had a feeling it would make me look weak in front of the smug git. And now I'm back in my not-really-a-cell again. I'm starting to feel hungry, which is making it harder for me to maintain my calm. I don't know what they want from me, but it can't be anything good.

CHAPTER TWO

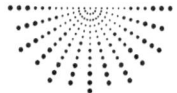

15 Senessay (I think)

I'm calling it tomorrow because the light went out at some point, and I finally fell asleep on the horrible gritty mat, and when I woke I felt better. Rested, at least. Two of them came in before that and grabbed my arms, and marched me down the hall to one of the interminable doors, which turned out to be some kind of commode. There was a porcelain basin like the ones I've seen in some of the big manors, only this one didn't have water sitting in the bowl, it had water flowing through it so it was constantly cleaning itself. I was glad to see it, because I had a pressing need to piss and there wasn't anywhere in my cell I could relieve myself. So *someone* is thinking of my needs, at least on that level.

They brought me food before I slept, and also took away the gray robe, though it's not like I could make that deception work twice. The food was a couple of slices of a dark bread I'd never tasted before and a bowl of thick, spicy red soup with beans and some grain that looked like wild rice, only white and bland. It was filling and strange, and if I didn't know I was in some other country before, I'd be sure of it now. Food is one of the things that varies most between places. I'm trying not to be worried that I don't recognize it, because that means I am definitely far from home, and I don't know how I'll get back.

Though—I wrote that, and then I wondered why it would matter. It's not as if I have ties to any of the places I've visited since I left Thalessa ten years ago. Not that I'd want to stay here, prisoner or no, but who knows what kind of pouvrin I might find in this far-off place? And that's really all I care about, giving this magic inside me space to grow. Who knows? If When I get out of here, I might find a country in this area where magic isn't illegal. *That* would be a place I could settle in.

I may have done something stupid, though. After I woke this morning, I decided to make another try to escape—not really escape so much as to see what kind of weaknesses I could exploit. So I used the mind-moving pouvra to unlock the door, and pushed it open a crack—and there were two women standing right outside the door, like guards. They looked surprised to see me poking my head out, and one of them started talking at me, very agitated. I shut the door as quickly as possible. About two seconds later I heard the door lock again, and more talking, muffled by the door. They were definitely having an argument. Then I heard some bumping, and a scrape, and I'm pretty sure at least one of them is leaning against the door right now. So they know I have a way to open locks. They're almost certainly going to keep a closer eye on me now. Damn it.

I wonder what they make of me. I wonder why they brought me here. It feels as if I took them by surprise, which is strange considering they must have put some effort into summoning me, or whatever it was they did. Maybe it was an experiment they didn't expect to succeed. Or maybe they were expecting something or someone else. But if that's so, why didn't they just send me back? Because they're certainly doing their best to keep me from leaving.

I don't

That was close. I was in the middle of writing that sentence when the door started to open, and I barely got this book tucked away in my trousers' deep pocket when one of the gray-robes came in, cautiously, like he was afraid I might set him on fire. Which is a reasonable fear. I was sitting on the floor—those cushioned cylinders aren't very comfortable—and he looked down at me and didn't say anything. He was several inches taller than me and had a pleasant face, round blue eyes, and brown hair in a tail that fell to his waist, and despite his caution, he didn't seem afraid of me, just a little worried.

He said something and held out his hand to me. I could see his sleeves were as smudged as the ones on the robe I'd stolen, but I don't know what that means yet; it's just strange that they'd wear such a light color if whatever they do all day makes them so dirty. I crossed my arms over my chest and glared at him, and he let his arm drop and said something else. Then he came all the way into the room and shut the door behind him, which I thought was brave of him, and that made me less angry. I'm not sure why.

He said something that sounded like a question, and made a motion like "get up" with his hands, then repeated it. It was such a polite gesture I stood and brushed off my ass from where the floor grit had clung to me. I probably look awful. Not that I care what these people think of me.

He smiled when I stood, which made him look almost handsome —I think "pleasant" is the best he can hope for—pointed at his chest, and said a word. It took me a second to realize he was telling me his name. (I hope that's what he was telling me. It might have been a title, or their word for "chest," but it makes more sense that it was his name.) So I repeated it back to him, "Terrael" (I don't know how to spell it, so I'm going to write it the way it sounds in my language) and he smiled really big and nodded vigorously and said it back to me.

Then he pointed at me, so I said "Thalessi Scales" and pointed at myself, even though I think he gave me his praenoma rather than a surname or placename. I've adapted to many foreign customs over the years, but I've never been able to bring myself to share my praenoma as casually as most people in other countries do. So I wasn't about to tell him my name is Sesskia.

Then he started babbling. I'd thought he was pretty smart until then. I don't know why he believed our knowing each other's names would make me spontaneously able to speak his language. I listened for a few seconds, then said, slowly and clearly, "I have no idea what you're saying." Not that I believed speaking slowly would make *him* understand *me*, but I hoped he'd take the message from my tone that his cunning plan wasn't working.

He cut off mid-sentence and looked sheepish. Then he chewed his lower lip in a thinking kind of way, and made a "stay put" gesture accompanied by some words I guessed meant the same thing, and left the room. No one locked it after he left, which I thought was odd, but I suppose if those women are still standing outside the door, I can't go anywhere. So I'm writing all this down quickly, in case he comes back soon. Or at all.

Later, same day

I'm in a different room now, one of the bedrooms lining the inner curve of the corridor. I learned in following Terrael—but I'm getting ahead of myself. Terrael did come back, after maybe half an hour, and gestured for me to follow him. The women didn't stop me from leaving, though I saw one of them look at the other with this expression that said she thought it was a bad idea to let the strange woman wander around with no one but Terrael to supervise. Terrael didn't seem worried I might run off.

I don't know what to make of him. He's young enough, I'd guess eighteen or nineteen, that he might not be sufficiently cynical yet, but...I don't know. He has this air of eager confidence about him I don't understand. But he's polite, and he's trying to communicate with me, and in general I'd feel bad about knocking him down and running away. So I followed him.

We walked down the corridor a little ways and everyone we passed stared at me. My clothes no doubt look strange to them, my wide-necked shirt with long, shapeless sleeves and the trousers with the big pockets that can hold books larger than this one. Though I left my stinking jacket in the other room. I hate giving up anything that might be an advantage, but I couldn't have cleaned it even if I created water, which would only have made a big wet mess. Terrael didn't pay any attention to the gawkers, and they didn't acknowledge him. He took me to another door on the same side of the hallway and indicated I should go in.

It was another sitting room, though a much nicer one; I think they crammed me into the first room because it was unused and they needed someplace to put me while they could think about what to do next. There were a couple of tall stools, still without backs, and a table with a tray holding a steaming pot of something that smelled nasty and some smaller jars, and a pair of porcelain cups with no handles.

Terrael pointed at one of the stools and sat in the other, so I sat down and watched him pour a bitter-smelling translucent green liquid into the cups. Then he waited. I watched his face, wondering what he expected me to do. After a few seconds, he nudged one of the jars in my direction. I took the lid off and found it contained a paste that smelled like roses. I dipped my finger in it, and Terrael made a grunting sound that sounded like suppressed laughter. I shoved the pot back at him and glared, and wiped my finger on my trousers. So this was a test, to see if I understood the custom. I stopped liking Terrael in that moment.

Except he immediately lost the smile, turned red, and started babbling again and making this motion with his fist closed over his throat and bowing in my direction, over and over. Then he picked up the jar and a tiny spoon with a bowl the size of my thumbnail, scooped out some of the paste, and tapped it into his cup with three little *tinks* on the edge of the porcelain. Then he offered the jar and spoon to me. I was still angry with him, but I repeated his gestures, and he smiled and nodded like I'd performed an exceptionally complicated trick.

Then he took another little jar, this one full of red crystals like dyed salt, picked up another tiny spoon and put two scoops into his cup, then took a different, larger spoon and stirred the liquid. So I imitated him, reasoning that keeping him happy might mean greater freedom for me, then raised the cup to my lips when he did the same. And it was good! Tangy and a little sweet, and somehow the combination of liquid and rose paste and red salt made it smell like oranges, which I love. Terrael could see I liked it and his smiling and nodding nearly took his head right off, and I had to smile at his enthusiasm, which made me decide to like him again.

I don't know what the point of the drink was, but I'm guessing it was some kind of hospitality custom. All I can say is they have a damn funny way of showing hospitality, locking me up in a bare room that, yes, might as well have been a cell. We drank for a while, and I stared at Terrael, and he stared at me, but he didn't try to speak again. There's supposed to be a pouvra that lets you hear what other people are thinking, and I wished I had it right then. Though if he was thinking in his own language, it wouldn't have done me any good. I've never heard even a rumor of a pouvra that can translate words from one language to another. Pity.

When the drinks were gone (Terrael poured me a second cup when I finished the first) Terrael got up and moved the tray to a different table, then sat down again and said something that ended in a question. I shrugged. Shrugging is another universal gesture, by his response. Then he said something else, and I could tell right away it was not in the same language he'd spoken at first. I shook my head, but I felt excited. I speak four other languages besides my own, though two of them I'm not exactly fluent in, and it was possible we might find one in common.

He spoke again, in a third language, and I shook my head and responded in Enthendil—no reaction. I'll skip to the end and say it was a failed experiment. Neither of us spoke a single language the other understood. I was so disappointed, and Terrael looked like I'd kicked his favorite puppy. I almost felt worse on his account than on my own, he'd looked so hopeful.

After all that, Terrael stood and made a shooing motion toward the door. Again, I don't know if he's stupid or just supremely self-confident, but it didn't seem to occur to him I might try to run if I left the room first. And I admit, at this point I was curious. Sticking close to Terrael might get me closer to freedom than sneaking about would.

So I went back into the hallway ahead of him, then let him lead me further along the corridor. Eventually we came to the cavern, and now I had time to examine it more fully. It's well-lit despite being made of such dark rock, mostly with those basket lights again, but also with tangles of glowing rope near the ceiling and around the walls below the ledges. One of the basket lights wasn't glowing, and I got a better look at the design on it. It looks like it's painted on, and it's not symmetrical at all. It looks almost like writing. I still don't know where the lights come from, but it has to be a pouvra of some kind, and I hope I can learn that one because wouldn't *that* be useful!

The tables were mostly occupied by gray-robes, showing each other their wooden tablets and talking very fast. Other gray-robes stood along the stone walls, writing in chalk or drawing pictures. And I discovered their sleeves are smudged because they use them to erase the chalk markings. I guess that's convenient, but it seems odd that they'd dirty their own clothes rather than use a sponge or a rag. Or maybe it's so everyone can see immediately what they are, whatever that is. I don't know.

I didn't understand what was happening at the center of the room. There were a dozen free-standing bookshelves, crammed with ancient books my fingers itched to touch, even though I was certain I couldn't read them. They were arranged radiating out from a circle on the ground about twenty feet across, an inch-wide gold strip set into the black stone floor. It took me a few seconds to realize it was the spot I'd "arrived" in. I left Terrael's side and ran toward it.

An unfortunately familiar hand grabbed my shoulder and brought me to a halt. Smug Git said something in that sarcastic tone of voice that made Terrael drop his gaze to the floor, silent for once. I wrenched away and said, "If I'm such a burden to you, send me back already, but leave Terrael alone. And don't bother locking me up again, I'll just keep escaping, if only to make your life hell."

Those eerie eyes narrowed, and he spoke rapidly this time, the sarcasm gone. Terrael responded, and the two of them had an increasingly rapid conversation in which Terrael ended up gesturing and tapping his forehead, and Smug Git kept shaking his head no, which I hope is another universal gesture, because imagine if 'no' meant 'yes' and how much more confused I'd be.

The conversation ended with Smug Git being very sarcastic at Terrael, who to my surprise didn't cringe at all, just glared at him in defiance. Then Smug Git turned his back on us and went back to doing something at the circle. Terrael looked furious. He actually walked several steps away before remembering me and beckoning me to follow. We left by the other corridor, and I was right, it's one big corridor looping around one side of the cavern. Terrael didn't say anything else, just led me to this room, bowed, and left. Without locking the door. I wonder if they've decided that's pointless.

This is a much nicer room, an actual bedroom with a narrow bed and dresser and wardrobe, more or less like the room I hid in. From what I've seen, all the bedrooms are on the inner side of the curve, and the rooms on the outer side are sitting rooms—that's more of a guess. The rooms aren't plain enough, or I'd think this was some kind of barracks. Maybe it's the uniformity of dress; I haven't seen a single person who wasn't wearing a smudged gray robe and black trousers. It's strange, and it makes my skin crawl, and the sooner I find a way out, the happier I'll be.

17 Senessay

I'm feeling overwhelmed, so I'm just going to start at the beginning and hope writing it all down calms me. I'm fairly certain about the date, but that's the only thing I'm sure of anymore.

The new bedroom was still a cell, if a nicer one. People brought me meals, and the lights dimmed by themselves after a time—I think the lights in my first cell didn't work properly—so I slept when it was dark and paced the room and practiced pouvrin when it was light. I gained enough control over the mind-moving pouvra that I could lift the bed, the dresser, and the wardrobe all at once. Only an inch or two, and only for a few seconds, but it was exciting. But that's not what has me overwhelmed. I went back and re-read the first page of this book, just to be certain I haven't forgotten my own language.

Though if I'm writing in it now—see how flustered it's made me? But I'm getting ahead of myself again.

I didn't see Terrael yesterday or today, and I was surprised at how disappointed I was. I mean, I couldn't understand him, but at least he was nice and didn't treat me like a problem. I poked my head out of the door a few times and there was a single guard, so either they were feeling more sure of me or they've given up on trying to contain me and that was a token. I smiled and waved at the guard (a man) and he watched me impassively until I got bored and went back inside. I decided I was going to make another escape attempt tonight when the lights went dark.

Except before that happened, Terrael appeared. He no longer looked confident. He looked like a boy about to do something that would get him into trouble. He came into my room, shut the door, and made a pinching gesture in front of his lips I guessed meant "be quiet." As if anything I might say would be meaningful, no matter how loudly I said it. Then he opened the door and gestured for me to precede him. In the hall, he said something to the guard, who nodded. He looked bored. I couldn't blame him.

I followed Terrael down the corridor and into the cavern again. It was quieter, less busy, like a marketplace where almost everyone has closed up shop for the day. Terrael was walking casually now, greeting the people we passed, stopping to exchange a few words with a pretty young woman whose hair was fastened with a jeweled clasp, polished jasper with cabochon garnets, reasonably valuable if only for the craftsmanship. It was the first sign of individuality I'd seen in any of these people in their identical clothes and hairstyles, and also the first thing I'd seen worth stealing.

Eventually we made it around the perimeter of the cavern to a door, metal like all the ones in the corridor, but wider, and Terrael took out a large key and unlocked it, then shooed me inside with the first hint of nervousness he'd displayed so far.

The room beyond was much larger than the corridor rooms, though of course nothing near as big as the cavern, and was brightly lit. And it was filled with castoffs. I didn't recognize a single thing there, but I've been stealing from great estates long enough to recognize a room where unwanted things are stored. Almost all of the things were made primarily of metal, and they were all intricately decorated with engravings that reminded me of the maybe-letters on the glass light baskets.

I tried to pick up a sphere of overlapping bronze strips like an enclosed basket, and Terrael yanked my hand away, shaking his head vigorously in a way that told me, first, that 'no' was in fact a universal gesture, and second, he absolutely did not want me to touch anything. Naturally, this made me want to touch everything I could get my hands on, but there was fear on Terrael's face that made me put my hands in my pockets. I was planning to go back there for some real exploration, but after what's happened, I'm not sure I'll be able to.

Terrael sidled to the back of the room, carefully not touching anything himself, and soon disappeared behind a tall slab of greenish copper that looked like a horse trough stood on end. I waited, jamming my hands firmly into my trouser pockets in case they decided to do some exploring on their own, and eventually he came back holding a helmet. No, it was more of a cap made of black iron, and for a wonder it wasn't covered with scribbles. There was a blank band all the way around the rim that was smoother and shinier than the rest of the cap.

Terrael held it out to me, and I took it. It felt like cold metal, and nothing happened to me when I touched it, so I turned it upside down to look into it. The inside of the cap had these hair-fine traceries all over it, as if someone had done lacework on it in molten iron. I ran my finger over the lines, and it still only felt cold.

Terrael nudged me, and made a gesture like he was putting something on his head. I looked at the cap again. Suddenly it seemed sinister, all this secrecy, Terrael acting tense and telling me not to touch anything, and *then* handing this thing over as if it were nothing. When I didn't respond right away, Terrael made an exasperated sound, took the cap from me, and put it on his head. Nothing happened. He took it off and offered it to me with a "see, it's harmless" look.

So I put it on. It was far too big for my head, and canted over my left ear. I must have looked so stupid—I certainly felt stupid, standing there in that room surrounded by mysterious cast-off things, with Terrael beaming at me as if, once again, I'd performed a trick and deserved a reward. Then he looked around, made that exasperated noise again, and cleared a spot on a nearby counter until he had a bare space about five feet across. He pointed at it, but it wasn't until he sat on the counter himself that I figured out that's what he wanted me to do. It wasn't a very tall counter, but I'm not a very tall woman, and my feet dangled.

Terrael started muttering to himself. It was the kind of muttering you do when you're going over a complicated project in your head, like planning to break into one of the royal manors, so I didn't feel obliged to pay any attention to him. He reached inside his robe and pulled out a pot with a stoppered lid and a small brush, its skinny bristles no longer than my pinky nail.

The pot turned out to be full of silvery ink or paint. Terrael came to stand close in front of me and began painting on the brim of the cap. Every few minutes he would rotate the cap on my head to paint a new section, making the lacework tug on my hair. I wished I could ask him questions—hah! That's funny now. Anyway, I stayed patient because I was curious about what he was doing. I don't know if it's good or not that I didn't run away.

Finally, he stepped back, and his eyes focused on mine again. He looked serious, like saying goodbye forever serious, and I got nervous and was about to take the cap off when he reached out with the brush and made a final mark on the cap.

It felt like my head exploded. It hurt worse than anything I'd ever imagined possible, and I wanted to rip the cap off my head and throw it at Terrael's face, but my entire body was paralyzed. I found later I'd fallen off the counter, but at the time I couldn't feel anything but the pain that radiated from my forehead through my entire body. Phantom smells of ash and rainwater filled my nostrils, and I tasted salt. I couldn't see or hear anything at all, not even the screaming I'm sure I was doing.

And then I could hear too much, all these voices shouting in hundreds of languages, none of which I understood. Somewhere in there I blacked out, I think, because the sound went from being hundreds of voices to only one, high-pitched like a woman's, chanting. I still couldn't understand it, but then I realized I could move—that's when I found I was on the floor. I had the cap off my head and flung across the room before I discovered I wasn't in pain anymore, and I could see.

What I saw, from my perspective on the floor, were two pairs of sandaled feet attached to two pairs of black trousers. Terrael was arguing with Smug Git, and this is the overwhelming part—I listened to their conversation for nearly a minute before I realized I understood what they were saying. It staggered me to the point that I can't remember now what their exact words were, just that Smug Git was furious with Terrael about what he'd done with the cap, and Terrael, surprisingly, was standing up to him and saying something like "it was worth the risk."

I got to my feet, and they both stopped arguing. Smug Git said, "We will have to watch her to see if any permanent damage was done." The way he said it, like I was some kind of injured animal, made me angry, so I said—I can't remember exactly, that's how angry I was—"Oh, yes, let's hope she didn't sustain any permanent damage, that would be *so* inconvenient for you" and that's as far as my anger took me before I realized I was speaking their language, and that startled me so much I shrieked and clapped my hands over my mouth.

Terrael's mouth fell open. Smug Git raised one eyebrow again—really, that makes him look even more arrogant and annoying than he naturally does. "It worked," he said. He made it sound like the whole thing was his idea.

It sounded like Terrael felt the same way, and he said, "Just as I said, Sai Aleynten," and I could practically hear him thinking *I told you so,* though he was careful not to sound rude. Smug Git nodded once, and said, "Take her back to her room, Master Peressten, and I will interrogate her in the morning."

I didn't like being referred to in the third person, and I *really* didn't like the sound of "interrogate." I said, "You brought me here, maybe I should be interrogating *you*." It wasn't much, but I couldn't stand there and not defy him. It's his face.

He turned that cold, indifferent gaze on me, then said "In the morning, Master Peressten," and walked away. So I lost my temper and summoned the fire in a circle around him. Terrael cried out and took a step toward the git, who turned smoothly on his heel, made a few gestures like writing on the air—and I flew back into the counter I'd been sitting on. It knocked the air out of me, and I lost control of the fire and it went out, but obviously what really stunned me was seeing him work that pouvra. Never mind that I couldn't do anything nearly so powerful; what was the gesturing for? Pouvrin come from inside you, something you encompass with your mind and then turn outward. If I gestured all the time when I did magic, I'd be captured instantly. So—

All right. I'm still overwhelmed. I was overwhelmed enough then I didn't strike back at Smug Git or whatever it was Terrael called him. Sai Aleynten. He walked away without another word, and Terrael helped me stand, babbling something about how I shouldn't attack people and Smug Git could have done far worse because he's some word I didn't understand. Whatever Terrael's cap did to me, there are apparently words it can't translate, or didn't bother translating, and there's probably some logic to it, but I can't see it at the moment. He brought me back to my room, and now I'm hurrying to write this before the lights go out.

There's too much. Here's what I know.

1. That cap did something to me that lets me speak their language.

2. These people have magic. Powerful magic, if Smug Git is representative.

3. They don't work magic the way I do.

4. They want to learn something from me, hence the promised interrogation.

I ought to escape. I have no reason to believe that just because I haven't been hurt before, their interrogation won't involve...maybe not torture, but physical duress at least. But—this is the first place I've ever been where magic not only isn't feared, but is openly practiced. Even if the way they use pouvrin is not at all like mine. I can't leave until I've at least learned why that is. And I'm increasingly curious about why I'm here at all. I think Smug Git's interrogation may give me more information than I give him. At least, that's my plan.

CHAPTER THREE

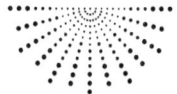

18 Senessay

Things I learned during my interrogation of Sai Aleynten, better known as Smug Git:

1. They have never seen magic like mine before.

2. This place is a sort of cross between a school and a co-operative of magic.

3. That cap, as I'd suspected, could have killed me.

4. My coming here was, as I guessed, a complete accident.

Obviously the thing I'm most concerned about right now is number 3, though number 4 runs a close second. How *dare* Terrael risk my life like that? Yes, I'm glad I can understand these people now, and no, there's no way he could have explained the situation to me and gotten my consent, but I'm still angry. Fortunately for Terrael, I haven't seen him since last night, when he escorted me (in silence) back to my room.

In the morning, a gray-robe brought me breakfast (gruel studded with raisins and sprinkled with sugar, better-tasting than it sounds) and waited for me to finish (it's hard to eat when someone's staring at you, did you know?) then escorted me down the hall to a chamber near the mouth of the corridor. It was a much bigger room than the "sitting rooms" I'd seen before, maybe thirty feet in both directions. There was a table made of some wood so dark it was nearly black, a long, plain thing like a stone slab, and two chairs facing each other across it, but near one end, so we weren't fifteen feet away from each other.

Sai Aleynten stood next to one of the chairs, hands clasped behind his back, smug gitty look on his face as usual. "Sit down," he said, pointing at the other chair. I tried to think of something rude to say to that, but in the end I just sat. So did he.

For a minute or so, we stared at each other. His face was completely expressionless. I don't know what I looked like; belligerent, probably. I've never been in a position to spend a lot of time looking at my own face, but I've been told I sometimes look as if I'm about to start a fight, which is never true. Starting fights only gets you noticed, and getting noticed only gets you a cell. In this case, I wasn't going to be the first one to speak. This interrogation was Sai Aleynten's idea; let him start the "conversation."

And speaking of conversations, how I wish I had the kind of memory that would let me remember everything word for word! My memory's good, what with all the memorizing I've had to do since the magic woke up in me, but it's not that good. So I'm going to write as much as I can remember, and I'm going to guess at the rest, and maybe that means it's not a totally accurate history, but I'll be as honest as I can, and this should make it more readable for whoever it is reads it in the future. Which, again, might only be me, but I don't see why my personal record shouldn't be entertaining.

Finally, Sai Aleynten said, "You're very lucky. That aeden Master Peressten used on you might have killed you." (I guess this means number 3 is actually number 1. Oops.)

That made me feel faint, but I said, "That would have solved your problem, wouldn't it?"

He didn't flinch. "I have no desire to see you dead," he said. "You are a curiosity."

"And one who keeps trying to escape," I said.

"We are keeping you here for your protection," he said. "Far worse things might happen to you outside the Darssan."

"I only have your word for that," I said.

He raised his eyebrow, which made me itch to slap him. "Why did you interfere with our kathana?" he said. (Number 4, which is really number 2. I should have thought more clearly before I made that list.)

"I didn't interfere with anything," I said. "*You* brought *me* here."

"Provably untrue," he said. "That kathana could not have summoned or created anything living. I repeat, why did you interfere with our kathana?"

"And *I* repeat, I didn't do anything. I was asleep when you and your kathana, whatever that means, dragged me to wherever this place is. I...had nothing to do with it." I was about to say "I don't even know how to do that kind of magic" when I realized I shouldn't tell him any more than I had to about my abilities. Better to keep him guessing.

Sai Aleynten frowned. It was the first genuinely human expression I'd ever seen him use. "I think you are lying," he said.

"And I think you're a smug git who wasn't spanked enough as a baby," I said. (This is untrue. I actually said something like "Am not!" but I came up with this when it was too late to say it, so I put it in here, but now I feel guilty about being deceptive, even if the only person I'm deceiving is myself. So this is me telling the truth.)

"Your magic is unlike ours. You might be capable of anything," he said. (New number 3.)

"I could," I said, "and so could you. But I didn't. So if you didn't bring me here, and I didn't interfere with your kathana, maybe you should look for a third option instead of accusing me of lying."

He raised his eyebrow again. "I can think of any number of reasons why someone might want to insert herself into the Darssan," he said. "You might be a spy. You might be a saboteur."

I started to get angry, but he shushed me before I could do more than begin to shout. I'm embarrassed to write that I backed down immediately. Smug git or no, he has a powerful presence, and I can see why everyone around here defers to him. It's infuriating.

"But I am inclined to believe you, because it is true I have never seen magic like yours before, and you could not have pretended to be affected by the aeden, which tells me you genuinely did not speak our language. And Master Peressten informs me you spoke none of the many languages in which he is fluent, which tells me further that wherever you have come from, it is very far away. So if you are not spy, nor saboteur, and you did not choose to come here..."

His voice trailed off, and his gaze slipped to a point somewhere above my head, where it stayed for long enough that I became impatient.

"Excuse me," I said sarcastically, "but if you're done, I'd like to leave this place. Though I imagine you'll just take me back to my cell."

That brought his attention back to my face. "Are you not comfortable?" he said. "I thought we had corrected the misunderstanding that put you in that unused storage room first."

"It's comfortable, but as long as I'm not free to leave, it's a cell," I said.

"You would not be safe outside the Darssan."

"I can take care of myself."

"Undoubtedly," he said, and he got this sour look on his face, "but not all the dangers you would face are the kind that respond to being set on fire."

That made me want to laugh. So he hadn't been so composed when I tried to burn him last night. I said, "Are they the kind that respond to being thrown into a countertop?"

He actually smiled! It was a thin, anemic little thing, but it staggered me. "You seemed surprised anyone might fight back against you," he said.

"Most people don't," I said, and immediately wished I hadn't, because that was the sort of information he did not need to have, and of course he jumped on it.

"You often use your magic aggressively?" he said.

Damn, damn, damn. "Sometimes," I said.

"Then you mean people in your homeland lack the ability to respond. Is magic something rare, where you come from?"

Damn times one hundred. "It is," I said. I don't know why I didn't lie to him, but I had a feeling he would know if I did, and that might mean he'd keep an even closer eye on me. So I suppose I do know why I didn't lie.

"And all magic is like yours? You do not use kathanas or th'an?" he said.

"Those words don't even translate." This was when I figured out why there were words the cap hadn't bothered to give me. Anything my language doesn't have a concept for gets left in their words.

"Th'an." Sai Aleynten waved his fingers in the air, again like writing, and the table shifted two inches to the left, startling me. "You saw them on the other aeden in the safe room, and no doubt on the walls of the cavern. And a kathana is using th'an in patterns, combined together, to work magic."

At this point, I have to stop and justify myself. I know I wrote I wouldn't give away any more than I had to. That I was going to get more information out of him than he did from me. And he's arrogant and I don't like him and I don't want him to have the satisfaction of thinking his interrogation succeeded.

But.

This was what I've dreamed of ever since the magic awoke—being in a place where I didn't have to fear being killed for what I can do. And Sai Aleynten's magic might be nothing like mine, but what if there's something in it that teaches me more about my own? I couldn't help myself. So if this decision causes a total disaster, and my future self reads this and wants to kill me, I want to point out you were me once and this was your decision too.

Anyway. I told him about my magic. I told him everything. All about pouvrin and how I learn the shape of them, and the research I've done over the last ten years, and the kind of pouvrin I can do and the ones I'm still not sure of.

I didn't tell him how magic is feared in my country, in the nearby countries even, and I didn't tell him anything about how scared I am sometimes when I realize I might be the only person who can do what I do, and I didn't tell him about the magic waking up inside me —I haven't told anyone that, haven't even written it in any of the record books I've kept, not that I have access to any of them but this one now—but everything else, I poured out to Sai Aleynten like water from an ever-flowing spring.

He sat there, his smug face impassive and therefore marginally less smug, listening without comment, until the flow dried up and I sat back, my throat and mouth dry from speaking. Then he stood up and went to a cabinet on the far wall, and returned with a pitcher and a couple of glasses, which he set in front of me.

He made a gesture, sort of an invitation, and I looked and saw the pitcher was empty. So I did the water-summoning pouvra and filled the pitcher about three-fourths of the way. And *he* wiggled his fingers again, and the pitcher floated off the table and poured water into the glasses, wobbling a bit and spilling a few drops. That awkwardness— I looked at Sai Aleynten, and he was smiling that thin little smile again, but this time there was actual humor in his eyes, and for a minute I forgot I don't like him.

We drank, and sat silent again for a minute or two. I felt drained, like I'd been practicing pouvrin all day, and I couldn't think of anything else I wanted to say to Sai Aleynten. Besides, I'd been doing all the talking; I decided it was his turn.

Finally, he said, "The kathana was to summon something. A book. We have been working for three days to discover why it brought you instead. As I said, it should not have summoned anything living."

"Do you know how to send me back?" I said.

There was another long pause. Then he said, "We are trying to discover this as well."

"What is this place?" I said. "This Darssan?"

A third pause. My momentary lapse of judgment that had me disliking Sai Aleynten less vanished. "If you're afraid of giving away your secrets, you ought to ask yourself who I could possibly tell them to," I said. "And I've already told you all of mine." This was untrue.

There are any number of things I hadn't told him that are frankly none of his business. But it was true in the specific context of our conversation.

He looked at me in silence for a moment longer, his face growing more expressionless, then he said, "The Darssan is a place where mages come to learn and to teach others. It provides resources and shelter and a certain amount of protection against those who would like to turn our magic to their own purposes."

His lack of specificity suggested there were things he wasn't telling me, but since I had my own secrets, I decided not to push. "So why were you trying to summon that book?" I asked.

"That is not something you need to know," he said, and once again he looked arrogant and smug.

"Then you don't need to know anything more about the pouvrin," I said. I wanted to fling fire at him again, but my hip still hurt from where it had struck the counter, and I decided it wouldn't get me what I wanted. So I took refuge in rudeness.

"If you explain your magic, we might have a better chance of returning you," he said.

"I might say the same," I said.

We glared at each other for a while until he stood and said, "Master Peressten will come to you later. I will instruct him to answer as many of your questions as he is allowed, if you will extend him the same courtesy."

I couldn't believe Sai Aleynten had bent even that much, so I only nodded and left the room, where I found a gray-robe waiting to take me back to my bedroom. It would be just like Sai Aleynten to make someone wait at the door that whole time—it must have been over an hour that we were talking. But I was too full of questions to have much room to be indignant on the poor man's part.

And that brings me to now. Terrael hasn't appeared yet, which is also typical of Sai Aleynten, leaving me here with nothing to do, as far as he knows. I'm trying to come up with questions for Terrael— more accurately, I'm trying to work out which of the hundreds of questions I have are the most important. And I haven't given up on trying to escape the Darssan. Sai Aleynten may be worried about safety, but I had to scrape a living for myself and Mam and Bridie since I was twelve, and I've been on my own since I was seventeen, and I'm not afraid of anything that might be outside these walls.

18 Senessay (evening)

Maybe I was wrong about that last sentence. Again I'm so over-whelmed by what I've learned I don't know what to think anymore. So I'll start with what I'm sure of, which is that Terrael wouldn't meet my eyes when he finally showed up, about two hours after the end of my interrogation. The first thing he said was "I'm not sorry."

"I was furious with you earlier," I told him, "but since I'm not dead, I decided to be glad it worked and forgive you. But if you ever try anything like that on me again I'll strangle you with your own robe." (That's actually what I said, not me being clever in retrospect. Though I don't know how I'd make it happen. Terrael's tall and I think he's stronger than he looks.)

"That's fair," Terrael said, and then he looked at me and he didn't look at all penitent. I get the feeling Terrael is the sort of person who can't stand not trying new things, even potentially fatal things, which means we have a lot in common.

Then we both started talking at once, stopped, started again, and then fell silent. It seemed Terrael had as many questions for me as I did for him. "Sai Aleynten said you'd answer my questions," Terrael said.

"He said you'd answer mine, too. So I think we should take turns," I said, and Terrael nodded. "You can go first," I added, because I could see he was about to jump out of his skin with impatience, another thing that told me he was fairly young. I realize, technically, I'm still fairly young myself—twenty-seven isn't exactly ancient—but when I was his age, I'd already had cynicism beaten into me by life, and Terrael is just so *eager* all the time. But I'm getting off track.

Terrael nodded, began to say something, then said, "Oh, we should probably go somewhere we can sit comfortably. This might take a while."

"That's fine," I said, but I was thinking *If this takes a while, there had better be food.* Terrael showed me to another sitting room, this one containing several chairs with actual backs, and I sat in one and immediately felt better. Soft chairs are so relaxing, and there's something about them that makes me think of reading, which is one of the things I like best. Oh! Maybe Terrael's Cap of Death made me able to read their language! I wish I'd thought of that when he was still here; he could have brought me a book. Something else to find out in the morning.

Terrael perched on the edge of his seat so no part of him touched the chair back. "What country do you come from?" he asked. No preliminaries. Just what I'd expect of him.

"Balaen," I said. He looked confused and said he'd never heard of it. "I could show it to you on a map, if you have the right map," I said.

"Good idea! Let's go—" he said, and I had to grab his hand and make him sit down.

"I don't think where I'm from is the most important issue right now," I said. "Besides, it's my turn."

"But that wasn't really an answer!" Terrael said. He can be a little whiny.

"Too bad for you. Why do you need—tan, was it?—to work magic?"

"Th'an," Terrael said. "It's how magic works. I might as well ask you why you *don't* need them. How did you learn to work magic?"

"That wasn't an answer," I said.

"Too bad for you," Terrael said, and he grinned at me, which made me laugh. That broke down the reserve between us, and from there the conversation went more smoothly. I'll summarize what I told him and what I learned from him, so I can get to the more interesting things.

What I told him: I explained about magic being rare where I come from, and people who can do pouvrin being feared. I didn't tell him about the magic waking up inside me—I'm never going to tell anyone about that—but I did explain how I'd spent ten years searching for old records and stories about pouvrin and learning to use them.

36

I also told him the pouvrin I could do and the ones I was trying to discover, like the invisibility pouvra, and that made his eyes go extra wide and round, and he told me that was impossible for their magic. So I guess that's one for my side, so there, Sai Aleynten and your flinging innocent women into convenient counters! (All right, so I attacked him first, but I was provoked.) Let's see...I think the only other thing I told him was about how it felt to use a pouvra, which he seemed very interested in, though he wouldn't say why and I didn't care enough to ask.

What he told me: more about the Darssan—how it was founded centuries ago by a woman named Audryn, with the help of Castavir's first king Eddon (Castavir is their country), and how it started as a place where mages could be safe from threat of persecution or death. It seems there was a time in their history where magic was as feared as it is in Balaen. And over the centuries it turned into a repository of knowledge and a home for mages, where they can study and create new kathanas to use for the benefit of Castavir.

Terrael's been here for three years. He didn't come out and say it, but from what he did say I worked out that he's a prodigy—mostly people don't qualify for the Darssan until they're at least twenty-one, and Terrael said he was nineteen. And he said Sai Aleynten is the head of the Darssan, something called a Wrelan, and has been for two years. It turns out "Sai" is a title, not a name; they call regular mages Master (and I don't know why that translates when Sai doesn't) and Sai means, basically, "great master." Which might explain Sai Aleynten's permanent smugness.

I asked him about the kathana that brought me here, but his explanation was too technical for me to understand. Maybe if I knew more about their magic—but he repeated what Sai Aleynten had said about it not being able to summon anything living, and how they'd been analyzing it for flaws ever since I appeared. He did tell me more about what it was *supposed* to summon, a book that would help them create a powerful kathana, but when I asked what that was supposed to do, he said I should ask Sai Aleynten. Which means I'll probably never find out, because the idea of going begging to Sai Aleynten, even for something like that, makes me irritable.

Let's see, what else... I asked him to explain more about his magic —like, if you work pouvrin by learning their shape and bending your will to the magic, then letting it come from within you, how do you learn th'an and so forth. Terrael had trouble with this; it sounded like it was something that came so naturally to him it was like trying to explain how to walk. But what I understood was that people studying to be mages have to learn hundreds of th'an and how to shape them perfectly. If you don't get a th'an exactly right, nothing happens. So they practice their penmanship a lot.

Then they have to learn the ways th'an can be combined into kathanas. Some combinations don't do anything, but mages are always learning, or rediscovering, new combinations. And some mages get to be so good at th'an they can scribe runes on air and have them work as if they'd been written on stone. One more reason for Sai Aleynten to look smug. Really, it's amazing he even deigns to walk among ordinary people.

Right. That was another thing. Castavir—the whole region, in fact —went through this awful catastrophe several centuries ago, where a lot of knowledge was destroyed, and mages were feared, and they still haven't recovered everything that was lost. I told Terrael my country had suffered something similar a long time ago, so it seems the catastrophe had a wider area of effect than either of us believed. We tried comparing histories, but couldn't find anything in common. Then

18 Senessay (later, same evening)

I had to stop before because Terrael came to ask me more questions. Then Audryn—I haven't written about her yet, I guess—she came to make Terrael leave me alone so I could sleep, but I really need to finish writing about this, because it has to be important.

So, we compared histories. After about three hours, we were both tired, and Terrael suggested we get some food. This time, he took me to a big room with ten or twelve long tables and little backless stools lining them on both sides. A lot of gray-robes were sitting there, eating, and all of them looked at us—at me—when Terrael and I came in. Terrael ignored the attention and walked to an opening in the far wall, like a five-foot-square window with no glass, and I followed him.

Beyond the window was the largest kitchen I'd ever seen in my life, and that includes the one in the royal house in Venetry where the cook hid me while the guards searched the house. A man came to the window, looked at both of us, and walked away again. When he came back, he had a couple of plates piled with food: a slice of meat in thick brown gravy, mashed potatoes (finally, a food I recognized!), green peas that had been dried and then reconstituted, so they were mushy, and a thick slab of the unfamiliar brown bread perched on top of everything.

Terrael handed one to me, thanked the man, and sat at the end of one of the tables where no one was sitting. He went at his food like it was the last meal he'd get all week. I was conscious of people still staring at me, so I used my best manners. Though now that I write that, it occurs to me I have no idea what these people consider good manners. Maybe Terrael inhaling his food is the pinnacle of proper eating etiquette in Castavir.

"Will you look at the maps after dinner?" Terrael asked. His mouth was full of food and, I'm sorry, but there's no way that's good manners no matter what country you're in. Since my mouth was also full of food, I nodded.

"Are they letting the stranger out now?" said a young woman, sliding onto a stool beside Terrael. It took me a second to realize she was the young woman Terrael had spoken to the night he ~~nearly killed me~~ gave me their language, the one wearing the jeweled hair clip.

"Her name is Thalessi, Audryn," Terrael said, and this time he made sure his mouth was empty when he spoke. He also sat up straighter and couldn't quite meet her eyes, and those are some more gestures, like nodding, that mean the same thing no matter what language you speak. I covered my mouth with my hand so I wouldn't embarrass him, because it seemed like the young woman didn't realize how Terrael felt, but I couldn't help smiling. Really, people in love are sort of cute.

Audryn turned to face me, put her palm flat against her chest below her throat, and said, "Welcome to the Darssan, Thalessi, though your arrival was unintentional."

To my surprise, she had the same green-gray eyes Sai Aleynten and I do. In my travels, I've seen maybe ten other people who had the same eye color I do, so two of them in one place was unusual. I wanted to ask about it, but I felt awkward about blurting that out. "That's certainly true," I said instead. I thought about mirroring her gesture, but decided it might not mean greeting, or at least might not be reciprocated by the same gesture.

"Well, if anyone can get you back home, Sai Aleynten can," Audryn said. She spoke his name with such pride and respect that for a moment I wondered if we could possibly mean the same person. I decided to be polite and not act as if Sai Aleynten puts my back up, which he does.

"I hope so," I told her, though as I said before, I'm not sure if I care whether I go home or not. Again, being polite to the people who are still basically keeping me captive is probably the best course of action. "Your name sounds familiar."

"I'm named for the woman who founded the Darssan," she said, and then I remembered what Terrael had told me. Well, I learned a lot of things this afternoon—I'm sure there are things I've forgotten to write down.

"We're going to look at the maps to see if Thalessi can show us her country," Terrael said. He was eating more daintily and seemed to be using that as an excuse for not meeting Audryn's eyes, though he did a fair job of still looking at her occasionally. Poor Terrael.

I wonder what their courtship customs are, here in Castavir. In Balaen, women are supposed to indicate their interest in a man before the man can reciprocate, and if it's the same custom here, Terrael could be in for a long wait, because I didn't see any evidence Audryn feels anything for him but friendship. But I'm not going to assume it's the same here. I've been in many different countries and they all seem to do things their own way. Still, I feel for Terrael. Not that I would know what being in love feels like.

Anyway, we finished eating, and Terrael took me back to the cavern. Audryn came with us. She seemed interested in what we were doing, and I wonder if she was in the circle of people when I arrived. She didn't say anything to me, just to Terrael, but I caught her watching me once or twice with this speculative look, as if she was waiting for me to do something interesting. It was unnerving, but not antagonistic, so I didn't react.

The maps are in a large cupboard near the room with the aeden. Each map is rolled up around a wooden rod, and the rods are stowed on metal stands on wheels, so they can be rolled out into the cavern, which is what Terrael did. He lifted one of the rods off the stand and laid it on the cavern floor, then unrolled it to its full length. It was big —maybe six feet long and nearly as many wide, and the minute I saw it I forgot to breathe.

I've seen many, many maps in the course of my quest. Some of them were ones I was using to find my way, more of them I found when I was looking for other things. So I know the geography of my own country, and the surrounding region, so well I could draw a map of my own. And I know what the two other continents look like, at least as well as anyone does, since few people from Balaen have ever crossed the ocean. And what Terrael was showing me was a map of Balaen.

I'm still overwhelmed at the thought. I have no idea what it means. And when I say it was a map of Balaen, that's not completely accurate. The continent was the same—*exactly* the same—and the major landmarks were all there, like the Myrnala River that runs north to south and nearly cuts off the eastern side of the continent. But the cities were all wrong, like the big one lying right on the Myrnala River, and nothing where Thalessa should be.

And—this is what really shocked me—there was a small range of mountains near where the western border of Balaen ought to be. When Terrael pointed to it and said "That's where we are now" I examined it closely and worked out it was close to the spot where I'd been sleeping the night they summoned me. Obviously I can't tell with any exactness, but it can't be coincidence.

Terrael asked me if I recognized anything, and I lied. I didn't know what else to do. I suppose it wasn't entirely a lie, given that I *didn't* recognize any of the cities, and I sure as hell didn't know what that mountain range was doing there, but I didn't know what to say. I don't know what it means! And I'm reluctant to give anything else away to these people—I know, I told Sai Aleynten about the magic, and I agreed to answer their questions, but this seems so big—

I'm taking refuge in lists again. It's my way of coping with things that are too big for me to understand.

1. This is all a huge coincidence.

2. I've been pulled forward, or backward, to a time so distant from my own the landscape and the culture have changed.

3. This is some kind of other-world, like in children's stories, where it's almost the same as my own but with key differences.

4. I've been knocked on the head, and this is all some elaborate hallucination from which I will wake at any moment.

Hell. All of those seem so unrealistic and impossible. I suppose someone who didn't know any better might say "anything's possible with magic," but that's just not true. Magic has rules and limitations —at least, mine does, and I bet Terrael's does too. In fact, he even told me invisibility was impossible for them, though how he'd know that, I have no idea. I've always assumed, when I couldn't do things, it was because I hadn't figured out the right way yet. But magic does have limitations, and everything I've listed does seem like a child's fantasy story.

But to resume: Terrael showed me several other maps, all of which were more or less familiar. There was one that was a far more detailed map of the continent south and west of mine, and one that showed all the continents laid out on a single map, and some that showed countries I didn't recognize.

Finally Terrael gave up, and I felt awful at keeping that secret, he looked so disappointed. I'm sure he was hoping to have some great success in front of Audryn, though she didn't seem disdainful of his failure. Her curiosity about me aside, she seems like a nice person. Then they talked for a minute, technical stuff I couldn't follow, and after that Terrael brought me back to my room, for which I was grateful, because I'm still not good at telling the doors apart. I wonder if it would be all right for me to mark mine—but that might make me seem weak, and not all these people might be as nice as Terrael and Audryn.

My hand is sore from writing. Terrael showed me how to disable the automatic light dimmer when he was here earlier, so I don't have to worry about finishing before the light goes out, but writing all of this hasn't clarified anything. I'm feeling guilty, now, about not telling Terrael the truth. I promised to be honest, and I broke that promise. It's just that it felt like such an important thing—

Damn. I'm going to have to talk to Sai Aleynten and his smug face. I hate the thought of confessing to him that I wasn't totally honest, but if he's the leader of the Darssan, he's the one who ought to know what I couldn't tell Terrael. I wish there were another option.

CHAPTER FOUR

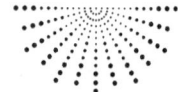

19 Senessay

I had breakfast this morning in the room with all the tables, eggs with funny orange yolks and some reassuringly familiar bacon and a glass of pink juice that tasted bitter, but grew on me over time. They don't seem to have coffee here—I don't know if that's just the Darssan, or if their country hasn't discovered it—and while I dislike drinking it, I miss the comforting smell.

No one came to sit with me, and I didn't see Terrael or Audryn, and while I didn't exactly feel lonely—I've traveled alone for too long to let solitude bother me—it meant I had no one to talk to but the inside of my own head, and that made me increasingly nervous about the upcoming conversation with Sai Aleynten.

It felt like I was coming at it from a position of weakness, since I'd made a mistake, and I hated—still hate—the thought of giving Sai Aleynten any power over me. I don't know why that is; he only used magic on me to defend himself, and he seemed more concerned for my welfare than Terrael was with the whole Cap of Death incident, even if that was only because he sees me as a puzzle he doesn't want damaged until he can solve it. I just don't like him, that's all.

But all last night, before I finally fell asleep, I kept going over the day's events and I was increasingly sure Sai Aleynten needed to know about the map. So when I finished eating, I went in search of him. It took a while. Nobody stopped me poking around the cavern, and I didn't give them a reason to by prying into their conversations.

Though I did find out, in looking at the walls, that I can't read their writing. I was so disappointed. They have a lot of books in the cavern, not just in the shelves surrounding the gold circle but on shelves here and there next to the walls, and they're the old kind I love because you're practically guaranteed to find something mysterious and maybe even magical within their pages. Maybe I can get Terrael to read to me, though I don't know how we'd figure out which of those books would interest me. All of them, maybe.

I wandered around for a bit and smiled at everyone. Nobody talked to me, and although they didn't stare either, I felt awkward. I don't think anyone, myself included, knows what to make of me. After I'd made the circuit of the room three times, Sai Aleynten came out of one mouth of the corridor. I know he saw me, but he didn't come to me immediately; he stopped to talk to a little knot of gray-robes, then was handed one of those wooden tablets by someone so tall he made Sai Aleynten, who isn't short, look like a dwarf.

I stood and waited. Eventually he finished his business and came to where I stood, and said, "Can I help you with something?"

Have I mentioned how much his tone of voice bothers me? I kept my irritation under control and said, "I need to show you something, and I think it should be private because I don't know what you'll want to do with it."

"Cryptic," he said, raising one eyebrow and HOW THE HELL DOES HE DO THAT? Is it something they teach in Sai school?

He followed me to the map room and watched me choose the first map Terrael had shown me, then helped me take it down from the stand. "Is there room enough in here to spread it out?" I asked.

He looked around, gestured, and two of the stands rolled back, leaving a big empty space in the middle of the floor. I'm so jealous. Maybe if I keep practicing, I'll be that good with the mind-moving pouvra someday. He unrolled the map and stepped back. "Well?" he said.

I said, "Is this your country? Castavir?" I knew it was, but I hadn't given much thought to how I was going to explain this strangeness, so I decided to stall. Or lay the foundation for my revelation. That sounds better. More noble.

Sai Aleynten squatted beside the map and traced lines with his forefinger. "This is the Castaviran Empire," he said. "Here, the central country, Castavir. East is Helviran, bordering on the ocean. Northeast, Endellavir, and southwest, Viravon."

"They all have 'vir' in the name," I said, once again stalling for time learning useful information.

"The names come from a much older language than the one we are speaking now," Sai Aleynten said. "'Vir' means 'land' in that tongue." His words were patient enough, but his tone said he wanted me to get on with it already.

I squatted next to him. "The lands on this map look exactly like my homeland," I said.

He went completely expressionless, his green-gray eyes fixed on mine. He stared, and I fidgeted, until he looked back at the map and said, "You don't mean they are similar."

"I mean I've seen maps like this many times in my travels," I said, "and with a few exceptions, this map is identical to those."

"What exceptions?" he said.

I pointed at the places where in my world there were cities, at the places where they have cities that in my world are empty, and at the ridge of mountains where the tiny dot of the Darssan sat. "And this should all be plains," I said, spreading my fingers to encompass the area around the Darssan.

Sai Aleynten went even stiller than before, enough that he might have been carved of stone. "Tell me," he said, extending a finger, "in your world, what is in this place?" He pointed at a spot where the borders of Castavir and Viravon met. "No, wait," he said, interrupting me. He stood and walked to the back of the room, where he rummaged around a bit and returned with a roll of tan paper, or parchment, or something, and a handful of smooth rocks.

He rolled the parchment out over the map; it overlapped it a bit on two sides, and was thin enough that the lines of the map showed through it. Then he set the rocks on the corners to keep it from rolling back up. They weren't ordinary rocks, but stones carved to look like animals, fat little turtles and low-slung horses, and I had to wonder why anyone would put so much effort into something that would only be used to hold paper down. Or maybe they have some mystical significance and only Sai Aleynten would use them for something so prosaic. I don't know.

Sai Aleynten reached inside his robe and took out what looked like a pencil, though it was fatter than the one I'm using, and when he started tracing the outlines of the land, what came out was a thick black line, more like ink than lead. He kept sketching until he had drawn the coastline and the major geographical features. He didn't include the country borders or the cities and he didn't include the Darssan. When he finished, he handed the pencil/pen to me and said "Draw what you know of your land."

Again I fought down my irritation and concentrated on remembering how my maps looked. I said before I could probably draw the map out myself, but I felt certain Sai Aleynten would want more detail than the general sketch I was capable of producing quickly. I drew in country boundaries and cities, and labeled the cities, and then I put in all the ruins I'd explored over the years, since I thought they were strange—all of them roughly the same size and shape, all of them in remote locations.

Sai Aleynten just watched me. He was able to keep on squatting long after my thighs started to ache and I had to get on my knees, which was cold and uncomfortable since the floor of the map room was the same uneven, rippling stone as the cavern. I became more impatient with Sai Aleynten's refusal to give me answers the more I drew. Once again he didn't seem surprised or shocked by something I could do—first the magic, and now the revelation that his country and mine were identical. I wanted to ask him which of my list of suppositions was correct, but I couldn't do that and concentrate on drawing, so instead I just let my impatience rise.

Finally, when I'd drawn as much as I could remember, I sat back on the cold stone and handed the writing tool to my silent companion. He squatted there, looking at the map, and when I started to speak he held up a hand for silence and, damn him, I shut up. Again I wonder if that's something he learned in order to be whatever-it-was, Wrelan, I think, or if it's just part of who he is, like his stupid smug face.

When I was nearly ready to explode with impatience, he said, without looking at me, "You're certain of this."

"Yes," I said.

He took hold of the parchment and rose, rolling it up as he stood. "I realize you are impatient," he said, "but there is one last thing I want to do. I promise you will have answers soon." He set the parchment aside, squatted again, and began making marks all over the map. I was shocked at that, because it looked like an old map and not one people ought to be drawing on, but I suppose when you're Sai Aleynten you can do anything you like and no one will criticize you. He worked rapidly, with no indication of what he was marking, just two quick slashes to make an X at spots all over the map.

Then he put the writing tool away and unrolled the parchment. "Help me line this up," he said, and I helped align the maps along the coastlines and what in my world is the Myrnala River, and then I had another shock, because those X's matched up almost perfectly with the ruins I'd marked on the parchment. I say "almost" because it wasn't a one-to-one correspondence; there were a few places I'd marked that he hadn't, and vice versa, but almost every X had a ruin overlaid on it.

"What does it mean?" I said.

Sai Aleynten stood and looked down at the map. "I dislike guessing," he said. "But it may explain how you came to be here, and why."

"So tell me!" I said. I might have sounded shrill, but the whole experience had me on edge. I'm still on edge, honestly, probably because he put me off *again* after assuring me I'd have answers soon.

He shook his head and said, "I must perform two kathanas before I am certain. If I'm wrong, well, I would prefer not to tell you something that may not be true."

Damn. I hate his logic. Because he was right; I much prefer knowing the truth than somebody's guess, even though (I can't believe I'm writing this) Sai Aleynten's guesses are probably more accurate than other people's truths, if only because I imagine he's the kind of person who hates being wrong.

Anyway, he rolled up both the maps and took them with him. I followed him until he came to a door on the sitting-room side of the hall and said, "This is not something for which I need an audience." I bristled at his sarcasm, but I couldn't think of anything to say in return. Nothing's coming to mind now, either. And I used to think I was so clever and witty.

So I tried a few doors until I found my room—fortunately I didn't come across any more naked couples—and now I've written it all down, and now I'm waiting. I can't decide what to do next. It's too soon for a meal, I don't want to bother all those people in the cavern, I refuse to go hunting for Terrael to entertain me, and there's nothing to read—oh, hell, there *isn't* going to be anything to read until I go back to my own country, is there? Just this book, and I know I'll get sick of my own writing sooner rather than later.

I just made myself homesick for a place I didn't even call home.

I hope Sai Aleynten's figured out a way to send me there.

I don't know what I'll do if I can't get back. Learn to read, probably, but am I going to be stuck here in the Darssan for the rest of my life? I doubt I have the aptitude, let alone the patience, to learn all those th'an, which frankly sound like a clunky way to work magic when you have the option to let it emerge from within you. And it's unlikely they'll have any of the books I'd need to learn more pouvrin.

Now I feel sorry for myself, so I'm going to lie down and indulge in that for a while. It's not as if I have anything else to do.

20 Senessay

There was no time yesterday to bring this record up to date. So much has happened—and yet I don't feel much has changed. One change is Sai Aleynten knows about this book now. I left it on the dresser when I lay down, and then I fell asleep—I've been sleeping restlessly, and I suppose I was more tired than I realized.

I woke to a knock at the door, and then Sai Aleynten came in without waiting for me to invite him, which might be a Castaviran custom but is more likely just Sai Aleynten being himself. "I could have been naked," was the first thing that emerged from my mouth, and then I wanted the floor to swallow me up.

Sai Aleynten raised an eyebrow and said, "Is it a custom of your people to sleep naked?"

"It's a custom of my people to wait to be invited before entering a room," I said, wishing once again I could come up with snarky responses to him.

"My apologies," he said, which surprised me, as I didn't think he was in the habit of apologizing to anyone. Then he saw the book lying on the dresser and moved to pick it up, so I jumped off the bed and snatched it up before he could touch it. "I meant no harm," he said.

"It's private," I said. The idea of anyone reading this book—yes, *now* I remember he couldn't read my language any more than I could read his, but at the time I was sleep-fogged and paranoid.

"I cannot read your language," he pointed out (see, *he* could think clearly!) and held out his hand, and I gave it to him. I wish I had half his presence, though really, if I did it would only draw attention to me, which is fatal for a thief and even worse for a secret mage.

He flipped through the pages, turned it over and looked at the cover, then handed it back to me. "Did you make this yourself?" he asked.

"Yes," I said. I didn't explain about how hard it was to find blank books, how I'd taught myself bookbinding with the help of a manuscript and scrounged the end pages from other books for paper, because that's not interesting to anyone but myself. But it's an accomplishment I'm proud of.

"It's very fine workmanship," he said. "And you are writing...what?"

I was going to say "My business" but when I opened my mouth, what came out was, "A record of my journeys." Damn him.

Sai Aleynten nodded, thoughtfully. "But you have been traveling for many years. Are the others lost?"

"They were in my pack when you—when I came here," I said, "and all of that stayed behind."

"I am sorry for that," he said. "It must be a great loss."

I couldn't think what to say to that. "Thank you," was what I eventually came up with. I put the book away in my pocket and said, "Do you finally have some answers for me?" I probably did look belligerent then. I know I sounded belligerent, because Sai Aleynten raised his eyebrow at me and smiled, just a tiny bit, and beckoned to me to follow him.

Now I wonder why he didn't send a messenger, Terrael or somebody, to fetch me. I'm still puzzling over that. I doubt the Wrelan has any time to waste going after inconvenient women who disrupt his institution. I suppose it's not important, but it's too strange for me to forget entirely.

We went, not into the cavern, but into the eating room, which was filling up fast. There have to be at least two hundred people in the Darssan, maybe more, and the room was barely big enough to hold them all. There certainly weren't enough stools, though someone near the front stood and gave me hers when Sai Aleynten and I approached. The front, that is, defined as the place where Sai Aleynten stood, since everyone immediately focused on him. I sat and waited. I don't mind writing that I was nervous, though at the time I had absolutely no idea how much cause for nervousness, let alone fear and panic, I had.

Sai Aleynten stood facing the room, hands clasped behind his back. He didn't seem as smug as he usually was, I think, more...he was almost eager, if he ever displayed that kind of emotion. It was just that there was a tenseness to him that made me think of how it feels the first time I try a new pouvra, the anticipation and nervousness and excited fear that maybe I'm wrong about it and this could be the time it kills me, though I've never seen references to improper use of pouvrin killing anyone. That kind of tenseness.

Eventually, the room settled down, and no more people entered, and Sai Aleynten waited a minute more before saying, "You all saw the kathana fail. It should have brought us the Codex Tiurindi, and it brought Thalessi instead."

He paused—I could see his face getting smug, like he was about to say something profound—and said, "It did not fail. The th'an described a literal interpretation of the kathana, and rather than bring us the Codex, it fulfilled its instructions perfectly. However, we were wrong in one key fact. We assumed Thalessi came to us from a time before the disaster. I have now confirmed that Thalessi is actually an inhabitant of the shadow world."

There was half a second of silence, and then everyone started talking at full volume. I sat there, stunned, because what Sai Aleynten said made no sense to me. Balaen isn't shadowy and neither am I. Sai Aleynten stood there looking smug at the commotion he'd caused, so I jumped up and shouted, "That's not an explanation, that's just you being a smug git and saying things that make no sense! I demand you tell me what the hell you're talking about!"

(More or less word for word what I said. The rest of this...I paid close attention, because I knew it would matter to me more than anyone else there, so I've only had to fill in a few blanks. Much more of this and my memory might actually be good enough to recall everything word for word. Maybe there's a pouvra for that.)

I actually got a reaction out of Sai Aleynten, the slightest look of surprise at my attack before the smug look descended again. "You're correct, you deserve more of an explanation," he said, and in a louder voice said, "Please calm yourselves. Thalessi has more questions than the rest of you, and I think she should have answers. Master Peressten, please explain to our guest what we know about the shadow world."

Terrael jumped up from where he was sitting, two tables over and a few seats back. "Of course, Sai Aleynten," he said. "Thalessi, a long time ago, nobody knows exactly how long, a group of mages was working on a powerful kathana. We don't know what it was supposed to do, but what actually happened was a catastrophe that caused the world to peel into two separate worlds, each invisible to the other. Not that anyone knew this at first. All we knew—all history records—is that there was widespread devastation. Cities were destroyed, people were killed, knowledge lost.

"If someone, or some place, disappeared, it was assumed they or it had simply been lost in the cataclysm. It wasn't until this decade that anyone knew what had truly happened. People started seeing ghosts, not only of people but of buildings and animals, all of them foreign-looking, and the mages of the Darssan discovered that those "ghosts" were, well, shadowy images of people and places that exist in the other world. That's why we call it the shadow world. We believe the same things are happening in your world—to you, if you were there, we would be the ghosts."

That raised a whole slew of questions, but I went with, "So why are these ghosts appearing?"

"Because the worlds are coming back together," Sai Aleynten said. "As they near one another, more of the shadow world becomes visible to us. And vice versa, probably."

More questions. "What does that mean? What happens when they recombine?" I said.

Sai Aleynten's face was still again, and much less smug. "Disaster," he said. "For both worlds. Destruction on a level not seen in millennia. Countries will fall, millions will die. We of the Darssan have been working for the last two years to discover a way to prevent it happening."

At this point, I was overflowing with questions to the point that I couldn't ask any of them. Fortunately, Sai Aleynten kept on going. "The Codex Tiurindi was a book referred to many times in later texts. It supposedly contained the kathana those first mages created, the one whose failure caused the division of worlds. We intended to summon it from the past, from a time before it was destroyed. But the kathana we used was not specific enough—could not be, because we know very little about the book—and instead it attempted to reverse the effects of the failed kathana, the one that separated the worlds.

"Since we use safeguards to prevent exactly that, it was able only to bring the worlds into contact briefly, at a single point—and, as its th'an still instructed it to summon something, it brought whatever was at that point from the shadow world into our own. It found you."

The shouting began again, though I remember thinking it was terribly distant and quiet now, and I found myself inexplicably fascinated with the smooth-rough texture of the table I sat at, how it felt like sandpaper under my palms, but pebbly sandpaper that's been used so often it's lost its bite. I couldn't stop looking at Sai Aleynten, whose face had gone expressionless again, and it felt as if—it's strange, but it felt as if despite the commotion he and I were the only people who really cared about what was happening to the world. To our worlds.

I opened my mouth to speak, and Sai Aleynten raised his hand for quiet, and of course he got it. "Ask," he said to me.

"It's not a question," I said. I still can't believe, even looking back as I am now, that everything was so obvious. "You can't send me back, can you? The worlds would have to touch again, and every time that happens, there's a chance the worlds will snap back together. You're not saying it, but I know I'm right."

Sai Aleynten paused, then nodded. "We did not realize the danger we were in with the kathana that brought you here," he said. "Those safeguards I spoke of become less effective as the worlds draw nearer to one another. In only a few weeks we will be unable to use certain kathanas for that reason."

"And how long before the...catastrophe?" I said.

Again, he paused, considering, then said, "Months. At the most."

That left me, once again, with nothing to say. I was trapped here. My world—it's still overwhelming to write "my world" so casually, as if it weren't the stuff of some child's fantasy—is going to be destroyed if the Darssan can't stop it, because no one in Balaen or anywhere else knows enough about magic to prevent the destruction. Right now I'm furious, because it's the only way I can keep from falling into despair—furious at those long-dead mages and their stupid, careless kathana that could not possibly have been worth what's happening to us now.

There. I did a couple of fire-summoning pouvrin and I feel better, though one of those window paintings is blackened now. I think I can focus on finishing this entry. Sometimes using magic relaxes me, and sometimes it makes me tenser, and I don't know what makes the difference, but that's not important now.

After Sai Aleynten said that, about it being a matter of months before the worlds came back together, the room got noisy again. This time it was the sound of a lot of people having technical discussions about what they were working on to stop the destruction. Sai Aleynten said nothing, just kept looking at me with that still, not as smug as usual expression, until I said, "What can *I* do?"

That shut everyone up, though not all at once—the silence spread out from around me to the farthest corners of the room until everything was quiet. Sai Aleynten said nothing. I said, "Do you really think that kathana brought me here because I was convenient? Me, one of the only people in my country, possibly in my world, who knows how to use pouvrin?"

Sai Aleynten said, "No. Had you not been in that place at that time, the kathana would simply have failed. I think whatever it is about you that can work magic...resonated with the kathana. I think your magic comes from a time before the separation. You are able to do many of the things we do with th'an, but in a different way, a way that has been lost to us."

"And you think that is the key to finding the kathana that will stop the worlds coming together," I said.

Sai Aleynten smiled that thin little smile again. "I see you need little explanation to grasp the essence of a problem," he said. "Yes, I believe your magic may be of use to us."

I didn't like the sound of that—as if my magic were something that could be separated from me, like the yolk of an egg—but I thought of the places I've visited, thought of them being destroyed by being mashed together with their Castaviran counterparts (though I don't know if that's how it happens, but then, does it matter?) and made a decision. "Then I'll help you," I said, and Sai Aleynten's smile grew fractionally wider.

"Sai Aleynten," Audryn said from somewhere behind me, and I swiveled around in my seat, craning to see her, "how will this affect our research?"

"For most of you, nothing will change," he said. "The general shape of the kathana will remain the same, and we will still need to determine whether it is possible to return the worlds to their original, fully separated state, or if it is only possible to halt the recombination. For those of you who have been searching the most ancient records for kathanas that might help us, you ~~will now work directly with me to interpret those records in light of the knowledge Thalessi brings to us. For the remainder of the day I expect each of you to reevaluate your research. Look for~~

All right. Enough of that. I'm lying at this point in implying I remembered all of that verbatim. And I'm being unfair to Sai Aleynten. I may dislike him, but throughout this speech it started to become clear to me why everyone here defers to him, and it's not because of his presence (which is powerful) and it's not because he's so much better at magic than they are (though I gather he's skilled beyond the reach of anyone except Terrael, who's hampered by his lack of common sense). It's his commitment to this cause.

Keeping the worlds from coming together is something that matters to him tremendously, and it was obvious even to me, who has trouble seeing past his smug face, that he respects and admires everyone who was in that room, and genuinely believes if anyone can find a solution to this problem, they can. And I could tell having his respect made everyone one of those people resolve to be worthy of it. It was strange, seeing him through their eyes, and it's made me reevaluate my first impressions of him. Though I still think he thinks too highly of himself, Sai or no.

So, basically, what Sai Aleynten said was they would have to go at their research in a different direction, but he didn't want to entirely throw away what they'd learned so far. And he told me he would work with me directly, which obviously didn't fill me with joy, but I could see the sense in it.

Then he asked everyone to separate into their "working groups," which I assume means the knots of people I observed while I was wandering around the tables waiting for Sai Aleynten, and come up with ideas for how to investigate my magic. Another thing that didn't make me feel happy, and made my opinion of Sai Aleynten drop again, because I'm afraid if I don't push back he's going to treat me like a thing and forget I'm a person. Well, I may not hate him as much anymore, but I sure as hell don't think he deserves my respect and he's definitely not getting my unthinking compliance.

All of this took until early afternoon yesterday, but then people kept asking me questions, then making notes on their writing boards and going away to discuss. Since it was usually the same questions over and over again, that made me irritable and bored at the same time, and I wish I'd thought to tell Sai Aleynten to keep everyone gathered together to ask their questions, but he disappeared and no one else seemed inclined to take the initiative.

That went on until it was almost too late for dinner, and I was starving, but Terrael and Audryn sat with me and asked more normal questions about my culture, and told me things about theirs, and that was almost fun. Then I was too tired to write, and that brings me to now.

I woke unnaturally early today and couldn't fall back asleep, so I decided to write, and now I'm thinking about breakfast. I imagine today is going to be more exciting than yesterday, and Sai Aleynten will have things for me to do, and I'll be able to see an actual kathana instead of just Sai Aleynten wiggling his fingers, as impressive as that is. But breakfast first.

CHAPTER FIVE

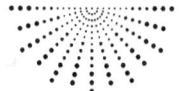

20 Senessay (afternoon)

Well, I was totally wrong. Damn Sai Aleynten and his stupid, smug, arrogant, keep everything to himself attitude. I spent the entire morning doing pouvrin at his command. Set this on fire. Move this. Walk through this. I refused to do the last, which made him angry, but what could he do about it? And he wouldn't tell me a thing about why he wanted all of that from me, just kept making notes on his stupid wooden board, or rather on papers he held on his stupid wooden board.

At first—probably for an hour, which is fifty-two minutes longer than I should have waited—I did as he asked without complaint. Then I got frustrated. Then I got stubborn and told him I was done "helping" him unless he told me what he was doing. And he had the gall to get smug and snooty about it and say "you wouldn't understand," in so many words. That was when I walked away.

I came back here so I could be angry in private, since nobody else was at fault for their Wrelan's arrogance, but then I realized I was hungry, so I stormed off to eat something. Everyone else was still gathered into groups, even though they were at lunch, so I didn't have to interact with anyone, which suited me fine. Then I came back to this room again and punched my pillow for a bit.

It's as if he's forgotten my world is at stake, too. He sees me as a tool to solve his problem, emphasis on "his" because he's so wrapped up in his own importance he thinks the whole burden is on him. Even though there are two hundred men and women here who are working every bit as hard as he is to keep this disaster from happening. I don't know why I ever thought we might be able to make common cause.

And yet I don't have any choice, do I? If there's even the slightest chance I could make this kathana work, if it could save both our worlds, I have to try, even if it means working with that smug git. Maybe I can attach myself to Terrael's group. No, Terrael may be willing to stand up to Sai Aleynten in some things, but I bet he'd defer to him in this.

I hate this. I hate feeling trapped and I hate Sai Aleynten for trapping me. There has to be an alternative.

20 Senessay (evening)

I just finished reading over what I wrote above and it makes me cringe to see how petulant I sound. Once again it turns out I was wrong in a lot of my assumptions. In my defense, Sai Aleynten was definitely at fault, too, but I shouldn't have given in to my anger like that. And I can admit, now, my first impressions of Sai Aleynten were all bad ones, and that predisposed me to dislike everything about him, even if he doesn't deserve most of it.

I don't think we can ever be friends, but I'm doing my best not to hate him and his smug face—there, I did it again. He only looks smug because of the way his eyebrows are crooked and his eyes are almost always half-lidded, like he's trying to hide the fact that he's laughing at you. But I've seen him talk to the rest of the mages, and he never laughs at anyone, or sounds dismissive or impatient. He does get sarcastic at times, and that makes me angry, because they all want his respect, or at least his approval, and I can imagine how his sarcasm makes them cringe. He has some definite character flaws, but after today I've decided not to assign him any more of them than are actually true.

About ten minutes after I finished writing the entry before this one and was sitting on my bed, wondering what to do next, there was a knock on my door. I waited, but no one came in, so I called out an invitation and Sai Aleynten opened the door. See, right there, that should have told me I was wrong about him: he'd learned from our earlier conversation. At the time, I was still angry enough not to give him credit for anything. I said, "If you want me to perform any more tricks for you, you can forget about it."

"No," he said. "That was wrong of me. I am afraid my eagerness interfered with my good sense."

That sounded like an apology, and I figured I wasn't going to get any more than that from him, so I said, "And what does your good sense tell you?"

"That we should work together, not separately," he said. "You know far more about your magic than I can understand simply by observing it. If anything, I should be showing you th'an and asking for your opinion on its similarities and differences to your pouvrin."

It staggered me—I was still operating on the assumption that Sai Aleynten was too arrogant to admit anyone might have something to teach him. I said, "I wish I could read your books. I've studied hundreds of ancient writings in my own world and I'd like to see what they have in common. I don't know how helpful it would be, but you did say you were trying to summon a book. If the worlds split, and some things ended up in one world and not the other, perhaps there's a book in my world that has some of the information you need."

Sai Aleynten nodded, and gestured to me to follow him. Again, it surprised me that he was listening to my suggestions, but it was at that point I started to feel ashamed of myself for damning him so thoroughly. We went to the gold circle and the bookshelves surrounding it, and Sai Aleynten removed a book that looked as if it had been in a fire. "Tell me if you recognize anything," he said, and turned the pages for me. The writing was gibberish, and I shook my head. "What does it say?" I said.

"Nothing any of us can read," he said, closing the book. "It is very old, but probably not as old as the separation. You said you have studied ancient books; were any of them in languages you did not recognize? Or languages you could not read but were able to decipher?"

Huh. I can't believe I didn't see this before. In asking that question, Sai Aleynten paid me a huge compliment by assuming I'd be smart enough to learn to read an ancient language. Now I feel *incredibly* guilty. But I still don't like him very much.

"I was able to work out two books because they were similar to one of the languages I speak," I said. "But most of them were unintelligible to me. I don't remember seeing any in this script, though."

Sai Aleynten put the book away and took down another. "This might become tedious," he said, "but if there is any chance you can read a book we have been unable to, it could mean the difference between failure and success."

That was another apology, I think. "I understand," I said. "You might try explaining things to me instead of assuming I can't."

"I should not have said that," he said. "I meant only that what I was doing requires a great deal of study in th'an to understand, study I know you lack. Does it help to know I would have said the same to half the men and women in the Darssan?"

It did, actually. "Yes," I said. "But you should have been that specific."

"As I said, I allowed my eagerness to get in the way of my good sense. I have a regrettable tendency to become so focused on a goal I have trouble expressing myself. I apologize."

That was the second time he'd used that word to me. I

I stopped writing there for about fifteen minutes while I thought about it. I really have been stupid and prejudiced, and it's embarrassing. Yes, Sai Aleynten has been insufferable at times, and I think we might be too different ever to be friends, and I'm never going to give him the respect he gets from the mages, but I have no reason to hate him. So, again, I repeat my resolution to give him more credit than I'm inclined to.

Anyway, his apologizing made the rest of my anger disappear. I said, "I'm afraid I get impatient when I'm not seeing progress. I'm sorry I stormed off like that."

"Then let us see if we cannot make progress together," he said, and smiled, so I smiled back at him, and that made me feel better, like we might actually be able to find a solution.

He showed me a few more books, none of which I could read. These were beautiful books. I've seen the new ones coming out of Venetry, the ones made by machine so they're all alike, and those are pretty, but there is something about a hand-stitched binding and tooled leather cover that satisfies me down to the core.

Some of them were illuminated with abstract designs, and some had animals I'm sure were fantastical decorating the capitals of the pages, and there was one where the cover was crusted with gems in a spiraling pattern that was simply amazing. Some of the gems had been added more recently; the glue holding them in was a different consistency from the older ones. It made me wonder whether this book was special, that it had been restored to its original condition, or if someone just couldn't bear to see it imperfect.

I touched one of the gems, then pulled my hand away quickly, thinking Sai Aleynten might object to my handling these books, but he said, "I think, having seen the book you created, I need not fear you would damage this one," and he gave it to me so I could open the pages and exclaim at the jewel-like colors decorating the front page. I wish I could read it, but again, it's not in a language I understand.

I asked him if *he* could read it, and he said, "I am not entirely fluent in this language, but I know it is a book of stories. It came from the library of the palace at Colosse and we believe it was made for the children of an Empress. I wonder if they appreciated it."

"They couldn't have handled it much, if it's in this condition," I said.

He nodded, and asked for the book back so he could put it away. We went through about fifty books, and I was starting to become irritated because we weren't succeeding, when he said, "I have been showing you books that are of relatively recent date, in the hope that our languages might not have separated as far as we feared. I have not given up hope that we will find one you are capable of reading, but the results of this initial exploration are not positive."

(He really does talk like this, though I'm not getting the words exactly right. Very precise and formal, like the rest of him.)

"I wish I could tell you the age of the oldest book I've been able to read, but when I find them in places like the ruins, places whose age I don't know either, it's hard to tell," I said. "Some of them are kept in dry, airless vaults, preserved so they don't look much older than the day they were written."

"The ruins," Sai Aleynten said. "Of *course*. I should have thought of it before. We must look at the maps again." He grabbed my hand and towed me rapidly after him, and I remembered he has a grip like a clocker crab. There was no point in trying to get free, and anyway I wanted to see what he had in mind.

He dragged me to the map room and pulled out the parchment— well, I've been calling it parchment, but it's far bigger than any parchment I've ever seen, and more translucent, too—that I'd drawn the map of Balaen on, and unrolled it. "Show me the places where you have found books you could decipher," he said curtly.

I ignored his tone and pointed at three ruins. Two of them had had books that were in the language that was a derivative of Enthendil, and in the other I found the book where I could barely make out nouns and a few verbs. Sai Aleynten stared at the map for a bit, then rushed out of the room, this time leaving me behind, so I said a few choice words in my exasperation and followed him at a slightly slower pace.

He ran back to the shelves and began running his finger across the spines, occasionally pulling out a book and setting it on a nearby table, which was already cluttered with books and papers and a few more of those carved animal stones. When he was finished, he had three piles of books—not many, really, compared to how many were on the shelves. "Look at this one," he demanded, and flipped open a cover.

"Ask me," I said.

He blinked at me. "I did."

"No," I said, "you ordered me. I understand you're excited about something, but I don't see why that entitles you to be rude." See how polite I was? Even though he was behaving like an arrogant git. And I don't think it's unreasonable for me to point that out.

He opened his mouth, probably to object, and that was when I realized we had an audience. Sai Aleynten rushing around was bound to draw attention, and while the gray-robes watching us were doing so covertly, I could tell by the way their activity went to almost nothing that they were intensely interested in this conversation. "My apologies, again," he said. I thought I heard a couple of people gasp, very quietly. "I meant, I believe we may have better luck with this book, and would you mind looking at it?"

"Thank you," I said, and took a look at the pages. The first two were meaningless. I turned a few more pages, opened my mouth to say, "I still can't read it," and then my mouth stayed open in astonishment when I realized I could.

I trailed my fingers down the page, then thought better of touching anything so old, and continued using only my eyes. Reading it was as slow as I remembered it being, the last time I'd read a book in this language, but that book had taught me the walk-through-walls pouvra, and I'll never forget that. And it was strange, reading a non-magical text in a language I associate so strongly with pouvrin.

"It's a history," I said, and Sai Aleynten's hand, resting on the table nearby, closed into a fist. "I think the first—wait a minute." I picked up the book and turned it face down, and now the gasps were louder, and I could tell Sai Aleynten wanted to snatch the book out of my hands. I lifted it to eye level and sighted along the place where the pages joined the spine.

"The first three pages were bound into it later," I said. "They might be an introduction for anyone reading it years after it was written. The rest...I can only summarize, because this language has tenses yours doesn't, but it begins "Eddon, God and King—"

That was as far as I got before the entire room erupted in shouting. Sai Aleynten rested both his fists on the table and bowed his head. Terrael came out of nowhere and grabbed me around the waist, then backed away when I juggled the book and nearly dropped it. He was too excited to speak, and honestly, I had no idea what they were so excited about, but I do now, and it's—well, Sai Aleynten thinks it's hugely important, and I think if I'd been working on this problem for two years, I would agree with him. What little I do understand is still exciting. To sum up:

1. Everyone in Castavir knows those words. They are the opening sentence of a famous book about the god-kings of Castavir. (They still have god-kings, or now god-emperors, though it doesn't mean what I think it means, according to Terrael, but there wasn't time for him to explain it to me.)

2. What I was holding was undoubtedly the original book.

3. They now know to within a few years how old it is, which gives them dates for several of their other books, some of which they can read.

4. This helps them work backward toward discovering whatever language it was the Codex Tiurindi was written in. (Why they were trying to summon it when they didn't know if they could read it baffles me, but I think it might be a measure of how desperate they all are. Which I can understand.)

I'm not an expert on languages, but Terrael is, and what he explained is if they have a text in an unknown language, and they know what that text is, they can use it to translate that language into theirs and read other books. Which makes sense. I'm less certain of the other thing he said, about being able to work out how a language changed over time and reverse that process, but, again, he's the expert.

The one thing I insisted on is being allowed to take the book to my room with me tonight. I argued it would help me understand their culture better, but really, I am so tired of having nothing to read!

And I think Sai Aleynten knew that, because he agreed to my request with a little smile. He never gives anything away, but I know he's relieved at having made some progress.

And Terrael—*he* was the one who objected to me taking the book, but that was because he was so eager to start translating you could see him vibrate. It took all of Sai Aleynten's force of presence to get him to calm down and join the others in ransacking the bookshelves. And it did look like ransacking, when I left. Sai Aleynten assured me they do this all the time, rearrange the books to represent whatever theory they're following at the moment. That's an interesting idea, that the shape of the library might have something to do with the knowledge that comes out of it.

What they're doing now is looking for all the books written in that language, and the ones they think are similar to it, and tomorrow we are going to begin translating those books. I'm supposed to read the first pages to get an idea of what kind of knowledge is in each book, so we can focus on studying the magic books first.

Terrael is going to work on this book, learning to read the language—he really is some kind of savant, Sai Aleynten seemed to think it wouldn't take him more than three days to become fluent—so I'd better read quickly, because I doubt Terrael is going to want to wait on me tomorrow morning.

Funny. I wrote "we" just a few lines ago. I'm a stranger to this world, I don't understand their society, and yet I feel now as if I'm a part of something. Like I've been accepted here, even if only as the strange cousin from across the ocean who has to have everything explained to her. It's a comfortable feeling.

Now I'm going to put this away and do some reading. Fortunately, it's not a very thick book, though it is a little heavy to hold comfortably in bed. But I'm so glad to have something to read that isn't my own writing I don't even care.

CHAPTER SIX

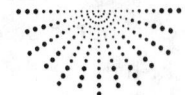

21 Senessay

I had a bath this morning, and I'm trying hard not to feel totally humiliated about it. I do have a sense of personal hygiene, it's just that sometimes I go days or even, once, weeks with no more chance to bathe than a couple of quick swipes in strategic places. And I'm usually by myself, so there's no one to be offended if I smell bad. So I admit sometimes I forget how long it's been. Really, though, your own smell grows so gradually, and is around you all the time, it's no wonder I can't always tell when I'm becoming ripe.

But this morning at breakfast, I saw Audryn wrinkle her nose in my direction—she didn't realize I noticed—and when the meal was done, she said, "I'm going to take a bath, Thalessi, would you like to join me?" and I wanted to die of embarrassment. Terrael had no idea what was going on. He's beautifully ignorant sometimes. Now all I can think about is how everyone must have been so disgusted all week, what with me wandering around trailing my unique stench.

Still, Audryn was perfectly well-mannered about it, and kept up the pretense she needed to bathe—I doubt she's ever smelled of unwashed body in her life, and her hair is never stringy or greasy as mine sometimes gets when it's humid. She took me through the cavern to a door that opened on a wider, straighter corridor, and we walked a short distance to what looked like a natural cave opening. It couldn't have been, though, because there were curving passages that went left and right that were shaped stone.

I smelled water near, hot water, and felt the wetness in the air that comes from a large body of water in an enclosed space. We went to the left, turned a corner, and the passage opened up into a large cave with a high ceiling. Five or six pools of varying sizes, the largest maybe fifty feet across, were scattered across the floor, one of them coming all the way to the right-hand wall, which unlike the rest of the cave was perfectly straight and smooth.

There were a few women relaxing in the smaller pools, and one woman swimming with long, smooth strokes back and forth across the largest pool. All of them were completely naked. It hadn't occurred to me to wonder what kind of modesty taboos Castavirans had, but now I know it's perfectly normal to go naked among members of your own sex, and completely embarrassing to be naked in front of someone of the opposite sex. This is true regardless of which sex you're attracted to, according to Audryn. So the bathing pools are segregated—that's what the wall is for. When we were sitting in one of the hot pools, Sovrin—never mind, I'm getting ahead of myself again.

Audryn shucked her clothes as she walked toward the back of the room, nodding at a few of the women, and I followed her example. It was uncomfortable, because Balaenic custom is that nudity is really only acceptable in front of people you're close to, male or female, but I make a habit of following the customs of whatever place I'm in, and the women in the pools seemed disinclined to ogle.

Audryn's beautiful, well-proportioned in a way I'm not, and when she loosed her hair from the day's clip (I still haven't seen her wear the same one twice, and they're all exquisite works of the metal-smith's art) it fell nearly to the small of her back like a chocolate waterfall. I try not to compare myself to other women, because I know I have a tendency to be overly critical of my physical flaws, but it was hard not to wish I had legs like hers.

The far end of the cave had a fold in it that led on one side to a room with three commodes, all of them with water flowing through them, and on the other side to a room where water poured in a steady flow from a couple of openings in the wall and disappeared down an iron grate. The floor was wet, but too rough to be slippery.

Audryn took a long-handled dipper with a wide, deep bowl, and an odd-looking sponge, so I did the same. She filled the dipper from one of the streams of water and poured it over herself, then began scrubbing with the sponge. "You drop it in that hole there when you're finished," she said, pointing, and went back to washing herself. I held my dipper under the water, then poured it over my shoulders. It was lukewarm, a little warmer than the ocean off Thalessa, but fresh instead of salt, and oh, how good it felt!

I started scrubbing and discovered the sponge had been treated with some kind of soapy liquid that foamed up wherever I rubbed. It wasn't a natural sponge, though it looked like one. I don't know what it was made of. I scrubbed myself pink, then rinsed off and poured more water over my head.

Audryn handed me a large dollop of a gritty brown soap that smelled like mint and demonstrated how to rub it into my hair. I could have rubbed my scalp with it all day long, it felt so good, but eventually I rinsed my hair—this took a while, I have a lot of hair— and squeezed the extra water out. Then I dropped the sponge into the hole and hung the dipper back on its hook.

"This is my favorite part," Audryn said, and we went back into the cave, where Audryn made straight for one of the pools. This one was already occupied, and steam rose off its surface, and as we approached I smelled hot water. There were steps carved into the pool's side, and Audryn gingerly descended, making a couple of squeaks, then swam to the side of the pool opposite the steps. I followed her.

The water was *hot*. Not boiling hot, not truly uncomfortable, just several degrees hotter than body temperature. The pool was too deep for me to touch bottom, so I swam to the side and discovered there was a ledge circling the pool that was just deep enough that when I sat on it, my shoulders were barely above the water. And it felt *amazing*. I stretched out my legs and every one of my muscles relaxed. I hadn't realized how tense I was until that moment.

"Your hair is incredible," the other woman said. I don't know how she knew that, given that her eyes were closed and I'd thought she was asleep until she spoke. "I've never seen that color before."

"I have," said Audryn. "A lot of Viravonians have hair that color. I don't suppose you come from there, Thalessi? I mean the corresponding place in your world."

"No, I was born near the ocean," I said. "You all have hair the same color, mostly."

"Sarial's hair is red," Audryn said, "but mostly we're all native Castavirans or Helvirites. Though there's more intermarrying, this last century."

"True. My mother's mother is Endellaviran," the other woman said. "I'm Sovrin, by the way. I'd salute you, but I think my muscles have melted in sheer joy."

That made me laugh. "We don't have anything like this where I come from," I said. "The rich houses have plumbing, and large baths, but all the natural hot springs I've seen are too hot for bathing."

"This isn't natural, it's a kathana that does it," Sovrin said. "And made the wall between the chambers, after creating the pools. The men's side isn't as nice as ours."

"That seems unfair," I said.

"It's their responsibility to clean it, so it's their own fault if it's not as nice," Audryn said. "I've heard they piss in the pools sometimes, but I don't believe it. That would get disgusting very quickly. There's a reason we bathe in the kiorka instead of out here. So we don't have to swim in our own filth."

"Fae sneaked in there with Haddan once, after midnight, and she said the men leave their towels lying around for the person on duty to clean up in the morning, when he makes the sponges," Sovrin said.

"I thought the sponges looked unnatural," I said.

"They are. Though with you coming from near the ocean, I guess you would know," Sovrin said.

"Thalessi, you'll want to wash your clothes, yes?" Audryn said. "Sovrin can lend you something. You're the same height."

I eyed Sovrin's breasts, which are quite a bit larger than mine, but said, "That would be nice. And I don't suppose anyone did anything about my jacket?"

"It's probably in the laundry somewhere," Sovrin said. "We can find it, and take your clothes there. Damn, it's my turn in the laundry tomorrow. I hate the laundry. Always leaves your hands wrinkled, no matter what th'an you use."

Audryn slipped off the ledge and swam to the stairs. "Sovrin, stop lazing about and come with us. You know how your group hates it when you show up late."

"What are they going to do about it?" Sovrin said, but she climbed out of the pool and I followed them both. We dried off, and I tried to get as much water out of my hair as I could, but I knew from experience it was going to stay wet for a while. I wished I had time for a real swim in the large pool. I think I'll go back tomorrow morning, after I find a way to keep my hair wrapped around my head so it doesn't get wet again.

Sovrin and Audryn both had plain green dressing gowns to wear, but I had to put on my own clothes for the walk back to Sovrin's room, and I couldn't believe how filthy they felt now I was clean. I don't think I've ever been this clean in my whole life.

Sovrin's room was a surprise. The furniture was all the same as the other bedrooms, just that one narrow bed and the wardrobe and dresser that looked like they'd seen a lot of wear, but Sovrin's bed was unmade and her gray robe lay crumpled on the floor, and her black trousers were draped over a corner of the dresser. "Yes, Sovrin is a slob," Audryn said, seeing my expression.

"No point in making a bed you're going to get back into later," Sovrin said. She opened dresser drawers and began pulling out clothes that were definitely not gray robes and black trousers.

"I've never seen you all wear anything but the uniform," I said.

Audryn said, "We rarely have the chance to, but sometimes there are rest days, once every two weeks now. It used to be more often, but...our work has more urgency than it used to, and I think we might never stop if Sai Aleynten didn't insist we take breaks."

I have to stop underestimating Sai Aleynten. True, I think he'd push himself past the breaking point if he had to, but I'd assumed he treated his subordinates (is that what they are?) the same way.

Sovrin came up with a long-sleeved shirt with a wide neck and tossed it at me. "If it fits, you can have it," she said. "I don't like how tight it is across the chest, on me, and you're nice and slender." Which is a polite way of saying "flat-chested," but I'm sure she meant it as a compliment.

She found a few more shirts, then some trousers and even a skirt, which I don't normally wear because they're hard to run in and even harder to climb the outside of a building in, even when you don't care if people can see your underwear. And speaking of underwear, there was a moment of embarrassment for all of us when Sovrin handed me some short pants made of soft unbleached cotton, and said, "I don't know if...you didn't seem to..."

I took them graciously and said, "Yes, I do wear undershorts. I wore through my last pair about two weeks before I came here, and I wasn't in a position to buy more. So thank you."

Sovrin chuckled, and said, "That's a relief, and I hope you don't wear breast bands, because I'm damn sure mine won't fit you." We all laughed at that. She's got a very generous figure, but the undershorts are only a little too large. And, not that I'm not grateful, but I can admit in the privacy of this book I hope someday I'll have clothes that fit again.

There were a lot of other things we talked about that I forgot to put in before. Like, Sovrin told me more about the construction of the bathing chamber, how the earliest mages built it when they carved out the rest of the Darssan, and how the wall between the sections was erected only eighty years ago, when the trend for separate bathing spread to all levels of society.

And I learned nobody starts work early in the Darssan. Leisurely breakfasts and chores and bathing all get done before work begins, on the theory that minds will be properly limbered up if they are well awake and aren't burdened by worry about other responsibilities. Though I would bet hard money, if I had any, that Sai Aleynten is an early riser. I don't think that's me being spiteful.

And somewhere in all of this, I asked them to call me by my praenoma, Sesskia, instead of my placename. I tried to make it sound casual, so it wouldn't embarrass them to know how much it meant to me, but...I felt comfortable with them in a way I've never felt with anyone but my family before. Maybe not friends, yet, but I think they will be, and I wanted to give them something in exchange for how kind they've been to me.

They of course didn't think anything of it, and wanted to know about placenames, and exchanged glances when I explained that Thalessi Scales refers to my work in the fishery and I'd kept it as camouflage even though I no longer worked in the fishery. I couldn't exactly call myself Thalessi Mage.

Then Sovrin went to join her group. She's group leader, which is why she said her group couldn't really do anything about her being late, but I think she was exaggerating, because she didn't waste any time getting dressed. After that, Audryn and I went to her room, where she loaned me a comb and I managed to get it through my tangle of hair, and I admired her collection of hairpins and clips.

I think it surprised her that I was so knowledgeable about the quality of most of her pieces (none of them are inexpensive, and one or two look old), but I chose not to tell her I'm more a thief than I am a mage, even if I only became a thief to steal books that would teach me magery. No, that's a lie, I became a thief so Mam and Bridie and I wouldn't starve to death. Damn it. I swore I wouldn't think about Bridie again, because I get so furious with Mam

More fire-summoning pouvra. That painting is all but obliterated now. I'm calm. I'm rational. Time for another list.

What I did today:

1. Read a lot of books. At least, read the first pages of a lot of books.

2. Argued with Sai Aleynten about which books were important. I realize he's been studying this for a long time, but I've been reading

ancient tomes for at least as long as he has and I've learned to recognize when a writer knows what she is talking about.

3. Had lunch and bitched to Terrael and Audryn about how unreasonable Sai Aleynten is, which got no sympathy because they think the sun shines out of his ass.

4. Felt guilty about once again being overly critical of Sai Aleynten, who after all doesn't know what I'm capable of. As far as he can tell, I'm just a strange mage who knows some tricks he doesn't and happens to be able to read a language he can't.

5. Made peace with Sai Aleynten, who unbent so far as to admit he wasn't taking my input seriously. We altered our method of study accordingly. He tells me what matters to him, and I read not only the first pages but skim some of the others as well, looking for those things. I also tell him when I find something that would be meaningful to *my* magic, which isn't often, but I've found at least one book that might give me a new pouvra, and I got to keep that one. Sai Aleynten was excited about that book, though he only shows excitement by becoming still and expressionless.

5a. I really wonder, now, what made Sai Aleynten the way he is. I would have sworn he was indifferent to practically everything, but the more I interact with him, the more I realize he's just so self-contained it's a wonder he doesn't erupt. He gets sarcastic instead. Good thing he doesn't turn that on me, because I would shout at him, since I don't share the respect the other mages have for him.

And that's not entirely true, either. True, yes, in the sense that I don't venerate him—and I don't mean that slightingly, it's just that I know the mages respect his person and not only his role—but I'm beginning to see how good he is at what he does. He's quick to grasp the implications of what I'm reading, and I know he's already memorized the new configuration of the library, and of course he can write th'an on air.

Which reminds me I still haven't seen a real kathana. I keep forgetting to ask someone when that will happen, there's always so much else going on. Besides, Terrael is almost totally occupied with translating the Eddon book. Audryn had to drag him to the refectory (this is what they call the eating room) so he'd leave the book behind, because of course you wouldn't eat while you were touching it. Audryn is in Terrael's working group, by which I mean Terrael is the leader, and I think one of her jobs is keeping him either focused on a problem instead of flitting about, or *not* focused on a problem to the point of forgetting to eat or, and I sympathize with this, bathe.

When I wasn't bitching about Sai Aleynten, I had all sorts of questions about the Eddon book. I stayed up far too late reading it, but aside from not wanting to give it to Terrael without finishing it, it fascinated me.

The short version: Eddon was a king of Castavir in the dark time after the disaster. The royal family still existed, but people were so busy scrounging for a living they didn't have time for kings. Eddon had a vision—Okay. This is the part I didn't understand. Eddon had a vision where he learned he was God and he had a duty to make Castavir the greatest nation in the world. So he used his personal resources and what was left of the kingdom's treasury to build an army and levy taxes.

Then he used the taxes to build up the kingdom's infrastructure, improve its economy and so forth, and by the time he died Castavir was the region's economic powerhouse. Interesting, because in my world most rulers would interpret "greatest nation" to mean "the one with the biggest army." So whatever else Eddon was, he was practical. And he taught his heirs they would become God, or at least God's avatar on earth, as long as they were worthy to hold the throne.

Well, I suppose most of that makes sense. What didn't make sense was I couldn't tell if the author of the book believed in Eddon's godhood or not. So that was what I asked Terrael and Audryn.

And they became really quiet and furtive, and Terrael started on this long and complicated explanation I couldn't understand, until Audryn shushed him and said, "As far as anyone is concerned, as far as people will say, the God-Empress Renatha is God on earth. She certainly believes it. Whether that means she's actually God is more complicated. But no one would ever come out and deny her status."

And she gave me a very meaning look that I understood perfectly.

It said, *She's not God, but who knows what she might do to someone who doubted that?*

So now I know more about the ruler of the Castaviran Empire, but it only raises more questions. Like: Is her rule benevolent or despotic? How far is she willing to go to enforce her dicta? Is she as unstable as Audryn hinted at? How much power does she actually have, versus the power of the individual countries' rulers? I've traveled in countries where the rule of law was overtaken by martial law, and it's not pretty. I'm happy it's unlikely I'll ever be in a position to care about what God-Empress Renatha does.

More I learned from the book: Another thing Eddon did was make Castavir welcoming to mages, who were hated and feared because of their role in the disaster. The book says they were blamed for things they hadn't actually done, which suggests the author was fairly sympathetic to mages himself. And of course I already knew about Audryn's namesake founding the Darssan.

Then there was the growth of the Empire. During Eddon's time, Castavir absorbed a couple of smaller countries, but peacefully— they saw the benefits of being part of the Castaviran economy. Castavir conquered Helviran a century later, when one of Eddon's successors realized not having a seaport (Castavir is land-locked) was hurting them, and since Helviran had a history of killing off its mages, Castavir and its battle mages conquered them readily.

That was where the book ended, so I asked Terrael and Audryn what happened next. They told me there was a Castaviran Empress, much later, who wanted to conquer the whole world, and she managed to triple the Empire's size before her death. Her successors weren't so talented, and the Empire shrank back to almost its original size, with the addition of Endellavir and Viravon. That was about a hundred years ago. Endellavir assimilated into the Empire well, though it has a strong cultural tradition and all these holidays specific to Endellaviran history, but Viravon is this tiny, scrappy little place whose people still resent being annexed, and there are rebels there who fight the Empress and whom the army hasn't been able to suppress. I think I like the Viravonians.

Let's see, what else...I had some interaction with the mages in the other groups. Sovrin's group had some very specific questions about the water-summoning pouvra, and we all went to the bathing room (her group is all women, I don't know why) so we could take turns summoning water in our different ways.

I asked them to show me how they draw th'an, and it turns out they all have fat writing tools they use to write on their boards. The th'an for summoning water is relatively simple, which means it's still incredibly complex, but it's fascinating—they use one of those fat writing tools to draw the th'an (I guess it's actually a pair of th'an linked or overlaid on each other) and then the th'an disappears and a gallon of water appears in midair and splashes into the pool, or whatever they summon it over.

The way the water from the th'an appears is identical to mine, though it turns out I have better control over how much I create (or summon from elsewhere, I don't know exactly), so Sai Aleynten's theory that my magic is the same as theirs, only done in a different way, might be true. They were disappointed that I couldn't show them the water-summoning pouvra—I mean the shape I have to bend my will to in order to make things happen, not the effect—and I tried to draw it out for them, but it was too difficult to show the three-dimensional shape on a piece of paper.

There was something else that happened, something I didn't tell them about. I had this feeling, looking at the th'an, that it was familiar somehow. As if I'd seen it before. But I know I've never seen th'an in my world, and though my first guess was that it was a visual representation of a pouvra, it was obvious the th'an wasn't complex enough for that.

Which, now I think about it, is strange, considering I don't think I'd ever be able to master their th'an, and yet pouvrin are more complex than that and—well, I wouldn't say it's easy to learn them, because it's definitely not, but they make sense to me in a way th'an and kathanas don't. I don't know. I'm going to pay closer attention to the th'an they scribe and see if I can figure out why they seem familiar.

Something I should probably ask Sai Aleynten tomorrow morning is why some of their th'an vanish when they've been executed, and others, like the ones on the light baskets and the aeden, are permanent. I don't know if it means anything, I'm just curious.

I'm going to read a little from the new book now, but I'm too tired for any real study. That will have to wait for tomorrow. I'm not even sure what pouvra this book hints at, which would be exciting if I weren't about to fall asleep.

22 Senessay

More reading. Another argument with Sai Aleynten, short-lived and completely my fault this time, and I managed to suppress my dislike of him long enough to apologize genuinely. No time to read the pouvra book, no time to write anything longer. Very tired.

23 Senessay

See above, except without the argument. I think—I wouldn't say I like Sai Aleynten, but I don't dislike him anymore, either. I don't I was about to write "I don't know why" but I do know why, it's because his annoying mannerisms no longer annoy me. I suppose I'm getting used to him.

There was an unexpected quarrel between two of the groups over resources, namely a book they both demanded, that turned into a fist fight before Sai Aleynten broke it up with loud, penetrating sarcasm. There's been quite a bit of muttering recently, nothing nearly so explosive as the fight, but tension is high, and I heard a couple of people saying they'd better have a rest day soon, or there might be real trouble.

I'm nervous because I don't know the politics of the Darssan and am now constantly afraid of saying or doing something inadvertently offensive. They'd probably laugh it off as just another example of my foreign ignorance, but I find I want these people to like me.

Read a few pages of the pouvra book but was too tired to focus. Bed now.

24 Senessay

I've decided I have to insist I be given time for my own research. I don't even care if this new pouvra helps their research; I've spent too many years working at becoming a mage to be able to pass up the opportunity to learn something new. I still don't know what it does, but from the reading I've been able to do, in pieces between doing other things, I'm certain this describes a pouvra I don't know.

Oh. I'm so stupid. This book was written *after* the disaster. I'm going to blame my constant tiredness on not realizing it sooner. If this was written post-disaster, and it contains instructions for a pouvra, AND these mages have never heard of pouvrin—

I have to talk to Sai Aleynten *right now*.

Later, same day

Sai Aleynten went so completely expressionless when I told him what I'd learned I thought he'd had a seizure. Eventually, he said, "How sure are you of this?"

"I can't be sure until I've studied it more," I said. "But every book I've ever read that taught about pouvrin had the same basic structure, and this book is the same. Or at least I think it's the same."

He looked at the book, raised its cover and flipped over a few pages as if the language would suddenly become comprehensible to him, and said, "We do not know its age. Surely knowledge of pouvrin could not have persisted many centuries only to be written down much later than the disaster."

"I agree," I said. "I think I should focus my efforts on this."

"Yes," he said. "Master Peressten has succeeded in learning this language and can now take over your responsibilities."

"Good," I said, though I felt bereft. "I'll let you know what I find."

"I would appreciate frequent updates, even if you learn nothing immediately," he said. "Unless that would be inconvenient."

That's exactly what he said. I was so stunned, it was so unexpectedly humble, that the words stayed with me all the way back to this room. I know I mumbled something incoherent in agreement—*those* words escape me utterly—but I didn't know what to say, because I felt so incredibly guilty about ever hating him. I don't know if it's his fault or not that he's the way he is, but aside from the sarcasm and the occasional rudeness, he's not a bad person.

He demands a lot from his mages, but I know he works himself harder than anyone else. I was late to dinner two nights ago, and I had to cross the cavern to get to the refectory, and he was still there by the gold circle, standing over the table and writing something as he read from one of the books. He didn't even notice me, that's how focused he was (well, that and I'm in the habit of moving silently). And I understand what it's like to be driven to learn something, though none of the pouvrin I've studied were potentially world-saving.

I think I do like him, after all.

CHAPTER SEVEN

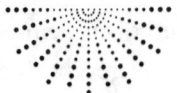

25 Senessay

Rest day. I was planning to study the new pouvra in earnest, but Sovrin barged into my room without knocking and said, "Put the book down and get out of bed, Sesskia, or I'll drop you in the pool wearing all your clothes." She's big enough I think she could do it, so I got dressed (I'm sleeping in that long-sleeved shirt and undershorts now, and the shirt is so comfortable I don't even mind that it's a little large) and went with her to the bathing room.

Most of the women were already there, splashing around in the big pool or lying back in one of the smaller ones. I took off my clothes and put them in one of the cubbies—I forgot to mention this, there are shelves divided into foot-wide cubbies for storing clothing off the wet floor. The large pool slopes at one end, like wading into the surf but without the waves, and at the far end I think it's about ten feet deep. I swam down to the bottom, forgetting I didn't want to get my hair wet, and felt a little current that told me the water was circulating. So Audryn was exaggerating about swimming in their own filth, but I still wouldn't piss in the pool.

When I came up, Audryn had arrived, and there were about ten other women I knew to speak to, most of them from Sovrin's group.

About half the women could swim well, and the others paddled and splashed closer to the shallow end. We ended up talking about the ocean, because some of the women were from Helviran and had either lived on the coast or visited there often.

It was strange, talking about a place I knew so well that was exactly like the one they knew in some respects and completely foreign in others. We worked out where Thalessa was, and it seems in this world there had been a few settlements there over the centuries that had eventually failed and disappeared, though no one knew why. I told them about Thalessa, the good things, and I made my job at the fishery sound funny rather than backbreakingly tedious and awful.

I didn't talk about Mam or my sisters, or how the magic woke up inside me, just that I'd left Thalessa at seventeen to travel the world in search of knowledge. And I downplayed the fact that I'm a thief. I don't know what they'd make of that, but in Balaen it's not something that engenders trust. So I glossed over some of the ways I'd acquired books, and focused instead on the books themselves. They were all interested in those, of course, and somewhere in the middle of the discussion I gave all of them my praenoma, and it didn't feel at all awkward or wrong.

At that point, all our hands were pruny, and someone suggested we move the conversation to the refectory, because no one had eaten yet. I had to borrow another comb, which makes me wonder if there's any way I can get some things for myself instead of borrowing all the time. Everyone's very generous, but I wish—I never had many things, but I left all of them behind, and I didn't realize how much I cared about being independent even on the level of owning my own comb.

We had breakfast, and the conversation continued, attracting some of the men, who hovered around the edges of our company of women, making comments about being excluded that the women laughed at. They all wanted to know about my life, and my culture, and all sorts of things, and I talked until I was nearly hoarse, telling stories that made them laugh, or gasp, or both at the same time. I can't believe how comfortable I felt. I know I wrote before that I was starting to feel like part of the group, but I meant I felt they'd accepted me as being committed to the same goals and capable of working alongside them. Now I feel I'm among friends. I haven't had friends since

I haven't ever had friends.

I never thought about it, and now I'm trying not to feel sorry for myself, but how could I, with the life I've lived? There have always been people I liked, people I worked with at the fishery, and before that kids I played with in the street, before Dad died and everything went to hell, but no one I'd call friend. It's a miracle I even know what friendship looks like. And no, I'm still not that close to anyone here, but I know Sovrin and Audryn are becoming my friends, and Terrael has no concept of *not* liking people. It's...unexpected.

There. I'm done being self-indulgent. The point is I had a wonderful morning that turned into a big, messy, noisy communal lunch, with people stealing food off other people's plates and the woman running the kitchen popping out now and then to complain that she wasn't having any of the fun, though she entertained herself by arranging the food on plates to make humorous or sexually graphic designs.

I asked where the food came from, if the Darssan was underground, and they told me about the growing cavern, with light provided by th'an that made sunlight. They described so many amazing things, like the huge storage chambers where the rest of the food is stored, and the cooling cabinets that contain frozen meat, also maintained by th'an.

I told some stories about working as a reaper every harvest for the last three years, and the great harvest feasts at the end of the season. By the end, it degenerated into a food fight, but I made my escape before I was drawn into that. The last I saw, Sovrin had upended a table and was rallying her group behind it, armed with rolls provided by their friend in the kitchen and a big tub of mashed potatoes.

Before that, though—it didn't occur to me to look for Sai Aleynten (I don't care what he said later, I have trouble not thinking of him as that) until just before the food fight started, and then I realized I hadn't seen him at all. It made me wonder where he ate, and I asked Terrael about it, and he said, "He eats in his room."

Two days ago that information would have made me think of him as superior and smug. Now I said, "Isn't he comfortable eating with the rest of you?"

Terrael said, "I don't know. He just never eats in here. Even on rest days."

"I think he thinks he makes *us* uncomfortable," Audryn said. "And I think he's right. Not that we don't like him, but—I know I'm always conscious that he's Sai Aleynten, whenever I'm around him."

"That must be lonely," I said, and Audryn and Terrael looked surprised, like it hadn't occurred to them to think of it that way. "What does he do on rest days?" I asked.

Terrael shrugged and said, "I don't know. He doesn't work, or at least he doesn't work in the cavern. I have trouble picturing him relaxing."

"When Sai Vorantor was here, they used to play this strategy game that leaves me cross-eyed," Audryn said.

"Who's Sai Vorantor?" I asked.

Audryn and Terrael glanced at each other, and I had the feeling I was about to get an evasive half-truth for an answer. "He was Wrelan before Sai Aleynten," Terrael said. "He...took a job in Colosse. He and Sai Aleynten were good friends."

"Still are good friends," Audryn said. "He comes back sometimes to...talk to Sai Aleynten about things."

I wonder if I should have pushed them to tell me everything. Something else happened with Sai Vorantor, I'm sure of it, and I hate not knowing the truth. But I didn't know how to force them to be honest, so I let it go. Still, I plan to poke around a bit more and see what else I can learn about the mysterious Sai Vorantor.

"I think I'm going to read now," I said. They both looked relieved I wasn't going to pursue that line of conversation further.

"Not your research," Audryn said. "That goes double for you, Terrael. It's a rest day. Give yourselves time to rest. You'll be more efficient in the morning if you do."

"All right, but you have to play a couple of rounds of *spo-rih-do* with me," Terrael said, which I thought was brave of him, since he was essentially inviting her to pair off with him. He still won't meet her eyes, though, and I still can't tell if Audryn knows how he feels.

"I will read something that has nothing to do with work," I assured Audryn, and bade them both goodbye as the first fist-sized mound of mashed potatoes flew across the room.

Despite what they'd said, I wasn't surprised to find Sai Aleynten in the cavern, looking through the books on the shelves. He was dressed in a plain brown shirt with an abstract pattern in black embroidered around the neck and cuffs, and brown trousers of a different shade than the shirt, so he looked less formal than usual, but he still had that distant, closed-off air he always did.

"I thought this was a rest day, even for Sai Aleynten," I said. I suppose I was teasing him, which shows how much my attitude toward him has changed.

"It is a rest day even for women from the shadow world," he said, not looking at me. I hadn't even startled him. I need more practice in moving silently. "I am looking for something to entertain me," he added, "but I find I am not in the mood for any of these."

"I came here for the same thing," I said. "But I'm not sure I'll be able to resist doing more research, if I get my hands on these books."

Now he turned his head in my direction. "Learning is a disease, with you," he said, and before I could protest, he went on, "I have the same illness. I recognize the need for occasional rest, but when there is a puzzle to solve...it is a great temptation to lie to myself about my motivations, when I choose a book to read."

I couldn't help smiling. "That's exactly right," I said. "That book, with the pouvra...I'm afraid to go back to my room without something else to read, because I won't be able to stop myself."

He smiled. I think he might not be capable of anything bigger than that little half-twist of the lips, as self-controlled as he is. "Then we are alike in that much," he said.

It makes me uncomfortable thinking I have anything in common with him, even if I do like him a bit now. I think

I just spent five whole minutes thinking about this, when it doesn't really matter. Except it does, a little, because I can't stand mysteries. I think it's because he's so reserved, so private, that if I have something in common with him, it breaches that reserve. And I'm increasingly disinclined to intrude on his privacy, because for him to stay that buttoned up all the time, his privacy must be deeply important to him. It feels as if I'm breaking down a wall I have no right to batter at.

And—I know why that matters now. Because as gregarious as I'm capable of being, I have so much inside me I'll never share that, on a deeper level, I'm as private a person as he is. I know how it would feel for someone to try to breach that wall, how angry and hurt that would make me. Maybe I'm wrong, and Sai Aleynten doesn't feel that way, but in either case I feel defensive of his privacy the way I'm defensive of my own. But if *he* doesn't mind—and in light of what happened later, maybe I *am* wrong about him—at any rate, I know how I'm going to behave, and he can make his own decisions.

Anyway. I felt uncomfortable, and I started poking around in "my" piles, the books I can read, and found one we'd both discarded as less useful, a history of some city I'd never heard of. I'd liked the clarity of the prose when I read the first few pages, so I picked it up and said, "I think this one will entertain me for a few hours."

Sai Aleynten nodded and went back to scanning the shelves. And I had an idea I'm not sure was a good one, but I remembered how I'd seen him in here a few nights ago, still working while everyone else was at dinner. I thought about what Terrael and Audryn had said about him not eating with them, and how it clearly hadn't occurred to them he might be lonely. Before I could stop myself I said, "I could read it to you, if you like. At least it's a book you know you've never read before. And it would keep me from falling victim to my disease."

I felt stupid immediately. I'd assumed he didn't like being alone without remembering I enjoy solitude very well, thank you, and certainly don't need pity or condescension or some well-meaning person "helping" me out of it. But Sai Aleynten turned to look at me again, his eyebrow raised, and said, "I would not want to intrude on your time."

"I wouldn't offer if I thought it was an intrusion," I said.

He smiled again, and said, "No, you would not," and I think he was making a joke! "I would enjoy that," he said. "There is a reading room down the hall, if you'll join me."

It was a comfortable room. There were four well-padded chairs, and a low table perfect for drinks, and while I settled myself into one of the chairs, Sai Aleynten disappeared and came back some minutes later with a tray holding a metal pitcher and two glasses. This time he poured the conventional way, and rather than water the pitcher held a pale yellow liquid that looked like lemonade, and it was. We talked for a few minutes about things that were the same in both our worlds, not that there are many of them, and then I read aloud for a while.

I had to keep stopping because the book referred to places I didn't know, and Sai Aleynten (big surprise) was familiar with all of them. It was an interesting book, though we'd been right in thinking it had no bearing on our research.

At some point we put the book aside and Sai Aleynten told me more about the government of Castavir—I don't know how we came to that subject. It was clear there were things he was skirting around, primarily the God-Empress issue, but if the God-Empress is as dictatorial as I think she is, it would make sense that he wouldn't want to criticize her out loud, even to an otherworlder who's unlikely to repeat his words to anyone who might care.

Anyway, I now feel I have a slightly better grasp of Castaviran politics, though my understanding of politics in general has never been strong; ground-level enforcement of the law has always had more of an effect on me.

And I told him—I still can't believe I did this—I told him about some of the things I've had to do to gain access to the books I needed. That led to me explaining I'd had to steal to survive for most of my life. I didn't talk about Bridie or Roda or Mam, and I didn't try to explain about the politics that lost my family its social and economic standing when I was no more than a baby (not that I understand them myself), just that Dad died when I was nine and we became destitute. He listened, and at the end he said, "No wonder we could never keep you locked up."

"No, that was the mind-moving pouvra, though it's true I need to understand locks to know how to move them correctly," I said, and then we both realized that although I'd told him about the pouvra, he'd never seen me do it. So I showed him how I could raise the tray with its pitcher and glasses, though only an inch or so, and then I worked the lock on the door a few times, and he showed his astonishment in his usual ebullient way, which was to raise one eyebrow until it threatened to climb off his forehead.

"The fine control to work that lock is beyond me," he said, "though I think my capacity for moving larger objects is greater than yours," and he wiggled his fingers and made one of the chairs, thankfully not the one I was sitting in, lift into the air until its back struck the ceiling. This time, I was watching his hand more closely, and I swear I saw traces of amber light following the movement of his fingers.

"Definitely," I agreed, "though it makes me wonder something." I concentrated on my glass, which had about half an inch of lemonade still in it, and the liquid flowed up the sides of the glass and emerged to make a pale yellow sphere that I flew around the room.

"*That* is truly astonishing," Sai Aleynten said. He traced a th'an on the side of his glass, which was fuller than mine, and the liquid quivered, but stayed in the glass. "It seems I have practicing to do."

"So do I," I said, laughing, and he smiled. I wonder if he ever laughs. I wonder why he never relaxes. Well, he was relaxed then, but his relaxation still looks like someone else's rigidity.

Right then my stomach rumbled, and I laughed again. "I think I should have dinner," I said, and then I didn't know what else to say. It felt rude to walk away, but I didn't think it would make either of us comfortable for me to invite him to eat with me in the refectory. And, honestly, I can't picture him eating in there. No one would dare to joke or laugh or even speak. Except me, possibly.

Sure enough, he said, "Then I will speak with you in the morning.

Or in the evening, if you prefer, when you may have something to report."

I said, "Then, good evening, Sai Aleynten, and thank you for an enjoyable afternoon."

He nodded, but when I had my hand on the knob and was realizing I'd left the door locked, he said, "You should not call me Sai."

"But everyone calls you that—did I misunderstand?" I said. I was embarrassed again. I hate looking like a fool, and if I'd been calling him Sai Aleynten when that was wrong—that's as bad as calling him by his praenoma when I wasn't invited—but that's not what happened.

"'Sai' is not only a title," he said. "It implies a relationship...not exactly of obedience, but of obligation. You are under no obligation to me."

That made me feel better, though still embarrassed. "Do I call you Aleynten, then?" I said.

He paused for a long time, then said, "My given name is Cederic. It would not be inappropriate for you to call me that."

That still makes me feel horribly embarrassed. Like I've written before, in Balaen names are important. We used to have a surname before Dad was stripped of power and he lost that along with everything else. And Sai Aleynten sharing his given name with me, when we don't really have a close relationship...that's an intimacy I'm sure he didn't mean, and I couldn't tell him that without embarrassing him too. He said, later, he was the only one who could invite me to use his given name, so I guess names do mean something to them, but nothing nearly so personal as they do to me.

So I've resolved never to be in a position where I have to call him *anything*. I don't know what I'll call him in the pages of this book. I kept writing Sai Aleynten because that's how I thought of him, right up until he gave me his name, but obviously I shouldn't do that anymore. It's stupid of me to be so sensitive, but I've already lost my whole world and almost all of my customs, and I feel as though I need to cling to *something* in order to stay myself. Also, how awkward will it be if I'm the only one calling him Cederic? That's the sort of thing that gets noticed!

Which is more or less what I said next, though it came out as, "That's not too informal, when everyone else calls you Sai?"

He smiled, and said, "You are not everyone else, and they know it. I think you will find they are happier when you, an outsider, do not presume upon the obligation all of them have earned."

"You mean they've all been cringing every time I refer to you as Sai Aleynten?" I said. I'd noticed my talking about him made them uncomfortable, but I'd assumed it was because I was always so critical of him. I thought I'd been embarrassed before, but now I didn't think I could face the refectory and all those people who thought I was...I don't know. Presumptuous, maybe?

~~Sai Aleynten~~ Cederic He shook his head. "I imagine none of them knew how to correct you without embarrassment. And none of them would feel comfortable giving you the freedom of my given name."

"I understand," I said, "though I'm surprised *you* didn't correct me earlier."

"It never occurred to me," he said. "And you never address me directly."

"I don't know whether to apologize for that or not," I said, "but I think most of our conversations haven't been the kind where our names are important."

"True," he said. He'd been sitting this whole time, and now he stood and said, "I think you will discover the door is still locked."

"I know," I said, and quickly unlocked it. "Thank you...Cederic."

He inclined his head to me. "Thank you for the reading, Thalessi."

And I have *no idea* why I did what I did next, which was to say, "My given name is Sesskia." It just came out. I suppose it was partly because I felt so awkward about him giving me his name that I wanted to restore the balance between us, and partly because something about him makes me tell him everything, even against my better judgment. But I did, and now I can't take it back. I hope I don't regret it.

So he said, "Then thank you, Sesskia," and we went our separate ways, him presumably to his room, me to the refectory. It was an uneventful dinner, probably because everyone had exhausted their stores of fun and was ready for an early bedtime and back to work in the morning. And now I'm finishing this record for the night.

I'm looking forward to studying the book in the morning. I still don't know if I can call him Cederic, particularly to his subordinates, but I suppose Sai Aleynten is out of the question now. At least I don't hate him anymore, because there are serious taboos about using the personal name of one's enemy. And he's certainly not my enemy.

26 Senessay

It's definitely a pouvra. If I hadn't had ten years of experience learning pouvrin from ancient, barely legible texts, I wouldn't have recognized it. I had to go to the refectory for a glass of that bitter pink juice that I hoped would clear my head, because my brain kept trying to cling to concepts it could barely understand until it whirled around like a dust devil, whipping up a storm that only made things worse.

This is what I know so far:

1. The book is nothing but speculation about magic. If I were a Castaviran mage, I would dismiss the author as a madman.

2. The madman who wrote the book had access to other fringe texts, some of which pointed him in the right direction.

3. The madman believed pouvrin shaped what he called residual magic, something thrown off by kathanas.

4. Completely by accident, he worked out a pouvra that conceals the user from sight.

I had to get up and pace the room again after I wrote that, because I'm so excited I can barely breathe. It's not invisibility, more of a powerful suggestion that the observer not see you, but how can that not be the most useful pouvra I've ever learned! When I think of all the times I was caught, or nearly caught, because I stepped into the light at the wrong time—there, I had to take a pacing break again.

All right. I'm calm again. Not really, but calm enough to apply myself to this book. I only made it about a third of the way into the pouvra book before I got to number 4 up there, and then I had to tell someone. ~~Sai Ced~~ This is ridiculous. I can't keep writing "he." I'll have to get used to calling him Cederic, at least when I'm writing. Anyway, Cederic was busy with one of the groups, so I collared Terrael and made him answer my questions. His answers:

1. Yes, there are other books in this vein, and yes, Castaviran mages think the authors are insane, because nothing they write of has ever been proven effective.

2. Terrael had heard of one or two of the texts the madman refers to, but has never seen them. Still, he estimates the book is well over four hundred years old. Which is impressive, since it's barely faded or foxed, though the pages are too brittle to be handled easily.

3. There is no such thing as residual magic. Terrael was emphatic about this. Magic is constrained by th'an and either flows into an object or is consumed by the th'an or kathana. He offered to show me proof, but I declined on the grounds that I wouldn't appreciate it.

4. Upon being shown the relevant passages, Terrael admitted that what I said hinted at a pouvra was meaningless to him, but the way the madman constructed th'an was unusual and bore further examination.

5. There was a bit of a tussle that ended with me rapping Terrael on the knuckles and telling him to find another book to examine, because he couldn't have mine.

I decided to write all this up before going back to studying, to give myself time to calm down. Later, I have to tell all of this to ~~Sai~~ Cederic. I think he will have a better idea of why the madman came to the conclusions he did—whether it was coincidence, or whether he actually did stumble on some secret we might be able to use. And tonight I'm going to start learning that pouvra.

CHAPTER EIGHT

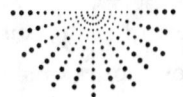

27 Senessay

I was so caught up in trying to learn the concealment pouvra I didn't take time to record the rest of yesterday before I went to sleep. I'm so tired this morning I'm having trouble concentrating on anything. I took my discoveries to Cederic after lunch yesterday, and he insisted (politely, he's learning) that I read out certain passages. Then he told me things to look for, key words and phrases, and I read those too.

By the time we were both ready for dinner, I'd read myself hoarse and Cederic was pacing back and forth across the circle, fingers of one hand pressed against his forehead. Finally, he said, "I think we should leave this for now. There is a book that might reveal something of what this author claims, but I would prefer to come at this fresh, in the morning."

"But you're going to read that book tonight," I said.

He raised his eyebrow at me. "And if I do?"

"Do you believe in rest at all?" I said.

"I find that amusing, coming from the woman who intends to stay up all night learning the concealment pouvra," he said.

I sputtered at him indignantly, but in the end I had to laugh. "It's a disease," I said, and he nodded, smiling.

"Well, I think we can both agree to have enough self-control to be able to function in the morning," I said. Except I don't think I did. I have no way of keeping track of time, here under the mountain, and I didn't fall asleep until I was so exhausted my eyeballs ached, which had to be only a few hours before someone banged on my door and shouted something about breakfast. They've taken to doing that, now I'm so engaged in research, and I appreciate it most of the time. Just not when I've had only a few hours of sleep and my head is pounding. I didn't go to breakfast immediately, but wrote all this in the hope that my headache would go away. I think it got worse. Maybe food will help.

After breakfast

Still headachy. I'm going to forgo a bath this morning—and no, that's not going to make me stinky, I bathed yesterday and I can afford to miss one day—so I can write more about the pouvra. I haven't come close to mastering it yet, of course, and I didn't expect to. It has a strange shape, much more angular than the others, and I think it's because the madman who described it was working from all manner of wrong assumptions.

But I know it will work. I can feel it, deep inside, where my magic responds to the pouvrin and my will bends to meet them. What's interesting is that part of what the madman did makes the underlying reasoning behind the pouvra more obvious, which means I'll probably learn this one more rapidly than the others, all except the fire-summoning pouvra, of course.

I've written so often about the process of learning a new pouvra that I don't know that I need to do it here—but then, I've lost the other five books, and it's unlikely I'll ever get them back. And although I don't intend anyone but myself to read it, there's always a chance this could end up important to historians in some far distant time—hopefully a far distant time, I don't want Cederic ever to see some of the things I wrote about him, assuming he learns to read my language—so I might as well be thorough.

The first step is to know a pouvra exists. I don't know how the first pouvrin were created, but as far as my experience goes, it's not enough to simply wish to be able to do something; you have to have a shape for it. But the shapes aren't physical, though I always describe them in those terms because they are able to affect the physical world. They're more like...no matter how often I explain this, I never do get it exactly right.

They're like the memory of a place, a room, for example. You never only remember the size of the room and the things that were in it, you also remember how it smelled and what the lighting was like and, most importantly, how you felt when you were there. And some memories of places are so strong that when you remember them, it's as if you were there once more.

Every pouvra has a different form that's multidimensional in that way. In my mind, they have texture and color and taste and smell, though they never have a sound. They're like physical things that only exist because your mind and your body make them real.

I suppose it's possible to create pouvrin, I just don't know how. All the pouvrin I've learned have been shapes laid down by other mages. But—think how hard it is to describe a place so well that the other person sees it accurately. Impossible, maybe. Then think of describing an object whose characteristics are completely non-physical and yet have a tangibility in memory. That's so much harder.

So it's not as simple as one mage writing a description that another can read and understand. All pouvrin are described figuratively, like poetry, and understanding them is a matter of learning the language of that description. I've written that I've read hundreds of books over the last ten years—well, only a few of them actually described pouvrin. The rest taught me how to understand those few.

Some of them I read and moved on, others I stole and hid again, with clues, in the hope that some other mage might find them one day. This is how I could tell the madman's book contained a pouvra; there's a consistency to the language that's like a clue for other mages that here is something worth knowing.

My stomach's growling at me again. I'd better go eat something before I have to get to work. I hope Cederic isn't dragging as much as I am.

27 Senessay, evening

Today was a near-total loss. Cederic was every bit as exhausted as I was, and irritable in a way I wasn't until I started talking to him, and we had an argument that was more of a squabble, in which he was sarcastic and I was rude. We managed to cut it short and apologize to each other, but neither of us meant it. Finally, he said, "This is pointless. Have your lunch, and take a nap, and let us see if we can salvage anything of this day after that."

"You'd better take a nap, too," I said. I think he did. I'm not sure. But he was less cranky when we met later that afternoon. We ended up in that sitting room again, talking for a long time about the concealment pouvra, and I explained what I wrote above about how I learn them. And he told me the book he mentioned explains more about residual magic, that it's not leftover magic but *pre-existing* magic, sort of where magic comes from before it's shaped by th'an. It's still speculative, but more in the sense of unproven theory than crazy impossibility. Cederic said it was a metaphysical question, a chicken-or-egg theory the mages of the Darssan don't have the leisure to contemplate, but at least we know the madman wasn't entirely mad, or possibly he was just lucky.

I'm still tired despite the nap, so I'm leaving the book alone tonight.

28 Senessay

Still wrestling with the pouvra. Read more of the madman's book to Cederic today while he took notes. I have no idea what, if anything, he's learning from it, but he seems satisfied.

Learned something surprising tonight, which is that Audryn is at least as enamored of Terrael as he is of her. He wasn't at dinner tonight, and when I asked why, Audryn said he was involved in the translation of one of the Castaviran mage books, and he was working himself to the bone, and she wished he would listen to her when she told him to eat. She's good at hiding it, but that concern wasn't at all what you'd expect from someone only worried about her superior. I wish I could tell one or the other the truth, but I don't poke my nose into other people's business. I hope one of them summons the nerve to speak up.

29 Senessay

Still no success on either front. Finished with the madman's book, but Cederic asked me to watch him draw several individual th'an and tell him if I saw anything familiar. Nothing. Not even that hint of recognition I got from the water-summoning th'an. I didn't tell him about that, because I'm increasingly convinced it was just my imagination, like when you have the feeling you've done something or been somewhere before, and I don't want us heading off down a false path when we don't have time to waste.

Cederic was disappointed at our failure, which he displayed exactly the way he shows every other emotion—complete lack of expression. I'm getting better at reading his actual feelings, what with spending so much time with him. Good thing I don't hate him anymore.

30 Senessay

I did it. The concealment pouvra works.

I didn't realize it at first, because it doesn't conceal you from yourself. But it makes you feel different, numb, like everything is happening just an inch beyond your fingers. That's going to be a problem if I use it while I'm stealing things, but I think it might be a matter of learning to compensate for the difference, like learning to grab a stone from a riverbed despite its visual displacement. So I knew *something* had happened, just not what.

I left my room and strolled down the hall to the cavern, and wandered around a bit. No one paid attention to me, but that's normal. Cederic was at the circle, kneeling on the floor and drawing th'an with his fat writing tool. I walked over to him and crouched opposite, watching him work. He didn't raise his head, but I'm used to him knowing I'm there, so I assumed he didn't see a need to greet me, which he usually doesn't. I said, "Does it matter what you draw the th'an with, or can you use any pen or pencil?"

He dropped his writing tool and shot to his feet. I've never seen him so surprised. "Sesskia," he said, and then he regained his composure and his expressionless demeanor. "I take it the pouvra worked," he said.

I stood and waved my hand in his face, and he grabbed it and brought it closer to his eyes. "I can see you, now that I know what to look for," he said, and released me. "When does it end?"

"Presumably, when I tell it to," I said, "though I didn't know it was working until I startled you. So I'm not sure how to turn it off." But I concentrated for a bit, thought about the shape of the pouvra, and almost immediately the numb feeling disappeared, and I could tell by the way Cederic's eyes focused on me that I was visible again.

"I didn't think it was invisibility," I said. "What did you see?"

"Nothing, at first," he said. "But it was as if I did not want to look in your direction. As if something far more interesting were happening elsewhere. Then, when I did see you, you seemed to take the shape of what was around you. You were a very short bookshelf, for a few seconds."

"That's unexpected," I said, laughing. "Well, I think I need more practice, but I was serious about the question. I never see you using that writing tool for notes, just for th'an."

"Any writing implement will work, for th'an," Cederic said. He retrieved his writing tool from where he'd dropped it and scrawled a th'an into the table; it vanished, and the smell of apricots wafted from the wood. "But we use these, or chalk, because they make the most definitive lines. One can even write th'an with water, or oil—anything that leaves a visible mark. Though those are always transitory."

"Why do some vanish, and others persist? Like the ones in the storage room?" I said.

He sketched the same th'an on the air, and this time I really did see amber light around his fingers. Apricot scent brushed my nose and cheeks. "Some th'an have an immediate effect that is powered by the magic bound up in the th'an," he said. "The effect happens, and the magic and the th'an disappear. Other th'an have ongoing effects. Their magic...replenishes itself, you might say, drawn into whatever object it is scribed on to power the effect, until the magic can no longer regenerate. Then a new th'an must be drawn if the effect is to persist."

"So what about the things in the storage room?" I asked. "Those th'an are made of metal."

Cederic grimaced, the faintest drawing down of the corners of his mouth. "Experiments," he said, "from years, sometimes decades, ago. Occasionally someone revisits the idea of permanent th'an with permanent effects. Those aeden still have power, some of them, but it's an unpredictable power, which is why they are locked away. Not that anyone but Master Peressten would dare to use them."

"You didn't want him to," I recalled.

Cederic shook his head. "I did not think it fair to you to subject you to such a dangerous experiment," he said. "I told Master Peressten to speak with you long enough to learn your language, so he could gain your consent. But he is often impatient. I'm afraid I lost my temper at him." He looked away from me and twiddled the writing tool in his fingers. I think he was embarrassed.

"I forgave him," I said. "But thank you for trying to contain him."

He smiled. "I am glad it worked," he said, "even if our conversations are occasionally... strained."

"That's because you're stubborn and irrational," I said.

He raised his eyebrow at me. "You are only able to say that," he said, "because you are so intimately familiar with those characteristics." He smiled as he said it, and that made me laugh.

"Can you use the pouvra again, while I watch?" he said.

"Maybe," I said, and reached for the shape of the pouvra in memory. It took a few tries, and Cederic standing there watching me made me nervous, but eventually the numbness spread over my body again, and Cederic's eyes watered.

"I can still see you," he said, "but it is difficult not to want to look away." He turned his head briefly, then looked back at me. "And now you are once again part of your surroundings."

I released the pouvra and shook out my fingers. "I wish I knew how this could help with the kathana," I said.

"Anything might help," he said. "What will you use it for?"

I knew what he was really asking. Why did I tell him I'm a thief? Why do I tell him *anything* personal? Even if I do consider him a friend, now. "I'm not going to sneak around and spy on people, if that's what you mean," I said, "and I have no need to pursue my former profession, since there are all these books lying around and no one minds if I read them. But practicing pouvrin makes me better able to learn new ones. So that's what I'll use it for."

"I did not mean to imply that I distrust you," he said in a low voice, though there wasn't anyone around to hear us.

"Then what did you mean?" I said. I swear I didn't intend to sound hostile, because I didn't feel hostile. Just disappointed that he thought less of me because of who I'd had to become to survive.

He paused, looking off into the distance, then said, "You see the world in ways no one else has thought of. The pouvra has obvious implications. I am interested in the non-obvious ones I am certain you will discover."

"Oh," I said. It felt like—still feels like—a tremendous compliment, and yet I'm not sure what he meant. I'm a mage because I see things others don't, or I wouldn't be able to learn pouvrin, but I could say the same of every mage in the Darssan. Aside from the obvious, I don't think of myself as anyone special. Well, I am, though, because after the magic woke up in me, I could have ignored it and not learned any more pouvrin. But seeing the world differently...I think he might be mistaken about that. But it was a nice compliment, so I accepted it at face value.

After that, he drew more th'an and we talked about kathanas, which I still haven't seen, and I began to grasp some of the underlying logic behind the shapes of Castaviran magic. I still don't think I'll ever learn to do magic their way. Maybe it's more flexible, but I'm so used to encompassing magic with my body and giving it shape there that I think I'd feel hampered by the need to learn all those fiddly th'an.

Learning the concealment pouvra, though, has made me think about the possibility of crafting pouvrin of my own. It's a huge stretch, because I don't even know what's possible, but what a challenge! Maybe learning more about th'an will give me some ideas. But I'm going to master the concealment pouvra first. And maybe see if I can find some non-obvious applications for Cederic.

CHAPTER NINE

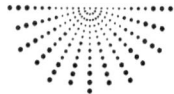

2 Lennitay

I'm writing this from the rear senet of the loenerel, where I can have some privacy because it's noisier than the others and no one wants to endure that. Everyone else is gathered in the senet behind the collenna, which is the thing that makes the loenerel go. I'm so full to bursting with new words and ideas I feel dizzy, a feeling not helped by how fast we're traveling across this horrible, hot, arid wasteland. I remember now what Cederic said about my not being safe outside the Darssan. I didn't realize he meant that literally.

The Arabel Mountains, under which the Darssan is located, sit squarely in the middle of the least hospitable desert I've ever seen, and I've seen more than a few. I looked back at the mountains when we left about an hour ago, before the loenerel kicked up so much dust I couldn't see anything, and they were these jagged black hills like the desert's teeth, jutting up toward the sky. Now they're far in the distance, and I wish I were back there safe beneath them. Even if it meant not seeing the sky for a few more weeks.

It's been a few days since I was able to write anything, and they were such eventful days I'll only try to record accurately a few important conversations, because I've already forgotten most of the details.

The night after my last entry *wasn't* eventful. I practiced the concealment pouvra and did some sneaking around before I felt guilty about it. Even though I wasn't trying to spy on anyone, and I only wanted to test its effectiveness, I knew they'd object if they knew. So I went back to my room, but discovered I was unexpectedly tired, so I told myself I'd write more

Cederic just came in and told me I was expected to join the rest of them. He was more expressionless than usual, which told me he wasn't happy, but then he hasn't looked happy since Sai Vorantor arrived. Not that I should call him that, but I don't know what other name to use. Cederic addresses him as Denril, but I'm guessing my calling him that would be inappropriate even by Castaviran standards. So I'll call him Vorantor in these pages and try to avoid addressing him personally.

He also said, "Don't let anyone see that book." When I asked why, he said, "The God-Empress does not like not possessing information she believes is important. A book she cannot read would fall into that category. She would likely have it destroyed."

I thanked him, and told him I would follow shortly. He never asks what I'm writing, though I think he's curious. I'm sure a foreigner's impressions of Castavir would interest him, even if I wasn't writing about people he knows. But he's too polite to pry. So I'm putting this away for now, but I intend to find more chances to write about what's happened in the last three days.

2 Lennitay, just after dinner

I'm hiding in my room—it's not so much a room as a cubicle, with barely enough space for a bed and window—having pretended to have a headache. It's not entirely a lie. The motion of the loenerel makes me queasy, and right now I've got my face hanging over a little vent that constantly blows cool air into the room, probably to compensate for how hot the loenerel is. The master, the one who keeps the collenna moving, said it would be much hotter if not for the kathana that shields it from the sun's rays. I can't even imagine walking through the desert unprotected, and I'm trying to be grateful, but since I'm still angry at Vorantor's manipulation, it's difficult to hang on to gratitude for anything.

I hate when I can't write every day. I know I'm forgetting things, and then I remember them and have to put them in out of order, and I'd like to summarize, but so much of importance has happened I feel as if I'm cheating myself to skim over it. So if this is confusing—but I suppose I'm the only one who'll be reading it, so there's no sense apologizing to myself.

So, as I wrote earlier, I was tired and went to bed instead of writing, not that that mattered because I hadn't done much worth writing about. In the morning, I went to breakfast and the refectory was practically empty. One of the mages was leaving as I entered, and he told me to be quick, because there were visitors on the way. Well, that excited me—any change is exciting, though the news that someone had discovered the right kathana for summoning the Codex Tiurindi would have been far better. I gulped down my food and hurried out to the cavern to find it was nearly empty, too.

(The loenerel just came to a stop again. They have to refresh the th'an frequently because the loenerel is so massive it swallows magic like a drunkard swigs brandy. When it stops, it becomes warmer, and the smell of hot metal becomes more pervasive, and then I feel really ill. It's a measure of how quickly I've come to take the casual use of magic for granted, that I can be annoyed at the loenerel's failings rather than awestruck that anything can transport fifty people across the desert faster than a horse can run and with greater endurance.)

Terrael was there in the cavern, and he told me everyone was cleaning up so the Darssan, and its inhabitants, would look their best for the visitors. But what he and a handful of other mages were doing was washing off the walls in places, and I think they were concealing some of their research from whoever was coming to visit. Now that I know it was Vorantor, that makes sense. Damn it, now I'm telling the story out of order again. At least I can take comfort in knowing my dislike of Vorantor is rooted in good reason, unlike my previous dislike of Cederic, which was just mutual misunderstanding and my unfortunate prejudice.

I asked what I could do, and he said I should dress as nicely as possible, which was useless advice because I have no idea what constitutes nice dress in Castavir. I certainly don't have a gray robe to wear. I compromised by going back to my room and dressing in the clothes I think look nicest on me, a pale blue shirt embroidered with white flowers around the neck, cuffs, and hem and a pair of gray trousers almost too fine a weave to be practical.

I couldn't do anything about my shoes—I don't think I've ever said that everyone here wears thin-soled sandals held on by cloth strips, and if they have other shoes, they maybe have a single pair, and there wasn't any need for me to borrow them. And of course if the sandals are too informal for something as important as this visit, they'd all need their own shoes and no one could loan a pair to me. So my worn and cracked leather ankle boots didn't look right, but there wasn't anything I could do about it.

Audryn knocked on my door just as I was about to leave and made me sit while she pinned my hair up with two of her clips, simple openwork brass loops big enough to keep my mass of hair in place. She's the one who told me our visitor was Vorantor, and she wouldn't say much more than that, which left me nervous because I still didn't know the truth about him and his relationship to Cederic.

We walked back to the cavern, which in contrast to earlier was full of people, everyone dressed neatly in their gray robes and black trousers. Some of the women wore hair clips and a few of the men wore earrings, nothing flashy, nothing that might get in someone's way while he or she was scribing th'an. I saw Sovrin across the cavern, and she saw me and gestured to me in a way I eventually realized meant "step back".

So I took a few steps until I stood behind someone else, partially concealed by the crowd. I realize now she meant to conceal me from Vorantor, but at the time I thought it was only a custom. It didn't matter, because at that moment Cederic entered, looked around the chamber, saw me immediately despite my being much shorter than the person I was standing behind, and made a little motion for me to stand beside him at the circle.

He was dressed as he always is, no extra jewelry or anything, though he was wearing shoes rather than sandals. "Say nothing except in direct response to something Denril asks you, and then be as brief as possible," he instructed me in a low voice. "You may want to argue, but say nothing. Promise me, Sesskia. This is important."

"I promise," I said, because his tone of voice frightened me, and if he thought Vorantor would make me want to argue, then something serious was happening.

We stood together and waited for a few minutes. Everyone was still, almost unmoving. I noticed Cederic clenching his hand into a fist and then forcing it to relax, clench/relax, at least a dozen times before a door on the third level, high above, opened with a loud clang, and a few dozen people emerged and came down the ramps to meet us.

(This is another thing I haven't mentioned. About half the living quarters are on the second level, and all the facilities and the other half of the living quarters are on the first, and the third is entirely unoccupied. The population of the Darssan used to be much bigger.)

They walked single-file, even though the ramps are broad enough for three people to walk side-by-side comfortably, and I was certain, looking at the procession, that they were doing it to look more impressive. Though that could just be my impression in hindsight, knowing more of Vorantor now.

Cederic watched them impassively, his hand now relaxed—or maybe it was only open rather than clenched, because I could tell by the way his jaw was tight that he was in no way relaxed about any of this.

Eventually the procession came to the bottom of the ramps and the man at the head of the line approached us, while the rest of the men and women following him bunched up behind him. The man held out his hands to Cederic, who clasped them by crossing his arms so right hand took right hand and so forth. "Thank you for the invitation," the man said.

"We are always happy to welcome you and our other friends to the Darssan, Denril," Cederic said.

"I am glad to hear it," Vorantor said, and then he looked at me, and I didn't like it. He had the smile of a shark, a toothy, humorless smile. He had a receding hairline, which made him look older than I suspected he was (early thirties, the same as Cederic), and wore his black hair pulled back the way all the mages of the Darssan did—all the newcomers wore their hair this way—but he and his friends wore richly colored and heavily embroidered robes that fell past their knees, tied with metallic-looking gold ropes that ended in tassels as thick as my wrist, over pale gray trousers almost the color of my own.

Vorantor also wore an earring made of a square-cut ruby that could feed a family of ten in Thalessa for a month, and that made me dislike him more. I don't know if the earring means something, or if he's just showing off how important he is, but I've stolen much better than that from the noble and wealthy of Balaen, and if he thinks it's something that will impress me, he is utterly wrong. Not that I imagine he worries much about impressing me; no doubt he cares more about what the God-Empress thinks. I suppose I'll find that out soon.

Anyway, he looked at me, and he said, "And you are Thalessi, our visitor from the shadow world," and that surprised me, because it had to be Cederic who told him about me, and I didn't know he understood how personal praenomi are to Balaenics or that he wasn't allowed to give my praenoma to a stranger on my behalf. It made me realize for the first time that we really are friends, and that's so strange, given that I once thought that was impossible.

Even with the buffer of my placename between us, I was uncomfortable having his attention on me, so I just nodded and said, "I am."

I wasn't sure at the time why he made me so uncomfortable, other than his resemblance to a shark, but now I have time to think, I feel as if I've been protected in the Darssan. Vorantor's arrival, even though I didn't know then that there was something sinister about it, disrupted that protective little world. I'd managed to convince myself I could stay there indefinitely, even managed to pretend the world's fate wasn't in the balance because I finally had friends and a place where I didn't have to conceal my magic, and that was stupid.

And speaking of the shadow world, I finally understand why they call it that. The loenerel is still traveling through miles and miles of wasteland, but every now and then we pass things that are, well, shadows. Barns or houses you can see through, or people walking around doing things that would make sense if you could see the world they were actually interacting with.

Once we drove entirely through some kind of gathering hall and we could see its interior, complete with people dancing. The shadows don't persist—sometimes we see them in the far distance, and they fade in and then out again—but they do appear frequently, and Sovrin said that although they never saw them in the Darssan (no idea why not) they knew from the news they got from outside that the shadows were showing up more often and staying for longer than they used to. Just more evidence of the approaching disaster. This also reminds me I didn't ask her how they get news from outside, if the Darssan is so isolated. Not that it matters anymore.

Audryn just stopped by to see if I'm still alive. I hid the book before she entered. It's not that I don't trust her, because I do, but the fewer people who know I have this, the less likely one of them will reveal its existence to Vorantor, even though I'm sure they wouldn't mean to. But I'm taking this as a sign I need to turn out the light and try to sleep. I can't believe I'm actually looking forward to arriving in Colosse. I can't believe I ever had the innocence to write that the God-Empress was never going to have anything to do with my life. More tomorrow.

3 Lennitay

I'm no longer faking illness. Cederic took one look at me when I came to breakfast and ordered me back to my room. Then he brought me food himself. This was to give him an excuse to speak to me privately, to make sure there wasn't anything more wrong with me than (as we determined) motion sickness. He offered to send Vorantor to me, as he knows some healing magic, but I declined, and he didn't push. I know Terrael and Audryn said they were still friends, but from what I overheard between them, it's a friendship on the brink of falling apart.

Right. I haven't reached that point yet. Vorantor didn't say anything more to me, and Cederic said a few things that sounded like hospitality ritual, and then Vorantor said something like "don't let us keep you from your work" and everyone broke into their groups and went back to their research.

Hahahaha.

What really happened was that everyone broke into groups and *pretended* to work, because Vorantor's people spread out and started "helping" by making corrections to their th'an or offering suggestions about which book to refer to. I followed Cederic to our table, since I had nothing else to do, and Vorantor came with us. More accurately, he strode a few steps ahead of us, as if he were leading the way, and that annoyed me. I know he was Wrelan here before Cederic, but he has no right to act as if he's still in charge. Cederic didn't seem to mind.

When we got to the circle, Cederic showed Vorantor the books we've been translating, starting with the Eddon book. They had a technical discussion I probably could have followed, since it was about everything Cederic and I have been working on with regard to pouvrin and th'an, but I was too busy worrying about why Vorantor was even here.

I was certain it was all due to me, even though he was putting on a good show of being interested in our research, and I was right, which makes me furious as I'm writing this. Vorantor wanted me for his own purposes, and it makes me even angrier to remember how they were talking as if they were collaborators instead of Vorantor waiting for the right moment to reveal the truth.

I despise him because he thinks of me as a prize, as a thing, and I swore no one would ever use me like that. But there isn't much I can do about it now. Maybe when we reach Colosse, Cederic will think of something, or the God-Empress will change everyone's plans.

They talked for several minutes, and I ended up flipping the pages of a book I couldn't read, looking at the pictures. I'm probably just as happy I can't read that one, because based on the illustrations, it's a sex manual, and what it's doing with the rest of these books is a mystery. Then Vorantor said, "Thalessi," and that brought my attention away from the picture of three people tangled together. "I would love to see your magic, if you don't mind," he said.

"Of course," I said, and did the fire-summoning pouvra almost in his face. I regretted it before the fire died away, and cursed myself for letting my annoyance override my good sense. I'm sure making myself seem dangerous was a *wonderful* choice that made Vorantor decide I had nothing to offer him and leave me alone. Fortunately, Vorantor didn't seem angry or frightened, and he didn't flinch. He might smile more, but he seems every bit as self-controlled as Cederic.

"Fascinating," he said. "Will you show me the others?"

I looked past him at Cederic, hoping he could give me guidance, but his face was completely expressionless, as always. And then I saw his hand was open, his fingers spread, and he flexed his fingers a few times. *Five.* But I know seven pouvrin, counting the walk-through-walls one I don't use—and then I realized what he was telling me, as clearly as if there were a mind-speaking pouvra we both had access to.

I said, "Yes, but I won't be able to show you how I can see in the dark," and I summoned water, then caught it and turned it into a sphere and flew it around for a bit (even in my nervousness, it was hard not to make it hit the back of Terrael's head, just for fun) and I had Vorantor go behind one of the bookshelves and hold up so many fingers, and I looked through it to tell him how many.

Cederic, standing with his back to Vorantor during this test, gave me another meaningful look, this one of thanks. He may trust Vorantor more than I do, but I saw he thought we might need the advantage of him not knowing about the walk-through-walls and concealment pouvrin, and he was right. I didn't realize he could be as paranoid as I am. It's funny how we have far more in common than I believed in the beginning.

Vorantor was impressed, and not in a child-doing-tricks way. He asked a lot of questions about pouvrin, how to learn them and what it feels like to use them, and were there any similarities between pouvrin and th'an. I told him what we'd learned, and I didn't hold anything back, in case Cederic had already told him things. I think it may be another advantage for him to believe I'm cooperating, so I hope he couldn't tell I was furious about being forced to go to Colosse, and in that way.

And I have to admit Vorantor is easily as intelligent as Cederic, because he grasped the implications of our work immediately. On the other hand, he said nothing about the Codex Tiurindi, nothing about the worlds coming together, and at the time I assumed it was because they both knew what needed to be done and talking about it was irrelevant. I was wrong.

Eventually, their discussion wound down, and Vorantor said, "I would like to speak with you privately, Cederic. We have so much to catch up on."

Cederic nodded, turned to me, and said, "Thank you for your help, Sesskia." Then he and Vorantor walked away toward the corridor, leaving me gaping for a moment at the abruptness of his farewell. It took me less than a second to decide I had to hear whatever they were about to say to each other.

Yes, I know I'd told Cederic I wouldn't use the pouvra like a thief, and I felt slightly guilty about using it on him, but I was tired of everyone but me knowing what his relationship with Vorantor really was. And he *had* told me to keep them a secret from Vorantor, which is close to giving me permission to eavesdrop.

I used to be better at justifications.

And I got what eavesdroppers are proverbially supposed to get, which is, nothing good. I don't regret it. Cederic would have told me the details later, but hearing Vorantor's words from his own mouth—I'm glad I know what kind of man he actually is. I

Dinnertime. I'm surprised Cederic is always the one who comes for me. I think he knows I'm writing and is trying to keep anyone from finding out about this book. I think writing while the loenerel is moving is making me queasier, but there's no way I'm going to delay any longer. It's supposed to take fewer than three days to reach Colosse, and I'm determined to have caught up before then, because who knows what might happen?

CHAPTER TEN

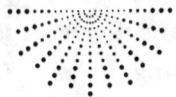

3 Lennitay, after dinner

So. Eavesdropping. I followed Cederic and Vorantor, keeping behind groups of mages and acting as if I were interested in their discussions. When Cederic and Vorantor left the cavern, I lagged behind them as they moved along the corridor until they were out of sight, but not out of hearing—fortunately they weren't wearing those sandals. I stayed close enough to know which one of the sitting rooms they entered, which was the one Cederic and I had used when I read to him, and then they shut the door and I stood alone in the corridor, trying not to panic.

I wrote that I've only used the walk-through-walls pouvra once. It's frightening. It makes you mostly insubstantial, which means it's impossible to breathe, and alters whatever you walk through to be insubstantial too. But you can still feel, and it feels as if you've been turned to liquid, and you're flowing through the cold stream that is the other object, and if you don't concentrate, you'll be swept away and mingled with it.

But I also feel if I try to pull away from the other stream, I could go too far the other way and become solid in the middle of whatever I'm moving through, which would make it become solid too, and that sounds like one of the more gruesome deaths I can imagine. But I was sure whatever Cederic and Vorantor were about to discuss was important to me and not just to them.

So I took a few deep breaths, did the concealment pouvra (because coming through the wall completely visible would ruin everything), prayed the walk-through-walls pouvra wouldn't negate the concealment, and went straight at the wall before I could think too hard about it.

I felt that moment of transition, that sensation of being fluid and the horrible feeling of having all my organs exposed to the wall's near-immaterial substance, and then I was through and standing next to the door. Cederic and Vorantor were seated across from each other, and Cederic was using a th'an to pour water for them. The pitcher was steady and he spilled not a drop, which made me proud and a little smug on his behalf, because I'd bet Vorantor couldn't do as much. He can't write th'an on air, either.

They were chatting, mostly small talk about people they both knew and I didn't. I paid close attention to this conversation, so I could record it more accurately later, but I didn't bother remembering that part. I leaned back against the wall and prepared to wait for a while, but a few seconds later, Cederic said, "I hope you are convinced by this, Denril."

Vorantor sipped his water, put the glass down, and said, "I was about to ask the same of you."

"Sesskia's arrival nearly brought down the Darssan around our heads," Cederic said, which was news to me. No one ever talked about the day I came here, and while Cederic had said the kathana was dangerous, I had no idea just how dangerous that was. "Imagine the devastation if the transfer had not been confined to a single individual."

"You know I have never downplayed the extent of the coming catastrophe," Vorantor said. "I know very well how bad it will be. Which is why we have been working so hard to find ways to minimize it."

"It will be impossible to protect everyone, Denril," Cederic said, in a voice that implied they'd had this conversation a dozen times before. "We have to prevent it happening entirely."

"If you would allow yourself to think rationally—" Vorantor began.

"*Do not accuse me of irrationality*," Cederic said, sounding so intense that Vorantor flinched back. "We worked side by side for *years*. I disagree about the results of our research. That hardly makes me irrational. *You* are the one who sits there and counts casualties and talks about acceptable losses instead of working with me to prevent the coming disaster!"

"I apologize, Cederic, my words were poorly chosen," Vorantor said, but I'm pretty sure he was lying. He wanted—still wants—Cederic to be off-balance in Colosse, so he can get him to do as he demands. "You are correct, we disagree, but time and again our research has indicated that complete prevention of the worlds' coming back together is impossible. Containment is the only solution."

"We are close to summoning the Codex Tiurindi," Cederic said, calmer now, and he definitely surprised Vorantor. "And thanks to Sesskia's input, we will be able to read it when we do."

"Astonishing," Vorantor breathed. "You did not put that in your letter."

Cederic actually smiled. "I wanted to tell you to your face and see your reaction."

"Well, I hope you're satisfied with my surprise and delight," Vorantor said, laughing. It was a strange conversation. At times, they sounded like mortal enemies, and then they could joke and laugh together like old friends.

"Entirely," Cederic said. "Now, Denril. *Please* see sense. The Codex Tiurindi will show us how to keep the two worlds apart permanently. No future generation will have to struggle to prevent chaos the way we are right now. I want us to work together again. Please."

"I was unaware Cederic Aleynten knew how to make requests," Vorantor joked, but it made Cederic recoil as if he'd been slapped. "You know the contents of the Codex are in large part a mystery. We don't know what we will learn from it. The end is fast approaching, old friend. We no longer have time to entertain your...optimistic ambitions."

"What is that supposed to mean?" Cederic said.

"I mean it is time for *you* to work with *me*," Vorantor said. "You have failed to prove your theory is correct. I, on the other hand, have a great deal of proof on my side. The God-Empress sees the need for action, now, and has entrusted me to carry out her orders. I am to collect what you have learned and bring it back to Colosse for the Sais to study."

"Denril—" Cederic said. His voice was rising.

"Don't shout, Cederic, you know it doesn't affect me," Vorantor said. "You have a choice. Stay here in the Darssan, with your mages, and face destruction—you know this is too far from civilization for my kathana to protect you. Or come with me and have a part in saving the world."

Cederic said, "This world, naturally."

"The destruction of the other world is regrettable, but there's no hope for it," Vorantor said. "Its mages will have to save it themselves."

"They have no mages," Cederic said. "You are condemning a world to death."

"As I said, regrettable, and the thought of all that death pains me, but I have an obligation to *this* world," Vorantor said.

I'm a thief. If I went around reacting in surprise or anger or fear or horror all the time, I'd be a dead thief. But hearing Vorantor talk so casually about the destruction of my world made me so furious I nearly dropped the concealment pouvra and throttled him there in that seat. Cederic said, "You cannot take the knowledge in our heads. We will still be able to summon the Codex Tiurindi."

"Possibly," Vorantor said. "With the help of the woman. I thought her name was Thalessi."

"Sesskia is not a name she shares with casual acquaintances," Cederic said, "and her magic is key to that kathana, yes."

"Unfortunate that the God-Empress has instructed me to bring her with me, then," Vorantor said, and he sounded so sly that I know,

I just *know*, the bastard waited until that moment to strike at Cederic when he was at his lowest point.

Cederic sat straight up in his chair. "She is not a thing you can simply carry away," he said.

"No, but she will not refuse the God-Empress's command, I think," Vorantor said.

"I would not count on it," Cederic said. "She has no more loyalty to this world than you have to hers."

"I have brought thirty-five mages, thirteen of them Sais, to ensure her compliance," Vorantor said.

"That might not be enough to contain her," Cederic said.

"They aren't to contain her," Vorantor said. "My orders are to begin killing the mages of the Darssan if she refuses. From what you wrote of her, we know she's developed an attachment to them. The God-Empress thinks she won't want to see them die when she can prevent it with a single action."

Cederic looked horrified, and that frightened me more than anything Vorantor had said. "Denril," he said, "how can you possibly condone this? Let alone preside over it?"

"Cederic, I have little choice in the matter." Vorantor said.

"No choice. That is never true, and you know it," Cederic said in a low, intense voice. "I warned you not to throw in your lot with hers. She's insane, Denril, you know she is. Only a madwoman could order such a vile thing."

"Do not make such accusations, even where only I can hear," Vorantor said. "She is our ruler, Cederic, and she deserved to know what was coming. We will need her temporal power in the aftermath, however well we are able to contain the destruction. She has amassed an army the likes of which no one has seen since the days of the Conqueror to maintain Castavir's stability after the coming disaster. But the God-Empress is preparing for war against an enemy she knows she can't fight, and her paranoia is increasing.

"She insists I produce results, regardless of the cost, and you and I agree on one thing: Thalessi, or whatever you call her, as an inhabitant of the shadow world, is crucial to our ability to preserve this one

—that's true no matter which of our theories is correct. And I am *sorry*, old friend, I am truly sorry, but you must give up this mad, doomed quest.

"I need your help. Your skills are unparalleled; I can even admit you're better than I am. Your continued refusal to join me *will* mean the deaths of hundreds of thousands, perhaps millions. You made a request of me. Let me extend the same to you. Help me. *Please*."

Cederic turned away—and looked directly at me. I'm sure he hadn't been aware of my presence until that moment. His face was once again impassive, but his eyes were pleading with me—for forgiveness? For approval? I nodded, though I wasn't sure what I was agreeing to. He turned back to look at Vorantor and said, "I will join you. And Sesskia will come peacefully."

"Thank you," Vorantor said. "And I truly am sorry for this."

"I am sorry, too," Cederic said, though he didn't say for what.

I wrote that Vorantor was smart; he stood up from his chair and said, "I will leave you to decide how best to tell the mages. They should be evacuated from the Darssan."

"And I suppose you have a plan for that as well," Cederic said.

"I have called for another loenerel to transport them to Trengia," Vorantor said. "From there they will be able to return to their homes."

"And forbidden the opportunity to save their world," Cederic said. His voice was as expressionless as his face.

"You know most of them lack the skills to give us any advantage. Choose your best, and thank the others for their assistance to date," Vorantor said.

"They were *your* best, once, Denril," Cederic said. "Are you so completely lost to human feeling?"

"This is a hard time, and we must make hard choices," Vorantor said. I couldn't see his face, but he sounded angry. "Past time you learned that."

Cederic said nothing, just made a small dismissive wave of his fingers as if to say the conversation was over. Again, Vorantor demonstrated his intelligence by leaving without saying another word.

When the door was shut, Cederic said, "I wish you had not heard that."

I released the concealment pouvra and said, "I'm sorry. I know I said I wouldn't use the pouvra like a thief."

"I am not angry at your eavesdropping, Sesskia, but you do not need to be burdened with the knowledge that we are at the mercy of a mad Empress who is willing to slaughter innocents," Cederic said.

I said, "Why not? It was me she wanted to coerce. I'm the one she's going to try to control. I think I have a right to know in what way I need to defend myself."

Cederic shrugged. "You have a point," he said. "And now I must decide how to tell two hundred mages that our work is not only over, but has been a waste of time. Without implicating Denril."

"Why not implicate him?" I said. "It's his fault!"

"He is the Empress's right hand in this matter. If I give them reason to murmur against him, and that murmuring gets back to her, their lives will be forfeit," Cederic said. "I will take the blame myself. I will explain that in light of new evidence, I have been convinced our work needs to take a different direction, and the Darssan must be closed for everyone's safety. If I am lucky, they will hate me and not Denril."

"That's not fair," I said.

Cederic looked up at me, and his eyes showed all the pain his face never would. "This has never been about fairness," he said. "Was it fair to pull you from your world into this one, make you a pawn in a game you never agreed to play? Denril was right, in part—this is a hard time that requires hard choices. The difference is he believes he has the right to make those choices for everyone else. I have never agreed with him in that respect."

"Do you still believe you're right?" I said.

"I do," he said, "and I will take with me the mages most capable of proving me correct. We will summon the Codex Tiurindi, and it will prove the truth to Denril. I only hope it will do so before it is too late."

"I'll help *you* find a solution," I said. "I don't have to be cooperative with him," and then I remembered what Vorantor said about killing the mages, and it made me so angry I couldn't go on speaking. I would be going to Colosse surrounded by hostages.

"You see the problem," Cederic said, drily.

"Damn him to hell and damn your God-Empress too," I said.

"Never say that again. Never even think it," Cederic said. "She is dangerous in ways you cannot imagine, because she is erratic and paranoid and is capable of destroying things, and people, even when that destruction hurts her cause. Your guess is correct: she wants you in Colosse so she can control you personally, and not because Denril has told her you are necessary to his work. But if she turns on you... God only knows what she might decide to do."

"I can defend myself," I said, "but I can't defend everyone around me."

"Exactly," Cederic said.

I sat down in the chair next to him and said, "How can I help *you*? Since it's clear I won't be able to help myself."

He smiled. "Behave as if you know nothing of this conflict. You don't have to be cheerful about it, naturally, but a desire to mitigate the coming disaster would be appropriate. Cooperate with Denril when he asks you about pouvrin. I'm glad you understood what I asked you earlier."

"Now I'm especially grateful I did," I said. "Having pouvrin he knows nothing about could save my life."

"I hope it doesn't come to that," Cederic said. "We won't leave until the second loenerel arrives to transport everyone—I won't let it seem I'm abandoning anyone. You and I will have to find a way to pursue the correct line of research without seeming to be insubordinate. It could be dangerous."

"Because nothing about the rest of this is dangerous," I said. "I don't understand 'loenerel.'"

"It is a machine powered by th'an that can transport large numbers of people more quickly than walking or riding," Cederic said. "They are made in segments, so those segments, the senets, can be added or removed depending on how many people it needs to transport. It will require a fairly large loenerel to move all the mages of the Darssan—minus the few I am to be allowed as part of my entourage," he added, sounding bitter. "I cannot believe Denril is so dismissive of their abilities, simply because he took many of our best mages when he left for Colosse two years ago."

That was a surprise. "Those men and women with him, they used to belong to the Darssan?" I said.

"Many of them, yes," Cederic said. "Some of them were privately employed before Denril coaxed them to work for him. But enough of those mages have friends here..." We both sat silent for a moment, and I'm sure he was thinking (as I was) about what kind of people could agree to kill their friends for any reason. Or maybe Cederic wasn't exaggerating about the Empress's madness. "And there were more Sais here, once," he went on. "Seventeen of us. They all believe as Denril does."

That made my heart ache for him. Seventeen people who might have been his friends in a way the ordinary mages could not. "So you were the only one who saw this possibility," I said, and he nodded. Then he stood, and said, "I hope for all our sakes you are as good a liar as you are a thief," and I could see he was trying to make a joke, so I laughed. It didn't hurt my feelings—I'm sure he meant it as a compliment—but it reminded me my life had suddenly become dangerous, and that I have secrets that could mean people's deaths, or even my own, if I reveal them.

The rest of it I'll sum up, because it's too painful to remember. I think Cederic told Vorantor to keep his stooges out of the way when he told the Darssan mages what was going to happen, and there was a lot of noise and furor. Cederic was so still during all of this I couldn't help thinking how painful it was for him, that they all thought he'd abandoned them and the research they'd all worked so hard on.

I tried to stay out of the way as they all packed up the books and washed down the walls, shut down the kathanas powering the commodes and the pools, and gathered up their belongings, because it felt as if my home were being destroyed. I had so many goodbyes to make that it didn't help that the thirteen mages coming with us (not including Cederic) were all friends of mine, ten of the group leaders, including Terrael (that was an obvious choice) and Sovrin, plus Audryn and two other men I knew well. I had to hide in my room often so I wouldn't make them feel worse by how miserable I was. This is why I've never had friends. It's too hard when you have to leave them behind, and you *always* have to leave them behind.

No, that's a lie, and if I'm going to be lying a lot in the days and weeks to come, I shouldn't lie to myself. I've never had friends because I never could trust anyone before, and as much as it hurts, saying goodbye, I'd rather have had friendship than not.

Sovrin was more miserable than the rest of us. Her lover isn't coming along, despite her arguments and even my pleas to Cederic to make an exception. He said, damn him for being right, "We can't look weak in front of the Empress, and Denril will know we didn't bring our best. Hard choices, Sesskia." So the best we could do was give them as much time together as possible.

Eventually, the second loenerel arrived, and I didn't go up to see it, but if the one we're riding in now is small, I can't even imagine how huge that one was. After it left, there was some uncomfortable shuffling around—I think Denril's mages had the decency to feel guilty about why they were there—for an hour or two before our loenerel was positioned for us to bring our things on.

It's beautiful, in a hard and gleaming way—lots of brass and rubbed brown leather, and some of the senets are rows of seats with lots of windows, and others have sleeping cubicles, and there's one for eating in. It smells of hot metal all the time, though as I wrote above, the smell becomes stronger when it stops, and there's also a bitter-oily scent I now associate with large quantities of magic, and never mind what Terrael said about magic being completely used up by th'an or kathanas.

I went up to look at the collenna, which is what actually contains the magic—the senets are all connected to it in a long row—and it positively reeked of that odor. The master, whose name I've forgotten, showed me where he draws the th'an, and it was so clever! There's an engraving on this brass panel in the shape of a couple of linked th'an, a groove thin enough for a skinny paintbrush to fit, and the master has a five-gallon bucket full of that silvery ink or paint Terrael used on the aeden to give me his language. He paints the th'an, following the grooves exactly, and that makes the th'an work.

That's how people other than mages can use magic, though I gather it's not as simple as filling in a line. The masters, not just of collennas but of other machines as well, have to be taught to write their rune in exactly the right way, and they usually only learn the one their job makes them responsible for. I'm not sure how that doesn't make them mages, though I suppose in Castavir being a mage is defined as knowing hundreds or thousands of th'an. But it is reassuring to know if anything happened to the master, we've got fifty people on the loenerel who can make it go, which is good because the idea of being trapped in this horrible, hot, arid, stinking wasteland makes me feel even more queasy.

And that brings me up to now. To sum up:

1. We're all going to Colosse to take part in research none of us believes in.

2. Denril Vorantor is dangerous.

3. The God-Empress is even more so.

4. Cederic still has hope the Codex Tiurindi will prove him right, and in time for that to make a difference.

We should be out of the desert soon, probably by tomorrow morning. I wish I knew how fast we've been traveling, so I could get a sense for how far we've come, but I suppose it doesn't matter. And despite everything, I'm eager to see Colosse. I've visited many cities in I don't know how many foreign lands, but this is my first time visiting a city in a completely different world. I hope it isn't a disappointment.

CHAPTER ELEVEN

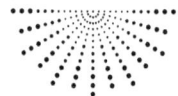

4 Lennitay, evening

This is how paranoid I am: There is a perfect little niche in the wall of my bedroom, behind the headboard of my bed, that my book fits into exactly. And that's why I'm not using it. I'd bet hard money, if I had any, that someone in the palace knows every single hidey-hole there is in every single room, and I'd bet even more of that nonexistent money someone's searched my room since we arrived this morning. So I continue to keep my book and pencil on my person, and keep it under my pillow at night, because it's the last thing I have of my world and losing it would devastate me.

Colosse isn't as big as I imagined, smaller than Venetry, probably, and not as sprawling as Thalessa, but it's impressive in a way neither of them ever dreamed of being. I don't know if it's how white the walls are, or how all the lines and angles are so exact, but it looks so clean I wonder how anyone can bear to live in it. Audryn, who comes from Colosse, says no animals are allowed within its city limits, as per orders of the God-Empress. (I've decided to call her that even in the privacy of this book, so I won't slip up when I'm speaking of her or, horribly, to her.)

So there's no animal waste in the streets and no smells of warm animal bodies. What kind of stink the humans make is something I haven't discovered, as the loenerel came straight through the city and inside the palace to unload us, so I've only seen a little of Colosse so far and nothing up close. But I saw lots of people walking, and some riding in bearer-borne chairs that in my world would only be used by the very wealthy, and there were some little wheeled carts that fit two passengers while a third person pulled it.

Audryn also said machines like very small versions of the collenna are becoming popular among the upper classes, but their th'an are so small and intricate it takes a lot of practice to learn how to operate one. I'm guessing the God-Empress has one of her own, but big enough that someone can drive her around in it. It fits what little I know of her.

What else did I observe about Colosse: it sits athwart what Castavirans call the Coell River but in my world is the Myrnala. (I think it's Coell, with the long 'o', but some people pronounce it as 'call', and I'm going with Audryn's pronunciation, since she's actually from here). The loenerel crossed it at one point, and it was the strangest feeling, because the Myrnala is so much greener and slower and it bears no resemblance to the Coell; I only know the two are the same, or at least in the same place, because I saw it on the overlapping maps.

This whole region is much drier and hotter than the corresponding places in my world, particularly that wasteland surrounding the Darssan, which in my world is nothing but grassy plains and a few very unwelcoming settlements. If Colosse is always this arid, the seasons might not even correspond. We ought to be heading into fall, by my reckoning—I'll have to ask Audryn or someone what time of year this is. Either way, I'm not changing the dates in this book.

I keep getting distracted. Well, Colosse was a distraction, a distraction from worrying about the God-Empress and what Vorantor might want from me and whether or not Cederic will be able to prove himself right. It might not be as big as Venetry, but it's still pretty damn big, and blindingly white in the sun because they surface all their buildings with white plaster or white marble, depending on the wealth of the owner. The roofs are like jewels in the sun, all different colors that don't come from paint but from this huge variety of slate that either comes from the nearby mines or is imported.

I learned the color of a roof represents someone's religious allegiance, in a way. They all worship the same God, but their God has so many traits that people here adopt one and let it define their lives. For example, someone might value Truth above all else, and they'd put a blue roof on their home and be known for always seeking for truth, however uncomfortable that might be. Not that someone who valued Strength couldn't be trusted to be truthful, and a seeker for Truth might not always be totally honest, it's just that Strength or Truth would be what drives that person.

And it's still true that you can count on an adherent of a particular virtue to behave in certain ways, because they see that virtue as an important aspect of who they are. To me, it seems like bragging about how truthful or strong or generous you are, but Audryn also implied that someone not adhering to the principles of their adopted virtue can be charged with impiety in front of the God-Empress, who probably doesn't appreciate people treating her (as avatar of their God) with such disrespect. One more reason not to declare one's allegiance, I'd think.

Anyway, what with the colored roofs, Colosse looks like a pile of gems snuggled up against the banks of the river, but with the white walls and the wide, paved roads that are perfectly regular, it also looks like a model city, something built by a giant and left behind when she went home for supper.

Even though I could see all the foot traffic, the loenerel is nearly soundproof and what noise it lets pass is muffled by the noise of its wheels and the thumping of the collenna, and the silence made the city seem even more like a toy, with people being made to move by that giant's pouvra. It was almost a relief to roll through the big, square opening in the side of the palace and into the darkness beyond.

It wasn't completely dark, just dim by comparison to the blindingly white buildings outside. The loenerel slid to a halt, though the collenna's thumping continued, more quietly now that it wasn't pulling anything, and Vorantor (we were all sitting in a couple of the senets filled with rows of seats) stood and walked forward to the door, which is a thing that is hinged in the middle so it folds on itself, and opened it. It was almost like a ceremony, he and his mages looked so solemn, and they all remained seated while Cederic and our mages and I stepped out past Vorantor and into the chamber beyond.

It was narrow, almost like a corridor, and low-ceilinged, and its shape looked as if it had been designed specifically for the loenerel. Cederic immediately walked forward, which is to say toward the front of the loenerel, without waiting for Vorantor to catch up. We all followed him, me at the end of our little procession that had to go single file because the room (tunnel?) had such little space between the loenerel and the wall. I kept close to Kaurin, who was immediately in front of me. I would have held on to her robe if I'd dared, because the whole thing made me claustrophobic in a way the Darssan had not, even when I felt most oppressed by the weight of the mountain hanging over my head.

We came to a pair of double doors at the end of the tunnel, and Cederic pushed them open as if he had a perfect right to be here. I wished I had a good excuse to push past everyone and stand next to him, to have some idea of what to expect based on how he felt, but I guessed by how abruptly he was doing things, how rapidly he was moving, that he was trying to control his anger. I don't blame him for being angry.

Now that we were actually in the palace (or, rather, I assumed we were in the palace and not just wherever the loenerel could be stowed) it was nearly impossible not to remember why we were here, and the manner of our being brought here. I don't think Cederic told any of our mages, the ones who came with us, what threats Vorantor had made—not something they needed to be burdened with, in my opinion, and not something they could do anything about. Though I imagine all of them knew better than I did what kind of danger the God-Empress presented.

The double doors opened on a space even larger and taller than the cavern in the Darssan, and far more opulent. The walls were tiled with mosaics depicting all kinds of heroic deeds, again in colors that reminded me of jewels—a hero slaying a giant, another wrestling with a dragon, yet another holding back the tide from a city on the edge of the ocean.

It took me a minute to work out what was wrong with the pictures, and then I couldn't stop noticing it. All the mosaics appeared to be the work of a single hand, which was impressive—it must have taken a lifetime to create them, based on the size of the room—but the heroes' faces had been put in by someone far less gifted, and they were all the same woman's face. No doubt what had happened there, and whose face adorned each mosaic. If I hadn't already been convinced of the God-Empress's self-aggrandizing lunacy, this would have done it.

The floor was tiled with larger tesserae in gold and copper, making a pattern far too large for me to make out. Maybe if I could find a way up to the upper levels—there were four of them, all with balconies that had nothing but a single protective rail keeping an observer from plummeting to a painful, skull-cracking death.

I saw no stairs, but five dark openings spaced evenly around the room separated the mosaics from one another, the one we'd entered by making a sixth. The room was completely empty except for us. Cederic walked toward the center of the room—no, I'm certain that, since he's Sai Aleynten, it was the exact center of the room, and now I can say that out of admiration and not annoyance—and stood with his arms folded across his chest, waiting.

After a minute or two in which the rest of us became increasingly nervous and fidgety, a woman emerged from the dark opening directly ahead of us, walking rapidly, her hand closed in a fist over her throat. She managed to bow, a rapid bobbing of her head, as she walked, and as she neared us I could tell she was terrified and trying not to show it. "We apologize, Kilios, a thousand apologies. Someone was meant to meet you—Kilios, please forgive—"

"We require accommodations and the wherewithal to wash after our long journey," Cederic said. His cold tone of voice made me shiver. The woman bobbed even more rapidly and waved her hands in the direction of one of the other alcoves. Cederic allowed her to precede him; everyone else followed in a line, with me again at the rear.

Now that I know that the palace has been built and rebuilt over the years, with sections being shut off and others rediscovered (literally; there have been rooms no one even remembered until a God-Emperor's building project uncovered them), I can understand why the woman led us in such a circuitous route. I've had years of experience in remembering my way out of homes and manors made to thwart thieves, and even I couldn't remember the path we took. I'll have to do some exploring later tonight.

At the time, I thought she was trying to confuse us, possibly in retribution for how rude Cederic was. But the servants here all seem thoroughly cowed, and while I don't know why they called Cederic Kilios, and I still don't know what it means, they definitely venerate him. And they're uncomfortably terrified around me. I have yet to make one of them look me in the eye. How that reconciles with my suspicion that someone is spying on us, I don't know, except that it's unlikely all the God-Empress's servants are this spineless.

The woman brought us through some narrow passages that smelled damp, which I thought was strange given how arid Colosse is in general. Then we walked up a fairly steep ramp into a wider corridor made of yellow bricks twice the size of my head, lined with doors on both sides. The doors were made of the same metal the ones in the Darssan were, and none of them had locks, which made me less nervous than if they had locks that could only be locked from the outside, but not by much.

The woman, bowing again (she'd stopped doing that briefly while we were walking along the narrow corridor), opened the first door and said, "Please accept the God-Empress's hospitality during your stay," and beckoned to Sovrin, who was at the head of the line, to enter. Sovrin glanced at Cederic, who nodded a tiny bit, and she went into the room and closed the door. I had time to wonder how they'd get our things to us when the woman moved on to the next door and repeated the ritual for Jaemis. Ultimately, everyone got a room to him- or herself, until it was just me and Cederic left with the woman.

Cederic still looked like a statue. I probably looked confused. The woman went through a doorway at the end of the corridor, where there were stairs leading up. She said, as we climbed and climbed, "Otherworlder, we have nothing that befits your status, I hope you will forgive our inhospitality. We will put you in the wing with the Sais, I hope that is acceptable."

We came out of the stairwell into a long, broad hallway paved with giant gray flagstones that had a roof open to the outside. The roof was a series of metal grilles that made diamond patterns of shadow and light on the floor. It wasn't nearly as hot as the waste-land, but the air was very dry and smelled of dust and, more distantly, of magic. Doors more widely spaced than the ones where my friends had been housed, these made of new, planed wood and bearing shining steel plates with locks by the doorknobs, stood along both walls of the corridor. I wanted to run down the hall and see what was at the other end, but that would probably have given the servant woman a heart attack, so I decided to save that for later. I have a lot of plans for later.

The woman walked a short distance down the hallway and stopped at the third door. "Again I apologize for the paucity of your accommodations," she said, and pushed the door open for me. I went inside and nearly fainted. I have *never* seen anything so opulent, and I have stood in the King's own antechamber and wondered which of his treasures I should take first while he slept in the next room.

The flagstone floor, identical to that of the hallway outside, was covered with a thick maroon rug like the pelt of a large, strangely colored bear. Glazed windows, their golden velvet drapes pulled back to admit the morning sun, looked out over the roofs and windows of the patchwork palace. A bed stood in one corner, covered in blankets that matched the rug and the drapes, with enough white pillows that I could have made a bed from them alone. Four pillars at its corners supported a gauzy golden curtain that was currently pulled back and tied at each post.

A dressing table made of the same mahogany as the bed, mahogany that would have cost a fortune in my world, stood next to a matching wardrobe large enough for me and Audryn and Sovrin to hide in together while we plotted tricks to play on the men. A mirror hung over the dressing table, and I don't know why that struck me as a far greater luxury than any of the rest of the furniture, but I've never had a mirror that wasn't cracked and certainly not one that could show me my entire body at once, supposing I cared to look.

There were more rugs scattered across the floor, and I went forward to open the wardrobe, because this all felt like a joke the God-Empress wanted to play on the otherworlder woman, and someone might be waiting inside to leap out and startle me. It was empty except for a few drawers and hangers. I didn't have nearly enough to fill it, which was good—always travel light, that's one of my many mottoes—but it made me feel awkward, as if they were giving me all of this because they think I'm more important than I am. I hope I'm not more important than *I* think I am.

"This will be adequate," I managed to choke out, and the woman bowed and bobbed even more than before.

"Someone will call for you, when it is time for our audience," Cederic said, and then he abandoned me—well, not really, but the woman closed the door and I was alone amid opulence I'm certain I don't deserve. On the other hand...it *is* awfully nice, and the bed looked soft, not that I'd jump on it until I was out of these travel-stained clothes.

I jumped on it anyway. I'm not ashamed.

I practiced locking and unlocking the door with the pouvra—I noticed the woman didn't give me a key, so it was important I learn to do that—and I took off my boots and jumped on the bed more, which is undignified in someone my age, I know, but I couldn't resist, and then I sat around trying to decide what to do next. I thought about exploring, but I didn't know when the God-Empress would call for us, and I didn't want to miss that audience. So I put off exploring until I could do it when no one would expect me to be running around.

This book was nearly discovered when a couple of men entered my room without knocking. I shouted at them and explained at length about my customs (what is it about Castavirans that they don't believe in waiting on an invitation?) and they bowed and groveled until I felt guilty. It turned out they came to measure me for my palace wardrobe.

Wardrobe? Yes, wardrobe. Etiquette is very strict here in the palace, and while as I am an otherworlder it's understood that my mistakes aren't meant as a slight to the God-Empress, I'm still expected to make an effort. The men had armloads of clothing, most of it the same rich brocades and velvets Vorantor's mages wear, and if I didn't know the God-Empress was crazy, this and the mosaics would definitely confirm it, because brocade and velvet in this climate is insane. Even if the palace does have some kind of cooling system.

Anyway, they made me put on everything, and some things they discarded and others they fitted to me, and there was one long-skirted dress with full sleeves, made of linen, that they said was a pattern for my other dresses. Since they'd already fitted me with ten robes of varying lengths and trousers with wide legs like divided skirts, I'm not sure how many more dresses I need. At least they're nothing I'd want to carry with me, because there's no way I could manage that lot.

While I was being fitted, another servant came in with my bag and began putting my things away. Good thing I keep this diary on me, though I had to undress for some of the fittings and it was tricky keeping it hidden inside my discarded clothes. It's too bad I've never had to do anything like *that* before. Hahahaha. This servant kept looking at me as if thinking "why does the otherworlder have so little?" and then he left and came back when the fitting was almost done with a box filled with all sorts of things: hairbrush and comb and hair clips, soaps and lotions, a file for my nails, and—this *really* shocked me—a flat box filled with jewelry.

Not fake jewelry. They go in for cabochons rather than faceted stones, and they use more semiprecious stones like agates and jaspers, but the workmanship is *incredible* and some of the filigree work is far beyond anything my world has produced. And they just gave it to me. No one's ever given me jewelry before; I've always had to steal it, and of course I never kept any of it because it was far more valuable in trade for books. It still shocks me.

I should stop if I want any time for exploring tonight. I didn't realize how late it was. Cederic just came in to say good night. He also said, "I would tell you not to wander, but I realize that would be pointless," and he's right, because there's no way I'm not going to investigate this palace. But I'll have to write about that tomorrow. That, and seeing the God-Empress this afternoon. It was nothing like I expected.

CHAPTER TWELVE

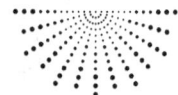

5 Lennitay, way too early in the morning

I've only had a few hours of sleep, but I want to write everything that's happened while it's still fresh in my memory. Especially what I learned from exploring last night.

But first, the God-Empress. I almost don't know where to begin. So I suppose I'll start with the clothing, because that was strange. I had about half an hour to play with the jewelry before the men with the clothing came back, with friends, and then it was like being at the center of a fuchsia-scented whirlwind of brocade.

Two of the servants hung clothes in the wardrobe and put away all sorts of garments I hadn't seen before, including underclothing, and then the men left and the women stripped me naked and began dressing me as if I were an infant. I protested loudly, but stopped when they all became hugely apologetic. I learned this was supposed to be an honor, a service normally performed only for God-Emperors, and if I rejected it they would all be punished.

So I mentally said some very rude things about the God-Empress, never mind what Cederic said, and let them wrap me in more layers than I'd ever worn in my life, including a breast band, which they don't have in my country. I tried one back in the Darssan, but I'm not exactly well-endowed and I decided a good shirt is enough support for me. It felt awkward and strange and I hoped it wasn't obvious from the way I held my arms that I was wearing it.

Then there was a thin thigh-length robe that went over the wide-legged trousers, both of them a beautiful cerulean blue I'd only ever seen on pottery before. After that came a sleeveless tunic made of a multicolored brocade that has tassels hanging from the hem to my knees. If they were allowed to swing free, they would be annoying, but they're constrained by the over-robe, which is gold velvet that matches the curtains so closely they might have come from the same bolt. It has shorter sleeves than the thin under-robe, so the blue shows, and it fastens only with a single button at the waist, so it's open over the brocade tunic and some of the tassels are visible.

And *then* they put a white thing like a sheet sewn up the sides over my head, so the whole outfit is covered up. I asked what the point was (I was more polite than that) and the gist of their explanation was that the God-Empress expects everyone to dress in their finest court clothing when they wait upon her, but not to outshine her. Hence the white sheet. Insane. Though with a certain logic.

I had to wait a little longer for Cederic to come for me, when the women were done, and it was strange to see him wearing the sheet, which looked pink because of the red robe he wore under it. He still managed to look composed instead of ridiculous. I'm pretty sure I looked rumpled. I hadn't dared look at myself in the mirror.

Instead of beckoning me to come, he entered my room and shut the door behind him, gesturing me to keep silent. He drew th'an on the air, and spots on the walls glowed with amber light. I went with him to look at the nearest one, which was on the left-hand wall, and he indicated I should put my eye up to it.

When I did, and my eye focused properly, I realized I could see into the room next to mine! I bit back an outraged complaint, and Cederic smiled, but it was a bitter, resigned smile. Every one of the amber lights indicated a peephole. It was infuriating. Suppose someone had been watching me dress!

Cederic went to my wardrobe and dug into the top drawer, and came up with, to my embarrassment, a pair of undershorts. He removed the drawstring and tore them down the back seam, then into smaller pieces he rolled up tight and fitted deep into the holes. Then he scribed more th'an, and the amber light flared again, this time giving off the scent of cinnamon.

When I looked again, I saw the cloth was now fused with the stone, completely blocking the holes. Cederic tossed the mutilated undershorts at me, and I set them on fire in midair so they came down in front of the window as nothing but black ash.

"I doubt anyone here knows those holes exist," Cederic said, "but I thought you might feel more comfortable not worrying that someone might be watching you. Or listening to us."

"How did *you* know about them?" I said.

"I didn't," he said. "I hypothesized their existence and then proved it in my own chamber. It is, by the way, the fourth door down the hall from yours."

"Thank you," I said. "Before we go, what do I need to know about the God-Empress? What should I expect?"

He put his hands behind his back and walked toward the door. "She is predisposed to like you," he said. "Show her whatever magic she asks for. Whatever she offers you, accept and say it is an honor you do not deserve, but *never* decline a gift, because she will take it as refusing God's bounty. You will know when she is pleased with herself; at those moments, admire her without sounding sycophantic. I think you will find that less difficult than it sounds, because the God-Empress is capable of great things. And she is not stupid, whatever else she may be."

He very carefully never uses the word "insane," not since his conversation with Vorantor. "Above all, do not go out of your way to have contact with her. Every encounter is a chance she might change her mind about your...novelty, and there is the rare possibility that Denril's insistence that you are needed for the kathana may not be enough to protect you."

"Is it all right that I'm a little afraid?" I said.

"That shows how sensible you are," Cederic said. "Now, follow me, and say nothing until you are spoken to."

I followed him back to where the rest of our mages were staying. They had either already received their instructions or knew how to behave without being told, because they fell silently into line behind us. Terrael gave me a look that said he wished he could tell me something, but there was no chance to exchange words. Our white-sheeted procession retraced our earlier steps, and even now it makes me shudder to think of how much we looked as if we were going to a funeral.

This was when I memorized the route, which only deviated from our earlier path when we were near the mosaic chamber. Cederic made a sharp turn to the left and we ascended a long staircase that had landings opening off it at intervals. I guessed (correctly) these landings led to the upper levels of the mosaic chamber, and filed that information away for later use. I went back, last night, but even with the see-in-dark pouvra there wasn't enough contrast for me to make out the pattern on the floor. That's really starting to bother me, not knowing.

We kept going until I was panting and there was a horrible stabbing pain in my side. Even Cederic was breathing heavily. Just as I knew I was going to collapse on the stairs, we walked through an arched doorway and into a round...pavilion, I think I should call it, because it was open to the sky on all sides, its domed roof held up by pillars of the same yellow stone as the passageway below.

The underside of the dome was painted in an abstract pattern of green and black and orange that was the ugliest thing I'd ever seen. Hot wind blew across the pavilion, carrying with it the same smell of arid dryness and magic I'd smelled outside my room, and it made all our sheets ripple, revealing the hems of our colorful robes. It was much higher than the roofs of Colosse, so high it felt as if we were floating above the city and clouds might drift past my knees at any moment.

The pavilion was already occupied by Vorantor and his mages, though they wore brown sheets rather than white ones. I learned later the brown sheets designated mages in direct service to the God-Empress, because ours were exchanged for brown ones after this meeting, though I don't remember saying anything explicitly pledging my service to her. And I remember almost every detail of this conversation. It was too surreal to forget.

Again, Vorantor and his mages were already there, surrounding a dais with ten steps leading up to a golden throne. Tacky, but a standard display of wealth and power. The God-Empress Renatha Torenz sat on the tacky throne, and it seems the one thing no one had bothered to mention is that she's stunningly beautiful.

I have no idea why she's worried about anyone, male or female, outshining her. She dyes her black hair gold—she was due for another treatment, I could see her roots—and it doesn't look cheap on her, it looks like she's wearing a crown of gold, because it was pinned up on top of her head in all these elaborate loops with emerald-tipped pins that were faceted to catch even the indirect light of the pavilion.

She wore the same kinds of clothing I was wearing under my sheet, but they were all cloth-of-gold trimmed with emeralds, and around her neck was a choker of more emeralds set in gold bezels, and emerald bracelets—ten or twelve of them on each wrist—glittered like her hairpins. Her perfectly oval face is made more perfect by strong but feminine cheekbones and full lips that didn't need artifice to be red.

And her eyes...they're dark with long lashes, and I've just re-read this and realized I sound as if I've fallen in love with her, or at least want to sleep with her, and that's not it. She just has the kind of beauty you want to look at all day long. I'm not attracted to women, but even if I were I wouldn't dare think of her in a sexual way. I am *so* glad I knew in advance that she's insane, because I might have fallen at her feet and given her anything she wanted otherwise.

Cederic gestured at us to stay where we were and took a few steps forward. "Kilios," the God-Empress said, and I swear I'm not exaggerating when I say her voice sounded like a heavenly flute. Honestly, I'm not attracted to her! Just because she seems to be the embodiment of female perfection! And I don't even feel jealous of her, probably because I know she's madder than a barrel of ferrets, and who can be jealous of that?

Anyway, Cederic dropped to one knee, though he kept his eyes on the God-Empress, and said, "God-Empress, thank you for your welcome." He stayed in that position for the whole time we met with her, never wobbling, though there were a few times I think he wanted to leap to his feet and argue with the woman. He really is the most self-controlled person I know.

"You choose to heed my summons now," she said, and it was obviously both a question and a rebuke.

"The time is right, God-Empress, as I am certain you know, since you in your wisdom renewed your invitation at this exact time," Cederic said.

"I did, didn't I," the God-Empress said with a trilling little laugh. "Come forward, otherworlder."

Fortunately, I remembered I was the otherworlder before she had to repeat her instruction. I copied Cederic's gesture, but said nothing, because I didn't think she'd actually spoken to me. "You may stand," the God-Empress said, so I stood and waited. She stared at me, tapping her forefinger against those perfect lips. Eventually, she said, "You appear to be Viravonian."

"I am not, God-Empress, though I've been told there are similarities," I said.

"And why do you suppose that is?" the God-Empress said.

"I can only guess, God-Empress," I said, "but I know our worlds were once one, and some of those who in your world are Viravonians are probably in mine as well." Vorantor was almost in my line of sight, and I saw him close his eyes as if I'd said something wrong, but I had no idea what. Now I know he thought I'd made a mistake in mentioning that our worlds had once been one, but the God-Empress disagreed, because she didn't lose her temper or order me executed.

What she said was: "And you will prevent the worlds from destroying each other when they are reunited."

I realized at this point that she was in the habit of asking questions phrased as statements. That was clever, forcing the addressee to own statements she probably didn't intend to make. "I will assist the mages who will perform this task," I said.

The God-Empress stood up and came down the stairs. She was taller than me, not by much, but enough that she could grab my chin and tilt my head up to look directly into my eyes. She stared at me, and I tried not to blink, and eventually she released me and went to Cederic and repeated the procedure. "Your eyes are the same," she said.

(I forgot to mention about a third of the mages at the Darssan have green-gray eyes. Nobody seems to think it's unusual, so I never remembered to ask about it. I've seen a few other people with those eyes in my travels, just not so many in one place.)

"It is a color that indicates a predisposition for magic," Cederic said, not flinching. I have no idea whether this is true or not. I forgot to ask him, like I forgot to ask him what Kilios means. I suppose it could be true. It was an explanation the God-Empress liked, because she strode back up to her throne and gracefully settled on it.

"We welcome the mages of the Darssan," she said in a louder, carrying voice, "and bid them put themselves under the supervision of the most high priest Denril Vorantor. We will hear their oaths now."

There was some shuffling behind me, and one by one my friends came forward, bent their knees briefly, and said something I couldn't understand, they spoke so quietly. It made me furious on Cederic's behalf. He'd already lost the Darssan, lost his research, and now he'd lost what little was left to him. Kilios or no, this couldn't be anything but a slap in the face.

Or so I thought. When everyone had gone back to their places behind us, the God-Empress said, "Kilios, will you make common cause with Denril Vorantor and turn your skills to his needs?"

"I will, God-Empress," Cederic said, his voice entirely neutral.

"Denril Vorantor, make your oath," the God-Empress said, and damn if Vorantor didn't cross the pavilion and prostrate himself in front of Cederic, and say, "I accept what you offer and swear to heed your words, Kilios," and Cederic laid his right hand over Vorantor's and said, "I give you my skills and will follow where you lead."

The whole thing sounded bizarre; who was making promises to whom? I still have to ask Cederic about that, that and the Kilios thing and about a million other questions, but I keep forgetting.

I wasn't finished being confused by that when the God-Empress said, "Otherworlder, will you give me the freedom of your name?"

I didn't have time to indulge my outrage at her asking such a personal thing of me, God-Empress or no. "I, uh...yes?" I said. "My name is Sesskia."

"And you may call me Renatha," said the God-Empress, which provoked a reaction from everyone except, naturally, Cederic.

Remembering what Cederic said about gifts, I said, "Thank you, God—Renatha, it is a generous gift I do not deserve," and she smiled more widely. I think it was a test.

"You will join me presently, and we will learn more of your magic," the God-Empress said, and that was apparently a signal that the audience was over.

Cederic stood, and we all filed out of the pavilion and back down the stairs. Vorantor and his mages didn't follow us, which was fortunate because as soon as we were back in the hallway at the bottom of the stairs, everyone started talking at once, and Cederic had to shush them.

"This changes nothing," he said. "You will turn your efforts toward assisting Sai Vorantor, because now we have a common goal. Summoning the Codex Tiurindi is of paramount importance. It does not matter to whom you owe allegiance."

"We owe our allegiance to *you*, Sai Aleynten," Terrael said.

"That may be, but I have sworn to aid Sai Vorantor, and I instruct you to do as he says," said Cederic. "That should satisfy the demands of honor."

"I don't like it," said Jaemis. He's short and wide and looks more like a wrestler than a mage, but his skill at transmutation kathanas is unmatched by any of his peers.

"Liking it is not the issue," Cederic said. "And remember you may be watched at any time. Say nothing that will draw unwanted attention. Now, dinner will be served in two hours, so I suggest you use this time to rest so you will be refreshed for the morning's work."

Everyone grumbled, but they all went to their rooms. Cederic and I went back to the Sais' wing, but he followed me into my room and said, "That was unexpected. Sharing one's name with the God-Empress means a sort of kinship. You may be unable to avoid being called often to her presence."

That frightened me. "What can I do?" I said.

"What you always do. Listen. Speak carefully. Be honest when you can and lie well when you cannot. And at worst, you can slip away from her and we will find another solution," Cederic said.

"Staying hidden from her forever seems impractical," I said.

He smiled. "This palace has places no one but a ghost can enter," he said, "and I daresay you can become a ghost when you want."

"That's less encouraging than you think it is," I said.

"We will worry about it when we come to it," he said. "I will see you at dinner. And please, Sesskia, if you must wander, do it when no one will be watching."

Which I did. Dinner was uneventful; the God-Empress, naturally, didn't dine with us, and the dining room seemed reserved for the use of the mages. I sat with Terrael, Audryn, and Sovrin, and Cederic ate with Vorantor and acted exactly as if they were friends. I don't think I could be friends with anyone who behaved the way Vorantor had. Fortunately no one was asking me to be friends with him.

After dinner I dressed in comfortable clothes (my shirt from the Darssan and some trousers that fitted more closely than I would normally find comfortable, except they were perfect for sneaking around) and waited in the dark until I judged everyone had gone to sleep. Seeing in the dark is a matter of altering the shape of your eyes, more or less, and it can be...not dangerous, exactly, but if you walk into a well-lit room in that state, it blinds you for a while and it hurts like hell. So you have to be careful where you go. Fortunately, I was planning to go places that would be empty of people.

When the moon was finally hovering on the horizon, preparing to set, I slipped out of my room and headed down the hall toward Cederic's room. I wanted to see where the hallway went. It turned out to end at another set of stairs, this one continuing up, so I followed it and found myself in a round room much like the God-Empress's pavilion, but with a smoked glass dome for a roof and wind-blasted pillars supporting it, all of it overgrown by some kind of twining vine with fat, five-pointed leaves. The wind had died down somewhat from earlier and the night was cool and refreshing.

I almost stepped out into the expanse when I saw it was already occupied. I ducked back into the doorway—I wasn't using the concealment pouvra because I didn't want to get used to it and become careless—and watched for a bit. The person stood looking out past the pillars, and it took me a while to discover it was Vorantor.

That made me intensely curious about what he was doing, because I was certain he wasn't there to admire the view, but I didn't exactly want to walk up to him and strike up a conversation. So after about ten minutes of watching him do nothing, I turned around and went back down the hallway to the other stairs.

I was tempted to stop in and talk to Audryn when I reached their hallway, but I realized in time that if I were caught wandering, and it got me in trouble, she would need to be able to say with conviction she knew nothing about it. So I kept going.

My first stop was the stairway leading to the God-Empress's pavilion, with the landings that led to the upper levels of the mosaic chamber. As I wrote, there was too little contrast for me to see the design, and that was frustrating, having a failure right at the beginning of the night. I considered climbing back to the pavilion to look at the city from that height, but the memory of how long a climb that was deterred me.

So I sat with my legs dangling over the edge of the highest balcony and thought about what to do next. Normally when I'm sneaking through a manor or a castle, I'm looking for the library, or maybe a secret room where the important books are kept, and after that I want to find the treasure room so I can buy the books I can't steal. But I can't read the books here, and the mages already have all of them. And I don't have any need for the treasure, not to mention that if I'm caught with it, the God-Empress (I can't call her Renatha in these pages, I just can't) would probably do something fatal to me and everyone I know.

Thinking about the God-Empress gave me an idea. It was still dangerous, but in a fun, let's-see-what-I-can-get-away-with way, and if I was successful, it could benefit me in the long run. So I went to map the boundaries of the God-Empress's territory.

A manor may belong to a person, but in practice, there are portions of that manor that are the personal rooms of the owner. Places that aren't secret (though sometimes they're that), but private. Those are the places a thief has to be especially careful of, because people take intrusions there as more of a violation. Though violating them can be effective, if you're trying to frighten someone by, to take a hypothetical example, leaving notes in their bedroom that say (again hypothetically) THE WATCHER KNOWS WHAT YOU DID TO YOUR WIFE. Very effective.

I wanted to know what the God-Empress called her own so I wouldn't trespass accidentally. I knew some places where her territory wasn't—the rooms where the Darssan mages were housed, and the Sais' wing, and our dining hall and the two common areas we gathered in after dinner. Places like the mosaic chamber were probably outside that territory, since too many people use them—I could hear lots of foot traffic coming from that chamber when we passed it on the way to the audience with the God-Empress. I think it's likely that when we arrived, it was cleared specifically so the Kilios didn't have to encounter any of the unwashed masses.

So I was imagining a map of the palace as I sneaked down to the ground floor. I may not have the most perfect memory for conversation, but I wouldn't be much of a thief if I couldn't keep the map of a building I'm infiltrating in my head. There were far too many blank spots, because the palace is *huge*, and having entered the way we did, I don't have as good a sense of its footprint, but the whole point of exploring is to learn new things, isn't it?

My first step was to learn where all the alcoves off the mosaic chamber led. I didn't get very far last night/this morning because, as I said, the palace is huge, but what I discovered was still a lot. I already knew one alcove leads to the loenerel's stopping place, and one leads to all the mages' living and working quarters and, less directly, to the God-Empress's cloud-kissing pavilion.

The one directly to the right of the loenerel alcove goes to the public areas of the palace, waiting rooms and audience chambers and finally to the God-Empress's real throne room. The actual, official throne is strangely plain, unadorned except for elaborate carvings, and it's built to a scale that would accommodate someone fifteen feet tall. The God-Empress probably looks like a child sitting in it, kicking her feet because they wouldn't reach the ground.

The throne room makes up for the throne's plainness by being lined with mirrors, all of them three feet wide (I used my arm span to measure) and as tall as that imaginary giant, framed in what was probably gilded wood (you can't see colors with the see-in-dark pouvra) decorated with scallops at top and bottom. The floor is marble tiles in contrasting colors, dark and light, and I had to be especially careful not to make any sound walking on them.

I wandered around in these rooms for a bit, admiring their scale and the beauty of the furnishings, which is more refined than my world goes in for. I was going to write that they were more sophisticated, which is true but gives the wrong impression; my world lacks things this world has, mainly with regard to what magic can do, but its cultural development doesn't lag that far behind Castavir's. So in my world, the wealthy go in for big, sturdy, unadorned furniture and architecture, which compared to Castavir's looks rough, but closer examination just shows that it's different. I don't think I'm trying to make excuses for my world, either. But I suppose this is another thing that's irrelevant.

The alcove to the right of that one, the alcove between it and the mages' alcove, leads to a warren of more personal sleeping and living quarters, and a big dining room and a kitchen. And it was completely empty. All those bedrooms, unoccupied. The kitchen hadn't been used in months, at least. I couldn't tell if this was meant as guest quarters, or as living space for the royal family, but either way it was eerie.

Now I've had time to think about it, my instinct is it's guest quarters. The royal family has to be protected, and it's easier to have them all in one place rather than splitting the guards' efforts—and this definitely didn't belong to the God-Empress. I don't know why the palace would have an entire wing for guests and then not have any, but it likely has something to do with the God-Empress's insanity. I can't imagine anyone staying here unless she was a hostage. That thought makes me queasy, because every one of the mages is a hostage if the God-Empress decides it's so.

By this time, it was getting very late, and I was tired, so I decided to leave exploring the rest of the alcoves until another time. I have a much better idea of what the palace looks like, even if I didn't find anything interesting. I don't know whether to hope the God-Empress's quarters are beyond one of the two remaining alcoves or not. Easier if it is, but if not, what a challenge to try to sneak into it!

So I went back to my room, but when I reached the hallway, I decided to take one last look at the...I'm still not sure what it is. An observatory? It's certainly high enough, though I wonder what anyone could see through that smoked glass. In any case, I figured Vorantor wouldn't still be there, and I really wanted to see the view for myself.

I was still cautious, approaching it—an overconfident thief is a dead thief, another one of my mottoes—even though I heard nothing, not even snoring from the adjoining chambers. Now that those holes are closed up, my room seems completely soundproof, and these stone walls are thick enough to keep most noises contained. I'm not going to experiment by standing in my room and screaming, certainly.

I was almost to the entry when I heard voices—not even voices, just a low cadenced hum I've learned to recognize as what voices sound like at the edge of hearing. I took a look into the observatory and saw Vorantor was still standing there, at the other side of the room, only this time he wasn't alone.

With my eyes more perfectly adjusted to the dark, I could see immediately that the second person was male, shorter than Vorantor, light-haired, and dressed in clothing that looked drab next to Vorantor's rich robes. Everything about him screamed "thief." I didn't even have to think about it; I did the concealment pouvra and started to sidle along the circumference of the room, trying to get close enough to make out their words.

Years ago, when I first learned the basics of the see-in-dark pouvra, I tried adapting it to enhance my hearing, but I was never successful. I can't believe there isn't a pouvra for that, so I haven't given up on finding it, but I don't think I've ever wanted it more than I did just then. The trouble with sneaking up on a thief is that she's, well, a thief—and if she's any good, she'll be constantly on the lookout for people doing to her what she'd do to them.

The closer I got, the less convinced I was that the stranger was a thief, simply because he lacked the alertness I'd have in his position. But...well, whatever he is, stealth and cunning are definitely some of his tools of the trade, even if he's never hung by his fingertips off a third-story window ledge while his bare toes grope for purchase on the irregular bricks of a castle wall.

I went as close as I dared and was frustrated to discover the conversation was nearly over. I suppose it would have been too much for me to coincidentally enter just as they started talking about a key piece of information that only mattered to me. As it was, it left me with more questions instead. The stranger said, "An upset for you, I think."

Vorantor said, "Cederic pledged his honor, so I'm not worried about him. And he's never been interested in glory. Everything will go on as it has."

The stranger said, "No matter what you have to do to ensure that."

"Exactly," Vorantor said. "Something I believe you understand."

The stranger nodded, then to my surprise walked past Vorantor to the edge of the observatory, where a low wall kept people from simply stepping off and falling, I assumed, to their deaths, slung his leg over the wall and dropped. Vorantor didn't react, and I heard neither scream nor fatal thud, so I concluded that he *was* the kind of thief I'd originally thought, and I confirmed this later—well, I don't want to put this out of order when I'm almost done.

A minute after the stranger made his dramatic exit, Vorantor turned and left the observatory, passing close to me without noticing anything amiss. This is why I don't wear scent. People forget there are all sorts of ways to notice a hidden someone that have nothing to do with eyes. I could smell Vorantor just fine; he uses a nice-smelling woody cologne, which is probably the only nice thing about him. I gave him plenty of time to reach his room, then tiptoed forward, still concealed, and leaned way out over the wall to see where the stranger had gone.

The observatory is at the top of a fat tower about fifty feet tall, with narrow windows marking out the layout of the interior. Based on the way the windows are arranged, the tower has three stories, and its base is set in one corner of what I've come to think of as the "main" palace, which is itself another four stories from the ground. So the observatory is fairly high up, based on those stairs about half a story above the Sais' wing, though not as high as the God-Empress's pavilion.

From my angle, dangling over the wall, it was immediately obvious someone had built a staircase from the base of the observatory to the nearest window, which was about ten feet down and three feet to the right of where I was. I say "staircase," but it was more a series of jutting blocks that offered hand- and footholds so you could reach the window without much—all right, not much effort for someone like me, and a crippling fear of heights would make it almost impossible, and the window wouldn't admit anyone much larger than the stranger, who wasn't much taller and broader than I am.

But it would be a good way for someone to meet someone else in the observatory without walking past a lot of Sais, who might want to know what that someone was doing there. None of my exploration had led to that tower, which made it even more interesting; it was something somebody wanted kept secret.

I pulled myself back up and returned to my room, not even pausing at Cederic's door. I know he knows th'an he's never showed me, and that there are all sorts of them that have offensive capabilities, and I'm certain he'd try to take the head off anyone who entered his room at night. And now I've written everything down, and I'm so tired I can barely keep my eyes open long enough to make a list of what I need to do in the morning:

1. Tell Cederic about Vorantor's well-after-midnight conversation.

2. Ask him about Kilios. And the eye color thing. And what happened between him and Vorantor in the God-Empress's pavilion.

3. Figure out what's directly below us in this tower. Yes, I could take the staircase to the window, but allowing myself to be outlined against the sky for a possible enemy to take a swipe at seems like a bad idea. Besides, I don't want to give away the fact that I know about the staircase if I can help it. It could turn out to be an escape route.

4. Begin work on the kathana to summon the Codex Tiurindi. As much as I dislike Vorantor, and find working for him distasteful, I'm excited to finally witness a kathana I'm not the focus of.

Sleep, finally.

CHAPTER THIRTEEN

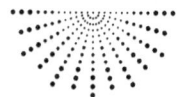

6 Lennitay

I'm every bit as tired tonight as I was last night, though this time it's because I spent half my day being ordered around by Vorantor, who's not very good at not sounding like he's ordering you around, and I resent him because I don't like him, so I feel like I'm being bossed. The other half I spent performing like a trained seal for the God-Empress, who remains endlessly fascinated by my pouvrin and has no concept of how wearying they can become over time.

This happened in the official throne room, which was even gaudier and more ornate than I'd imagined snooping around it last night. The hanging lamps are made of crystals that send sparkling light over everything, and she has mages to refresh them constantly because the th'an that power them run out quickly.

She showed no sign of insanity and was pleasant and friendly, even informal, as if I were her younger cousin (I think I am younger; closer observation puts her age nearer forty than thirty, and let me just say I hope I age that well, though if I have to become mad to get that wish, never mind) visiting from a strange land. Some of my tiredness is probably due to how tense I was the whole time, worried I'd say something wrong or respond too slowly to a demand, but this time, at least, my manners were acceptable.

This was also the first time I'd seen mages other than Vorantor's and the Darssan mages. It hadn't occurred to me there would be others, or that they would use magic for practical things. But I suppose the th'an on the collennas have to come from somewhere, and someone has to teach the masters how to draw them. And the God-Empress has to have an army to keep her empire intact, and since I know there are offensive and defensive kathanas, there must be mages attached to the army as well.

I wonder how many mages there are in the Castaviran Empire. I wonder what the countries outside the empire are like. There are so many things I want to know, and no time to learn them all.

Speaking of wanting to know things, I caught Cederic early this morning (I doubt I've had more than three hours of sleep, so no exploring tonight) and told him what I'd heard. He didn't even look a little surprised, though he did look sad, and he wouldn't explain what the conversation meant even though he clearly understood it. He did tell me that based on my description, the stranger was probably Perce Aselfos, the God-Empress's chief spy, and that he wouldn't want to guess why Vorantor and Aselfos were meeting secretly, but I think he *did* have a guess he didn't want to share with me until he was certain.

On my other questions: Kilios is a title (thank you, Cederic, I figured that one out on my own) that identifies a mage who has mastered all known th'an and can perform all of a certain type of kathana without assistance. Cederic is the only living Kilios and has held that title for almost four years. (He sounded embarrassed at telling me this. He's reluctant to talk about himself if it sounds at all like bragging.) It conveys all sorts of privileges, most of which Cederic doesn't take advantage of, including one that says he takes precedence over every mage and Sai in Castavir, which is the reason for that odd ceremony I witnessed yesterday.

Despite being "most high priest," Vorantor has no authority over Cederic, wouldn't have unless he were still Wrelan of the Darssan, but as the one with the most experience at preparing the kathana we're here to do, he has to be in command. Ugh. So Cederic had to cede part of his rights, and Vorantor had to swear not to usurp any more of those rights than Cederic had given up.

This all explains why Cederic was allowed to stay at the Darssan when the God-Empress put her support behind Vorantor's theory; even the God-Empress can't force the Kilios in matters magical, at least if she's sane. I'm guessing Cederic has been using the distance between Colosse and the Darssan to keep well out of the God-Empress's notice, because (as we learned) she only abides by this rule when she feels like it.

To my surprise, Cederic was telling the truth about the eye color thing. It doesn't mean you can instantly master any form of magic, or that you're guaranteed to be better at magic than people who don't have green-gray eyes (case in point: Terrael's eyes are blue), but it means you're drawn to magic, that you have a desire to learn it. In Cederic's case, he began practicing th'an when he was old enough to mimic other mages' script, and in my case, once the magic woke up in me I couldn't leave it alone.

But Cederic's being Kilios is due entirely to a lot of hard work, though I'm sure his being intelligent helped. I have no idea how I compare to the other mages of my world, assuming there are any—no, I have to believe I'm not the only one, if only because the alternative makes me feel ill. I almost hope the others are better than I am, because the idea of learning pouvrin directly from someone else... suppose it's easier that way? Faster? It's not going to matter unless we can keep the worlds from coming back together, and then we have to find a way to send me home.

If I still want to return.

~~This is already far more of a home than I've ever had before, even in the years before Dad died and Mam became a drunk and Roda left and Bridie~~

It's more a home than I've had in a long while. I have friends. I have value, even if only as a novelty. But if I stay here, the likelihood of me continuing my study as a mage is virtually nonexistent. Finding the concealment pouvra was sheer accident, and the madman who created it did so also by accident. I might be able to create my own, but that's also a slim possibility I wouldn't want to count on. And the idea of giving all that up makes me feel even more ill than the idea that I'm the only one of my kind in my own world the way I am here.

I'm not going to worry about that now. Retrieving the Codex Tiurindi is the most important thing, as Cederic said, and even if my role in the kathana hasn't been determined yet—that was most of why Vorantor was ordering me around this morning—I can already tell it will be important.

And Vorantor's mages have been tracking the process of the worlds coming together, and the news is not good. Cederic had predicted months; the mages are saying it might be more like eight weeks. So we all feel a sense of urgency that has everyone on edge. I think Vorantor doesn't appreciate how lucky he is to have Cederic there. Cederic keeps people calm just by being who he is, though he's always perfectly deferential to Vorantor (ugh again) and redirects most requests to him.

Later

I just had a wonderful chat with Sovrin and Audryn, who came to my room to see if I was all right. I developed a bit of a headache during my session with the God-Empress, which is unusual since normally pouvrin don't cause me physical pain, except for when I maintain the see-in-dark pouvra for too long. It was gone by dinner-time, but I think Sovrin and Audryn wanted an excuse for some girl time, and we ended up talking and giggling until I was so tired I couldn't stop yawning.

But I saw my first kathana! Even if it was only a little summoning Sovrin and Audryn did on my floor to snatch some hand-sized fruit pies out of one of the palace kitchens for us to snack on. They pushed aside the red bearskin rug and chalked a circle on the floor—they are both really good at drawing nearly perfect circles—with single th'an at the four cardinal points and the four ordinal points.

Then they chalked runes on their right palms, sat across from each other with those palms pressed together, and slowly pulled their hands apart to reveal a sort of window in the air that looked into the kitchen. Sovrin used her left hand to take hold of the window so Audryn could let go, then Audryn chalked what I can only call instructions on the floor that made the view shift until we could see the pies.

It was my job to reach through the window and grab as many as I could before we heard someone shouting, and I rolled out of the window and it snapped shut. Then we laughed like loons and stuffed our faces.

Sovrin's cheerful enough, but it was clear she's still miserable about being separated from Marleya. It wasn't a serious relationship yet, but they'd been friends a long time before becoming lovers—had grown up together, even—and losing something like that is hard, I think. And Audryn confessed, with many blushes, that she's in love with Terrael. That left me horribly conflicted, though in the end I stuck with my policy of not interfering in other people's business. The furthest I was willing to go was to suggest she take a chance on telling him.

Audryn blushed even harder at that and insisted it was impossible, which I thought was because in Castavir the men are expected to speak first, but that's not it, it's that he's her superior. Not that he is, anymore, now the Darssan has been disbanded and there are no more working groups, but she can't stop thinking of him as such. And she's older than he is by a couple of years, though I still don't understand why that's a problem. It was one of those everyone-knows things cultures have that it takes outsiders a while to understand.

I almost wished I had a lover to gossip about, since I was the odd one out, and I almost confessed I'm still a virgin, but as intimate as the conversation became, I still felt awkward about saying that. Especially since I still know almost nothing about Castaviran sexual customs and taboos. For all I know, being a twenty-seven-year-old virgin is shocking on the level of eating puppies. (Though Castavirans might do that too. See how little I know?)

Eventually we got to the point of laughing our heads off at stupid things, like dust motes, and I made them leave so I could get some sleep. Tomorrow we begin combining aspects of the new kathana with my magic, and I have no idea what to expect, except I'll have to be polite to Vorantor, which means I can use all the sleep I can get.

7 Lennitay

I'm being required to learn a single th'an and scribe it in fire. This is so much harder than it sounds, and since I just re-read that first sentence and realized it doesn't sound easy, it's probably damn near impossible. Fortunately for everyone's peace of mind, Terrael was assigned to teach me the th'an, and as impatient as he sometimes is with lack of progress, he's got quite a lot of patience when it comes to teaching.

First, I had to study this th'an using only my eyes and my mind. For a very long time. It felt like hours, though Terrael told me when I bitched about it that it had only been twenty minutes.

The th'an is shaped like a two-pronged fork (note: forks in Castavir have four tines instead of three) with the right-hand tine bent at the tip at a right angle away from the other. Terrael had me stare at it, following its lines in an exact order: tip of left tine down to base of handle, lift gaze, start again where right tine meets handle, right tine from there to bent tip. It sounds easy, but after a while all I could see was that shape, burned black on the inside of my eyelids.

After several hours (Terrael: forty-three minutes) I was allowed to begin writing the th'an with one of those fat inky writing tools. But I wasn't allowed to just write it anywhere I wanted. Terrael drew a dotted-line version of it on a board—obviously if he just wrote it, it would activate and do no one any good—and put a square of glass over it. Then he made me draw the th'an, then erase the glass, then draw again, at least a million times (Terrael: two hundred twenty-three) until my hand ached. I still wasn't very good, because the th'an never activated, but that was when Terrael judged I needed a rest.

I sat, and rubbed my hand, and watched everyone else working on their part of the kathana. This was all happening in a domed, windowless room with slate set into the walls and a gold circle inset in the floor at the center of the room. It was obviously meant to imitate the Darssan, which made me want to laugh. Vorantor might have left the Darssan behind, but it's clear he still feels inferior and is doing whatever he can to boost his importance.

At that moment, Vorantor was off to one side with some of "his" mages (I know, they're all his mages now, technically, but knowing "his" mages were willing to kill ours makes it impossible for me not to make the distinction) and they were going over the order of th'an again, since the order in which they're scribed makes a difference to the kathana. I can't stop watching him, and I'm not sure why. Possibly because I feel he's dangerous, and I want to know exactly what kind of danger he poses.

I've gone over that fragment of conversation many times, and all I can figure is that Vorantor is counting on Cederic's honor to keep him from interfering with whatever Vorantor is planning. That could be the kathana, or it could be something more sinister; I, being a professional paranoid, am counting on the latter. Why else would he be meeting with the God-Empress's spymaster?

Though come to that, shouldn't the spymaster have primary allegiance to his mistress, and in that case, why would Vorantor be meeting with the man at all? Or is the spymaster a go-between for the God-Empress, and there's some reason Vorantor can't meet with her publicly? I've decided I'll need to explore further tomorrow night— still achy now from today's work.

Anyway, I watched Vorantor for a while, until I was so angry I had to think about something else. He interacts a lot with Cederic during the day, comparing research—they're each tackling a different aspect of the kathana—but every single damn time he manages to make himself sound like he's indulging Cederic's input, like Cederic is his inferior. And I *know* that's technically true, I *know* Cederic chose to take a secondary role, but Vorantor is so smug about it!

I cannot believe I *ever* thought Cederic looked smug, now that I've seen what it looks like on Vorantor. Cederic, for his part, remains perfectly expressionless and deferential, and I can't tell what he's actually thinking. How he can still consider Vorantor his friend is beyond me.

We don't speak much these days, since his part of the research is separate from mine, and I miss that. He's the only one who understands my magic as more than just a useful tool, and I liked being able to compare th'an and pouvrin and feel as if we were learning about some structure that underlies both. Which might not be true, but it was an interesting thought exercise, and I wish we had time for more discussion. I didn't realize how much I enjoyed spending time with him.

After I had only a few minutes for rest (Terrael: thirty-five minutes) he set me to work again, drawing over the shape repeatedly until I had drifted off into a reverie about what we might have for dinner when something in front of me went *pop* and the glass pane shrank in on itself as if it were clear fabric someone had grabbed in the middle and twisted.

I admit I shrieked like a baby and jumped back, but then I was surrounded by mages congratulating me on my first th'an. Cederic explained it was a binding that, when performed by me using my magic, would tie the kathana to both worlds and provide a link to the time before the worlds were separate. The time before the Codex was destroyed.

So now I have to do it with fire.

It's made me wonder what magic looked like before the worlds were separated. Each world's magic is so different now—different from the other, I mean—so does that mean they were combined, once? And what would that even look like? I have trouble even comprehending how pouvrin work, let alone th'an, so imagining them together is beyond me. I doubt they could even occupy the same space. It's something I could talk to Cederic about, assuming we ever had time to talk.

I'm so tired. After my success with the th'an, I wanted to go straight to trying it with fire, but Terrael insisted I repeat my success at least a dozen times before moving on. I managed to do it twice more before my efforts became too wobbly and Cederic told me to stop for the day and have something to eat. He stayed behind with Vorantor when the rest of us went to the dining hall. I wonder what they talk about when we're not there. I wonder if Vorantor ever rubs it in Cederic's face that he won. I wonder if Cederic ever thinks about punching him in his stupid smug face. I know I have.

Sleep now, work tomorrow, explore tomorrow night.

9 Lennitay, very early, maybe just past midnight

More research today. I mean yesterday. Still not enough successes for Master Terrael, so I'm still working on the glass instead of with fire. Though we took a small break in the middle of the morning for me to demonstrate some of the pouvrin, mainly fire and water. I'm getting better at juggling water, which is fun, and this time I did splash Terrael in the face. Just a little. He laughed with everyone else.

I don't know how much longer it will take before they can do the kathana. I have this horrible feeling they're waiting on me, which makes me work harder but makes my work less effective. The mages in charge of tracking what they call "the convergence" (presumably because it sounds less awful than "unavoidable catastrophic destruction") have stopped saying how long until it gets here, which makes me even more nervous. But, again, that makes me less capable, and my hands start to shake, and then I have to sit in a corner and watch everyone else until I regain control.

It's interesting to watch Cederic and compare him to Vorantor. Vorantor bustles a lot. He likes to draw people's attention to what he's doing, even if what he's doing is complimenting someone else's work. Which he does, frequently—gives compliments, I mean. But he's the sort of person who thinks he's being a leader because he read some-where that's what leaders do.

Cederic, on the other hand, is always quiet and rarely makes comments, but when he does, everyone stops to listen, even people who aren't involved in whatever he's talking about. And he does a lot more listening than Vorantor does, and listens with his whole atten-tion—I know this from experience.

So when he does give praise, you can see it really matters to the person he's giving it to. They may listen to Vorantor, because he does most of the talking, but they pay attention to Cederic, especially when he doesn't say a word. Even Vorantor's mages give him a kind of respect Vorantor can't command. It makes me feel proud on behalf of him and the Darssan contingent, even though we're so much smaller.

I don't know why I'm going on about this. The exploring I did was far more exciting than writing about stupid Vorantor. Though I have to write about him, because I decided I need to spy on him more closely, in case he has any more clandestine meetings. I haven't told Cederic, because he would definitely object—he still believes Vorantor is his friend, and I know he hates that I sneak around the palace at night. But I think Vorantor is more dangerous than he seems, and I won't be satisfied until I know why he met with Aselfos.

Fortunately, he has a routine he rarely deviates from, in the evenings: he eats dinner with Cederic and some of the other Sais, then all of them go to their common room, which is around the corner from the dining hall, where they sit and talk and have after-dinner drinks. (Our common room is larger, and the conversation is more lively, and there's more use of th'an for amusement.)

Vorantor always retires early, no later than nine o'clock, and goes to sit in the observatory for half an hour, then retires to his room, where he reads for another half hour before going to sleep. I know the last part because I sat concealed in his room last night, watching him. He's really very dull. He didn't sneak out later, and he didn't meet with anyone in the observatory.

But his meeting with Aselfos didn't sound, even what little I heard of it, like a chance encounter or a one-time event, so I'm certain he'll meet with the man again. Unfortunately, I can't just follow him around, concealed, waiting for it to happen, so I'll need to make a better plan. Last night was only to confirm his pattern, so I didn't spend much time watching him before I got down to real exploring.

This time, I used the concealment pouvra immediately and went down the stairs, counting, so I could keep track of where I was with regard to the tower. There are no doors off the Sais' stairwell, which descends in a series of landings in a sort of tall chimney, and by the time I reached the bottom, I'd determined I was at the floor above the base of the tower.

So then I started looking around for a way into the tower, or failing that, a flight of stairs that would take me one story lower where an entrance might reasonably be found. Part of me wanted something mysterious, so I was disappointed when access to the tower was as easy as following the hall off the stairs to a junction and then turning right.

That led me to a short double door made of brass that filled the width of the hallway. I used the see-through pouvra to verify no one was standing immediately behind it, learned it opened on a hall that curved downward immediately to the right, and went through it—the conventional way, since the walk-through-walls pouvra still makes me nervous.

The curving hallway actually rose and fell in both directions, with a gentle slope that suggested it followed the contours of the tower, and wasn't so dim that I needed the see-in-dark pouvra. I walked uphill for a bit and soon found one of the narrow windows on my left, which let in the light of the moon. It looked out over the palace rather than Colosse, which told me "my" window, or the one that would give me access to the "staircase" to the observatory, was on the opposite side of the tower from here.

I continued walking, occasionally passing doors on my right I itched to explore, but first I wanted to see if I had an exit from this place. All the doors were made of brass like the first, but single rather than double. Once I passed a brass double door on my left that I guessed led to another level of the palace, and I *really* wanted to explore that one, but I kept going, and my persistence paid off when I reached the final window, looked out, and saw a jutting brick inches from the top of the window frame.

I climbed up on the sill and reached for the brick, tugged on it to satisfy myself it was solid, then sat on the sill with my back to the open air and thought about what to do next. The spymaster had come in this way, but was it just a convenient passthrough, or was there something important about it? It hadn't exactly been easy to find.

I ascended all the way to the top of the tower, where the passage went right up to the roof (the underside of the observatory) as if it had once been open to the air and some giant, possibly the same one that had built Colosse, had slapped the observatory over it like capping it off. Then I came back down until I passed "my" window and reached the first of the single brass doors. It was unlocked. I opened it cautiously, then slipped inside.

It hadn't occurred to me, because I am occasionally stupid, that none of these tower rooms would have windows because they were all on the inside. I had to stop to do the see-in-dark pouvra, and then I was stunned at what I saw: shelves and chests and wardrobes piled high with every imaginable type of fur, all tanned and clean and ready to be turned into clothing or rugs.

I've said before my expert appraiser's eye is hampered by my not knowing the value of things in Castavir, so I'll put everything (and there was much, much more) in my own terms, and to the right buyer, this room would be worth a fortune. Furs aren't as popular as they once were in Balaen, at least they aren't as much a symbol of nobility as they used to be, but they're still the province of the wealthy, and though they're not as portable a form of wealth as you might like, they're still valuable.

I petted a mink and took a better look around. Definitely a fortune. There were five other exits from the room, all of which led to smaller rooms, all of those rooms filled with ingots of precious metals like bricks for a mad God-Empress's palace. I released the conceal-ment pouvra and wandered through them in a daze, because I'd never seen that much wealth accumulated in one place. Eventually I had to shut the doors and move on, before my twitching fingers could collect a souvenir.

The part of me that is a master thief would like to describe, in loving detail, the contents of the God-Empress Renatha's treasury—because that's what the tower was, seventeen rooms of jewels and precious metals and art and things I couldn't even put a value on because we don't care about them in my world.

There were coffers of jewels (I love jewels, they're so portable and everyone wants them) and strings of silver and gold chains and paint-ings whose frames alone were probably worth a coffer of jewels, and it was so hard not to take something, especially now I know I like jewelry for myself and not just for what it can buy me. But aside from the practicalities, which is that someone like me isn't likely to have a lot of personal wealth in any form, I wouldn't put it past the God-Empress to know down to the last two-carat diamond exactly how much treasure she has, and to be able to figure out who walked off with whatever's missing. Really, this place was not well protected and it wasn't guarded at all. Unless...

It was at that point my imagination started running wild about the possibility of th'an that sounded a silent alarm, and soldiers with large swords and muskets, and mages who could do who knew what kind of martial kathanas. My heart pounded faster for a few beats before I reminded myself I'd been there for a while, and I'd handled some of the treasure. If there were silent alarms and martial kathanas, I'd have found out about them by now. Even so, I didn't linger in any more of the treasure rooms.

I looked through, but did not enter, those brass double doors I'd passed before, and saw only a short hall that made a sharp right turn about five feet from the door. I was planning to come back up and see where it led after I reached the base of the tower, but I changed my mind when I found what was there. More exploration for another time.

But now, the base of the tower. Actually, it wasn't the base of the tower but the base of the palace below the tower, all seven stories to the ground instead of just the three of the round tower below the observatory. At the end of the curving, descending passage was another brass double door, but this one looked beaten, as if someone had tried to break it down once.

It was also locked, as I learned when I pushed on it, and then I very nearly became a dead thief for my carelessness, because the person on the other side of the door immediately unlocked it and flung it open. I'd skipped backward a few steps when the door began to open, and I worked the concealment pouvra and pressed myself against the wall, grateful for the pouvra's protection even though it made it hard for me to feel my fingertips and my toes.

Light came through the open door, blinding me, forcing my eyes shut. "Up there," a deep voice said, and two people jingled past me, the second coming close enough that the wind of his passing ruffled my shirt. It took me a minute to recover from the see-in-dark pouvra to see who'd opened the door. At first, I thought I hadn't recovered enough, because the man who stood in the doorway looked as if he was wearing a chicken on his head.

I blinked harder and realized it was a helmet made to resemble a falcon, with wings folded to either side and head thrust forward, beak slightly open as if crying out. He was looking up the passage toward two other men wearing matching helmets, who were carefully searching in all directions for invisible thieves. Fortunately for me, they used their eyes and not their hands, and I pressed back so far into the wall I might not have needed a pouvra to go through it.

"Nothing," said one of the two men, and they both came back down to join their comrade at the door. All three wore, in addition to the ~~chicken~~ falcon helmets, short-sleeved shirts made of a fine steel mesh over long-sleeved black linen tunics, snugly-fitting black leather pants, hard black boots I would not like to be kicked with, and sword belts with sheaths for a longsword and a nine-inch-long knife.

"I told Prenz these hinges needed work," the first man said, and all three went back inside and shut the door, and locked it. I stood there breathing peacefully for a while. Nothing guarding the treasure, but three men, possibly more, standing a very careful watch over whatever was beyond these doors?

I retreated up the passage a long, long way, maybe two stories, then dropped the concealment pouvra and rubbed feeling back into my fingers and toes. Getting past those men would be difficult, because there was no way in hell I was going to try passing through living flesh. All my instincts told me it was a bad idea. Hard enough maintaining my identity against a stone wall; how much harder against another creature, whose instinct to remain complete was as strong as mine? And if two of those men stood in front of those doors at all times...more reconnaissance was needed.

I crept back down, feeling my way in the blackness because I didn't want to be blinded again when I did the see-through pouvra, and carefully patted the wall with the tips of my fingers until I was certain I was facing the door. Then I did the see-through pouvra and took a look around.

Only one man stood in front of the door; the other two were in position a short ways off down a long corridor the door opened onto. I couldn't see where the light came from, but the corridor became dark just past where the other two men stood. They were all three of them very alert despite the hour, and after giving it some thought, I turned and went back up the sloping passage, finding my way in the dark to make it a bit of a challenge, until I reached the door I'd come in by, then I went silently back to my room. Which brings me to now.

I've been trying to think of what might be beyond that passage. The most logical explanation is that it leads to the God-Empress's personal chambers. The only thing a ruler wants to guard more closely than her treasure is herself. And she might want to maintain a direct route to her treasure rooms, even if she doesn't care enough to protect them more fully. But logic only applies if you assume the ruler is sane, which the God-Empress is not, in which case, who knows what's beyond those doors? There could be any number of things she might want closely guarded, intrinsically valuable or not.

I should just leave it alone. I'm in enough danger as it is. I certainly can't tell Cederic what I've learned, because he would definitely tell me to leave it alone, and I'd feel bad about disregarding his wishes. The thing is, I've never regretted gaining knowledge, even when that knowledge has been personally painful. I have, on the other hand, regretted not knowing enough. The God-Empress has an unhealthy interest in me, and the more I know about her, the safer I'll be. And that includes discovering as many of her secrets as I can.

I'm running out of pages in this book, and I don't know how I'll be able to make another. Maybe Cederic will let me scrounge paper out of the books, but that still leaves me with no leather for the cover and no thread and needle for the binding. I'll have to find an alternative, I suppose.

CHAPTER FOURTEEN

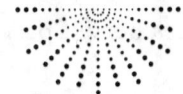

12 Lennitay

I haven't had time to write for days, which considering how few pages are left might be a good thing, if it keeps me from wasting space writing "same as before" all the time. I come back from dinner so exhausted I fall into my bed unconscious and sleep for ten hours until it's time to start again.

I don't think I've mentioned that Vorantor is *not* an advocate of the leisurely Darssan morning; he has an obnoxious belief that early rising is a virtue nigh unto Godliness, something I believe he learned from her actual Godliness, the God-Empress Renatha Torenz. So it's up at 6 a.m. and off to work again, every morning, and even if I weren't exhausted from practicing th'an and pouvrin, I still wouldn't have the energy to poke around.

It's afternoon now, and I got a reprieve in the form of Cederic, who stopped to look at my th'an (I still haven't achieved the requisite twelve successes, two more and I'm ready to move on to fire), then looked at my face, took the writing tool out of my hand and said, "Go take a nap. You're exhausted."

I started to protest, realized I wanted a nap, and thanked him. But when I was leaving, Vorantor appeared in front of me and said, "You're not leaving us, are you?"

"I'm going to take a nap," I said.

He said, "But that's not fair to everyone else, is it? Should everyone be allowed to take a nap? You're so close to success, Thalessi, you don't want to give up now, do you?"

"Sesskia has been working harder than anyone else, Denril," Cederic said, appearing as suddenly as Vorantor had, "and she will have no success if she pushes herself past breaking. I instructed her to rest."

"Did you," Vorantor said, and then the two of them faced each other in silence. Vorantor was glaring. Cederic was impassive as usual. They were fighting, but on no battleground I could see. Then Cederic raised an eyebrow at Vorantor, whose face flushed. Without looking at me, Cederic said, "Go and rest, Sesskia."

"Yes, of course, you need rest," Vorantor said, but it came out as a kind of stammer and his face went redder than before. I fled before their battle could go further. It's comforting to know Cederic can trounce Vorantor without a word, but it's only just occurred to me to worry about what might happen if Vorantor ever pushed his authority to a point that Cederic might have to disobey. I don't understand the details of the oath Cederic swore, but I'm certain he won't let it stop him fighting Vorantor if Vorantor ordered me, or anyone, to do something evil or dangerous.

I'm going to nap now, and see how I feel afterward.

Afterward

I can't believe how much that nap helped. I slept for two hours, woke when Audryn came to call me to dinner, ate heartily, and felt completely refreshed. And then I wasn't sleepy. Thank you, Cederic, for insisting I rest, because what I found later—well, I'm still not sure what it means, but it's all down to you that I found it.

So when full dark came, and all the sensible people were in bed, I sneaked back down to the bottom of the tower. This time I was dressed in my own dark gray trousers, a close-fitting dark shirt, and a

166

pair of soft-soled boots the wardrobe servants had brought me, and I was prepared to do some proper sneaking about.

The see-through pouvra confirmed the door was still guarded by one man standing next to it and two others standing a short distance away. I took a few deep breaths, released them slowly, then filled my lungs, held my breath, and slid through the brass door as far from the guard as I could manage without inserting myself into the corridor wall.

The guard didn't notice me; as I entered, he shifted his weight and looked off into the distance down the dark corridor. I didn't stop moving or let out my breath; the last thing I needed was to give my position away by exhalation. My shoes made hardly any noise on the uncarpeted stone of the hallway, just a couple of scuffs no louder than the guards' breathing. I slipped on between the two other guards and kept on walking, slowly, and didn't breathe out until the shadows surrounded me. Behind me, one of the guards sneezed, and the other said something in response. I stopped to do the see-in-dark pouvra, then moved on down the hall.

It went on for several minutes. I think the passage goes the full length of the palace and beyond; there's no exit on the far side, and I wasn't certain how thick the walls were, so I didn't dare go insubstantial and try to find a way out that way. But it was straight, and lightless, and boring, or would have been if I hadn't been keenly aware of being somewhere I wasn't allowed. Eventually I saw a light ahead, at enough of a distance that I could drop the see-in-dark pouvra before I was blinded. I concealed myself again and moved forward more cautiously.

That turned out to be unnecessary. There were no guards at this end of the passage, and the lights were th'an-powered, not torches as they'd been at the other end. I don't know why the lights were there at all, since there was no one to take advantage of them. There were also no doors; the passage simply ended at a room maybe half the size of the mosaic chamber, and that comparison occurred to me because like that room, the walls were covered with mosaics. But that was all I noticed before my attention was drawn to the things filling the room.

They looked like metal wagons, really heavy iron wagons that could not possibly move despite each being mounted on four wheeled axles. None of them had yokes for horses or oxen, either. Each one carried a tapered cylinder I could barely wrap my arms around (that's a guess, because *of course* I went up and hugged the mysterious metal things, I'm not insane) with a hole the size of my doubled fists at the narrow end and a funnel the same diameter at the fat end, with a blank brass plate fastened to the cylinder below it.

I circled the nearest one and found it became more complicated at the rear: there was a metal stool permanently attached to the wagon behind the cylinder, and a metal tankard of some kind that looked as if it had been melted to the side of the cylinder, just below the funnel, and another brass plate whose shining gold surface looked incongruous next to the rough, blackened iron the rest of the wagon was made of, fastened where it would be at waist level to whoever sat on the stool.

Engraved into the brass plate were several complicated-looking th'an, and this time I was certain I'd seen them before, or something like them. I don't know what seemed familiar—something about the shape, maybe. It's been bothering me since I returned from snooping around. I'll have to remember to tell Cederic, see if he has any ideas. Or—I don't know. I feel as though I take all my problems to him. Maybe he finds that annoying. I'll have to think about it.

But first, the wagon. I thought about climbing onto the seat, decided against it—if anything were going to have a silent alarm attached to it, this thing would—and circled it again. Some kind of collenna, then, but what? A th'an could make the thing go, might make up for the heaviness of its construction, but to what end? The stool couldn't be comfortable for long-distance travel, and I couldn't see the point of the cylinder. It baffled me, so I stepped back and examined my surroundings more closely.

The mosaics were pale where the ones in the main chamber are robust, and it took me some time to work out what they depicted. It was immediately obvious the craftsmanship here wasn't nearly as fine as that of the mosaic chamber, more at the level of the person who'd put the God-Empress's face on all the heroes. A closer look suggested this artist *was* the same person who'd defaced those mosaics. Then the pictures came into focus, and I almost walked backwards into one of the wagons. They were pictures of Death.

I shouldn't sound so certain about that. It's only that I've traveled in so many countries where Death is given a shape—not like Balaen, where we symbolize it by absences, things missing from places where they should be, like a gap in a hedge, or a hole in a sleeve, things like that. In fact, Balaen's in the minority on that, because in most places the grieving want something on which to focus their grief, and it's astonishing to me how often Death is given human form. To me it feels like bad luck, like drawing Death's attention to the fact that humans are vulnerable to it.

Anyway, I suppose the mosaics of dancing figures robed in white might have been anything. But my instincts tell me the chamber was a celebration of death, and it made me feel as if I'd entered my own grave.

I walked the perimeter of the room, growing increasingly afraid and counting wagons to stave off that fear. I reached three hundred before I couldn't bear it anymore and bolted. Safely down the dark passage, out of sight of the lights in both directions, I squatted and put my head between my knees until my breathing returned to normal.

I sneaked back through the guard post, still without any trouble —I'm afraid I'm going to grow too dependent on that pouvra—and crept back to my room, where I curled up on my bed with all my clothes still on and shivered. Then I wrote all of this down, in very tiny writing because there are now only a couple of pages left.

I'll have to tell Cederic about this in the morning. He might understand what I saw. Whatever it was, the God-Empress thinks it's important, and I would bet the hard money I don't have it's dangerous to someone. That someone might even be me.

13 Lennitay

This will have to be my last entry. I still have no new book and no way of making one.

I told Cederic the details of my nighttime adventure this morning, and he nearly killed me. Which is to say, he became so expressionless it was hard to believe he was still alive. He said, "How were you going to explain your presence to those guards when they caught you?"

"But they didn't catch me," I said.

"Because your God-given reserves of good luck are not yet exhausted," he said. "That concealment pouvra is by no means a guarantee of security. It does not make you invisible."

"They didn't know to guard against it," I said, "and you yourself said it makes you want to look elsewhere. Besides, that's not the important part."

"The wagons," he said. "I can only guess as to their purpose."

"Which means you won't tell me," I said. At this point I was starting to be annoyed, because I was proud of myself and I wanted him to at least acknowledge I'd done well. He may not like that I'm a thief, but he ought to at least appreciate that I'm a good one.

"I believe we agreed once you prefer knowing the truth to conjecture," he said, and smiled.

"That's true, but I would like at least some idea of what general type of thing they might be," I said.

We were in his room, standing by the windows, and he took my arm and drew me to the center of the room, away from potential eavesdroppers and anyone who might be capable of seeing through windows one hundred feet off the ground. "Weapons of war," he said in a low voice, as if those precautions still weren't enough.

"War?" I said, matching my voice to his. "But who does the God-Empress think she has to fight?"

"She is preparing to bring order out of chaos, when the disaster occurs," Cederic said. "What concerns me is, if we succeed in preventing the disaster entirely, she will have a large army and no one to turn it on. Which means we may be giving her the means to build her empire."

"But we can't let the worlds destroy each other!" I said.

"No, and it is a risk we will have to take," he said. "You said there was no way for the wagons to exit the room where they were stored?"

"Not that I saw, but I admit I didn't look very closely," I said. "And I can't imagine she doesn't have a plan for that."

Cederic frowned, and said, "This is good information to have, but at the moment I don't see what we can do with it. I wish I could ask Denril if he has trained any masters in the th'an you showed me" (I'd sketched it out for him, and he said it would make two things move in tandem with each other, but couldn't be more specific than that) "but I think that would be...unwise."

"You seem to be working well together," I said, which was both a lie and a leading question, but Cederic chose not to respond. He shrugged and said, "He is still committed to his solution, and does not believe the Codex will tell him anything he does not already know. I have been planning what I will do against the day he is proven wrong."

"Do you think there might be a problem?" I said.

"Possibly," he said. "Denril has convinced the God-Empress of the truth of his position, and she is not someone who takes well to looking like a fool. He might be in danger. But I am not in a position to warn him."

"So what should I do?" I said.

Cederic smiled and shook his head, and said, "Is there any way I can convince you to stay quietly in your bedchamber every night?"

"If I did that, we would never learn anything interesting," I said, and he shook his head again as if in despair. That ended our conversation, and we went to breakfast together, me in a better mood despite my late night. I didn't tell him about feeling like I recognized the th'an because I forgot. No, that's not completely true. I did forget, yes, but I also feel awkward about making a big deal out of some nebulous feeling that might or might not matter.

I'm embarrassed I wrote that. So what if I feel awkward? For all I know, this is the information that gives us a clue about how my magic relates to Cederic's. I'll tell him about it tomorrow, awkward feelings be damned.

The rest of the day was uneventful

Hah. I should never tempt fate by writing things like that. I just received a note summoning me to attend on the God-Empress tomorrow after breakfast, which means seven o'clock, far too early for a meeting with a divine avatar. No details, nothing saying she was going to have me beheaded and disemboweled for discovering her war wagons, just a polite little note stamped with her personal sigil, a falcon with some angular characters below its beak.

I suppose this excuses me from th'an practice, which is actually a disappointment—I did my twelfth successful shriveling of glass, and tomorrow I was to have begun practicing with fire. Terrael will just have to contain his eagerness. I hope they send the wardrobe servants again—the last time, I wore my own clothes, and I'm not sure what I'm supposed to wear for this private meeting with a mad God-Empress. I hate

Cederic just came to my door to say goodnight. He also handed me a small book and said, "I thought you might need this soon. It is of course not the same as making it yourself, but I hope it will do," and was gone before I could say anything. It's a blank book, machine-made but with a beautiful leather cover impressed with stylized leaves, dyed dark blue. I don't know how he knew I needed one, but it's such a lovely gift I don't care. I can't believe I ever hated him.

PART II
BOOK SEVEN

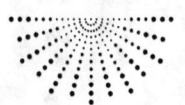

CHAPTER FIFTEEN

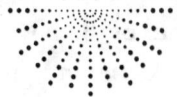

14 Lennitay

My first entry in my beautiful new book, and I feel like I'm defiling it from what I have to write. I'm tired, but not from physical exertion, and I wish I were back in the Darssan, where I could sink into a hot pool and let the water soak away the tension that's making my back and neck hurt.

Of course, if I were back in the Darssan I wouldn't have spent the day with the God-Empress, which is the reason for the tension. Having to constantly monitor my words and actions put me on edge, especially since for the first part of the day it didn't seem I needed to. It wasn't until later that I was reminded of the kind of person she is.

One of the wardrobe servants came for me in the dining hall, before I was half finished with my breakfast. He used a lot of polite words, but the gist of it was it was going to take some time to attire me properly, and if I was late, he and his fellows would be punished.

The God-Empress definitely enjoys manipulating people by threatening others. I think it gives her pleasure to know that it's a form of persuasion that would never work on her, because she doesn't give a damn what happens to other people. It works all too well on me, and I abandoned my half-eaten meal, exchanged despairing glances with Sovrin, and went back to my room.

They didn't strip me this time, but allowed me to take off my own clothes down to my undergarments (still wearing the breast band; I've become accustomed to it, and thank the true God for that) before presenting me with an actual choice between two dresses, one full-skirted with short sleeves and a fitted waist, the other tight through the hips and knees but flaring out below that, so my stride would be seriously constrained. Neither of them would be good for running in, and I had to leave both books behind, hidden more or less in plain sight (wrapped loosely in my discarded clothes), but I noted the loose seams of the second dress and decided I could tear them open if running did become necessary. Paranoid, remember?

The servants seemed pleased by my choice, which in addition to being impractical was a shade of brown that wasn't particularly flattering to me, and I remembered how the God-Empress didn't like being outshined by anyone. And I certainly wouldn't be doing any shining in that thing.

They piled my hair on my head and secured it with far too many pins, which is to say that it's heavy enough it needed almost all the hairpins I'd been given to keep it up, and even then if I did end up running, it would probably fall down anyway. Then I was allowed to wear some of my new jewelry, so I chose a very nice necklace of gold filigree with dark red rubies and had to struggle not to laugh at the servants' consternation at discovering my ears aren't pierced. No need, when I would never wear earrings that might catch the light at the wrong time, but they were so upset I think if we hadn't been pressed for time they'd have pierced my ears right then. They settled for bracelets of amber and gold I could quickly shed and shoes that pinched my toes but would come off as easily.

As I read over this, I realize I sound paranoid, but given my experiences today, I think everything I did and planned for was reasonable. If anything, I might have underestimated the correct level of paranoia. But everything in its time, and at this time in my account I was dressed properly and ready to be escorted to the God-Empress's chambers.

The last time, I was taken through the palace by the woman who'd met us when we first arrived, and handed off to a steward or something when we reached the public wing of the palace. This time, four soldiers dressed in the uniform I'd seen beneath the tower, complete with ~~chicken~~ falcon helmets, were standing outside my door when I left my room. Their appearance was so unexpected I nearly shut the door in their faces, which were as impassive as Cederic's ever is, but I recovered in time and waited for them to indicate what I should do.

They turned to face the stairwell, spreading out some, and I realized they wanted me to stand in their center, so I did. Then I had to hobble rapidly to keep up with their longer, unconstrained strides as they marched away. It felt exactly as if I were being marched to the gallows, assuming they have those in Castavir, and that was when I first began feeling tense.

The shoes became uncomfortable after only a few flights of stairs, the dress made me feel as if I were going to trip and fall and tumble to the bottom, hopefully carrying some of those soldiers with me, and my mind insisted on coming up with scenarios in which this *was* a death march and I was cooperating far too readily. The soldiers didn't speak, and I didn't have anything to say, and we saw no one at any of the landings and halls we passed. I think now maybe they'd cleared the halls so no one could see us.

I'm glad I didn't think of that at the time, because that would have bolstered my death march theory, and while I like to think I'm disciplined enough not to panic in stressful situations, I can't say I might not have made excuses and tried to run. Which would likely have been fatal.

The route they took me by was different from the first; it went through the mosaic chamber, which was every bit as impressive now as it was when we first arrived, and that reminds me I *still* haven't gone to look at the floor in daylight. We went through one of the archways I'd never been able to explore, the one between the God-

Empress subduing a dragon and the God-Empress laying the foundations for a vast city—funny, she's giant-sized in that one, maybe my fantasy about Colosse being built by a giant wasn't so absurd—and into a very different part of the palace.

The mages' wing is all narrow passages with low ceilings more suited to catacombs than a palace (everywhere except the hall in the Sais' wing) and old, pitted stone. This place had wide halls with arched ceilings painted blue and walls plastered with abstract frescos in cool colors, and arched doorways instead of doors. The hall we entered by terminated in a courtyard with a glass roof high above, revealing a circle of cool blue sky that looked as if it hung above some temperate landscape not blasted by the heat of the sun, which heat I could feel coming off the breeze that swept through the courtyard from both sides.

A fountain fifteen feet tall at the center of the courtyard kept it from being too hot, and the breeze carried a faint mist toward me that was beautifully cooling. My awkward dress was surprisingly comfortable; court brocades would have been awful in this heat.

My honor guard, or whatever they were, separated and went to stand at the four corners of the courtyard, still silent and impassive, leaving me clueless as to what to do next. So I walked forward to the fountain and inhaled the cool, damp air coming off it. I thought about taking a drink, but decided it might be taboo, or poisoned, or something. Of course that only made me thirsty, but I clasped my hands together in front of me to keep them from being stupid and waited.

And waited.

I walked around after a bit, admiring the courtyard. It was open to the outside on two sides, and the sunlight even at seven o'clock in the morning was blinding thanks to the white stone paving the paths that led away from the courtyard to some other part of the palace. Ahead of me, with respect to where I'd entered, was another archway that led to a short hallway identical to the one we'd come in by, but I couldn't see far thanks to the sunlight.

I went to stand at its entrance, glancing at the guards for some hint, but they ignored me. That was when I became angry. I was so afraid of what the God-Empress might do that I'd forgotten how far I've come, how many dangers I've faced, and I was ashamed of my cowardice. The God-Empress might decide to have me killed no matter what I did, so I decided to hell with her, and set off down the hallway. When I think back on how defiant I was, it makes me feel sick.

This area, too, was completely empty of people. If I hadn't known better, I might have thought the palace was abandoned, and I wondered how its population could disappear so thoroughly. I suppose the servants, not being otherworlder women with strange powers that fascinated the God-Empress, would take every opportunity to stay out of their mistress's sight.

I wandered the broad, frescoed halls, mentally keeping track of my route, until I reached an actual door. It was unlocked, so I pushed it open and found what I can only call a boudoir. The walls were invisible thanks to all the filmy draperies that shrouded the room, most of them moving lightly in an intangible breeze. The floor was so soft it was like walking on a pillow, every step throwing me off balance.

Cushioned, backless chairs stood at random throughout the room, some of them canted due to the pillowy nature of the floor. Everything was in shades of red, from deepest maroon to lightest pink. The God-Empress, who was reclining on a divan at the center of the room, was dressed in a thin shift of pale red—not pink, but pale red, there's a difference—so sheer I could see her nipples. Not that I was looking. They were impossible to miss.

"You are late," the God-Empress said, and here I should probably admit I'm making up almost everything I write her saying in this conversation. Not the intent or meaning, and I'm not doing it to make myself sound impressive and clever. When we were in her pavilion, she spoke in straightforward language, but every time I've met her privately, she's used what sounds to me like formal or archaic words.

Understanding her put a strain on my aeden-acquired language skills, and I found I couldn't remember her exact words most of the time. So this conversation is more extrapolated even than most of what I write. I really do think there's a pouvra for memory. If I ever have time, maybe that's the one I'll try to invent.

Anyway, she said, "You are late," but she didn't sound angry.

I said, "I apologize, but your palace is too beautiful for me to rush through it. And I didn't realize how constraining this dress would be."

"You dislike my gift," the God-Empress said.

"It's beautiful. I meant only to indicate my ignorance of Castaviran clothing," I said, trying not to panic. Insulting her before half a minute had passed was not a good beginning to this day.

"You chose well. It is an old-fashioned cut that shows you appreciate tradition," she said. "I would have been displeased if you had appeared in the other."

Already I was navigating the twisty maze that was her mind. Even my wardrobe was a test. "Thank you for the honor of the gift, which I do not deserve," I said.

"Sit," the God-Empress said, and I found a slightly canted chair and settled into it. "Drink," she said, and a servant emerged from a door hidden by the draperies and handed me a squat golden cup with two handles; I drank, and discovered it was lukewarm water, tasting slightly of minerals but welcome after the rapid walk I'd had.

The room was comfortably cool, and I think I've mentioned the palace has some kind of cooling kathana that I've been grateful for. Balaen is quite a bit more temperate than Castavir despite occupying much of the same territory. I wonder if Cederic knows why the same places in each world can have vastly different climates.

And yes, it did occur to me the water might be poisoned, but there was nothing I could do about that. There's only so much I can protect myself from, and refusing to drink on the slight chance the water might kill me would only be trading the possibility of danger for the near-certainty that the God-Empress would have me executed for insulting her.

We sat and drank in silence, me mindful of the instruction not to speak unless spoken to. The God-Empress had a cup matching mine and drank with both hands on the handles, which gesture I mimicked. Eventually she set the cup down and said, "I will show you my city. You should know what it is you are going to defend."

"Thank you, Renatha," I said, only barely remembering to use her name, and she stood up, which was a sign for servants to come rushing out of hidden doorways to dress her in tunic and robe and another tunic and a sash that went around her waist three times, all of it in shades of red and decorated with rubies, and a matching ruby-studded silver choker. The God-Empress is unusual in preferring faceted stones to cabochons, which is probably the only thing we have in common. That and being female. She was gloriously beautiful, and I felt dowdy next to her, which was probably the idea.

Once she was dressed, and her golden hair (which was freshly dyed) was piled on her head with ruby-studded hair clips, we left the room and went by a completely different route back to the courtyard, where the God-Empress went down one of the brightly-paved paths to where a strange-looking collenna waited, its thumping higher and more rapid than that of the loenerel.

It was...I can't even think of anything to compare it to. It reminded me a little of a tortoise's shell, if tortoises were dusky rose; its base was circular, and two seats surrounded by a silver rail were perched in a depression on its back, which was about five feet high. The seats were shaded by a canopy of rose velvet fringed with silver, and the seats themselves were upholstered in the same colors.

At the front (what I guessed was the front, which guess was later proven correct) was another seat, this one black lacquered wood, with a smallish bucket to the right of where the master would sit and a tray of brushes above it. The plate containing the th'an engraving was silver rather than brass, or it might have been steel, and I couldn't see the th'an because a woman dressed in a master's uniform, but in rose pink, was standing at attention near the collenna, blocking my view.

"Lift me," the God-Empress said, and a pair of tall and muscular men actually put their hands on her and raised her to where she could step into the collenna. I was watching her settle herself when I felt those hands on me, and I squeaked, but managed not to fight them.

My ascent was considerably less graceful than hers, but I eventually got my dress arranged around me and gripped the rail of the seat as the collenna lurched forward. I'm not afraid of heights, but there was something about the movement of the collenna, and being just far enough off the ground that falling would hurt, that made me nervous. Then again, it might have been the company.

Surrounded by a detachment of ten armored and helmeted guards, we left the palace grounds through an unattended stone arch. It was tall enough that we passed through with a good five feet of headroom to spare. I immediately began to sweat. I don't know if I stayed comfortable until that point because the cooling kathana extends to the palace grounds, or if it was all in my head, but Colosse was *hot* and the dress I was wearing, while comfortable enough, was still too heavy to be the right kind of clothing for this climate. I'm sure it was just me and my acclimation to a much more temperate climate, because it was still morning and could not possibly be as hot as I remember, and if I think about it, that was true.

Once we were some distance from the palace, where there were people filling the streets, I could see everyone else dressed sensibly in short trousers and sleeveless tunics, or loose-fitting dresses, and wore the same kind of sandals everyone wore at the Darssan. Of course, looking at how comfortable they all seemed made me sweat more. I discovered when I returned to my room, much later, that my nose was sunburned, which makes me look ridiculous. The God-Empress looked as if she were still in her cool, breezy chambers, despite her wearing many more layers than I was. All right, now I'm a little jealous of her. Just a little.

Our collenna took up most of the street, but no one paid any attention to us. Everyone from pedestrians to those people pulling the wheeled carts simply stepped out of our way, as if the collenna was shrouded in a concealment pouvra. The God-Empress stared straight ahead, her hand raised and moving in a strange, complicated wave at the unseeing passersby, thinking who knows what. It seemed so out of character that I finally said, "Do they always ignore you like this?" and then cursed myself for using the word "ignore," which made them sound disrespectful. Then I cursed myself for not remembering not to speak unless I was spoken to.

But the God-Empress didn't take issue with either of my mistakes. She said, "It is a rose day. I am invisible. It would be disrespectful if they acknowledged me when I don't choose them to."

Rose day. Rose-colored collenna. "May I ask what other kinds of days there are?" I said.

The God-Empress never once turned her head to look at me during this conversation. When she spoke, her voice sounded as if it were coming from far away. "Honey days, when I am accompanied by the mages and all must bow before God's presence and that of her priests." (Mages as priests. I keep having more questions for Cederic.) "Moss days, in which all must present God with tokens of faith. Sky days, in which the streets are cleared entirely and those found outside are punished."

"I see," I said, and then couldn't think of anything else to say. I tried not to imagine what punishment that might be.

The collenna lurched to a halt. "My God, I am sorry—please accept—I will be more diligent—" the master babbled, turning around in her seat, and this time I could see the th'an. It was far more complex than the ones on the loenerel and the war wagon had been, and I was struck so hard by the feeling I ought to recognize it that I felt dizzy in addition to my fear for the collenna master's life.

But the God-Empress said nothing, still staring off into the distance, and soon the collenna moved on. I breathed more easily; I'd been afraid I was about to witness a punishment first-hand. I relaxed too soon, but that's a different part of the story.

The God-Empress seemed completely sane all morning. She lost her distant look after a while and pointed out landmarks, and I began enjoying myself. Colosse is almost as old as the disaster, and has grown up in much the same way as the palace, if less haphazardly; the palace has the disadvantage of being seen by its possessors as an outward representation of their divine power, and being frequently rebuilt accordingly. Colosse is just a big city that's adapted to the needs and desires of its residents over the centuries.

And it's nothing like anything I've seen in my travels, but then I don't think anything in my world is as old as Colosse. There are tall domed buildings where mages perform kathanas for those who can pay (and sometimes for those who can't, depending on the mage) and buildings containing nothing but swimming pools and facilities for exercising, as if people don't get enough exercise walking around and doing manual labor, but I suppose if you have magic readily available a lot of the manual labor is done for you.

There are three buildings that look like that giant's building blocks dropped out of the sky, completely unadorned, that the God-Empress said contain books, and if you pay money you can go in and look at any of them you want. I don't know if I believe her. They're bigger than the biggest libraries we have in Balaen—the size of even one of those buildings would be enough to contain thousands, tens of thousands, of books, and that there are three of them...!

Though that was another thing I learned; buildings that perform a particular function all look alike. So the libraries look like rectangular blocks, and the mage buildings are all domed, and some of them are smaller than the others but they all have the same shapes. So there are almost no signs anywhere, even marking the streets. It's expected you'll know what services are offered based on the shape of the building.

I don't know if this is laid down by law, or if it's tradition, and I couldn't begin to guess. But since there are only so many types of building, even this otherworlder woman felt familiar with the city after only a short time. I saw a few shadowy people, but only three or four, and all of them were dressed and laden like travelers. I suppose if nothing occupies this space in my world, it makes sense that there wouldn't be many things to be shadows in this one.

Around noon, the collenna stopped in front of a single-story red-roofed building (honoring the virtue of Patience) that had arched doorways opening onto a central courtyard filled with little tables, which meant it was an eating place, and half the God-Empress's soldiers went inside. We waited for about ten minutes before they returned, trailing an elderly man who didn't meet anyone's eyes.

The God-Empress stepped off the edge of the collenna's seat exactly as if she expected to be caught, which of course she was, so I mimicked her and was conveyed to the ground with barely a wobble. The moment the God-Empress's foot touched the pavement, the elderly man prostrated himself and said, "It is an unlooked for honor, my God, and I hope you will be satisfied with my humble offering."

The God-Empress walked past him without a word, and I followed her into the cool darkness beyond the courtyard. Here, there was only one table, an oblong thing about six feet long with chairs set at the far ends, and it's only a slight exaggeration to say it was bowing under the weight of a feast that could have fed twenty.

I realize now the man knew the God-Empress was coming that day, but my first thought was astonishment that he'd pulled the meal together so quickly. We sat, and her soldiers ranged themselves around us, and more people came out from what smelled like the kitchen and served us. I thought it all looked delicious and only realized I'd let myself become complacent when I was startled by the crash of a plate the God-Empress knocked out of the elderly man's hand.

"I will have red," she said, "red is the color of the day, you will give me red," and the elderly man looked as if he were going to faint. A younger woman stepped forward and offered the God-Empress a new plate, on which was a slice of beef cooked nearly raw and some slices of tender beets. I breathed more easily—even the plate was red. This was a clever woman.

The God-Empress allowed her to place it before her, then delicately began cutting her meat and chewing with pleasure. I pointed at dishes randomly and was served by people who clearly had no idea what to make of me, but were grateful I didn't make any outlandish demands. I was so worried on their behalf I don't remember what I ate, except it tasted good. I do remember the final course, which was something sweet and creamy and cold topped with candied cherries, and I asked for seconds and nearly ate myself sick on it.

Afterward, the collenna took us down to the ~~Myrnala~~ Coell River, which has sandy shores and reeds that move with the current, which is faster than the Myrnala's. We dismounted again and the God-Empress walked toward the river, slowly, removing pieces of her clothing as she went until she was once again dressed only in her thin shift and her ruby choker. And she kept walking.

She didn't stop until she was waist-deep in the river, swaying in part because of the water's movement and in part because she was caught up in some reverie. I stood watching her from the shore until she said, "You are ungrateful for the river's gift."

"Oh!" I said. "I apologize, Renatha, I believed it was...something for God alone." I struggled to remove my dress, hesitated about my underclothes, then decided to leave them and my jewelry on and waded out to meet her. And it felt wonderful, so cool in the afternoon heat, though I felt my shoulders begin to burn the way my nose already had. I mimicked her swaying and wondered what else I was supposed to intuit. She could probably have had those soldiers drown me. I wonder what would happen if I tried to use the walk-through-walls pouvra on water? Nothing good, probably.

Anyway, we stood like that for several minutes. Boats floated past —it's a big river—and in the distance I could hear children shouting. I'm glad the God-Empress didn't take offense at other people using her river, because I don't think I could have stood by quietly and let her hurt children. But she just stood there, swaying, and I stood there, uncomfortable but at least cool for once. Then she said, "Raise the river."

"I'm sorry, I don't understand," I said, and that was true both on a semantic level (because she'd used really archaic language that time) and on a comprehension level. She opened her eyes and looked at me, and I took a step back, because for the first time I saw true madness there.

"Make the waters move," she said. "I'm displeased with the river's inability to understand my commands. It is the priest's job to invoke power on God's behalf. Make the waters move."

Now I was terrified. Not just because what she wanted was impossible for me, but because she thought I was a priest the way she did her other mages, and I had no idea what kind of behavior she expected. So I said, "Of course, Renatha, but I apologize if my...priestliness is different from what you know. My world is very different."

She kept staring with those mad eyes and said, "Do it, or I will give your body to the river."

I looked back and saw the soldiers approaching the banks. Of course she meant it. I shut out my awareness of the soldiers, and my fear for my life, and my uncertainty, and used the mind-moving pouvra on the water parting on either side of the God-Empress's body. There was no way I could move the whole river, but I could do something dramatic that might satisfy her mad whim.

I pushed the water where it met her body, shoving it back as if it were running up against something much larger than the God-Empress, and desperation gave the pouvra strength I know I'll never be able to duplicate. The water piled high, cresting white at the top and making a wave that built until it towered over her like a gray-green canopy flecked with white.

The higher it got, the harder it was for me to contain it, and the way it strained against my pouvra felt as if it were alive and desperate to drown the woman beneath it. I was tempted. Her death would be no loss. But I couldn't guarantee it would kill her, and there was a part of me, the part that still can't burn flesh, that cried out against taking even a life so cruel and terrible as hers.

So I held onto the wave, and said, "The river knows you are God," which I hoped didn't sound terribly sycophantic, and waited for her to see what I'd done, then I released it harmlessly to flow away to both sides of her.

She beamed at me, happy as a child. "Of course I am," she said, and waded out of the river. She left all her clothes on the shore, so I did the same, and we got back into the collenna in our underclothing and continued our tour of the city. I've never been so embarrassed in my life, nor so grateful that the Empress's insanity dictated that no one pay attention to us. Oh, and *incredibly* grateful I was wearing the stupid breast band. I've decided never to be without one again.

Nothing else exciting happened, and we returned to the gate we'd started from, and the God-Empress stepped off as lightly as she had before. I stumbled when I reached the ground, had to catch my balance, and was about to thank the God-Empress for her generosity in giving me her time when she said, "Kill the driver."

I whipped around just in time to see two of the soldiers lift the woman off her seat, and another take her head in his two massive hands and twist so rapidly the woman didn't even have time to scream. The sound of her neck snapping was almost inaudible over the roar of the blood rushing through my temples.

The soldiers dropped her, and the God-Empress came to stand next to the body and prod it with her big toe. "Tell the priests to train me another," she said, and walked away, her damp shift still clinging to her perfect ass and thighs. Fortunately my body knew to ignore my shocked brain, and propelled me after her, because for all I knew I might have been next.

"Don't worry, I have many drivers," the God-Empress said, and to my further shock drew my arm through hers and patted my hand. "I can see you dislike waste as much as I do. But she broke the rule and acknowledged me on a rose day, and God cannot be disrespected."

"I thought...it was the bad driving," I managed.

"What bad driving?" the God-Empress said.

We reached her filmy red chamber, which was empty of servants, and she stripped off her shift and walked naked to a wardrobe in one corner, which she flung open, revealing richly embroidered robes in all shades of, that's right, red, accented with gold and copper and silver. She took robe after robe from the wardrobe and tossed them on the floor behind her, held one for a few moments before wrenching at its back seam until it tore, then finally found something she liked. But she didn't put it on; she held it out to me. "You must be rose, too," she said, "for you are God's chosen."

I did not like the sound of that, but I said, "Thank you, Renatha," and wrapped it around myself. It was far too big for me, too big for the God-Empress even, but it was wonderfully opaque and fastened high enough in front that only a hint of my cleavage showed. She beamed again, childlike, but with a body that was definitely not that of a child. She found a robe for herself and then sat on the divan with her legs crossed under her.

"I expect to see the kathana performed soon," she said, and her voice and her features became sharp in a way they hadn't been all day. "How soon, do you think?"

"I, uh, wish I knew, Renatha," I said, "For my part, I'm working as fast as I can, but focusing on my own work means I don't know much about how the rest is progressing. But I know everyone is performing to their utmost abilities." I prayed to the true God I hadn't inadvertently said something that would condemn every mage to a sudden, neck-snapping death.

"I see," the God-Empress said. "Then I will allow more time. Thank you for bringing this to my attention."

"You're welcome," I said. Talking to her is like maneuvering a maze of knives blindfolded, though that might be easier. At that point I wanted to run back to the Sais' wing and tell Cederic we now have a deadline—though he and Vorantor probably already know this better than I do. I've resolved to be more diligent and to stop complaining at Terrael, now I understand what's at stake.

The God-Empress sat looking at me, and I belatedly realized I was dismissed. "Thank you again for the generous gift of your time and company, which I do not deserve," I said, and backed out of there as rapidly as was polite and sensible. Then I ran. I only made one wrong turn before reaching the Sais' wing, and the safety of my bedroom, and then I'm not too proud to confess that I ripped the robe off, stomped on it, then stood there in my underclothing and cried.

That poor woman. All those people. Had the God-Empress decided the men and women at the eating place had paid her too much attention, and sent her soldiers back to burn it to the ground? It was so overwhelming, all the tension of worrying about whether I was going to say or do something wrong. Could I turn the pouvrin against someone in defense of my life? I hope the answer is "yes," but I don't want to only find that out when my life is in danger.

After I finished crying, I dressed in comfortable clothing and wadded up the God-Empress's robe and stuck it in the back of the wardrobe. Then I got it out and hung it up instead. She might expect me to wear it again.

I don't want to call her Renatha again. She may not have hurt me today, but I'm convinced she is my enemy, and for me to use her praenoma...it's degrading to my true friendships to put my relationship with my enemy on the same standing. Even the thought of it makes me feel uncomfortable and sick at breaking that taboo, after all I've done to keep those customs.

But I don't have a choice, do I? The God-Empress might take lethal offense at my rejecting the gift of her name. And she might not direct that lethality at me. But as far as I'm concerned, 'God-Empress' is her aenemica now, her name turned curse, and I'll think it every time I'm forced to say 'Renatha' instead.

Well. I feel better now I've written all of this down, but I think I won't go exploring tonight; I'm still on edge. And I've just realized I have more to tell Cederic about what's happened, not only the part where it sounds as if the God-Empress is losing patience with her pet mage-priests; I have to tell him about feeling like I should recognize the th'an. And I have questions for him. And I'm starving because I forgot to go to dinner, I was too busy crying.

At least all I have to look forward to tomorrow is failing to work th'an with fire. No, I can't afford to think that way. If the kathana really only lacks my part to be ready, I have to redouble my efforts or I could cost many people, some of whom I care about very much, their lives.

CHAPTER SIXTEEN

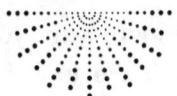

15 Lennitay

Before I can scribe my th'an with fire, I have to find a way to do the pouvra so the fire manifests as a trailing line, like ink flowing from a pen, rather than as a single mass all at once. I tried all day and failed every time.

By midafternoon I was too exhausted to do it any longer, and Terrael made me sit in a corner and watch how other people create th'an, and it should have had a calming effect, but it only made me more tense, thinking that all their lives were at the mercy of a madwoman with command of thousands of armed warriors.

I didn't get a chance to talk to Cederic today; he was busy with some of the Sais doing I don't know what. I'm not exploring tonight. Too jumpy—alertness, even a little paranoia, those things are a thief's friends, but too much anxiety leads to carelessness.

16 Lennitay

Dreamed about the soldier twisting that collenna master's head until her neck snapped. Woke in the dark and couldn't get the see-in-dark pouvra to work, then couldn't sleep without seeing the dead woman's face.

Cederic once again unavailable. I should have pushed my way into the conversation, but I couldn't bear the thought of looking like I go running to him for every little thing.

Another day of failures. I asked Audryn if she knew of anything that would help me sleep, some th'an or other, and she brought me a sweet, oily-tasting drink. I only sipped a little of it and it's making everything fuzzy. It should help.

17 Lennitay, very early

The drink gave me nightmares. Everyone in that eating place had the dead woman's face, with the look of confusion she wore just before she died. Then they all fell down and shattered like the plate into ruby shards the God-Empress stitched into her clothing, except they became golden because it was a honey day—I have to remember this, I know it's important and I can't sleep again until I've written it all down—it was a honey day, and I had to dress in gold and perform a kathana by myself in worship of the God-Empress, and the kathana was to write all over Terrael's body and

I just threw up Audryn's drink. I'm writing this huddled in bed. I don't dare sleep again.

18 Lennitay

Well, I did sleep, eventually, and woke clutching this book against my chest, just in time to hide it under my pillow when the servant came to rouse me. She was aghast at the vomit, which did smell horrible, and brought in a couple of other servants to clean it up and bring me water and some soft, tasteless food—they think I'm ill. I didn't correct that misapprehension.

I couldn't face the mages again. I've never been so low in my life. I was certain they were all going to be killed because I couldn't master the one tiny thing that was so crucial to the kathana's success, and every time I closed my eyes I still saw that woman's face, only after that nightmare, sometimes it was Sovrin, or Audryn, or one of the other Darssan mages. I ate a little, then set the tray aside and curled up facing the wall, my hand on this book under my pillow.

The door opened, and a moment later Cederic said, "You are not asleep. And you did not tell me everything. What happened when you were with the God-Empress?"

I rolled over to look at him. He was dressed in the gray robe and black trousers he still wears to work in even though, as Terrael had told me, he's entitled to wear red as Kilios (Vorantor's people wear brown and gold, and they always look as if they're going to a party compared to the simple Darssan uniform). "I don't want to talk about it," I said.

He came closer until he stood next to me. "Whatever happened is making you ill," he said quietly, "and will continue to do so as long as you allow it to fester inside you. Tell me."

So I sat up and told him everything, keeping my eyes on my clasped hands, managing not to break down when I described the collenna master's murder. I think I glossed over the thing about the th'an because I was still overwhelmed, or he didn't think it mattered, because he didn't seem interested.

He listened silently until I was finished and looked up at him finally. He wasn't looking at me; he was staring out the window, his jaw clenched and his face impassive. "Tell me I'm wrong about all this," I said. "Tell me I'm wrong that everyone's safety depends on me."

He shook his head. "You are not wrong." He looked down at me and said, "Lie back," and put the tips of his first and middle fingers in the center of my forehead and pushed. I lay back on my pillow, wondering what he had in mind, but he walked away and leaned on my dressing table the way he had on that table when I translated the Eddon book.

"This is not a burden you should bear, but I cannot take it from you," he said. "But I may be able to ease it."

He came back to my side and reached for the neck of my shirt, opening it slightly to expose my throat. "This will make you sleep, and will keep you from dreaming," he said, "and it may also clear your mind to make your task easier. Do not go wandering tonight, Sesskia. That is not a request."

I nodded, and the tips of his fingers brushed my chin as I did. He pressed up on my chin, baring more of my throat, and I felt the lightest pressure as he traced th'an on my skin, there and then across my forehead. I immediately felt sleepy, the good kind of sleepy where you've worked hard all day and your muscles are relaxing, and the last thing I felt before I dozed off were his fingers brushing against my cheek.

It was nearly dark when I woke, rested and happy as I haven't been in days—weeks—and with the nightmares a distant memory, sad, but something I could deal with. I sat up, which drew the attention of a woman sitting on the floor next to my wardrobe, who hopped up and bowed to me repeatedly. She explained, in between bows, that she would bring me food and it was the Kilios's instructions that I not disturb myself.

Though I did use the chamber pot in the kiorka as soon as she disappeared; I doubt Cederic meant me to exercise superhuman control over my bladder. I ate sitting up in bed, and now I feel sleepy again, but I wanted to write all this down before falling asleep again. I owe Cederic a debt.

Now that I'm thinking more clearly, I realize I took on too much responsibility for what is ultimately the God-Empress's evil. It's true she expects results out of the kathana, and it's true that as soon as I master my th'an, we'll be able to perform it, which means it's also true everything depends on me. But it's not true that that means I hold everyone's lives in my hand. It's not true that I would be to blame for any deaths resulting from the God-Empress's dissatisfaction with how her priest-mages are performing. All of that is to her damnation.

I can't do more than I've been doing, which is learning to use a kind of magic literally alien to me. And I haven't given myself enough credit for what I *have* accomplished, which is successfully scribe a th'an in only ten days without five years of preparatory penmanship exercises first. I know I can do this. And I refuse to let the God-Empress cow me again.

19 Lennitay

Made fire like a string of burning thread, first attempt. It's actually easier than the other version of the pouvra and takes less concentration. Drew everyone's names in the air to show off my own language's alphabet until Vorantor insisted I get down to work. Everyone annoyed with Vorantor, including his own mages. Cederic not-so-secretly amused.

20 Lennitay

Small setback—not sure how thick to make the thread. Lots of experimentation until Terrael suggested practicing the th'an until that's successful, then working out how large it has to be for the kathana. Terrael is definitely the brightest of us all and I'm pretty sure he's angling to be a Kilios himself someday.

Gaining control over the fire pouvra. Dinner was unexpectedly nasty, but they had some of that cold creamy stuff for dessert and that made up for it.

21 Lennitay

Still no progress.

22 Lennitay

I've found something I don't understand—no, that's not true, I understand it perfectly but I—this is stupid, I'm so tired from practicing the th'an I'm not thinking straight. I came back to my room directly after dinner, because of the aforementioned tiredness, but I wasn't sleepy; in fact, I was restless.

So after trying to fall asleep for about twenty minutes, I gave up. I didn't want to get dressed again and go to the common room, so instead I walked down to the observatory and sat on the ledge and let my feet dangle, and looked out over the pile of dusty gems that is Colosse in the light of the setting sun. It's a beautiful city, but then most cities are, from a distance.

I put my hands on the pillars so I could lean out farther, and my left hand brushed something soft that wasn't leaves. It was about waist-high (my waist) on the pillar above where the staircase begins and was the same color as the pillars. I picked at it, and discovered it was a roll of paper the length and diameter of my middle finger.

I unrolled it, and remembered I couldn't read their language just as I had it open and saw lines of meaningless, tiny script. So now I know how Vorantor and Aselfos communicate; there's really no other explanation. The note was hidden exactly where Vorantor always stands, exactly where someone standing on the hidden staircase could tuck it away without being seen.

It explains why I never see them together, why I never find Vorantor wandering the halls like I do. They must only meet face to face when one or the other has something that's too long to be entrusted to a note.

But now I have a problem. If I take the note, it could reveal to Vorantor that someone knows he's plotting something—for example, if he and Aselfos have a regular communication schedule. Vorantor *might* conclude that the note blew away or fell down the cliff, but that's too big a gamble for me to steal a note that might not have anything of importance in it.

The bigger problem is I don't know who I'd take it to. Cederic is the only one who knows about my suspicions, but he might be angry enough about my snooping around to refuse to help me. I certainly can't take it to any of the other Darssan mages without involving them in something that could be dangerous; I trust them, but none of them has the right outlook for this, which is to say, none of them are devious and paranoid enough.

So I had to leave the note where it was, though I did conceal myself and wait long enough to see Vorantor retrieve it. Confirmation of my theory, but I still don't know what to do about it. I'm going to observe a few more nights, see if those notes come with any regularity, and see if a solution presents itself.

23 Lennitay

We need a rest day. We're not getting one. Cederic lost that argument with Vorantor. Vorantor's mages close to rebelling—I think everyone wishes Cederic were in charge. No note tonight.

24 Lennitay

Success! The binding th'an works! But there wasn't time to either celebrate or experiment further to determine what size it should be, because it was a honey day and all of us, including me, were expected to put on golden robes and accompany the God-Empress to an amphitheater filled with citizens, then demonstrate kathanas for the crowds.

I now understand the mages are also priests because magic is considered divine power, which the priest-mages perform in service to and with the permission of the God-Empress. I wanted to ask what would happen if the mages decided to rebel against her, set themselves up as the rulers of the empire, but that's the sort of question that's dangerous to ask.

The God-Empress stood on a platform that raised her fifteen feet above the amphitheater floor, waving her hand in the same complicated, flowing salute she'd used the day we toured Colosse. Even though Vorantor is "most high priest," Cederic had to wear his red robe and officiate, which both he and Vorantor hated. It's increasingly clear that Vorantor is deeply jealous of his "old friend" and regrets bringing him back to Colosse, not that he had any say in the matter. I don't know if Vorantor always felt this way—he isn't a bad mage, actually he's very talented, he's just not in Cederic's class and I'm sure that bothers him. And I can't blame him for that.

Well, yes, I can, but that's because I dislike him and his habit of doing things that are the opposite of what Cederic suggests, just to spite him. Cederic never acts as if he notices, just politely accepts whatever Vorantor decrees. I'd say I wish Cederic would spit in his eye sometime, but if he ever lost control to that degree, I'd be too shocked to appreciate the spectacle.

I've been practicing the binding th'an in my room before I go to sleep at night. It's getting easier, but I'm trying not to relapse into the state of gut-wrenching anxiety that nearly destroyed everything. Ten more tries, and then it's bed for me. I checked the observatory already —there was a note. I wish I could read.

25 Lennitay

It was as if something connected inside my head this morning, and suddenly the fire rope pouvra was as easy as thought, any shape, any size, whatever I imagined, it would do. There was total silence from my observers when I tested the final pouvra and the fire th'an hung in the air, then shrank in on itself with a deep bell-like tone that made the walls resonate. Nobody cheered, but I could feel the excitement, see it on their faces. Vorantor embraced me and said some meaningless and patronizing things. Cederic just smiled.

The mages are setting up the kathana for tomorrow. The God-Empress has been notified. I'm sure I won't be able to sleep tonight for excitement. Tomorrow, we'll have the Codex Tiurindi, and Terrael can start translating it, and soon Cederic will have his proof, and we can *really* begin work.

26 Lennitay

That was the most astonishing experience, on so many levels.

And yes, it worked.

We woke extra early, long before sunrise, and ate a quick but filling breakfast—Vorantor wasn't sure how long the kathana would take, and we all needed to stay alert and undistracted by physical demands, so there was a lot of use of the chamber pots as well. Some of the groundwork was done yesterday, so the floor inside the gold ring was dotted with th'an, a type that are inactive until some other th'an wakes them up.

Vorantor walked around, chatting with people in his "I'm a great leader" way, while Cederic sat to one side with his hands resting on his knees, apparently meditating. I tried to do a little meditating myself, but I was too excited to manage it. So I watched the others. Four of Vorantor's mages, all of them men, were stripping out of their robes to only their trousers for the body-scribing aspect of the kathana.

This is what I know, as per Terrael's explanation:

A kathana, in essence, brings th'an together in a particular order at particular times to achieve a result larger than anything single th'an or small groups of th'an can produce. Most of them require multiple mages to complete, if only because people only have so many hands. And the mages have to practice together for hours to get the timing exactly right. That's what everyone else has been doing while I struggled to master my single th'an: practicing scribing th'an in the right order at the right time.

And this is a hugely complex kathana, a summoning kathana,

that describes a reality in which something that was not, is. We're trying to create a reality in which the Codex Tiurindi wasn't destroyed so many hundreds of years ago, but exists here and now. My part is to unite those two realities for long enough that the kathana can make the Codex part of this one.

Personally, I think the fact that they can do this is evidence that Cederic is right, because what else are we dealing with but two worlds, two realities, that are coming together? And if it weren't natural for realities to spring apart, we wouldn't need my part of the kathana to keep them together. But Terrael shook his head when I brought this up and said realities and worlds aren't the same thing, and then I think he became technical just to annoy me.

So I'll explain all of that as it happened, which was directly after the God-Empress and her chicken-headed minions arrived, one of them, a fat, gray-haired woman, wearing a red tunic instead of black and carrying her helmet under her arm. The God-Empress was dressed rather plainly, for her, in gold brocade over creamy silk and pearls the size of quail eggs dangling around her neck.

Cederic and Vorantor greeted her with regulation bows, Cederic's much shallower than Vorantor's, and they had a low-voiced discussion that ended with the God-Empress beckoning to me and, when I approached, saying, "You will sit with me, won't you, Sesskia? I would like someone to observe with."

I looked to both Cederic and Vorantor for advice, and got nothing, because Cederic looked impassive and Vorantor had his eyes closed in his "that's a really bad idea" expression. "Thank you for the invitation, Renatha," I said, "but I must stand here to perform my part, or the kathana might not work."

The God-Empress gazed at me, her eyes slightly unfocused, and then she said, "Of course. My priests, I will sit where you direct me," but it took a while for them to "direct" her to a spot she liked. I returned to my position, which was at the base of the circle (it's marked with the four cardinal and four ordinal directions, so the base of the circle is south), and balanced lightly on the balls of my feet, trying to stay relaxed and not to think about what the God-Empress might do if we failed.

Eventually, though, she was settled, and her soldiers were disposed throughout the room in a manner that did not suggest in any way that they had orders to begin slaughtering mages if the God-Empress was displeased, and Vorantor waved to everyone else to take their places. He signaled to the mage serving as drummer, who began beating the count, and when everyone had picked up the rhythm, Vorantor nodded to the first group to begin.

The first part was the easiest and required the most people. Those mages scribed th'an to complete the "phrases" already written in and around the circle. Terrael explained to me that it "wakes up" the magic (that was my phrase, not Terrael's, and when I said it he rolled his eyes and said, "you're almost a savage, you know that?" and I had to soak his head. Really, I had no choice) and gives a base shape to the kathana.

Savage or no, that part I did understand, since something similar happens when I learn a new pouvra. I was in a perfect position to watch, and it's beautiful, like a dance, with people passing back and forth across the circle, bending and swaying. Then they step away, and the body-scribers take their places at the four ordinal directions, sit down just outside the circle, and begin writing th'an on their chests and faces.

It's awe-inspiring, how perfectly synchronized they are. The body-scribing is to attune those mages to the kathana. It's extremely dangerous because they're linking their hearts and lungs to the kathana so it will persist beyond the instantaneous effect of activating the final th'an, and it could kill them if we aren't perfectly accurate.

They didn't look afraid. It took only a few minutes for their bodies to be crisscrossed with inky markings. As they each drew a final mark from the bridge of their noses down over their lips and to the point of their chins, those markings began to glow with a blue so bright it was painful to look at. I kept my eyes focused on the spot painted in red on the wall beyond the circle. It was my guiding mark for when it was my turn in the kathana.

The room was growing very warm, and I had trouble not rubbing away the sweat prickles under my arms. Because I was focused on my mark, I didn't see the next part, but I'd watched the Darssan mages practice, so I knew they were drawing th'an in a loose pattern surrounding the circle and the body-scribing mages.

With the magic made ready by the first th'an, and given duration by the body-scribers, the Darssan mages now defined the reality they wanted with a series of complex th'an. On the west side of the circle was a definition of our reality, and on the east side was the same definition with some key differences, namely, the existence of the Codex Tiurindi. I waited, and counted, my heart beating in time with the rhythm and not accelerating at all.

Then Cederic was in front of me, a pot of silver ink in his hand and a brush in the other, painting a th'an on my forehead, and the second he removed the brush I summoned the fire and scribed my th'an in lines of gold as thick as my wrist, halfway between myself and the red mark, which put it exactly over the circle.

White light sprang up from both sides of the circle, blazing brighter than the mages' blue bodies, and I squinted hard, blinking away tears, and watched the fiery th'an shrink in on itself and then hover, distorted and frozen, over the center of the circle. I was aware of Cederic and Vorantor directly ahead of me, Cederic drawing th'an on the air and Vorantor scribbling on the floor, and then the white light filled my vision, and I closed my eyes and threw up my arms to cover them.

Nothing happened. The drumming stopped and the room was completely silent. I heard someone walking toward me and opened my eyes, blinking away afterimages. Vorantor bent to pick up a small book, no larger than one of my hands. It was bound in gray leather and was locked shut. Vorantor pried at it, with no success, and Cederic gently took it out of his hands and gave it to me. "Sesskia," he said, and I used the mind-moving pouvra to unlock it. That set my head to pounding, so I handed the book back to Cederic and massaged my temples.

Cederic opened it, then handed it to Vorantor with a bow. I'm pretty sure he only did this because he knew Vorantor wouldn't be able to read it, and he could afford to look gracious. Vorantor turned a few pages and tried to appear wise and contemplative, but I thought he only looked like a fool.

"It is the book," the God-Empress said, and everyone moved aside while trying not to look like they were fleeing. She walked right up to Vorantor and took the book from him. The air hummed with the sound of fifty-one people, myself included, trying not to shout at the divine madwoman who had no experience in handling ancient books. Though it didn't look ancient, something the God-Empress pointed out immediately. "This can't be the right one," she said.

"God-Empress, the book comes from a time when it was new, so it has not experienced the passing of time," Terrael said, surprising everyone except Cederic. Then he shocked *everyone* by taking the book from her and turning to the first pages. "I can't read it yet, God-Empress, and I apologize for asking for more of your patience" (I had no idea Terrael could be so diplomatic!) "but I can verify whether this is the book we wanted, if you'll allow me a moment."

He skimmed the first few pages, turned to the back and examined the binding, then turned to a page about two-thirds of the way through and looked at it closely. "The first pages contain the name Veris, the binding has been repaired where an extra signature was inserted—a signature is a bundle of pages, God-Empress—and this is the page where Veris gave the book to her successor, Barklan; the handwriting changes. This is the Codex Tiurindi.

Now it didn't matter that the God-Empress was standing among us; everyone cheered, or gasped, or cried, or did something to express their excitement and relief, which meant Cederic turned away with his head bowed, and I hugged Audryn and we both tried not to dance. Terrael was already trying to read the book, but Vorantor took it gently from him and said, "All in good time, Master Peressten! God-Empress, thank you for allowing us the joy of your presence on this day. I assure you—"

"Don't bore me with your assurances, Denril Vorantor," the God-

Empress said, all traces of her earlier lack of focus gone. "You told me the book would keep my empire safe from this disaster. Show me."

That shut everyone's celebrating down. Vorantor's mouth sagged open. "We—God-Empress, we need to translate it, it's not so simple—"

"Show me *something*, Denril Vorantor, or I will make your life very simple indeed," the God-Empress said.

Vorantor's eyes were wide and panicked. "What do you—what should I show you, God-Empress?" he begged.

"The Codex Tiurindi was written in a time when defensive magics were more refined than they are now, God-Empress," Cederic said. "Would you care to see one of them?"

Vorantor's eyes were even wider now. I know a good lie when I see one, and I prayed to the true God Vorantor wouldn't do or say anything to give Cederic's game away. Of course there was no way the Codex Tiurindi could show the God-Empress anything, but she didn't know that, and I was certain by the expressionless look on Cederic's face that there were a lot of other things about magic she didn't know.

"The book, please," he said to Terrael, who was as wide-eyed as Vorantor, but handed the Codex to Cederic. He flipped it open (at random, I guessed) and said, "We will need to translate it to create the ultimate kathana, of course, but there are smaller pieces to the puzzle —here."

He shut the book, tucked it into his trouser pocket, stripped off his robe and used it to scrub the floor to remove the residue of the th'an. He's slim, with a scattering of short dark hairs across his chest, and he has more muscle than I would have guessed, for an academic. He was nearly done before it occurred to anyone to join him. He threw the stained robe away and chalked some th'an on the floor, looked at the book again, chalked a few more th'an, then said, "Step back, please," and made a few final marks.

A shimmering hemisphere about two feet tall sprang up around the th'an, glowing with a greenish-gold light that swirled like a film of oil across the hemisphere's surface. Cederic stood and rapped on the hemisphere with his knuckles, making the oil ripple out from that point of contact as if his hand were a stone thrown into a lake. "You might ask one of your soldiers to strike it," he said, "but I am not entirely certain it will not turn that force back on him."

The God-Empress shrugged and snapped her fingers in the direction of her soldiers, and with some hesitation, one of them came forward. She pointed, and the soldier drew his knife and approached the hemisphere, then brought the weapon down as if he were stabbing an enemy in the back. The knife met the oily surface—and shattered.

No one spoke. The soldier looked impressed. All the mages looked stunned. I don't know how I looked, awestruck probably. Cederic looked bored. The God-Empress nodded once, slowly. "I am satisfied," she said. "Teach the others. And tell me when the book is translated." She gestured at her soldiers, and they surrounded her as she left the room.

The instant she was gone, and the heavy door was shut, Vorantor was in Cederic's face, shouting, "*What in hell's name were you thinking?*"

"I was *thinking*," Cederic said, not shying away from Vorantor's ire, "that I would prefer none of us be killed by the God-Empress's soldiers."

"You had no idea whether that kathana would work!" Vorantor shouted. "Kilios or no, you could barely have understood what you were reading—how could you even know it was what you said it was?"

"I didn't," Cederic said. "I made it up."

That left Vorantor gaping with nothing to say. "Even Master Peressten cannot read that book," Cederic said. "I gambled that the God-Empress would not believe we were telling the truth that it would take time to translate all of it, and I...invented a kathana that would satisfy her."

I think I was the only person watching Vorantor at that moment —everyone else was staring at Cederic in awe—and I was enjoying his look of stunned chagrin when it turned, for the briefest instant, into something much darker, something that frightened me. Then he smiled, and threw his arm around Cederic's shoulders. "You never stop amazing me, old friend," he said. "Cheers, everyone! It's time to celebrate!"

The first cheers were weak little things, but they grew into robust, happy noise as it settled on everyone that we, first, had succeeded in the task that had driven us these many days, and second, were not dead. The room wasn't conducive to celebration, so we moved to the dining hall, and I ended up at the tail end of our procession next to Cederic, who looked as calm as always, though a bit scruffy in his reclaimed, wrinkled robe. He congratulated me on my part in the kathana, and I expressed my admiration at him making up a new one out of whole cloth.

"That may turn out to be a bad idea," he said in a low voice. "It probably saved all our lives, so I do not regret it, but now the God-Empress will want us to turn that kathana to her army's use. Just one more way in which we are giving her more power. And I am not entirely certain I remember how to repeat it."

"I don't believe you've forgotten a kathana in your entire life," I said, making him smile, "and I don't see that you had much choice. She wouldn't have been satisfied with a kathana that showered her enemies with rose petals."

He smiled again. "Not unless they were rose petals that exploded," he said.

That brought us to the dining hall door, and I thought about inviting him to sit with me—he couldn't possibly want to sit with Vorantor after that, could he?—but I hesitated too long, and he nodded at me and moved off to his usual table. So I sat with my friends, and we laughed, and drank too much wine, and had a wonderful time. My head hurts from the wine, so I'm going to sleep it off, and in the morning—strange, I don't know what I'm going to do next.

I've been so focused on the kathana that I'm used to having direction, and now it's a matter of waiting for Terrael to translate the book. And I really don't know what happens then. Will Vorantor be able to accept that he's been wrong? I think he'd be capable of violence if threatened, and I'm sure he sees Cederic's competence as a threat to his position. Never mind that Cederic wouldn't want to be the God-Empress's chief mage even if—well, no, if it meant saving both our worlds I think he'd accept the position. But certainly not for anything less.

CHAPTER SEVENTEEN

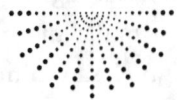

27 Lennitay

Very boring. Terrael is preoccupied with the Codex and the Darssan mages are half-heartedly cooperating with Vorantor's mages on the kathanas he's developed for "minimizing the damage" when the worlds come together.

Cederic was gone today, teaching the shield kathana to the God-Empress's battle mages. He didn't look happy when he returned, and I can't blame him, but he really had no choice. He told me he wishes it wasn't quite so simple a kathana, and I told him he should have thought of that before he went around being brilliant at people, which made him smile. What he needs is a good laugh, but I have a hard time imagining him laughing.

Terrael won't talk about what he's learned so far—says talking is a distraction, and makes him jump to conclusions—but I know he's in ecstasy over being the first to read the Codex Tiurindi in centuries, maybe millennia. We still don't know exactly how long it was after the disaster that civilization began repairing itself.

Nothing for me to do, though I could look at it as a good thing that the God-Empress hasn't called on me to entertain her. Today I finally went to look at the picture in the floor of the mosaic room. It's a falcon. It looks much more like the real bird than the helmets, but at least now I know where the inspiration came from. Exploring tonight for sure.

28 Lennitay

I've finally encountered Aselfos, though "encounter" is probably the wrong word, because it implies we met face to face, and I'm just as happy he doesn't know I exist. Though that might not be true, depending on what he noticed last night.

I decided I was going to make more of an effort to figure out where Aselfos went, the night I saw him talking to Vorantor. He'd gone down the secret staircase into the treasure tower, and I already know the treasure rooms only lead to one another and to the spiral passage inside the tower, and the room with the war wagons has no visible exit other than the guarded one. He might have left the tower by the corridor I'd originally entered by, but there were also the brass double doors on the outside wall of the tower I'd never investigated, so I decided to try my luck there.

I waited for Vorantor to finish his meditation, or whatever it is he does in the observatory after dinner, then I used the secret staircase to get into the treasure tower. I probably could have taken my original route, but Aselfos's way is more fun.

Once inside, I trotted down the spiral passage to the double door, looked through it to be safe, then pushed it open (it was unlocked) and went inside. As I wrote before, it opened on a corridor about five feet long that made a sharp turn to the right. I peeked around the corner and saw a hallway extending off into the darkness, which I proceeded along, quietly and cautiously. I recalled my mental map of the palace and concluded that I was beneath the Sais' wing. This was certainly close to the same length as that hallway, though much narrower.

Eventually I came to an iron door held only loosely in place by rusted hinges. The door was locked, and the strange thing was the lock was much newer than the rest of the door. That seems foolish to me, given that someone could easily break the door down, bypassing the lock, but then there's a lot about this that makes no sense to me.

I used the see-through pouvra and discovered the corridor continued a short distance to another door, this one wooden. Also strange. I unlocked the iron door and walked down the corridor to the wooden one, which was also locked, but with a simpler lock that wasn't any newer than the door. I looked through it, but whatever was beyond it was too far away to make out details.

So I started to unlock the door and got a nasty surprise: someone had set a clever little trap on the locking mechanism. It wasn't intended to harm anyone, just to show anyone who knew how to look that someone had passed through the door. A warning to the trap-setter. It was complicated enough it would take at least three hands to prevent it from going off while the door was being unlocked, and would be impossible to stop if you were entering from the other direction. Now I was certain Aselfos used this route, because I bet he's got that kind of devious and suspicious mind. So that's one thing we have in common.

I examined the trap until I was sure I knew how it worked, and carefully removed the trap with my hands while I used the pouvra to unlock the door. I might have been able to do the whole thing with magic, but why take unnecessary chances?

I set the trap on the floor inside the corridor, out of the way, and shut the door behind me. The room beyond looked like it might be a music room, though the instruments leaning against the walls weren't familiar to me. I peeked outside and was able to orient myself; I was in the wing containing all the empty guest chambers.

At this point I had nothing to go on. I felt it was safe to assume Aselfos had exited the tower through this door, and that he suspected someone might follow him on his trips up to leave notes for Vorantor. But I could only guess where he'd gone from here. I took the most obvious option, concealed myself, and went toward the one alcove off the main chamber I hadn't yet explored.

I'd only gone about a hundred feet when I was nearly caught. I admit I was careless, just as I've always feared using the concealment pouvra too much might make me. And I was getting tired. So it was mostly luck, and the fact that I've been doing this for a long time and my reflexes are excellent, that saved me.

I was nearly to the mosaic chamber when a door opened ahead of me and I had to dodge to one side and press myself flat against the wall. There was no convenient doorway for me to hide in, and I was grateful for the concealment pouvra even as I cursed myself for depending on it so much.

A man and a woman emerged from the open door. The woman said "...past time."

"It will have to be enough," said the man, and I recognized Aselfos's voice. When he came closer, I got a better look at him. He was older than I'd guessed, nearly fifty, but lean and athletic, and he moved with assurance. That he could navigate the secret staircase did not surprise me at all.

His companion was about the same age, with close-cropped hair that was gray in the dim light, and although she was fat where he was slim, she moved with the same assurance, like someone accustomed to command. I recognized her after a few moments as one of the God-Empress's soldiers, the one who'd worn a different uniform than the rest at the kathana. If this were Balaen, I'd assume she was a general, though again, I don't know the Castaviran Empire's military ranks.

"It would help if we had a better estimate," the woman said.

"Vorantor says the time is shrinking," Aselfos said.

The woman snorted. "Vorantor is a problem."

"He'll validate my claim, and I'll make him powerful," Aselfos said. "Whether he's right about this catastrophe or not. And his work on this supposed disaster is keeping the Kilios occupied."

"I suppose as long as his summoning puts our resources in the right place at the right time, it doesn't matter," the woman said. "But you should tell Vorantor sooner is better. Who knows what idea the crazy bitch might take into her golden head?"

"Have patience," Aselfos said, and he walked in my direction. I held my breath. "We'll have a day's warning, and that will have..." and they were out of earshot. I continued to hold my breath for a few more seconds, then released it slowly and retreated to the music room, through the door and into the hall, where I again paused before resetting the trap and locking everything behind me. Then I returned to my room as quickly as I could. That brings me to now.

I'm a thief, not a politician, but that sounded like a plot against the God-Empress to me. And Vorantor is involved. *And* they're afraid of Cederic interfering, I think. I should tell Cederic. But...if Aselfos is planning to act against the God-Empress, how is that a bad thing? He might be a better option than her—almost certainly would be.

I just don't know enough about Castaviran politics to know how a coup would affect the mages. They might be associated closely enough with the God-Empress that Aselfos would want to destroy them with her, and Vorantor has been negotiating with him for their protection. Or, knowing him, his own protection, and to hell with what happens to the rest of us. No, that's too cynical even for me.

I'll tell Cederic in the morning, wait for him to stop being sarcastic at me, and figure out what I can do.

29 Lennitay

Something is wrong with Terrael. I think. I mean, it's probably normal that he's avoiding people while he's working on the Codex, but avoid Audryn? I doubt even Terrael could be that obsessed. And I've seen him go out of his way to keep from meeting Cederic in the hall. He acts...furtive. As if he has some secret he's afraid he might give away if he steps wrong. Audryn couldn't find him at lunchtime, so she had me and the Darssan mages look for him, and I found him in the circle chamber, scribbling on the walls.

But he wasn't writing th'an, it looked like ordinary handwriting, not that I can read that. When he saw me, he turned absolutely white, then scrubbed off the wall as fast as he could and said it was just a theory he was trying on some I don't know what, it was technical linguistic things and I didn't understand him. Which, I think, was the idea. He wanted me distracted. If he's so upset about something that he doesn't remember I can't read his language...something is definitely wrong with Terrael.

I told Cederic about what I learned last night, and he was furious, not that anyone but me could tell. When he calmed down, he said, "I think you are correct that Aselfos is planning some kind of power play. What Denril has to do with it...I dislike guessing, but it sounds as if he intends to turn his magical abilities to Aselfos's benefit, though I cannot imagine what kind of interference they think I might represent. From what you overheard, Aselfos intends to take the God-Empress's place, and it would legitimize him if the chief priest-mage asserted that his claim is more valid than hers."

"So what should *we* do?" I said.

"Nothing," Cederic said. "We know too little to do anything but meddle, and I don't know how that might upset the balance of power. The upcoming disaster is far more important than anything Aselfos might have in mind, though what you overheard suggests their timing might be related to it. And if he does intend to eliminate the mages along with the God-Empress, I think he will find we are not so easy to kill. Now, is there any chance I can persuade you to leave this alone?"

"No," I said. "But I promise to be more careful. Does that help?"

"Not as much as you hope," he said, but he was smiling, and I think he's growing accustomed to the fact that this is what I am.

Terrael will finish the translation soon, and then Cederic will have to deal with Vorantor somehow. I don't know what part I might play in his strategy. I hope there's some way I can help.

30 Lennitay

I feel like such a fool. "I hope there's some way I can help." How pathetic.

I've made a nest for myself in these furs, and I've cried all the tears that are in me, and now I'm going to write all of this down, though I don't know what the point is. Maybe it's so I can look back later and remind myself not to be a fool again. I don't even care if the God-Empress learns that someone's been in her treasure rooms. Not that she'd know it was me. Aselfos can't be that good, or he'd have caught me already.

We found out what was wrong with Terrael. And the secret of the Codex Tiurindi. But I'm going to write it all down as it happened, leaving nothing out, and these are the sort of conversations I wish I could forget. What Terrael said—I know I'm going to make mistakes, and there are gaps, and I've made it seem my memory is perfect and I *know* that's not honest. But right now *I don't give a damn about honest* because when everything is falling apart, fiction is more comforting than fact. But I'm doing my best.

I spent the morning practicing pouvrin until I had a bit of a headache, then I took over a scrap of wall and doodled, nothing real, just experimenting to see if I could reproduce the shapes of pouvrin. It wasn't successful, but it gave me some ideas for other things I might try. I have no idea what the point would be, now, and I can't believe how hopeful I was at the time. I'm such a fool.

All the mages were there except Audryn and Terrael, and I think everyone was doing variations on what I was doing—sketching kathana plans, or practicing th'an. Cederic and Vorantor were at the circle, talking quietly about something on the board Cederic held. They looked so friendly. I guess that shows how impossible it is to tell anything just by looking.

I wish—remembering them standing together, I wish I could have warned Cederic somehow...but what would I say? I've already shown what a failure I am at saying the right thing—damn it, now I'm crying again. Enough. This is me writing it down, no more self-pity.

So. Audryn and Terrael finally arrived. Terrael still looked awful, but now Audryn did too. I started to approach them, but Terrael said something to Audryn, who shook her head and clutched at his sleeve to make him stop. He pulled away from her and hurried straight to where Cederic and Vorantor were, and said something to Cederic in a low voice.

Vorantor said, "I see no reason why you can't tell all of us what you've learned, Master Peressten. Unless you think no one but the Kilios deserves to know."

Terrael looked devastated. Cederic said, "Go ahead, Master Peressten, Sai Vorantor is correct."

Audryn seemed ready to cry, and I went quickly to her, but when I asked what was wrong, she shook her head again and covered her mouth with her sleeve. Terrael's shoulders slumped, and he took the Codex out of his trouser pocket and opened it.

"I've translated enough to know it has the information we—the information about the coming disaster," he said, loudly enough that everyone could hear him. "It has most of the kathana the mages used when they created the first disaster. We can use it to...to..." He stopped, swallowed, and turned back a few pages.

"Veris wasn't a mage," he said. "She was responsible for chronicling the acts of the mages, back then, which means the Codex isn't as useful as a record by an actual mage would be in terms of giving us a complete kathana we could use. But because she's an outsider, she sees their magic—what existed before the disaster—the way we might, and in that sense the book is more useful—"

"Please skip to the important part, Master Peressten," Vorantor said in that indulgent way he has when he's talking to the Darssan mages, like they're clever children, though some of them are older than he is.

"*This is important!*" Terrael shouted, startling everyone; he looks so harmless, so innocent, and it breaks my heart to think of how much all this hurt him. "Veris, and then Barklan, didn't understand much of what they wrote about magic. What they describe was something of a combination of our magic and Sesskia's—th'an expressed not through writing, but through the power of will. That's a part I don't understand yet.

"But the experiment that went wrong was intended to make magic more accessible, make it easier to learn and to use. They wanted to remove some of the...the inherent requirements of the magic. Barklan writes about it as if the magic were alive and could make demands, and that may or may not be true, but it's what those mages were counting on."

"So they tried to remove the magic, and separated their world instead," Cederic said.

"Maybe," said Terrael. "There wasn't anyone left to record what actually happened, and the Codex was destroyed in the disaster, so the last record is simply a note that they were ready to try the kathana, though they call it something else. It's the...the earlier records, the experiments, that tell what must have gone wrong."

He turned more pages. "They practiced—I don't know how they isolated magic, but they did, and they practiced removing the parts they didn't want. And it worked, for short periods of time. They would...they would separate the magic into identical pieces, exactly the same except that one had the magic they wanted and the other didn't. Just like how we summoned the Codex. But they could only keep them separated for seconds before they drew back together. Irresistible attraction. Because the magic calls to itself."

"I fail to see the point, Master Peressten," Vorantor said, exactly as if Terrael hadn't snapped at him before.

"I'm coming to it," Terrael said, though he sounded as if the words were being dragged out of him. "So with the final kathana, the one that caused the disaster, the plan was to suppress the magic long enough to take out what they wanted and recreate it in their image. Because if there was no magic, the pieces stayed separated. And if there *was* magic, nothing...nothing could keep the pieces from recombining."

By this time he was talking directly to Cederic, as if no one else were in the room, and I could tell Cederic was as mystified as the rest of us, but he nodded encouragement. That probably made Terrael feel worse.

"The rest is somewhat conjecture, but I swear to you, Sai Aleynten, I've gone over this a hundred times and I know it's true," Terrael said. "The kathana was too powerful, and it tore the world in half, two almost identical pieces with key differences and all the magic gone, or at least spread so thin it couldn't be used for anything. And they stayed apart for hundreds of years while the magic gathered itself and people learned to use it again, until there was enough of it to reverse the process.

"Every th'an, every kathana, even Sesskia's pouvrin bring the worlds closer together. And there's no way to stop it. They aren't meant to be apart. Sai Aleynten, I'm sorry, but there's no way to keep them apart. It's impossible."

Cederic was completely motionless. He didn't even blink. "I see," he said.

Vorantor said, "Oh, Cederic. You still held out hope, didn't you? Are you convinced now?"

"No way to prevent it," Cederic said, his lips barely moving. "You were right."

Vorantor put his hand on Cederic's unmoving shoulder. "Don't worry about it," he said, too cheerfully. "No harm done, in the long run, and there's no shame in being wrong, is there?"

"Of course not," Cederic said.

"Pity all that work was wasted," Vorantor said. "More than two years, wasn't it? Still, there's time—"

"I think I should begin...evaluating a new approach," Cederic said. He sounded so distant that I wanted to cry for him.

"You should do that," Vorantor said, clapping him on the back again. "I'll have some suggestions for you later, how does that sound?"

"Very good," Cederic said, and left the room, his face completely expressionless, his head held high. Vorantor's mages were whispering to one another and I saw one of them smirk at a comment his friend made. Somebody laughed. The Darssan mages stood frozen in place. Audryn was crying. I put my arm around her shoulders and hugged her, though I wasn't sure why I wasn't crying myself—probably because I was so furious with Vorantor I wanted to hurt him more than I wanted to weep.

Terrael stood in the center of the room, book held loosely in his hand, head bowed. I steered Audryn toward him, took the book from his hand, and walked over to slap it hard against Vorantor's chest to get his attention. He reached up automatically to take it, but I whisked it out of his reach and put it into my pocket.

"Master Peressten is exhausted from his labors," I said, "and he's going to rest. Master Engilles will do the same. I'm going to take them to their rooms now. That's all right, *isn't it*." I stared him down, willing him to see my readiness to hurt him in my eyes, and he flinched and did a poor job of hiding it. He muttered something about "overwrought, time for everyone to rest" and I took Audryn and Terrael by the hands and dragged them out of the circle chamber and through the palace to the Darssan mages' wing.

Once there, I opened Audryn's door and dragged them both inside with me. I'd made a decision along the way that violated one of my principles, but I was tired and heartsick and it was a principle that didn't matter much anymore.

"Sit," I said, shoving them both gently at Audryn's bed. "Audryn, Terrael is hopelessly in love with you," I said, causing Terrael to go red and Audryn to gasp. "He goes out of his way to be near you because he doesn't know how to tell you how he feels, because you're older and never become clumsy or awkward or any of the things he's sure he's doing anytime you're near.

"Terrael, Audryn is completely in love with you." It was Terrael's turn to gasp. "And she's afraid to tell you because you're her superior, sort of, and she's in awe of how brilliant you are and thinks *you* think she's not smart enough for you. And I was going to let this go on until you were both brave enough to tell each other the truth, but it sounds as if the world's ending and I think neither of you should waste any more time. And now I'm leaving."

I took the Codex out of my pocket and tossed it at Terrael, who caught it, his eyes still wide. Then I turned and walked out the door, and shut it before I could hear more than Terrael saying, "Audryn—"

I ran the rest of the way up the stairs to the Sais' wing. I can't believe I didn't see any of this coming. My later self is probably reading this and laughing herself sick at how stupid I was. All I wanted was to help. That's what I thought, anyway. That helping Cederic was all that motivated me.

I stopped at the top of the steps and waited for my breathing to slow, then I walked the rest of the way to Cederic's room and knocked. There was no answer. I remembered a Castaviran wouldn't expect someone to wait for an invitation, so I pushed on the door and found it locked. So I pounded on the door and shouted his name, and when that didn't work, I unlocked the door and went in. The room was empty.

That made me afraid, though I'm not sure why. I think there was a part of me that wondered if Cederic might not do something stupid, if losing his life's work and being humiliated by his "old friend" might not push even him past breaking. But I couldn't quite believe it. Mostly I worried that it was a large palace, and I didn't know where to begin looking for him. And then I did.

I left his room and ran all the way down the hall and up the steps to the observatory. Cederic was there, standing where Vorantor had the first night I'd seen the room, looking over the edge at what lay far below. I had another moment of fear, but pushed it aside and walked toward him. He always knows it's me, though I don't know how. This time he probably heard me shouting. He said, "There are stones in a strange pattern here."

"It's a way into the God-Empress's treasure tower," I said.

"I suppose I should expect you to know these things," he said, not turning around. I didn't like the sound of his voice. It was empty, and bitter, and sounded nothing like him.

"I'm a thief," I said, trying to make a joke, but it hung in the air between us and then fell to the ground, disregarded.

He didn't say anything. I swear I thought all I wanted was to help him. To show him no one who mattered thought less of him for having been wrong. I cast about for something that would adequately express that feeling, and came up with, "Terrael feels terrible for having been the one to reveal that."

"Master Peressten is an honest man. He would not have concealed it, even for me," Cederic said.

More silence. It was as if everything I wanted to say was running up against the brick wall that was Cederic's humiliation. "What will you do now?" I said.

"You mean, now it is clear to everyone that I am a fool, and that I have wasted two years of my time and that of Castavir's finest minds?" he said.

"You're not a fool," I said. "Don't say that."

"The evidence was clear enough for Denril and the other Sais to see the truth," Cederic said. "I let my pride in my rank convince me I could find success where they could not. That makes me a fool. An arrogant, selfish fool."

"Don't say that," I said. "You *are* better than they are, and you made a mistake—"

"What do *you* know of it?" he shouted, turning on me so quickly I took a step back in surprise. "You, another of my many mistakes, snatched out of your world because of my carelessness! You simply cannot leave things alone, can you? I did not ask you to follow me. I did not ask for your patronizing sympathy, your cautious tiptoeing around the truth, and I cannot understand why you believe anything you have to say means anything to me!"

I remember every word of it. His face, no longer expressionless, his voice, raging at me, I remember it all. It hurt so badly that for one confused moment I thought he'd stabbed me, and I put my hand up to my chest and felt nothing but cloth. The fury faded from Cederic's face. "Sesskia," he said, "I didn't..."

I turned and ran for the door. He shouted my name, and I heard him coming after me, but I was already leaping down the steps and plunging through the floor as into the ocean's depths, into blackness, from one open space to another, anything to get away from him.

I ran through long galleries where the servants flung themselves out of my way—I have no idea what they thought, I probably looked like a madwoman—and through rows of tiny, sealed-off cubicles; across the floor of the mosaic chamber, where I lost one of my shoes; then into one of the God-Empress's kitchens, where I kicked off the other to be a mystery for one of the servants to find.

I wasn't thinking at all, just running, and passing through walls, and at some point I became lightheaded from all the insubstantiality, and I stopped, and I was here in the fur room. I tore all the furs off the walls and the counters and piled them in a corner, and I flung myself down on them, and I cried as I haven't for years.

Because I didn't know I loved him until he told me how worthless he thinks I am.

I swear it's true. How stupid does that make me? How incredibly stupid was I not to realize my longing to ease his pain had nothing to do with friendship? I realize, *now*, I've loved him for a long time. Of course I go to him for every little thing, because I feel better when I'm with him, happier and more comfortable than when I'm alone.

I trust him more than anyone, even more than Audryn and Sovrin —I don't know why that is, because in most ways I'm closer to them than I am to Cederic. It's just—I think it's because he makes such an effort to be...not truthful, exactly, but he never says anything without being certain he's not misleading you, because truth and honesty and accuracy matter so much to him, and that goes so far beyond truth and lies it's like a bedrock foundation I know I can always count on.

I love it when I can make him smile or joke. I thought that was because it's a challenge, like it was a game I was playing, but the truth is even though his smile is tiny and thin, his eyes get this amused gleam to them that warms my heart. And I love the way his lips quirk just a little bit when he's intent on a problem. I'm pretty sure he doesn't know he does that. The thought of it makes my heart ache more because it reminds me of how confident and powerful he is, or was before that bastard Vorantor took such joy in tearing him down.

Did I write once that his face was smooth and arrogant? I don't know why I ever thought that, why I never realized how handsome he is, with those crooked eyebrows and high, strong cheekbones and those eyes I have trouble looking away from.

I love him, and he despises me. He's right, I don't belong here, and if I *had* something to offer him, I wouldn't have fumbled around like that in the observatory, I would have known exactly the right thing to say. And I didn't.

This isn't the worst day of my life. Not even close. That was the day I came back with the medicine for Bridie, and she was lying sprawled on the bed, dried foam at the corners of her lips from her final seizure. Mam was passed out in a gin-soaked stupor in the corner so Bridie hadn't even had someone who loved her to hold her when she died. I had to pick up her little body and carry it into the street to find someone who would help me bury her. I was fourteen. Nothing's ever going to be worse than that day.

So I don't know why this hurts so much more. Probably because

I'm a fool, and I need to stop lying here mopping tears out of my eyes. The world is still ending. There might still be something I can do to —not stop it, obviously, but make it less terrible. Even if that means working with Vorantor. Even if it means giving the God-Empress the chance to expand her empire.

It's been about fifteen minutes since I wrote that last sentence, and I feel calmer now. I can think about this more rationally. Cederic was hurt, and angry, and I probably looked like an easy target, fumbling around and hurting him more with my awkward words. So I doubt he meant any of what he said. But how much worse is that, that he knew exactly what to say that would hurt me and didn't even try to hold it back?

Remembering makes me feel small and worthless, because I'm just as bad as the Darssan mages, I want him to respect me and think I matter. I want him to love me. And this all proves he doesn't.

I'm going to wait here until I'm sure my face looks normal again, then I'm going back to my room, I'm going to sleep, and in the morning I'm going to go to Vorantor and ask him what he wants from me. And I'm never speaking to Cederic again.

CHAPTER EIGHTEEN

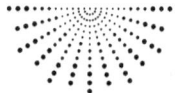

1 Coloine

It's amazing the difference a new day makes. A new month, a new day, new beginnings all around. I feel as if I could leap from the observatory and fly to skim the ground below.

After I finished my last record, I dismissed the see-in-dark pouvra and lay there in my pile of furs worth more, probably, than the Darssan and every mage in it, at least according to the twisted mathematics of the God-Empress's mind. I let my eyes go unfocused and my thoughts wander to more pleasant things, like how far Audryn and Terrael's conversation had gotten, and had they moved on to more physical activities yet—I still don't know the answer to that, because I haven't even had breakfast yet, but I feel too invigorated to sleep any longer.

At some point I realized I'd dozed off, and decided I should probably return to my bed. A pile of furs is nice to sleep on in theory, but in practice it shifts too much to be comfortable, and there are very few furs it's actually nice to rub your face against.

I passed through the wall into the spiraling passage running around the tower, and decided to use Aselfos's route to leave it. I was feeling reckless, and there was still a part of me that was hurt and humiliated and wanted to feel powerful again. I've found dangling off the face of a high wall with gravity trying to wrap its fingers around me gives me a feeling of power that's like nothing else in the world.

I was halfway up the wall before it occurred to me Cederic might still be in the observatory, even though it was full night, probably just after midnight. I clung there for a minute, wavering between continuing and going back, and decided I wasn't going to be deterred by the possibility that he might have more cruel words to hurl at me. But the observatory was empty.

I sat on a window ledge and looked out at Colosse in the darkness and thought about what it might look like when the disaster comes, whether Vorantor would be able to save anyone. My thoughts were still bleak, but I wasn't feeling nearly so much in despair as I had an hour earlier.

The wide passage was clear, with moonlight making the diamond pattern on the floor faint and blue-gray, and I amused myself by tiptoeing through the lighter patches until I reached my room, where I stopped, because there was light coming from under my door, and I hadn't left anything burning, flame or th'an.

I used the see-through pouvra and discovered Cederic was standing by my window, directly in the pouvra's line of sight. It irritated me that he knew exactly where to stand, as if he knew I'd use that pouvra, as if he were approaching me with his empty hands spread wide to show he wasn't a threat.

I thought about returning to the fur room for the night, but I was fairly certain that would only delay whatever Cederic had in mind. So I went in and closed the door behind me. "What are you doing here?" I said.

"Wondering if there is any point to asking your forgiveness," he said. The drapes were drawn, but he was standing at the window as if he could still see outside, with his hands clasped loosely behind his back.

"You think you deserve forgiveness?" I said. Once I was speaking to him, I no longer felt grief and embarrassment, I felt anger. I'd reached out to him in love and he'd struck at me. If he hadn't meant what he'd said, he had certainly known the exact words that would hurt me most, and how could he have done that if he truly was my friend?

"I think we need forgiveness most when we do not deserve it," he said. "I said things I deeply regret and I am—I cannot express how sorry I am."

He didn't sound sorry. He sounded dispassionate, the way he always sounded, and it made me want to strike him in some way, physically, verbally, anything that would break through that composure and make him feel pain the way I had.

"Sorry because you hate making mistakes?" I said. "Or sorry you haven't had a chance to correct this one?" He bowed his head, but said nothing. "I don't know why you care about my forgiveness," I went on, "since nothing I say means anything to—"

"Sesskia, *no*," he said, turning around. He looked anguished, he who never showed anything of his emotions on his face, and it startled me so much I lost track of what I intended to say.

"You mean *everything* to me," he said, "and I beg you to forgive my hasty words, because I cannot forgive myself for saying them."

There was so much pain in his voice I forgot I was angry with him. I forgot the pain he'd inflicted on me. I just crossed the room to put my arms around him and hold him, resting my head on his shoulder. He embraced me, first tentatively, then with a fierce grip as if he intended never to let me go.

His whole body was trembling with the effort to control whatever emotion threatened to overwhelm him, and out of nowhere I said, "I won't let you fall," and this time I knew the right thing to say. I held him as he shuddered, knowing he would never let himself cry. I don't know why he can't, or won't, or what happened to make him the kind of man he is, but I wept for him, my heart aching with sorrow even as it was filled to bursting with joy because he loved me, because he trusted me enough to let me see him in his weakness and despair.

I held him, and waited for the storm to pass, and every shred of bitterness I'd felt toward him vanished. It was impossible for me to hate him when he needed so badly for me to love him instead.

When he was calmer, he said, without releasing me, "Tell me you love me." It sounded more like a plea than an order, which made my heart ache for him again.

"I love you," I said. "And not because you told me to say it. I love you."

"Tell me I am not useless and a failure."

"You could never be useless, and you are not a failure."

"Tell me I still have something to offer this world."

"Vorantor's an ass. You may have to save the world over his objections."

He actually laughed. I had never heard him laugh before. I don't know if anyone ever has. "Denril hates me," he said. "I wanted to believe otherwise, but the summoning kathana nearly failed because he tried to take too great a role, thinking it would make him look important in the God-Empress's eyes, hoping it would lessen me. I had to fight him to keep it under control. And then I made him look like a fool, inventing that shield kathana as easily as breathing, something he knows he could never do."

"Inventing a kathana on the fly, or breathing?" I said. "Because I know he used to be your friend, but I personally would be just as happy if he forgot how to breathe."

He laughed again. He's laughed a lot since that moment, enough that I'll have to stop emphasizing it. His laugh is deep, and unconstrained, and maybe that's how he releases emotion and he'd forgotten how, under the stress of the last two years. I love his laugh. I love everything about him. And *he loves me.*

He loosened his grip enough that we could look at each other. "I cannot wish Denril dead, though I do wish I did not have to walk back into that chamber today and submit to his patronizing scorn," he said. "I have been too proud, Sesskia, and now I will have to pay for it."

"You still understand magic better than he does," I said, "and everyone knows it, and this will pass, and you'll make Vorantor's kathana work better than he ever could. And we'll save the world."

"Part of it, anyway," he said, and the bitterness was back in his voice, and I couldn't think what to say to make it go away. So I took his face in my hands and I kissed him.

I'd never kissed a man before, just my sisters, and my Dad when he was alive, and Cederic's lips were warm and shaped themselves to mine, and it was the most wonderful feeling I'd ever had. We kissed some more, long, slow kisses that made me forget I didn't know what I was doing. Then they were harder, more urgent, and then we were trying to take each other's clothes off without breaking that delicious, heart-pounding contact. That's a lot more difficult than I would have imagined, supposing I'd ever imagined anything like it.

Finally, Cederic removed my breast band, and we stood before each other naked. I had a moment of intense, self-conscious embarrassment, because my breasts are too small and my hips are too wide, and in general I've never been happy with the way my body looks. Then I saw how he looked at me, saw myself through his eyes, and I felt like the most beautiful woman in the world, because to him, I was. And his was the only opinion I cared about.

So, naturally, that's the moment I chose to blurt out, "I've never done this before."

Both his eyebrows climbed nearly to his hairline. "Never?" he said.

I *know* there's nothing wrong with being a twenty-seven-year-old virgin, and really, when have I ever had the chance to develop that degree of closeness with someone? Even so, I wanted to run away from his astonished gaze. "No," I said.

He slid his fingers through my hair to cup the back of my head and kissed me, gently. "Are you ashamed?" he said.

"Afraid I'll be awkward and terrible," I said.

He smiled, a real, tender smile, and kissed me again, and said, "You could never be awkward and terrible, and I promise to show you the truth of that."

I won't write the rest. I could never do it justice, and really, I don't think I'll need this book's help in remembering. It's enough to say Cederic was right, and if I thought kissing was wonderful, making love with him was so far beyond that I have no words for it. I cried a little at the end, which worried him, and I had trouble explaining how overwhelmed and happy I was, and how this was the only way I knew to express that emotion. So he kissed those tears away, and then he began kissing the rest of me, and we did it all over again, and it was even better the second time.

Afterward, I lay in the curve of his arm and played with the little dark hairs on his chest. There didn't seem to be anything to say, and I felt cocooned in the safe space that was our bed, as if there were no oncoming disaster and no Vorantor and no mad God-Empress and no—

"I wonder what Aselfos has planned," I said.

Cederic craned his head to look down at me. "I would ask where that came from," he said, "but I have learned it is better for me not to know the paths your mind takes at times."

"It was a tortuous road," I said. "It's only that I don't like not knowing what's coming. And I don't know how to find out more."

He held me more tightly. "Your safety has been uppermost in my thoughts since we arrived here," he said. "The God-Empress's interest in you is dangerous, and your nighttime wanderings put you at risk of drawing her wrath, should she learn where you have been and what you have seen."

"I'm at risk every time she summons me," I said. "And it also bothers me to know Vorantor has a secret plan we don't know about. I think I should investigate it."

He sighed. "Is there any point to me forbidding it?" he said.

"None. And don't think you can get away with threatening to withhold sexual favors, because I know you won't be able to stick to that threat," I said, poking him in the stomach.

He captured my hand and brought it to his lips. "I would never dream of doing that," he said, "when I could entice you to do what I want by *promising* sexual favors instead." So that was the end of that conversation.

Later, when I lay atop him trying to remember how to breathe properly, he wrapped his arms around me and said, "I had no idea, when I woke this morning, that this is how my day would end, humiliated by my former friend and then lying with you in your bed. It seems unreal, except you are so wonderfully tangible."

"As are you," I said, and I rolled over to nestle against him once more. He turned out the light, and we lay like that for a while, not speaking, and I was drifting off to sleep when he said, "I dream about you, you know. About this. I have dreamed of you so many times. You have been my foundation, even though you did not know it. My foundation, and my surety in the dark times."

It sent a chill through me, not of fear but of joy, that I might mean so much to anyone when I have been alone and disregarded for so long. And because he had opened himself to me, I wanted to do the same for him. So I told him what I swore I would never tell anyone, though as I write this it occurs to me this was inevitable, because from the beginning, even when I hated him, I have always told Cederic Aleynten everything.

I told him about the man at the fishery who never stopped watching me.

About the day he forced me into an alley in the warren behind the docks and knocked me to the ground, and tore my trousers and my undershorts down while he choked me with his other hand.

How he forced my legs apart, and I flailed at him and tried to scream, not that anyone would have come to my rescue.

How knowing that sparked something deep inside me, and I worked my first pouvra without knowing what I was doing and he burned from the inside out, burned to ash that filled my mouth and splintered bone that rattled down around me.

I was sixteen, and I had killed a man in a way that could mean my death if anyone knew about it. And even with the horror and the disgust at myself and the terror at what he had almost done, I knew I could not stop learning magic, because it was all I had in the world.

I told him all of this, and he held me and listened in the intent way he does, and said nothing for several seconds after I finished. Finally, he said, "If that is what it takes to make a mage in your world, I am surprised there are any of you."

"There have to be others," I said, "and I doubt most of them have been nearly raped. But there are other terrors that can make you fight for your life, or for your identity."

"True," he said, and held me closer. "My instinct is to protect you from all harm. But that instinct is wrong. You would not be who you are if you were not willing to risk yourself. Even so—allow me some fear on your behalf, please."

"It makes me feel loved, that you want to protect me, and even more loved that you know you can't," I said.

We lay together, not speaking, until I finally did fall asleep. When I woke about two hours ago, he was gone.

I'm ashamed to admit my first reaction was fear, followed closely by embarrassment that I'd misunderstood, that he'd only said those things because they were what I wanted to hear, that he didn't love me. I have no idea why I was so insecure. It was completely ridiculous.

I hadn't quite convinced myself to stop being stupid when he knocked, and entered without an invitation. "I'm sorry," he said, "but it isn't safe for me to be seen loitering outside your door." Then he looked at my face, and smiled at me with wry amusement. "You thought I'd left," he said.

"Because you left," I said.

He came to take my hand and squeeze it. "No one can know what we are to each other," he said. "If the God-Empress discovers it, she will use one of us to threaten or manipulate the other. So I could not be seen coming out of your room this morning. I shouldn't even be here now, but after you fell asleep, I went back to my room and lay awake in my cold bed cursing the God-Empress for keeping me from you, when you should have woken to find me next to you. And I had to risk coming now, so you would not misunderstand me. I would have stayed, if not for that danger, you understand?"

He sounded so urgent I nodded, even though I *didn't* understand why it was so important to him. He kissed me, then left as soundlessly as he'd arrived. So I've been writing for two hours, and it's time for breakfast now, and I'm trying to work out a way to ask Audryn if there's some significance to waking up with someone I should know about. But mostly, I still feel like I'm flying.

After breakfast

I had another shock just now, and I'm still working out what to do about it.

Terrael was not at breakfast. Audryn and Sovrin were at our usual spot when I arrived. Audryn looked radiantly happy. I hoped I didn't. I hadn't decided if I should tell them what had passed between me and Cederic. Sovrin I could trust not to give me away, but Audryn has an expressive face, and while she would carry my secret to her grave as far as telling anyone went, I wasn't sure she could keep her face under control.

So I decided first to tackle Audryn, who at least knew *I* knew something had happened. "Well?" I said.

Audryn grinned and hugged me. "Thank you for interfering in our business," she said. "I can't believe neither of us knew what the other was feeling. Who knows how long that might have gone on?"

"And they spent the night together. The *whole night*," Sovrin said with a meaningful smirk. "On purpose."

"I don't know what that means in your culture," I said, trying not to blush.

"It means they're married," Sovrin said, and Audryn blushed harder than I was trying not to. "Married, but without the public vowing, of course."

"Married," I said.

"It's symbolic of the commitment you make to each other," Audryn said. "Because you're most vulnerable when you're sleeping, and sharing a bed with someone means you trust that person with your safety, physical and spiritual."

"I see," I said.

"And every day is a new beginning," Sovrin said, "so waking together is like a promise to meet the future as one."

"But what if you fall asleep by accident? You have to be married?" I exclaimed.

"No, it's not binding unless you both agree," Sovrin said.

"Though there are a lot of stories, plays and poems and things, about accidental wedding promises. They're very popular," Audryn said. "Even if they're fanciful."

"Then I guess that's...beautiful," I said. "So what are the public vows for, if you're already married?"

"That's the legal commitment," Audryn said. "You speak them in front of a priest during a special ceremony and they grant certain legal and social rights. Who knows if that will even be possible for us any time soon, what with everything that's happening! But we didn't think we should wait, given how uncertain the future is. Like you said, Sesskia, we don't want to waste any more time."

"That makes sense," I said, but my voice sounded distant to me, because I felt as if I might fall over if someone breathed on me the wrong way. He sees us as married. He's pledged himself to me, as we'd say in Balaen.

And the shock isn't that he took that step without explaining it to me first, which bothers me a little—the shock is that it doesn't bother me *more*. That the idea of being married to Cederic, even so soon, fills me with joy. Maybe it's like Audryn said, that we don't know how much time we have, but I want nothing more than to be with him for the rest of my life, even if that's only a few more weeks. I am his foundation, and he is mine.

I don't have more time before I have to be in the circle chamber, or I would write about re-reading my early entries in the other book and laughing over how much Cederic annoyed me. I'm nervous on his behalf right now, wondering how he's going to behave to Vorantor, how he's going to reclaim his reputation. But Cederic is the greatest mage living—I don't think it's just my love for him saying that—and he won't let Vorantor's pride and jealousy stop him from saving as much of this world as he can. He might even manage to save some of mine as well.

CHAPTER NINETEEN

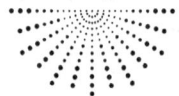

1 Coloine, evening

That was the strangest fight I've ever witnessed. Cederic won, but in a way Vorantor can't use to accuse him of insubordination. And that is because my husband—yes, I'm calling him that, and it makes me tingle all over when I do—my husband is brilliant, and frankly, Vorantor never stood a chance once Cederic decided to stop pretending he was anyone's subordinate. The situation is too serious for that.

But, back to the beginning: not only didn't I see Terrael at breakfast, I didn't see Cederic either. I didn't think that might mean they were together until Audryn and Sovrin and I arrived at the circle chamber and they weren't there either.

Vorantor was, and he looked so smug I think I could have popped him if I had a long enough pin. He was standing at one of the walls, writing something and holding forth to a couple of the Sais, and he caught my eye and smiled at me. It was a nasty little smile, though it didn't last long, and I didn't need the hypothetical mind-reading pouvra to know what he was thinking: *otherworlder, your side has lost.*

So I started doing pouvrin, fire and water at the same time to make great clouds of steam, which definitely caught his attention, though he pretended not to notice me. The other mages didn't have any problem coming to admire my work, and for about half an hour I demonstrated what I could do (not the secret pouvrin, but the other things) and we discussed possibilities for other pouvrin.

I need to give Vorantor's mages credit, and remind myself that about two-thirds of them used to be Darssan mages; they're all bright, and talented, and every one of them takes the coming disaster seriously. And it was fun to have an excuse not to work, since we didn't have Terrael to explain what he was learning from the Codex. Regan, one of the Sais, had some clever ideas about adapting the see-in-dark pouvra to enhance hearing, and I think he might be on the right track, so we arranged to work together during the rest periods Cederic made Vorantor believe were his idea.

So, as I said, we did this for about half an hour, and then Cederic came in alone and went straight to Vorantor, who pretended not to see him at first, then greeted him cheerfully, saying, "I was afraid you might not return, old friend."

"Why would I not return?" Cederic said, raising an eyebrow as if this were a completely absurd question.

"Well, you did seem upset about learning what a mistake you'd made," Vorantor said, smiling even more broadly. "I'm glad you didn't let your pride lead you to make another."

"No, Denril, I can admit I was wrong," Cederic said, pleasantly. "I should have listened to you from the beginning. I hope you won't hold it against me."

"No, of course not," Vorantor said, clapping Cederic on the shoulder. "As I said, I have some ideas for your research. I'm grateful you were willing to follow the God-Empress's suggestion and put yourself under my supervision. I think that's better for everyone, don't you? Given as how you're two years behind the rest of us."

"Of course, Denril," Cederic said. "Tell me what you'd like me to do."

At this point I was becoming suspicious. Cederic sounded far too affable, and I couldn't believe Vorantor didn't suspect something. But I couldn't figure out what Cederic's plan was.

Then Terrael came in, holding the Codex, and since he's even worse about controlling his face than Audryn is—really, I don't know how the two of them managed not to reveal their mutual feelings to each other—I could see immediately Terrael and Cederic were in collusion. Vorantor still didn't suspect anything. My estimation of his intelligence dropped by a lot today.

"Sai Vorantor," Terrael said, "I've translated a bit more, and I think it's important."

I glanced at Audryn, who had the tiniest wrinkle to her brow. "When did he have time to translate more?" I whispered.

"He didn't," Audryn said. "I can guarantee that."

"Master Peressten, thank you for joining us," Vorantor said in that patronizing tone he takes with the Darssan mages and especially with Terrael; Vorantor doesn't take him seriously because he's so young, despite Terrael's brilliance. "What have you learned?"

"Well, you know about Nialak's Conjecture, yes?" Terrael said with such wide-eyed eagerness I was certain Vorantor would realize Terrael was playing him. Vorantor looked mystified.

"He theorized mages have inherent abilities that allow them to manipulate th'an," Cederic said in a low voice, sounding as if he were prompting Vorantor.

"Of course," Vorantor said. "He...naturally, he was wrong."

"Only for this world," Terrael said. "The Codex reveals that in the time before the disaster, it was true. And it remained true for mages in Sesskia's world. Just not in ours."

"Oh, of course," Cederic said. "You are correct, Master Peressten, that *is* important."

"Yes," Vorantor said, but he sounded uncertain.

Cederic looked at him in surprise. Really, someone had to notice how unusually animated he was. "Denril, you see the implications, don't you?"

"I—well, of course," Vorantor said. "It's an example of how the magic reformed in each world."

"No," Cederic said, "no, it gives us part of the structure of the original kathana, of how they intended to reshape magic. Obviously they wanted to remove, among other things, the requirement that someone have inherent ability to use magic. They wanted to make magic more widely available. Sesskia's world contains the things they thought interfered with magic as it should be. I mean no slight on your world, Sesskia," he said, and I had to admire how he could speak to me without a trace of the love that had been in his voice last night, even as his seeming indifference left me feeling hollow. I nodded in acknowledgement.

"So we're justified in allowing that world's destruction," one of the Sais said, and I felt like slapping him with five gallons of water in the face, which is a lot more painful than you'd think. "Since it's essentially spare parts."

"I am sorry to contradict you, but I think perhaps you have not seen the implications of this. Our Codex-summoning kathana only worked because of Sesskia's magic," Cederic said, his tone of voice not at all humble. "Two kinds of magic in tandem. Magic calls to magic, didn't you say, Master Peressten?" Terrael nodded eagerly. "The worlds are not trying to obliterate each other. They're trying to meld."

Vorantor gaped. "Cederic," he managed, then cleared his throat and regained his smirk. "Old friend, I think you haven't quite learned your lesson," he said in a low, confidential voice. "Are you so unable to swallow your pride that you insist on challenging me? Again?"

"I'm surprised you could accuse me of that, Denril," Cederic said, "since it is your research that proves my assertion. At least in part."

He went to one of the boards—I forgot to mention this, because I can't read their language and that means most of what's on the walls is a mystery to me, but about a third of the wall space is taken up by Vorantor's explanation of what will happen when the worlds come together and notes for the kathana that will protect as much of this world as possible.

Anyway, Cederic went to the wall and used his sleeve to scrub out some of the writing, which made Vorantor protest. "No, I am sure you will agree when you see this," Cederic said, and then he began writing, and I won't even try to reproduce what he said, it was so far beyond my comprehension. But Vorantor stopped in mid-rant, and the other mages were nodding, and Terrael, who'd come to stand beside us, couldn't stop grinning.

"Did you plan this?" I whispered in his ear.

"Sai Aleynten found me this morning," he said, blushing, which told me Cederic had found him while he was going back to his own room from Audryn's, "and told me what I needed to say. None of it came from the Codex. There's no such person as Nialak. I think Sai Aleynten was down here studying Sai Vorantor's research early this morning."

"So he didn't get *any* sleep last night," I said, unthinking, and then wished the floor would swallow me up, but my gaffe didn't register with them, probably because they were paying closer attention to Cederic's explanation than I was. I want to tell them. I'd like to tell everyone. Damn the God-Empress.

"I am sure you would have gotten there in the end," Cederic said when he wound down, "but as long as I have agreed to assist you, I should no doubt do my utmost to aid this endeavor. Of course my skills are at your service."

Vorantor walked to Cederic's side in a daze. "Melding," he said.

"No shame in being wrong, is there?" Cederic said cheerfully, but his eyes were cold, and Vorantor flinched before he could gain control of himself.

"Of course not," he said. "How fortunate you were here to aid me."

"As I swore," Cederic said. "Now, if you'll direct me, I'm certain you understand *exactly* what the implications of this new development are, and we're all eager to hear what you want us to do."

Vorantor glared at him, but what could he say? Cederic had behaved with perfect adherence to the letter of his vow. "If I could make a request," Cederic added, "I would be interested in working on the problem of how our magic can work with Sesskia's to encourage melding rather than destruction, but of course the decision is entirely yours."

"I—certainly, since you seem familiar with the concept," Vorantor said, and began handing out assignments. He was desperately trying to regain control, but it was too late—every person in that room knew who was really in charge.

We spent the rest of the morning laying the groundwork for our new research, the Darssan mages and Cederic and I, talking about what we already knew about the similarities and differences between our magics. Except for Terrael, who followed Vorantor around, reading things out of the Codex to him in a cheeky voice just this side of insubordination, but Terrael is the one person Vorantor can't afford to alienate, not and still have the information in the Codex. Vorantor, of course, is designing (redesigning) the kathana, because that's where the glory is, but no one in our group cares about that.

This afternoon I wanted to ask Cederic what it meant, in practical terms, that the worlds were going to meld—does that mean Thalessa will join this world, or Colosse join mine? What will this single world look like? But there was never time, because after lunch he immediately directed us in practical matters, setting half our mages to creating th'an that would perform pouvrin and the other half, with me, trying to teach me to manifest th'an without going through the exhausting process I did for the summoning kathana, which would simply take too long.

Cederic asked Vorantor's mages, the ones timing the coming catastrophe, how much time we have left, and it's much shorter than it should be. Cederic looked grim, and said (to me, privately) that he believes our using magic is not just causing the convergence, but accelerating it. But there's no help for that. Without magic, the worlds will simply collide and annihilate each other. So what we're doing is both saving and destroying us.

So I'll have to ask him tonight, right after I pounce on him for deciding we should be married without consulting me first. I love him, and I think he's brilliant, but it hasn't occurred to him that one of us is capable of passing between our rooms without anyone being the wiser. Even so, I'm waiting until well after everyone's retired before going to him. But we're spending the whole night together. We might even sleep for some of it.

2 Coloine

We didn't do anything but sleep. In fact, Cederic was asleep when I came to his room, still fully dressed and lying on his back, mouth slightly open, snoring. I managed to wake him enough that I could help him take his clothes off, but I don't think he was conscious. He'd had a very full thirty-seven hours.

I made sure the door was locked, undressed and hid my clothes in his wardrobe—if someone came in on us unexpectedly, I could conceal myself quickly, but women's clothing on Cederic's floor would be bound to draw attention—turned out the light, and snuggled up next to him. It's nice, sleeping with someone you love, and I lay awake enjoying the feeling for a while before falling asleep myself.

He woke me in the morning, not on purpose, but by making a sudden movement that jostled me awake. I think he was surprised to find me there, which was reasonable. "Sesskia," he said, "this is far too dangerous. If you're seen—"

I worked the concealment pouvra, then went insubstantial and sat up, dramatically sweeping my hand through the pillow, not that he could see it. "I'm sorry, did you say 'isn't it fortunate you can be virtually invisible and walk through walls so we can spend every night together and not get caught'?"

He rolled onto his back, threw one arm over his eyes, and laughed. "Of course. I should have remembered. I wasn't thinking clearly yesterday, was I?"

"You were not, but I think you had a good excuse, what with everything that happened," I said, dismissing the pouvrin and lying down next to him so he could put his arms around me. "But you should feel ashamed of yourself, taking advantage of an ignorant otherworlder who had to find out she was married from someone else."

He groaned and held me tighter. "I truly was not thinking clearly," he said. "I assume you decided to forgive me, since you are here now."

"I decided you were worth being married to," I said, and then he kissed me, and we forgot about talking for a while. That left us with no time for anything else before we had to be at the breakfast table, not that I'm complaining, but it means I still don't know what will happen when our worlds come together.

It's hard during the day, him treating me with the same polite, self-controlled attitude he's always demonstrated toward me, me doing my best to respond in the same vein. I'm so eager, as I'm writing this, for the rest of the Sais to return to their rooms for bed so I can go to him, and not because of the sex, which is admittedly wonderful; when we're together, I can forget we have a deadline and very little idea of how to bring two worlds together safely. Vorantor discovered today there will still be destruction, even if we're successful, and while I was moderately amused that no one took him seriously until Cederic confirmed his conclusions, it fills me with dread.

Still no idea how I might manifest th'an the way I do pouvrin, though I don't know why I thought we'd figure that out quickly. I'm impatient, and worried that even if I do learn how, it won't have any effect on the final kathana. I refuse to fall into despair, though. That will do no one any good.

Time for me to join Cederic. If I'm filled with dread, I can only imagine how he feels, bearing not only this burden but the need to keep Vorantor in check and the fear of what demands the God-Empress might make on us, though I share that last fear. She hasn't called me into her presence since the disastrous tour of Colosse, and I know it has to come soon; I wish it would, so I could stop feeling as if a tidal wave were somewhere on the horizon, unstoppably approaching. I am so grateful to have the comfort of Cederic's support, grateful too that I can do the same for him.

3 Coloine

She's called me to attend on her tomorrow. I came back here to change my shirt, since Jaemis managed to spill soup on me at lunch. Small comfort that I drenched him in retaliation, but we both ended up laughing, and I was still laughing when I reached my room and found the note pinned to my locked door.

I panicked, and that's how Audryn found me about an hour later, sitting on my bed clutching the note in my hands, once again seeing the dead collenna master's face and unable to convince myself it wasn't going to happen to me or, true God forbid, someone I love. Cederic's assurance that mages are not easy to kill was no comfort, because I still haven't seen a mage perform a single martial th'an or kathana, except for Cederic's experimental shield that he's only taught to the God-Empress's battle mages.

She—Audryn—tried to talk to me, and I don't remember what I said, but she left about twenty minutes ago and I had to write something or go mad with fear. I shouldn't be this frightened. I can defend myself against the God-Empress's soldiers, and she never has those battle mages with her, who knows why. I'm stronger than this, I know I am.

It's been a while since I wrote the last, and I feel better, probably because Audryn came back with Cederic, and he knelt in front of me and drew me into his arms, completely disregarding Audryn's presence, and whispered comforting things to me until I could unclench my hands from the note and put my arms around his neck.

I could tell from how tense he was that he was not nearly so calm about this as he wanted me to think, but that, strangely, made me feel better—that he doesn't want his worry to overwhelm me, to suggest this is something I can't endure. And I can. I've faced things beside which the God-Empress is nothing. All she can do is kill me; she can't destroy who I am.

Finally, when I was rational again, Cederic kissed me, stood up, and told me to rest for half an hour before returning to the circle chamber, and that Audryn would come for me when that time was up. Then he left without glancing at Audryn, whose expressive face as she watched him leave was utterly stunned, but she went away without saying a word. I'm sure she'll have plenty of words for me when she comes back.

And now I'm going to lie down, and practice breathing quietly in between working the concealment pouvra and improving the speed with which I can do it. I doubt that's what Cederic had in mind when he told me to rest, but it will calm me more than napping would, because it makes me feel as if I'm learning to defend myself. He was right when he said once I could become a ghost if I had to, and I'm not going to be afraid of the God-Empress anymore. My friends can defend themselves, and I can too.

3 Coloine, after dinner

Audryn, with Sovrin in tow (I'm not sure how she managed to extricate her from the other mages), had *many* words for me when she returned, starting with, "When were you going to tell me about this?"

"Or me?" Sovrin said. "And how long has this been going on? Sesskia, if you're carrying on a secret affair with Sai Aleynten, we deserve to know!"

"We're married," I blurted out. That left them both speechless. I took advantage of the silence to explain when that had happened, and some of the details surrounding the event—not many, this wasn't the kind of conversation where you talk about your sex life—and they stared at me a little while longer, while I felt an intense desire to sink through the floor.

Then they both squealed and hugged me, and said things like "it's so wonderful!" and (Audryn) "both of us married on the same night!" and then they wanted more details, so I explained why it had to remain a secret, which they both completely understood and swore never to reveal the truth.

So then I ended up telling them about the secret pouvrin, which meant I had to demonstrate, and Audryn said, "I wish *I* could do that. Terrael is old-fashioned and doesn't want us to move in together until we've said our public vows, and he feels that means we have to sneak around to be together. But he looks so incredibly guilty every time he comes to my room, no one could have any doubt what he's doing. He'd be thrilled with those pouvrin."

"I'm still shocked," Sovrin said. "No offense, Sesskia, but it's hard to imagine Sai Aleynten unbending enough to have any kind of romantic relationship, never mind being married."

"Oh," I said, "he unbends," and *then* it was the kind of conversation where you talk about your sex life, and both of them were shocked I'd been a virgin, but not in a bad way. Now I feel guilty about sharing that with two women who don't need to look at their leader and imagine him having sex. But I couldn't help myself, it was so good not to have to keep it a secret. And when we finally went back to the circle chamber, neither of them gave any hint that they knew anything about Cederic and me that they shouldn't. I should have given Audryn more credit.

Now it's after dinner, and I can go to Cederic soon, and we'll talk about what might happen tomorrow, and what I might need to do. And I'm finally going to ask him what it will look like when the two worlds come together, if only to give myself something to think about other than the God-Empress.

I feel as if we're all fumbling around, probably because we are. Vorantor is desperately trying to cling to his authority, a task made more difficult by the fact that Cederic is still acting humble and deferring to him in ways that make it sound like Vorantor is even more incompetent than he is, without giving Vorantor any excuse to challenge him. Even Vorantor's mages go to Cederic now for advice. I'm afraid Vorantor's pride is going to drive him past the point of reason, but Cederic seems not to worry, and he knows the man far better than I do, so I'm not going to worry about it either.

CHAPTER TWENTY

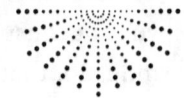

4 Coloine

It's been the strangest day. I don't know what to make of it. Especially the part where I felt I played a vicious game with the God-Empress, and may have won—it's hard for me to tell when I don't understand Castaviran culture well. Or, possibly, at all. I don't want to think about it, but I can't leave things out of this record just because they're unpleasant and uncomfortable and frightening.

But I have to get to the question of the worlds coming together first. After our lovemaking last night, which felt a little desperate, me wanting something good to hold onto and Cederic showing more than he probably intended of how afraid he was for me, we lay together and talked for a short time about the question of what the worlds would look like when they were reunited.

Cederic, surprisingly, said, "I don't know," and then went silent for about a minute. Then he said, "You said the place where Thalessa is in our world has never been successfully settled, correct?"

"That's what the mages from Helviran said," I said.

He was silent for a bit longer. "And the ruins all overlap," he said, but it sounded like he was talking to himself, so I didn't respond. Then he rolled out of bed and began dressing.

"What are you doing?" I said. I felt miffed at his abruptness.

"I am going to get some maps," he said. Then he saw my face, and closed his eyes briefly—he looked like he was wrestling with himself. "I am sorry," he said, "but I am not used to having to explain myself to anyone. Let alone to the wife I am about to leave alone in our bed for the sake of an academic pursuit."

"I think there are a lot of things we're going to have to learn to understand about each other," I said. "I've been alone for a long time, and I'm used to doing things without consulting anyone, too."

He smiled at me—a real smile, not that thin little twist of the lips, a smile he saves for me—and said, "I intend to retrieve some maps that may help me answer your question. I further intend to bring them here rather than examine them in the circle chamber, so I can make use of your perceptions. Will you pardon my abruptness?"

"Of course," I said, and got out of bed and pulled on my trousers. "I'll be waiting."

I didn't have to wait long. Cederic returned with what turned out to be small versions of the large maps we'd used the day he figured out I was from the "shadow world." He spread the Castaviran map out, then overlaid it with the Balaen map. "Where did you get this?" I said.

"I had Master Serelssor make copies of the large ones. She has an accurate eye," Cederic said. "Look at this. None of the major cities overlap any others. In your world, what exists where Colosse lies?"

"Nothing," I said, starting to feel excited but not sure why. "There are a lot of smaller towns along the river, but none of them have ever grown very large. Except Garwin, and that's much farther south."

"Unusual, since river traffic usually encourages settlement," Cederic said. "Can you think of any other cities located where Castaviran cities are?"

"None," I said. "What does it mean?"

He shook his head. "I don't know, and I—"

"Don't want to guess," I said, grinning at him.

He smiled back. "I am rather predictable in some ways, aren't I?" He turned his attention back to the map and touched it, right at the center of Colosse. "Though it seems as if each world has left space for its counterpart. And the ruins overlap exactly—that is the greater mystery." He touched three of the X's, one after the other, then let the maps roll up and stared off into the distance for long enough that I became impatient, and said, "What will you do?"

He looked at me, and his smile became teasing. "I will remove every scrap of clothing you are wearing," he said, "and explore your body until you forget everything except the feel of my skin against yours, and then I will make you cry my name—" at which point I pulled his shirt off over his head and kissed him, and then he did exactly as he'd promised.

Just remembering that makes my body respond as if he were still touching me, which I wish he were. But he and Vorantor are working late, and while I still intend to spend the night here in his room, I don't know when he'll join me. And now I have no more excuses; I have to write what happened with the God-Empress today.

No one came to dress me, so I dithered for a bit over what might offend the God-Empress least, then realized I can't begin to guess what her twisted mind might find offensive, and put on my nicest clothing that wasn't a dress. It turned out I didn't need to run away from her, but I still think it was a good precaution.

When I stepped out of my room, four soldiers in chicken helmets were once again standing there, waiting for me, and I stepped into their protective square and marched away. This time, no one had cleared the corridors, and people had to jump out of our way because the soldiers moved as if they had a walk-through-walls pouvra and didn't care who they used it on.

Most of the people we passed gaped at us, making me wonder if they knew who I was, or if they were just curious about anyone who rated such a guard. Or (this has only just occurred to me) they thought I was a prisoner being marched off for execution. I was too busy being nervous to pay much attention to them.

We went to the alcove leading to the public areas of the palace, and I thought we might be going to the throne room again, but the soldiers took me through a series of arched hallways, wide and tall enough to admit the loenerel but paved in a checkerboard pattern of black marble and green travertine, and into a breezy, light chamber whose windows all stood open.

Gauzy pale blue drapes billowed as warm air flowed into the room, fighting with the cooling kathana for dominance. Seven identical cedar wardrobes—I like the smell of cedar, but this was like being hit in the face by a warm, pillowy brick of the stuff—lined the blue walls. I don't have to describe the rest; the God-Empress likes monochromatic decorating schemes.

The God-Empress herself stood at one of the windows, letting the air blow her filmy white dress (more of a long, loose shift) around her. Her golden hair was loose and hung to her knees, and I had the beginnings of a pang of jealousy at how smooth it was that was suppressed by a memory of Cederic winding his fingers through my hair and telling me how much he loved its color and thickness.

And then, to my shock, I actually felt sorry for the God-Empress, who has no one to love her. It didn't last long, thanks to what happened next, but it's true, she's more to be pitied than envied. And more to be feared than either of those things.

The soldiers left me at the door, and I walked forward, not sure whether I should draw attention to myself or in what way I'd do so. But the sound of my footsteps on the smooth, caramel-colored wood floor alerted her, and she turned, shrieked in delight, and flung herself at me. I very nearly fell over beneath her weight. "Sesskia!" she exclaimed. "Isn't this the most beautiful, perfect day? I'm *so* happy to see you! And I know you must be so excited, but everything in its time, yes?"

She clapped three times, and a file of servant women emerged from a hidden door near the windows. "Clothing for my dear sister," the God-Empress commanded, and women flung open the wardrobes to reveal gowns in every shade of the rainbow and a few never found in nature, all of them made from silks or brocades or velvets, some richly embroidered, others studded with gems, every gown fit for a queen.

I stood, unable to speak, as women brought gowns to the God-

Empress for her approval. The God-Empress said, "You must tell me which ones you like! Isn't this fun, dressing up, when there are all these beautiful gowns? And then you can help me choose mine!" She began holding dresses up to my body, flinging some away, handing others back to the servants with a "Sesskia will want to try this on" or "Oh, this is divine, I simply must see if it fits me!"

Despite her words, I didn't ever have time to express an opinion, not that I cared which of these many gowns I ended up wearing. They were all exquisite, but completely impractical, and I spent my time while the God-Empress debated which was more my color, lilac or lavender (Note: they are EXACTLY THE SAME COLOR) wondering what she had in mind. Were we going to tour the city again, this time dressed like royalty? Or was all this simply for the sake of some elaborate tea party? Of course, the truth was far worse, but at the time I was innocently curious and wary.

The gown the God-Empress eventually chose for me was beautiful and, surprisingly, suited me well. It was silk, fitted through the bodice and waist to leave my shoulders bare, flowing softly to my ankles. It was pale blue at the top and became increasingly dark until it was midnight blue at the hem, as if the color had all bled from the top of my gown and pooled at the bottom.

I was admiring myself in the full-length mirror and thinking I should find a way to wear this back to the mages' wing, where Cederic could see me, when the God-Empress reached around my neck and said, "I know Mother would want you to wear these," and I nearly fell over because she had clasped several fortunes' worth of diamonds, not one of them smaller than ten carats, around my neck as carelessly as if they were a child's shell necklace.

For about five seconds I *really* wanted to keep those diamonds. Then common sense asserted itself and reminded me there was a good chance the God-Empress would look at me ten minutes from now, accuse me of stealing her mother's diamonds, and take them off by way of removing my head.

I was also trying not to think about what it meant that she clearly believed we were sisters today. The God-Empress has no family, having had all her siblings executed when she came to the throne, so my being her "sister" was no guarantee of safety.

The servants found me a pair of silver shoes with an impractically high heel that the God-Empress rhapsodized over and I could therefore not refuse, then I stood in the corner ("Don't muss yourself!" the God-Empress shrieked when I tried to sit down) and watched her choose a gown. "You must be the most beautiful today, of course, but that doesn't mean I can't be lovely, too!" the God-Empress exclaimed, and proceeded to choose a sleeveless gown of dazzling white, crusted with pearls in sizes ranging from as small as pinheads to more than an inch in diameter, that made her look more beautiful than ever. It was like she was going to the funeral of a nation.

Then the servants arranged our hair, brushing mine until it shone and then winding it around my head and pinning it fiercely in place with silver combs sparkling with more diamonds. I stood in front of the mirror again, admiring myself, and the God-Empress came to stand beside me, took my hand, and squeezed it. "I'm so happy for you," she whispered. "Thank you for allowing me to join you for this perfect day."

"I—it's my pleasure, and your company is an honor I don't deserve," I said, and she beamed more widely at me and squeezed my hand so hard parts of it went numb.

"Now we should go, and don't worry, everything's been arranged," she said, so of course I really started to worry. I've been thinking about this, and I've concluded there's no way I could have guessed what she had in mind, since our cultures are so different, but I should definitely have been more on my guard. Especially since everything she said suggested she was deep in some delusion. If I'd tried harder to work out what that delusion was, things would have gone differently—but, then, I'm alive, and so is Aselfos, so I'm not going to reproach myself too much.

The God-Empress linked her arm with mine and skipped—yes, actually skipped—out of the room, forcing me to skip along with her in those stupid silver heels. It's a miracle I didn't fall and take her down with me. When we came to the checkerboard floor, she went from skipping to hopping, always landing on the black marble. "It's not a moss day, can't touch the moss!" she said happily, and I stumbled along after her. Even so, I was thinking this was far from the worst thing she could do to me. And that was true, right up until we came to our destination.

The room was almost identical to the throne room, with the black and white patterned floor and the crystal lamps, though the walls were painted dove gray instead of mirrored, and of course there was no throne. Instead, there was a dais of black marble at the far end of the room, surrounded by men wearing chicken helmets and knee-length black tunics all standing with their backs to it.

The God-Empress slowed from her manic hopping to a slow, measured walk with an erratic beat: step-slide, step, step, slide-step, over and over again, and after a few missteps, I was able to follow her. It took several minutes for us to reach the dais this way, which gave me plenty of time to speculate on what would happen when we got there.

When we were within fifteen feet of it, I was able to look more closely at the men and realized they were wearing full armor under their poorly-fitting black tunics, which were thin linen stretched taut over the metal plates at their shoulders and chests. All of them were focused straight ahead, not on us, which was probably safer for them and for me; I was just as happy not to be noticed by them.

The God-Empress brought me up the three steps to the top of the dais and gently pushed me one way and then the other until I stood exactly where she wanted me, which was to my eyes a random spot left of center. She took my hand again and stood next to me, and we waited. My feet became sore, but I was afraid to shift my weight, because my mad companion was motionless, but poised as if listening for something.

"Don't worry, he won't forget," she whispered, and I was trying to decide whether I should ask her for clarification when a concealed door in the dove-gray walls opened, and more soldiers in black tunics came through single-file and marched toward the dais. Three men dressed in the costumes I'd seen courtiers wear when they attended the God-Empress in her throne room, but entirely in black, walked in the center of the line. I didn't recognize two of them, but the man in the middle was Perce Aselfos.

He has a handsome face, with a strong nose and deep-set brown eyes, but his appearance was marred by the beginnings of a large bruise on his right cheekbone and a split lower lip. He looked furious. The other two men watched him warily, exactly as if they expected him to bolt, or hit one or both of them.

"Oh, Perce, you look *wonderful*," the God-Empress said in a breathless, happy voice. "Come up here and stand next to Sesskia."

Aselfos glowered, but came up the steps and stood where the God-Empress pointed. The God-Empress took my hand, then Aselfos's hand, and to my surprise put them together. I clasped his hand automatically. It was dry, and limp. The God-Empress beamed, and took a few steps back. "What a perfect day!" she said. "Don't you think it's a perfect day, Sesskia? I'm so pleased for you both."

I realized what she had in mind, and jerked my hand away, or tried to; Aselfos's grip became suddenly firm, and he gave me a warning look. "You want us to be *married*?" I said.

I might have sounded the tiniest bit shrill, because the God-Empress's eyes narrowed, and she said, "No, Sesskia, *you* want to be married. I only agreed to witness your marriage vows. You're not having second thoughts, are you? Because I truly am *so* happy for you, and I would hate for this perfect day to be ruined."

I glanced at Aselfos again, and he shook his head, almost imperceptibly. My hand was starting to sweat. "I don't—" I began, then words deserted me.

"Marriage is a sacred act, Sesskia," the God-Empress said, waggling a perfect finger with a rose-enameled nail in front of my eyes. "You don't want to spurn God's blessing, do you?"

"I—" A delaying possibility suggested itself. "I am an otherworlder, Renatha, and I know nothing of your marriage customs. Would you explain them to me? Because I think making those vows without understanding them would be disrespectful to God."

Aselfos looked at me as if I were as mad as the God-Empress. "Of *course,* Sesskia, I should have realized!" the God-Empress said. "It's very simple. You and your beloved come before God—actually, most people come before a priest, but naturally I'm happy to perform the service for you, because you are God's choice—and declare your names, so God knows who stands before Her.

"Then each of you announces your intent to marry, and God asks you to name the man or woman of your choosing. And of course you say each other's names, because it would be silly to want to marry someone who didn't want you, yes?

"Then God asks some questions to be sure you understand how serious it is and tells you what the law settles on you as a married couple. And then you promise loyalty and love to each other, though you're free to say it however you like. And then you're married! Isn't that beautiful?"

It would be if Cederic were here, I thought. I was starting to panic. Obviously Aselfos had no interest in marrying me, and this was all some sick fantasy the God-Empress had dreamed up to "reward" one or both of us. I had no idea how binding this ceremony was, if neither of us meant it—and what happened if I swore marriage vows to one person when I was already married to someone else?

"You should begin," the God-Empress said, frowning, "or God will believe you have brought her here frivolously."

Aselfos dropped my hand and took two steps away. "I will not," he began, and one of the soldiers stepped up behind him and put one of those very sharp knives against his throat. He stopped speaking. The God-Empress screamed, *"You will do as God says or your blood will water this floor!"*

"Don't worry, Renatha, um, Perce and I want to be married," I said, reaching out to take Aselfos's hand. In the instant before I clasped it, the beginnings of an idea struck me. Just as our fingertips brushed, I worked the walk-through-walls pouvra and let my hand slip through his.

It felt *awful.* I could feel the blood flowing through his hand, felt bone grate on bone even though we were both insubstantial, and Aselfos cried out and jerked his hand up, making the soldier with the knife take half a step back. A thin line of blood beaded up along Aselfos's neck. "Our vows are rejected!" I screamed. "God will not allow me to take his hand!"

The God-Empress stared at my hand, then grabbed it and pinched the skin between my thumb and forefinger, hard, making me cry out. "I have done no such thing," she said. "Your love is meant to be. I would never reject your vows."

"It must have been an accident," I said. "We should try again. Renatha, please ask that man to release my love. There should be no violence on such a...a sacred day."

The God-Empress nodded, the soldier moved back, and Aselfos raised his hand to wipe the blood away. He was breathing a little too heavily and looked as if he were even more afraid of me than of the God-Empress.

I held out my hand to him, and he reached out to take it, and I did the pouvra again. It was still awful, though at least this time I was ready for it. Aselfos looked as if he were going to be sick. "Renatha, why is this happening?" I exclaimed, making a big show of examining my hand. "It surely means we are not meant to be married!"

"But I have decreed it!" the God-Empress wailed. She pushed me aside, ran down the dais, and snatched a longsword from one of the soldiers, who made as if to stop her before coming to his senses. The God-Empress raised the sword and swung hard at the dais; it made a strange sound somewhere between a clang and a thunk. "I am God and I will not be thwarted!" she screamed.

I felt lightheaded, like I was spinning, or maybe that was the room turning around me, as if the God-Empress's madness were infectious and I had caught the disease. "But it is this marriage that would thwart your will, Renatha!" I shouted. "Our desire to be married is wrong!"

The God-Empress turned on me and dropped the sword, which landed with a *clunk*. "It is," she agreed, her voice low and vicious now, her eyes narrowed. "Why would you waste my time like this, Sesskia?"

Now I was terrified. There were at least twenty soldiers, and I was certain I couldn't keep all of them at bay with fire, and concealing myself and running was a very short-term solution. "I...made a mistake," I said. "God is forgiving of mistakes."

"God dislikes waste," the God-Empress said, "but she is understanding of human frailty. And you *are* my sister, Sesskia." She turned toward Aselfos. "But he...he is nothing to me. Destroy him."

Aselfos had recovered from the shock of feeling my incorporeal hand pass through his, but now he went ashen. "I can't," I began, and the God-Empress said, "You will do as God commands, Sesskia, or I will be forced to watch these men kill you. God must be obeyed."

Aselfos's eyes met mine. He was pleading with me. I closed my eyes, willed him to hold still, and said, "God's command, then," and wreathed Aselfos in fire. He screamed, and I put the fire out before he could truly panic and flee.

"Renatha!" I shouted. "How dare you use your sister that way!"

The God-Empress took a step back. "What?" she said.

I drew myself to my full height and glared at her. "You dare command me to do something God has forbidden? This man is protected by God. Is this some sort of test?"

I had her thoroughly confused now. The God-Empress looked at Aselfos, who stood in the same place, shuddering, then at me. "But I —" she began.

I cut her off. "I only have power because God gives it to me," I said. "My magic has no power to harm that which God has protected. God must not be mocked. You are trying to trick me into betraying God."

"No," the God-Empress said, sounding once again like a child, but afraid rather than cheerful.

"I understand now," I said. "It *was* a test, wasn't it? A test of my loyalty? Did I pass?"

Confusion cleared from the God-Empress's face. "Oh, Sesskia, it *was* a test!" she said, and embraced me. "You are truly God's choice." She released me, went to Aselfos, and embraced him as well. "And you have been marked by God's power," she said, fingering the charred neck of his formal tunic. "I am sorry about the marriage. I know Sesskia is your heart's desire."

"My God, I will turn my heart elsewhere," Aselfos said, his voice barely trembling, his eyes fixed on me. When the God-Empress turned away, he nodded to me, slowly, as if acknowledging a debt.

"Oh, Sesskia, I do love you more than my other sisters. They never visit me," the God-Empress said, hooking her arm through mine once more. "We will eat together, and then you will return to Denril Vorantor and tell him God smiles on his work. I'm sure he'll find ways to make use of you."

"I think you're right, Renatha," I said, but my heart continued to beat like a rabbit's until we were seated in one of the formal dining rooms at opposite ends of the table, too far apart to converse, and I could concentrate on chewing and swallowing tasteless food. It probably was very good, but I was too keyed up to appreciate it.

I matched her madness for madness, and now I wonder if I've finally exhausted my stores of luck. The only good thing that's come of this morning is that I saved Aselfos's life, and he knows it. But I have no idea how that might benefit me. Maybe if Aselfos really is planning to kill all the mages, he'll spare my life. Or maybe he'll think twice before attacking the mages, if he thinks my magic is representative of what they can do. I don't know. I'm still jittery.

The God-Empress was back to being her usual cold, distant self by the time the meal was over, and dismissed me without any friendliness. She also didn't suggest I return to change into my own clothes. When I said, "I think you should have someone put this away for me," attempting to remove the diamond necklace, she said, with some anger, "Mother always liked you better," and walked away.

I don't know what to make of that. Either she's going to forget I have it, or she's going to send soldiers to retrieve it from me some day when I've forgotten I have it. So I walked back to the mages' wing, holding my head high and pretending no one was staring at me. That was hard, because everyone was staring.

I got as far as my own room before I realized it was impossible for me to get out of the dress without help. Everyone had already finished their lunch, so I had to go into the circle chamber dressed like the God-Empress's life-sized doll and submit to the exclamations of the women and the teasing of the men. Cederic went totally impassive when he saw me, and Vorantor said something about the God-Empress's favor; I think he was jealous, because I'm sure the God-Empress has never given *him* a fortune in diamonds.

Sovrin came back to my room with me to help me change. "I was watching Sai Aleynten," she said with a grin, "and he had a look in his eye that nearly made *me* melt, and you know he's not my type."

"I couldn't look at him and keep my composure," I said, and at that point I realized I'd left some of my favorite clothes back in the God-Empress's dressing room. I shook my hair out and put the silver combs on the dressing table next to the necklace. They're beautiful, and I wish I had some reason to wear them more often. Then I remember who gave them to me, and I wish I dared throw them away.

"So why are you dressed up?" Sovrin asked.

"I...we can talk about it later, so I don't have to repeat the story for Audryn," I said. That was only partly my reason. I was starting to feel panicky about how close I'd come to being married to the wrong man, and I needed time to calm down.

"Oh, if you have to be sensible," Sovrin said, pretending to pout, and we walked back to the circle chamber, where we both went back to work as if nothing had happened. Cederic treated me as he always did, with respectful indifference, and we made no more progress than before, partly because I simply could not stay focused. When I wasn't remembering the God-Empress's mad, confused expression when I challenged her, I was seeing Aselfos's eyes when the fire surrounded him. Th'an couldn't keep my attention.

Sovrin and Audryn came with me to my room right after dinner to hear my story. I felt guilty about telling them before telling Cederic, but I didn't even make eye contact with him at dinner before he and Vorantor went back to their research, and by that time I really needed to talk. We sat on the red bearskin rug, Sovrin wearing the necklace, Audryn with her hair pinned up with the combs, and they were perfectly silent as I told the story. When I was finished, Audryn said, "You are brilliant."

"I think I'm lucky," I said.

"That too," Sovrin said. "Saying marriage vows to one man when you're already married to another...even if neither of you mean it..."

"I was afraid of that," I said. "But I couldn't exactly tell the God-Empress the truth."

"At least you got something nice out of it," Sovrin said, running her fingers across the rows of diamonds. "And the dress is beautiful. You looked stunning."

"I doubt I'll get to wear it again," I said.

Audryn and Sovrin exchanged meaningful glances. "I think Sai Aleynten will figure something out," Sovrin said with a wink.

That's probably true. I almost asked them to help me put it back on, so I'd be wearing it when Cederic comes to bed, but as I wrote, I don't know how late that will be, so it will have to wait for another time.

It's nearly midnight now. Still no Cederic. I'm going to sleep now, and hope the God-Empress doesn't decide she needs her "sister's" company again anytime soon.

CHAPTER TWENTY-ONE

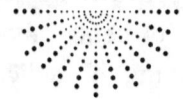

5 Coloine

Terrael has almost worked out all the details about the kathana that separated the worlds, though he told Audryn he had to guess at about a tenth of the th'an, since Veris and Barklan weren't mages and assumed there would be people around after the "success" to write it all down more fully. Or maybe some of those mages did keep records, and we just don't know about them.

Even though Terrael is uncertain, Vorantor's plan is to reconstruct the kathana, then invert it to describe the world as it used to be. I think of it as "reminding" the worlds how they're supposed to be united, something I won't tell Terrael in case he calls me a savage again. He ought to thank me for being so considerate of him, not forcing me to soak his head. It's so undignified.

We're having no success blending the two worlds' magics, and I'm starting to wonder if Vorantor is more clever than we thought, setting Cederic to work on research that's a dead end. Cederic behaves as if our work is important, and I know he's determined not to waste his time again, so I have to believe he knows what he's doing. He was collaborating with Vorantor again today, and then after dinner, and if he comes to bed before I fall asleep, I'll ask him whether Vorantor is actually accepting his input. Because I think if Vorantor can get away with it, he won't.

6 Coloine

I still have no idea what's going on between Cederic and Vorantor. Cederic's climbing into bed woke me briefly, very late last night, but he was up and dressing himself when I woke and we barely had time for a kiss before he was gone again.

It's frustrating, because I gave up exploring last night so we could talk, but I can't blame him for being preoccupied with the kathana. The mages have stopped trying to predict how long it's going to be until it all happens, because their kathanas give conflicting predictions, including some that say the convergence has already happened, which we know isn't true.

Vorantor and several mages, none of them from the Darssan, started reconstructing the first kathana today. Cederic didn't volunteer to help and told us to go on as we have been. Everyone was tense, and there were two or three discussions that nearly turned into arguments that Cederic had to break up, since Vorantor was ignoring everything except the kathana. The only good news is Alessa and Sovrin had an interesting idea for teaching me th'an that might work. No idea if it will work in time.

7 Coloine

Vorantor came into the circle chamber this morning looking far more smug than usual. No idea why, because he enlisted Cederic's help on the kathana, to confirm Terrael's guesses about the missing th'an. Cederic acted as if this were nothing out of the ordinary, but I'm suspicious. I hate that I have nothing concrete to attach my suspicions to.

The possibility of me learning to use pouvrin to manifest th'an is looking less likely every day. Cederic told us to focus our efforts on creating th'an that are based on the structures of pouvrin. I feel useless. Our discussion on the topic went nowhere, and I think some of the other mages were laughing at us, which made me feel worse. I don't know why I can't explain things better. This kathana is going to fail, and it will be my fault.

8 Coloine, very early

I was right to be suspicious of Vorantor, though I still don't know exactly what he's up to. I've decided to write all this down before taking it to Cederic, since there's nothing he can do about it now, but there were things that happened before I found Vorantor in what I'm sure are illicit activities, so I have to make a quick list before I forget the details:

1. snake, arch, fork

2. pictures (he's a good artist, maybe that's something all mages in this world learn)

3. why did he spit?

4. rhythm tap tap taptaptap thump

Before that: last night Cederic finally came to bed before I fell asleep, and though we were both too tired for sex, we cuddled together and I poured out my fears to him. I love how he listens like what you're saying is the most important thing in the world.

When I was finished, he wiped away the few stupid, self-indulgent tears I'd cried and said, "It doesn't matter if our mages succeed. The kathana Denril has invented has no room for your magic, and it is bound to fail."

"So why aren't you doing something about it?" I said, sitting up in outrage.

He pulled me back down to lie close beside him. "Because he is not listening to me," he said, "and there is a smugness about him that I do not understand. I may have the allegiance of the mages, but Denril still has control of the kathana, and he is relying far too heavily on the th'an Master Peressten extrapolated. He is clearly building the kathana to his glory without regard for whether or not it will work."

"I don't understand how he can do that!" I said. "He'll suffer as much as anyone if we can't bring the worlds together safely."

"I think he intends to make the failure look like my fault, to make me look like a fool, and then he will reveal another kathana, this one effective. This is my fault. I should not have humiliated him so thoroughly," Cederic said.

"If you hadn't, he would have found another way to strike at you," I said.

"Probably true," he said. "At any rate, I have asked Master Peressten to observe him; he can get closer to Denril than I. And I am studying the false kathana when Denril is not present, to see if there is any way to salvage it. If we make corrections...and don't worry that your efforts don't seem to be successful. Just keep working at what you've been doing. If it doesn't affect the kathana, it will almost certainly matter after the worlds come back together."

He kissed me, then said, "I apologize, but I have to leave you now. I have very little opportunity to study the kathana without Denril hovering behind me."

"But—" I began, then realized I was being selfish. "I understand," I said. "Just as *you* will understand I intend to go exploring now."

His face went impassive in the way it does when he's trying to control a strong emotion, then he said, "Where do you intend to go?"

"Somewhere you're happier not knowing about," I said, then, when he began to protest, I said, "I'm going to snoop around in Vorantor's room. If he's trying to get you out of the way, I want to know about it."

"You are correct, I was happier not knowing that," Cederic said. "Though I was afraid you were going back to examine those war wagons again. I admit to being curious about them myself, though I think it is less safe for you to pass those guards than any of the other places you have gone wandering."

"I agree, and I'm not going there tonight," I said.

"Which implies you will do so some other night," Cederic said.

"I knew you were brilliant," I said, and he laughed and held me tight for a moment, then released me to rise and dress. I did the same, then concealed myself and watched him move silently down the hall to the stairs before going, equally silently, to Vorantor's door. No light came from beneath it, so I sneaked to the end of the hall and checked the observatory.

Sure enough, Vorantor was there, sitting where he always did. It was too dark for me to make out any details, so I don't know if he had a note or not, but that wasn't important. I crept back to his room and passed through the wall, then used the see-in-dark pouvra and took a look around.

Vorantor—this wasn't new, I'd learned it the last time I'd been in his room—is neat and has almost no personal belongings aside from his clothing. I went through his wardrobe and found several ceremonial robes of different levels of splendor, though I'm sure I'd have been more impressed with them if I could have seen colors.

He also had a *lot* of shoes; I think he could wear a different pair of shoes every day for a week. He uses only one drawer of his dresser, for underclothing, and I poked through that in case he was a fool and kept important things there. Nothing.

There were no rugs on his floor, which is one of the places I look first when I'm searching for hidden documents. The lack of rugs almost got me caught, later, and I still wonder why Vorantor doesn't have such basic amenities. Though I suppose, based on what I witnessed in his room, he might have had them removed on purpose.

I checked under his pillows (he has more than I do), between his mattresses and in the frame of the bed, felt along the top of the canopy frame, and found nothing. Since I didn't know what I was looking for, I wasn't terribly disappointed. I slipped behind his bed, which had been shoved nearly all the way against the wall into a corner (that made no sense at the time, but I get it now), and checked underneath it and along the wall.

There was a niche very like the one in my room, the one that's practically an invitation to hide things, and I was about to feel around inside it, just to be thorough, when the door opened and Vorantor came in. I closed my eyes in time to avoid being blinded by his lamp. I was crouched behind the bed, so between that and the concealment pouvra I wasn't worried about him seeing me, but I went still anyway until the effects of the see-in-dark pouvra wore off.

When I opened my eyes again, he was removing his gold and brown "working" robe; fortunately for my peace of mind, he wore a sleeveless tunic under it, because what I do not need to see again is

Vorantor's very pale skin and bony back. Just one more reason for him to be jealous of Cederic, who is wonderfully handsome.

I closed my eyes again, in case he was undressing for the night, but I heard him taking things out of his wardrobe, so I opened my eyes again and saw him pulling a richly embroidered red robe around himself, and despite my well-trained self-control I nearly made an indignant noise, because he is *not* entitled to the robe of a Kilios! I don't even know how he got one!

I managed to stay quiet despite my outrage. Vorantor dressed himself with great care, unfastened his hair and brushed it and secured it again with a wide gold band. Then he knelt on the floor, took out a piece of black charcoal or chalk, and began drawing. I couldn't see a thing with the bed in the way, so I carefully slid out from that narrow space and moved to stand behind him. It was insane, I know, but I had to know what he was doing.

This is what it looked like: He drew a circle—the mages are all good at drawing nearly perfect circles—and then a much smaller circle inside it, centered on it. (I'm having to check my list from the beginning of this entry, because I'm already forgetting things. I feel very smart for having made it.)

In the space between the circles, he drew th'an, some of which I recognized from the Codex Tiurindi summoning, others which were unfamiliar to me. Inside the small circle, he drew a tiny picture, and he is an excellent artist, because it was obviously a war wagon.

Then he sat back on his heels, breathing hard as if he'd been running, then with his left hand began tapping out a rhythm, *tap tap taptaptap THUMP*, over and over again. He did it for long enough I almost started tapping myself. Then, at the top of the pattern, he leaned over and with his right hand began making new th'an, following the beat.

I didn't know these th'an, but they looked so much like real things it was easy to remember them: one like a snake, or an S with two extra curves, one like an arch that curled outward at the ends, and one like a Castaviran fork, with four tines. He drew these in several places around the outside of the circle, and then totally surprised me by spitting a great gob of saliva at the war wagon at the center of it all.

All the chalk lines went from matte black to shining gold, as if inlaid with metal, and the spaces inside the circle that didn't have lines drawn on them glowed with white light, not bright or painful, just a soft white glow.

And then I did something stupid. I inadvertently took a step back because the glow caught me off-guard, and I wasn't as balanced as I thought. My boot scraped across the bare floor (no rug!) and made a small but distinct sound. Vorantor's head whipped up and around, and he stood up and scanned the room, his eyes slowly passing over the walls and the floors.

I closed my eyes, which was terrifying, but I had a feeling if our eyes met, the concealment pouvra wouldn't protect me. So I had to stand there, motionless, blind, waiting for him to grab me and unable to do anything about it.

Nothing happened. Finally Vorantor took a few steps in the direction of the window, and I opened my eyes and tried not to breathe loudly. The chalk marks on the floor, and the light, were gone as if they'd never been. Vorantor had the curtains open and was looking out at Colosse (my room is on the other side and looks over the palace roofs).

I dared take a silent step backward; he didn't react. Slowly, one cautious step at a time, I moved toward the door—and then I stopped. I should have left, but I wanted to know if he kept anything in that niche behind the bed. So I leaned against the wall next to the door and waited. Eventually he got undressed (I kept my eyes closed for this too) and I waited for him to finish reading, then he turned off the light and settled in for the night.

I waited a while longer until his breathing slowed. I hoped he'd start snoring, but unfortunately that's one annoying trait he doesn't have. So I did the see-in-dark pouvra again, crept up to his bed, slid between it and the wall, then crouched low and felt along the base of the wall, wishing there were enough room for me to wiggle under the bed. Instead I knelt there with my face pressed against the cold wall, telling myself I was being stupid and there was nothing to find, and then my fingers reached the crack and I reached inside.

Something moved beneath my hand and made a rustling sound that in the dark seemed louder than an explosion. Vorantor shifted his weight, and I held my breath, but he didn't wake. The wall niche seemed full of dry leaves, or small papers—I teased one out and brought it to where I could look at it. Meaningless writing, but I was certain it was one of the notes Aselfos had sent Vorantor.

And now I had a dilemma. I *really* wanted to know what was in those notes, but I was equally desirous Vorantor not know someone had been snooping in his room. There was a chance he'd notice if one of them were missing. I crouched there with the note in my hand, weighing the possibilities.

Then I tucked the note inside the waistband of my trousers and retraced my slow, silent steps. Vorantor hadn't checked the niche when he came in, which means he likely only looks inside when he puts a new note there. I can show the note to Cederic, then return it during the day tomorrow when Vorantor is at the circle chamber, before evening when he might receive a new one.

That's my plan, anyway. I've been waiting for Cederic for nearly an hour now and I have no idea when he'll return. He can't go forever without sleep, though he doesn't seem to need as much of it as normal, sane people do, so eventually he'll have to come back, and then he can read the note and we can decide what, if anything, we should do about it.

CHAPTER TWENTY-TWO

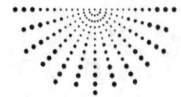

8 Coloine, evening

I had nodded off when Cederic returned and prodded me awake, telling me I shouldn't sleep in my clothes. The note was crumpled in my hand—I had to smooth it as best I could before returning it—and I told him what I'd seen and what I'd found, leaving out the part where Vorantor nearly caught me.

Cederic was very interested in the kathana I'd witnessed and asked me a lot of questions about it. I was surprised at how much of it I remembered, and I was able to draw the th'an Vorantor had used at the end.

"It was a transference kathana," Cederic finally said, "to move things from one location to another. The spit...it is a way to allow one person to perform a kathana that would normally take two or three mages. It is easy, but we try to train ourselves out of using it, not only because it is disgusting but because it often prevents a mage from moving further in his or her training. Denril was likely moving those war wagons. It might explain why there was no other exit from that chamber."

"But he couldn't have been doing it officially," I said, "or he would have used the circle chamber, and asked for help. So he was doing it for Aselfos."

"That is far too much speculation," Cederic said.

I thrust the note at him. "Maybe this will confirm it," I said.

Cederic read it quickly. "It is a list of items, most of them martial in nature," he said, "and a few that are unfamiliar to me."

"I bet one of those is whatever the war wagons are actually called," I said.

"Possible," Cederic said. He gave the note back to me. "But not proof, unfortunately. It is unsigned and Denril's name is not on it."

"I could bring all the notes here," I said. Cederic shook his head.

"That is unnecessary," he said, "and I don't say that because I dislike you risking yourself, because you could certainly do it tomorrow—later today, I suppose—when Denril is gone. This may not be proof good enough to accuse Denril of collusion in whatever plot Aselfos is behind, but it is enough to convince me of his involvement. But, as I believe I told you before, we still don't know enough to do anything but confuse things. And an attempted coup by Aselfos is not necessarily a bad thing."

"What I'm worried about is that Vorantor is planning something to hurt you," I said, "and I don't like not knowing what it is."

"This does not seem related," Cederic said, "and if you were not able to find anything indicating what Denril might have in mind, it is likely there isn't anything to be found. I believe it is nothing more sinister than trying to take all the credit for the melding kathana, and it doesn't matter to me who gets the credit for that."

"You said you thought he would try to make it fail and look like your fault," I said.

"Which cannot hurt me, since those whose opinions I care for will know the truth," he said, and brushed my hair gently away from my face. "What matters is that the kathana works, and we will deal with whatever else happens afterward."

"All right," I said, "but I'm going to keep an eye on him anyway."

"You and Master Peressten can protect me," he said with a smile, "and I will do my best to allow myself to be protected. Now, let's sleep, and make what we can of what's left of this night." And that's what we did. We probably won't be making love tonight either. Damn Vorantor anyway.

The day was just like yesterday. More Vorantor planning his kathana and keeping Cederic out, more of us (meaning the Darssan mages and me) failing to get our magics to combine. I didn't tell anyone what Cederic said about our efforts possibly being useless, which would have been cruel.

I ran back after lunch to put the message back in its niche, then went to the observatory to see if Aselfos had left a new note. He had. I wish I could read. Terrael would teach me if any of us had time. If the world doesn't end, that's the next thing I'm doing.

9 Coloine

BREAKTHROUGH!!!

I've been going back and forth from elation to feeling like a complete idiot, trying to tell myself there was no way I could have known this, when really it's that with one thing and another I forgot about the collenna. Well, no wonder, when all I could see for days was the master's neck snapping. And I know I told Cederic, but I can't have made it make sense or *he* would have seen it. Probably.

Oh, I'm so excited—everyone is, even though we don't know what use it will be—but I'm having trouble keeping my thoughts from flitting all over the place like a pod of baby dolphins, so:

1. Pouvrin and th'an ARE related.

2. We may be able to combine a pouvra with the merging kathana.

3. Creating new pouvrin is now more likely.

4. Using pouvrin in the merging kathana is unlikely no matter how successful we are, thanks to stupid Vorantor and his pride.

It was a dream I had last night that did it. I was touring Colosse with Cederic, and we were both in our underclothes (no mystery about that; it had been six days since we made love), and Terrael was driving the God-Empress's rose-colored collenna. Only instead of painting the th'an in the grooves of the brass plate, he was drawing them in mid-air, making it three-dimensional instead of flat.

And I saw it.

The reason it felt familiar is that it's the mind-moving pouvra! Missing pieces, and flat instead of multidimensional, but once I saw it in the dream it all fell into place.

I wrenched myself out of the dream and startled Cederic awake, and then I started babbling until he hushed me (that still works on me, and I hope it doesn't become a problem for us later) and made me explain everything more slowly. He went very still, of course, as I explained, then when I'd wound down he said, "But you never recognized th'an before."

"No, it all makes sense now," I said. Honestly, I thought I might leap out of the bed, I was so excited. "I've been looking at individual th'an, or maybe two or three combined, and that's like...like recognizing a person by being shown their heel and big toe. Pouvrin are far more complicated than that, have many more parts—many more th'an, is another way of looking at it. So on the lowest level, there's the single th'an you use to lift things—not to disparage your ability—"

"I understand," Cederic said. "Then the next step up are the th'an combinations used to power a collenna, and your pouvra is another degree of complexity beyond that."

"Right," I said. "And if the collenna th'an is similar to, but isn't as complex as, the mind-moving pouvra, that means there are individual th'an that could be added to it to make it do what the pouvra does. Which means I might be able to turn any large group of th'an into a pouvra by adding the right th'an to it!"

Cederic nodded, slowly. "But you don't know enough about th'an to know which ones," he said.

That sobered me up a bit. "No, and I have no idea how it can help the kathana," I said. "I mean, I could see how, in theory, a pouvra could be substituted for a group of th'an or a step in the kathana, but I only know the seven pouvrin, and even if we could use one of them, Vorantor would never agree to it."

"We need to look at Denril's kathana and determine which groups you can turn into a pouvra," Cederic said. "And you are correct that he will resist. So leave him to me. Tomorrow you and the mages will begin work on the collenna th'an to turn it into a true representation of your pouvra. That should be good practice for the real thing. And if I cannot convince Denril to cooperate, I can at least extrapolate from what I do know and possibly establish what th'an you should work on."

I think that's what he said, there at the end, because his hands were sliding under my sleep shirt and pulling it off over my head, and I was so busy kissing him while he stroked my skin that I wasn't paying attention. We really shouldn't go that long without sex again, though I have to admit it was probably more spectacular for being so long delayed.

Anyway.

Today I shared the news with our mages, and they were as excited as I was. Then we were all angry that Vorantor is still monopolizing Terrael's time, because he knows more th'an than anyone except Cederic, and what we needed was a lexicon of th'an that might be the missing parts of the pouvra.

But Sovrin had the clever idea of drawing out the collenna th'an a piece at a time, in colored chalks so it was obvious which part of the two-dimensional shape went to which th'an, and then letting me fill in the spaces as best I could with ink. Then she erased the chalk and what was left was...well, not much of anything that made sense, but she directed everyone to start looking up th'an to see if we could find anything that matched those shapes. We didn't have any luck, but morale is high because at last we have a direction!

Cederic, on the other hand, looked as if he were barely containing his anger. I saw him talking to Vorantor a couple of times, and the first time Vorantor didn't seem to pay him much attention and continued to write on his board the whole time Cederic was talking to him.

The second time, Cederic pulled him off to one side and they had an increasingly heated exchange, which ended with Cederic storming off (except, because it was Cederic, "storming off" meant he walked away at his usual pace but more expressionless than he'd been all day). It's only a matter of time before one or both of them explodes.

11 Coloine

Kathana almost done, according to Vorantor, not that anyone else would know because he's keeping it all to himself. Some argument today between Vorantor and Cederic over whether we should perform the kathana now (Cederic) or wait until the convergence is upon us (Vorantor). Vorantor's reasoning is that we'll have a better chance of success the closer the worlds are, and he has a good point.

Cederic, on the other hand, wants us to minimize the damage the convergence will cause by doing the kathana before the worlds are close enough to start disrupting each other. What he didn't say was he wants to have time to perform the correct kathana after Vorantor's fails. It wasn't so much an argument as a difference of opinion, carried out in reasonable and polite voices, which tells me Vorantor is definitely planning something. He's certainly not letting Cederic near any of the plans for the kathana now, telling him that he (Cederic) needs to work on his part of the research and not try to do everyone's jobs for them, in a supercilious tone of voice that to me sounds as if he has a nasty secret he's just waiting for the right time to reveal.

This is the closest I've seen Cederic come to really losing his temper—other than when he shouted at me, but that's best left forgotten. It would be easier if we knew when the convergence will occur, because it will take time to set the kathana up, and that's the best argument against Vorantor's position—we need to be better prepared.

We've identified two th'an that fit the pattern of the pouvra, but although I'm fairly sure it only needs one more to complete it, we don't have any idea which one that is. And it's only just occurred to me to wonder what this th'an will do when we've made it match the mind-moving pouvra—will it exactly duplicate what I do, or will it still have to be scribed on a surface?

I asked Alessa and Jaemis to give that some thought. It would be so much easier if we had a piece of the merging kathana to work on! Because right now we're starting to feel discouraged again; even if we make this work, there's nothing it can do in the kathana.

12 Coloine

Vorantor agreed to begin setting up the kathana, doing the same preparatory work they did for summoning the Codex. He was so agreeable I *know* he's planning something. Cederic was very polite about it, but when Vorantor left the room, he quietly wandered in our group's direction and whispered a few things to Sovrin, who's become the Darssan mages' leader in Terrael's absence—personally I think she's better at it than Terrael, who's easily distracted.

Then Sovrin gathered the rest of us and drew a complicated set of linked th'an I didn't recognize at all. She says it's part of the kathana and we need to see if I can learn to manifest it as a pouvra. It's daunting, but I had the mages deconstruct it and we'll see what we can do. At least we know it will be useful, if we succeed.

Cederic had me look at the maps a few minutes ago and asked if I saw anything strange, other than how the large cities don't overlap. It just looks like a map to me. There's not even a pattern to the ruins, even if you assume we haven't discovered all of them. Cederic nodded, but he stared at the maps himself for several minutes while I waited for him to speak. Finally he said something about it not mattering and walked away. I tried not to feel offended. He's been working harder than anyone.

13 Coloine

This was a *really* bad day. I'm starting to feel afraid, about so many things.

Cederic forced Vorantor to reveal his kathana. He was clever about it, put it in terms of "we'll all have to understand it" and "don't know how soon we will need it" so he sounded too reasonable for Vorantor to refuse. So Vorantor did—still smug, still completely affable, which made me suspect him more.

And it *almost* did what it was supposed to do.

Like Cederic said, it had no room for my kind of magic at all. Vorantor explained that my magic only exists because the original disaster created it, and therefore including it would just make the kathana unstable. He made it sound logical, but Cederic immediately countered him by pointing out that my magic was actually half of what had originally existed, and therefore his argument was invalid.

That's when Vorantor became furious. He accused Cederic of undermining him at every turn, of insisting on pursuing irrelevant research, in short, of breaking his oath. And Cederic lost his temper and rose to new heights of sarcasm, claiming Vorantor had abused his responsibility and misused the Kilios's abilities.

The fight went on for half an hour while everyone stood and watched, terrified to intervene or leave. It ended with Vorantor challenging Cederic's loyalty and insisting on a judgment, and Cederic saying he could take it up with the God-Empress if he wanted, and then Vorantor stormed off.

Except I was watching him the whole time—I already know how Cederic looks when he's furious—and I'm certain Vorantor planned it all. He wants the God-Empress to make a ruling on whether the oath was broken, and who did it, and I know he's got some plan to make it so Cederic is the one the God-Empress blames. Cederic is still angry enough that he won't talk about it, though I think part of that anger is that he agrees with me and despises himself for being goaded.

The other frightening thing is there was a message for me, in my room, my *locked* room, when I came back after dinner, sitting on my bed where I couldn't help but notice it. It was in the same hand as the messages Vorantor received from Aselfos. It frightened me enough that, after I thoroughly checked my room to see if there were any secret entrances I didn't know about, I went to the Sais' common room and made up some reason for Cederic to come with me. It was dangerous, I know, but *I can't read* and I didn't want to wait for Cederic to eventually come to bed.

We went back to my room, and Cederic read the message silently, then set it aside and stared off in the direction of my wardrobe. "Tell me," I insisted after it became clear he might sit there like that all night.

"It says, 'Three days from now the palace will not be safe,'" Cederic said. "It seems Aselfos is repaying his debt to you."

"Three days," I repeated. "No wonder Vorantor was transferring the war wagons. Aselfos is planning his coup."

"The convergence could happen any day," Cederic said. "In three days nowhere might be safe."

"And tomorrow Vorantor will have prepared his challenge," I said. "Anything might happen, when the God-Empress is involved."

Cederic put his arms around me, and I held onto him and closed my eyes, wishing I could shut out the world that easily. "Why isn't everything simple?" I said. "Why does Vorantor have to be jealous and the God-Empress have to be insane and Aselfos want to take over Castavir? I would like just one night where none of those things exist."

"I think I can give you that," Cederic said. "Go to my room and get into bed. I will return to the Sais' room and join the discussion so no one remarks on my absence, and then I will come to you. I only wish I could find you wearing that dress."

"Did you like it, then?" I said.

"I found the sight of your bare shoulders intoxicating. It was with great difficulty that I refrained from carrying you off to my bed and ravishing you," Cederic said. "But then I have the same trouble when you wear nothing at all."

"When I wear nothing at all," I said, "I don't mind being ravished."

So now I'm waiting here in Cederic's room, naked and writing all this down, and I feel less frightened. Whatever tomorrow brings, we'll be able to handle it.

CHAPTER TWENTY-THREE

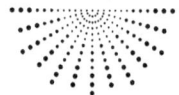

14 Coloine

Did I actually write that? That we could handle anything tomorrow brings? My hands are shaking so hard I can barely

Trying to stay calm. This book does no one any good if it's illegible. I'm going to write it all as it happened, and then I'll let myself think about what has to come next.

This morning I woke when Cederic kissed my forehead and said something about going to the circle chamber. I never used to sleep this soundly. You'd think sharing a bed with someone would make me *more* likely to be roused at unfamiliar movement, but no, he can rise and dress and be out the door while I snore peacefully away. (That was a figure of speech—I don't snore. I know, everyone says that, but trust me, if I were a snorer, I'd be dead several times over.)

I didn't remember what had happened between Vorantor and Cederic until I reached the dining hall. I was in a good mood thanks to a wonderful night with a wonderful man, but when Audryn said, "What is Sai Aleynten going to do?" it brought me out of my peaceful contentment like a gallon of ice water to the face.

"You probably know more about it than I do," I said. "I barely understand the oaths they swore. What judgment was Vorantor talking about?"

Audryn and Sovrin exchanged glances. "Only the God-Empress can determine if they've broken their vows," Audryn said. "Sai Vorantor will try to show her Sai Aleynten failed to follow his leadership. What we want to know is if Sai Aleynten decided to counterchallenge."

"I don't know," I said. "Can he?"

"Sai Vorantor hasn't been listening to Sai Aleynten for days now," Sovrin said, lowering her voice to a whisper. "Sai Aleynten can claim Sai Vorantor wasted the Kilios's abilities after accepting what he offered. If he counter-challenges and wins, he can request Sai Vorantor be removed."

"That sounds like a good idea. Why wouldn't he do that?" I said.

"Because the God-Empress is...not consistent," Audryn said, after nearly three seconds of groping for a word that didn't sound like a criticism. "She might see being asked for a judgment at all as an affront to God. Sai Aleynten might be better off staying quiet. It's not as if Sai Vorantor can prove his case."

"So why is he bothering?" Sovrin said. "This is a waste of time. We should be preparing that kathana. I swear I've felt tremors this morning."

"We don't even know what the signs of the convergence are," Audryn said. "It's your imagination. Sesskia, hurry up and eat, and let's go to the circle chamber. Whatever happens, we should be there."

I gobbled my food, and I wasn't the only one; if Vorantor did bring a challenge against Cederic, it would affect all of us. When we arrived, though, Vorantor and Cederic weren't there. We found places with the rest of the Darssan mages and resumed our work on the complicated th'an.

I wish I could write that it became instantly obvious it was a pouvra and I could use it with ease, but all I can say is it feels like it has the same shape as a pouvra, just with missing parts. I was debating with Kaurin whether it made more sense for me to figure out those missing pieces first, or just try to make it work, when Vorantor came in. He was dressed in one of his most ornate robes (not the red one, so he wasn't insane) and there was a smug gleam in his eye I didn't like.

He started ordering people around immediately, both his mages and the Darssan mages, but he ignored me entirely. I stood and watched and wondered, first, where Cederic was, and second, whether I should try to annoy Vorantor by asking for instructions when he clearly didn't believe I was necessary. I decided to watch for the moment, and see how much of the kathana I could understand.

It was another twenty minutes before Cederic appeared, and all movement stopped when he entered, because he was wearing the Kilios's robe and looked every inch the leader Vorantor wished he could be. He came to Vorantor's side—Vorantor was supervising a pair of Sais crouched on the floor who were having trouble scribing an inert th'an, it kept activating and disappearing—and said, "I believe if the two of you switch places, you will overcome your difficulty."

"You have no authority here, Cederic," Vorantor said. The two Sais looked up at him, then at each other, nervously.

"You made that clear, Denril," Cederic said. "I think you will find the Kilios still has a right to participate. And there is nothing wrong with the Kilios making a suggestion." The two Sais quietly began to switch places with as little movement as possible.

"Stay where you are," Vorantor said to the Sais. "Full of yourself today, aren't you, Kilios? Feeling the need to impress your lowly inferiors with the red robe?"

"Just a reminder," Cederic said, though he didn't say who needed to be reminded.

Vorantor turned on him, grabbed his shoulder and got right up into his face. "As if you haven't gone out of your way to remind me of it every day for the last four years," he snarled. The two Sais looked like they were thinking about crawling away. "You couldn't let it go, could you?" Vorantor said.

"You are the one who craved glory, Denril, not I," Cederic said. He was the only one unmoved by Vorantor's aggression; everyone else went tense, waiting for a fight to start. I began making plans in my head, ways to defend Cederic, ways to attack Vorantor and anyone who might want to side with him.

"I only wanted what was mine," Vorantor said, his fingers tightening on Cederic's arm. "And you always got there first. Well, that's not going to happen again. I'm going to ask the God-Empress to strip you of that robe."

"She lacks the authority to do so," Cederic said. "Release me, Denril. If the God-Empress comes, I will submit to her judgment, but until then, I will exercise my right to be present. Unless you believe you should usurp her authority in that as well."

Vorantor cursed (I think. It was a word that didn't translate) and shoved Cederic away; Cederic rocked, but otherwise stood firm, then stepped away from the circle and went to stand by himself at one side of the room. I nodded once at him in acknowledgment, then looked away toward where Sovrin was having a discussion with one of Vorantor's mages that had an edge to it that promised violence, even if only verbal.

Vorantor was pretending he still had control, but everyone kept glancing at Cederic, who looked bored. The only time I'd seen him look bored before this was when he created that shield kathana, and since I now knew he'd been ready to attack the God-Empress's soldiers if they raised their swords, I was really worried about what might happen next.

But nothing happened. People calmed down, once it was clear Cederic and Vorantor weren't going to turn their verbal battle into a magical one. The kathana began to take shape. One of the Sais had just suggested to Vorantor that it was time to break for lunch when soldiers suddenly filled the doorway, pushing mages out of the way until they could make a double file along the southern wall of the room.

I wonder what kind of person can serve the God-Empress as a soldier. Never mind the awful uniform; she's insane, and sometimes she's the funny kind of insane that makes me dress up in beautiful but useless clothing, and sometimes she's the unnerving kind of insane that makes her think she's God, and sometimes she makes horrible demands of her soldiers, like killing that collenna master, and how in the name of the true God can anyone justify doing those things? Is it just that they're afraid of her? Or do they enjoy being given freedom to indulge their own evil desires? *I don't understand.*

So they all lined up along the southern wall, and I was bumped by people moving out of their way (I was standing near the northwest point). Then the God-Empress came in. She was dressed entirely in white today, thick white satin with a neckline that plunged to her navel and no jewels or anything that might distract from the sight of her perfect body outlined in white. Was that coincidence, or do Castavirans associate white with death the way we do in Balaen?

Vorantor went to her and bowed, all very proper, and she touched the top of his head to acknowledge him and allow him to rise. Cederic approached to make his bow as well, but she ignored him, so he was forced to continue kneeling through everything that came next. "Denril Vorantor, you have asked for a judgment," she said, in that remote, formal voice that meant she was God.

"I have, my God. I accuse Cederic Aleynten of treason," Vorantor said, and I gasped, but since everyone else was making similar incredulous noises, I didn't stand out. Cederic raised his head to look at Vorantor, but said nothing.

"Your word is not enough," the God-Empress said, raising a finger. Her nail was enameled pearly white. Four soldiers came to make a loose circle around the group that was Vorantor, Cederic, and the God-Empress. Vorantor was even paler than usual, and his self-control slipped enough that he grimaced with anger at the God-Empress's words. I'm sure he thought Cederic's word would have been good enough for her.

"I have proof for you, God," he said. He reached inside his robe and pulled out a handful of familiar scraps of paper. I made a sound and Cederic's gaze flicked to me, blazing with the message to *Stay silent.*

The God-Empress regarded the papers as if he were offering her a mass of writhing worms. A soldier in what I thought was a general's uniform—in fact, the soldier who was Aselfos's co-conspirator—stepped forward and took the papers from Vorantor's hand, which was shaking. "I found these in Cederic Aleynten's chambers," Vorantor said. "Carefully concealed, but nothing is hidden from God's true servant, which God knows I am."

The general read the scraps of paper silently. "They are half of an ongoing communication between two people, one of whom requests that the other perform certain magical services in benefit of a proposed coup against God," she said.

"Cederic Aleynten," the God-Empress said.

"Yes, God-Empress?" Cederic said. I still can't believe how calm he sounded.

"You plot against God?" the God-Empress said.

"I do not," Cederic said. "Denril Vorantor is trying to discredit me. He has no proof of anything he has said."

"God sees how he wears his Kilios's robe though it is not a honey day," Vorantor said. "He believes his rank puts him above everyone, including God. He wants to take God's place."

"Untrue," Cederic said, and then he couldn't say anything else, because a soldier stepped up behind him, grabbed his hair to lift his head, and put a knife to his throat. I opened my mouth to scream, and he gave me another look, warning me off. I should have struck that soldier. I know I could have found a way to make him drop the knife without hurting Cederic. Everything would have been so different—

Yes, different. And probably many more people would have died. I —I have been sitting here, trying to figure out how I could have stopped it all. I hate that the God-Empress makes me feel so helpless. That she has the power to make men and women do evil things, or convince them they have to. I realize it isn't the same, but what's the point at which all your choices narrow down to just one? And what do you do then?

Well, I did nothing, except glare at Cederic so he'd know he had damn well better have a plan, or *my* plan would be to start setting people on fire. I'm not sure how much of that went through, but I could tell he knew I wasn't going to wait much longer. I kept glancing at the God-Empress, though it was hard for me to take my eyes off Cederic and that so-very-sharp knife. The God-Empress wasn't looking at him; she had her eyes fixed on Vorantor. "Would you serve God, then?" she said, her voice distant.

"With my life, my God," Vorantor said. I spared a glance for him; he was glowing with ecstasy, the poor bastard.

"As God's most high priest?" she said, still in that same distant voice.

"Until the end of my days," he said.

"You seem interested in your life and the end of it," the God-Empress said, and stepped around the still-kneeling Cederic and approached Vorantor, followed by a soldier. "God knows the count of your days, you know," she said. "All of them. And she is merciful." To the shock of everyone, she took Vorantor's face between her hands and kissed him full on the lips. Then she took a step back, leaving him motionless, his eyes wide, and made a little gesture with her finger. The soldier whipped out his knife and drew it across Vorantor's throat in one swift motion that sprayed the God-Empress with arterial blood.

Everyone screamed except Cederic, who probably didn't dare move. Vorantor's blood was everywhere. I couldn't stop staring at his body, which landed across the gold circle to obliterate half the th'an he'd so meticulously guided the mages in scribing.

The God-Empress's white dress was spattered with scarlet, her breasts and face were smeared with it, but she simply stood there, looking down at the body. "He offered to serve God all the days of his life," she said. "God alone knows that number. Do not presume upon God's gift."

She turned back to Cederic. "Kilios," she said, and the soldier holding Cederic moved slightly, making the knife press too firmly into his throat. Cederic let out a hiss. I took half a step forward, and his eyes went to me again, warning me.

And the God-Empress saw it.

She turned around fast, and her eyes had that terrible sharpness to them. "You care," she said, and the room went completely silent. "He is Kilios, but I think that's not it, is it?"

I have a feeling Cederic was trying to tell me something, but I was afraid to look away from her, the way small animals know not to look away from the fox. "He is Kilios," I agreed, wondering how I was going to get out of this.

The God-Empress smiled. Her gory face made the smile look like something demonic. "Cut him," she said, and I couldn't stop myself, I took another step forward and did the mind-moving pouvra on the knife, but I wasn't strong enough to stop the soldier cutting the finest thread of a line across the base of Cederic's jaw. I looked at him long enough to see his wince of pain, then the God-Empress's bloody hand grabbed my chin and forced me to meet her mad, evil eyes. "You care," she repeated.

"I care," I said.

Her smile broadened. "What will you give me for him, Sesskia?" she said. "Your heart, still beating? Your eyes, those strange green eyes, still blinking? What is he worth to you?"

I don't know what I should have said. If she hadn't slaughtered Vorantor in front of us, maybe I would have kept my composure enough to bluff. But it was too late. "Everything," I said. "I will give you everything for him."

The God-Empress licked her lips, and made a pleased sound. "Life tastes like salt," she said, and her eyes went unfocused again. "You always were the lucky one, Sesskia, yours is still moving and mine always fall down and break," she said, and gestured to the soldier to release Cederic, who stayed frozen in place as if he could still feel the knife there.

"Thank you, Renatha," I said, "it is a most generous gift I truly do not deserve."

"No, you don't," the God-Empress said. "I am such a wonderful sister! Don't let him break, I will be angry if you do." She walked out of the circle chamber, the long train of her gown smearing blood across the floor that her soldiers' boots made prints in.

The sound of their feet faded away, and still no one moved. I was focused on the empty doorway, and now I can't remember why—I know I had a reason, but it's gone now. I didn't come back to myself until I felt a hand on my arm, and Cederic said, "Sesskia."

I turned to look at him then. The thin line of blood was already clotting. "I don't know what I just gave away," I said, and then we were clinging to each other because it didn't matter anymore who knew.

"It was my fault. She saw me look at you," Cederic said.

"I let her rattle me. It's my fault," I said.

"I think we can agree it is actually *her* fault," Cederic said, and I tried to laugh, but it didn't sound right. But I felt better, with Cederic's arms around me, and the God-Empress gone for now, and Vorantor no longer able to interfere with the kathana—though I felt horribly guilty for that thought. I certainly didn't wish him dead no matter how much I'd disliked him.

Anyway, I was starting to feel better, so of course that's when the first signs of the convergence occurred.

Even now that I've had time to reflect on it, and discuss it with Terrael and Audryn and Sovrin, I still have trouble describing it. There was blurriness, at first, like coming up out of the water and blinking your eyes clear, only it lasted longer. Then everything went clear, but distorted; that first time, I was standing toward the northwest side of the room, so opposite the door, but it felt as if I were standing right next to the door at the same time.

That lasted for a few seconds, then faded, giving the sensation of being pulled slowly back into place. It felt like the much harder pulling I'd experienced when I was brought to Castavir. When I described it to my friends, they all said it was nothing like what they experienced, and none of us could agree on anything except the sensation of being pulled.

It's happened three more times since then (four times in the last nine hours) and there hasn't been any pattern to it, or any better warning than the blurriness, or whatever it is everyone else feels.

But that was later. Cederic and I held each other for a few moments after the convergence's warning passed, then he stepped away from me and said, "We no longer have any time to waste. Everyone gather your materials and your slates, go to your rooms and change your clothes. Return here with what you are wearing now so it can be burned. This room will have to be abandoned. I will arrange for Sai Vorantor's body to be cared for. Sesskia, take Master Peressten to find us a new chamber. He will know what we need. We will mourn Sai Vorantor later. For now we have two worlds to save."

It's a good thing Cederic had already established himself as the true leader of the mages, because no one argued, and he was right, there wasn't time. I don't know why our clothes had to be burned, since none of them were bloody, but I'm just as happy not to be reminded of what happened by putting on the wrong trousers one morning.

I changed quickly, washed Vorantor's blood off my face from where the God-Empress had touched me, and met Terrael at the stairs near the mages' quarters, and I took him to the empty wing of guest quarters. We didn't talk much—I think he was in shock, still, so it was mostly me asking what kind of room we needed and him explaining why he'd rejected yet another one.

Though at one point, while I was opening doors that all led to tiny bedrooms, he said, "So. You and Sai Aleynten."

"I'm surprised Audryn didn't tell you," I said, feeling pleased that Audryn had kept my secret even from her own husband.

"Not a word," he said. "Though it makes sense, in retrospect."

"Why is that?" I said.

He suddenly couldn't meet my eyes. "Um...Sai Aleynten became a lot more...relaxed... about two weeks ago, just after he proved the worlds were merging. Not that it was obvious, but now I know he was...that you were..."

"Yes," I said, which wasn't really an answer, but I thought it might stop Terrael babbling. Audryn doesn't seem to have any complaints, but it's funny how embarrassed Terrael gets about sex even now he's a married man; it reminds me how young he is. How young a lot of them are.

Terrael chose a room whose original purpose I don't know. It has a fancy wooden floor with no rugs, so maybe it was for dancing. I don't know if Castavirans have dancing rooms the way the King and nobles of Balaen do. It doesn't matter. We got back to discover servants had removed Vorantor's body and Cederic had locked the door to the circle chamber and done something to melt the lock shut, after burning away all the blood and the contaminated clothes.

Then we ate something—I don't remember what—and everyone followed Terrael and me to the new chamber and began setting up the kathana again. The second tremor—Sovrin's word, and yes, I know it's nothing like a tremor, but to me the convergence is like two overladen carts hurtling toward each other, each so heavy it makes the road vibrate, and I don't have a better word for it—happened right about that time. I think for a few seconds when it was over, everyone gave up inside.

Cederic doesn't flinch, fortunately for all of us. He drew me to one side when everyone was working and set me to doing pouvrin in a steady rhythm, all of them including the secret ones. "I don't want to frighten you," he said, "but there is a chance you will need to be attuned to the kathana the way the body-scribing mages were, in order to make your pouvra fit into it."

"You can't be more specific than that?" I said.

"We lost a lot of work," Cederic said. "At this point I am making up large sections of this kathana out of whole cloth. I don't want to tell you anything more until I am certain. But I can assure you that you will be in no more danger than any of us."

"Do you know how long we have?" I said.

"No," he said, and there didn't seem to be anything more to say, so he left me there and I did pouvrin until I could barely remember what they were for.

We've had dinner, and I'm in my room writing because I need time to myself before I join the others in the new kathana chamber. I don't know where Cederic is. I wish he were here, because I'm finally able to write what's really worrying me, which is that stupid Vorantor was so eager to see Cederic dead he gave away Aselfos's plan!

How could he let his lust for revenge, or whatever it is he wanted, destroy what might be Castavir's chance at having a better government, or at any rate a sane ruler? I'm not stupid. I've seen civil war—not on a large scale, but still war—and I've seen the results of revolutions, and it's vicious and brutal and only madmen enjoy it. But I've also heard something of what the God-Empress sends her soldiers to do, particularly what's been happening in Viravon, and I'm not sure Aselfos's plan *isn't* better for Castavir in the long run.

In any case, Vorantor's mania might have ruined everything Aselfos has planned. Unless that general is able to convince the God-Empress that Vorantor made it all up.

There's another tremor. If Aselfos is still on schedule—and that's a big 'if'—he'll discover the convergence has thrown all his plans into confusion. I don't know if it's writing all of this that's calmed me down, or if I'm too overwhelmed to panic because now I'm in danger not only from the convergence and a possible war, but also from whatever insanity the God-Empress might decide to rain down on me. At least I don't have to worry about anyone finding out about me and Cederic now. I wonder if sex will be less wonderful now it's not secret, semi-illicit sex. Probably not.

Tomorrow should see the end of it. It might only be a few hours from now. I won't write that we can handle whatever that is, because I'm superstitious now. But.

But.

If it is the end—I don't regret anything. There were days when I would stop in the middle of an empty road stretching from one tiny, xenophobic town to another and wonder why I bothered taking the next step. I had no family, no friends, nothing but the urge to learn more magic, and on those days I couldn't picture any more to life than that.

But it was magic that brought me here to a place where I have friendship and love and the chance to let my magic grow. I had no idea my life could be so full. I never thought I would know what it's like to love and to be loved. If the world doesn't end tomorrow, maybe I'll be embarrassed and tear this page out. But if it does—I know this record won't survive the disaster any more than I will, but this is how I want it to end, even if no one ever reads it. Here at the end, it was all worth it.

CHAPTER TWENTY-FOUR

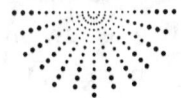

14 Coloine, an hour before midnight

It hasn't ended yet. I'm sitting in a corner of the kathana room, writing while the mages change the kathana's configuration yet again. There's a diagram of the original kathana, the one that caused the whole damn mess, drawn on the northern wall in thick black inky lines. The paintings that used to be on that wall are propped below the diagram in a long row. Most of them are landscapes of the same hilly country in early spring. I hope they're of a real place, because I look at them when I start to feel overwhelmed and tell myself we're doing all of this to keep that place from being destroyed.

Now I'm wondering why I'm not letting the thought of saving millions of people motivate me. I feel bad about that, but not much. Millions of people is too much for me to keep in my head; I can just about manage a picture of a grove of trees surrounded by daffodils.

The diagram is there so the mages can refer to it when they reconfigure their kathana. Terrael explained it as being like a puzzle: they have most of the elements of the original, but only one arrangement of those elements will do what they want. So they start putting it together until it becomes clear the direction is wrong, and then they start over. It's not something I can help with, and writing keeps me calm. So that's what I'm doing.

Vorantor was right about one thing—the original kathana needs to be inverted. Cederic says they can alter the key parts and get the new one close enough that it will be effective. He didn't sound convincing.

Terrael is in despair because he blames himself for not being able to read the minds of those long-dead ~~bastards~~ mages and produce the missing th'an. Cederic had to lecture him for a full minute until Terrael felt he was properly chastised, then told him to take a walk for five minutes to give himself a rest. It's funny to remember when I resented Cederic's ability to command, and how I'm so grateful for it now.

They've gotten a lot further than before. Looks like they're ready for me to take part. I wish I'd realized sooner what the connection between th'an and pouvrin is. With more time we might have been able to translate the th'an he gave us into a pouvra. Cederic is certain part of the kathana must be performed using my magic, but that's as much as he knows, and at this point we're just experimenting.

Right now I'm going to sit in the circle, in a spot that's been marked off by th'an, and go insubstantial when I'm told. It's difficult, because I start to fall through the floor, and of course I can only stay that way for about two minutes before I need to breathe, but the hard part is all on them, trying to scribe the right th'an in that two minutes. No guarantee it will work, but at least it's direction.

15 Coloine, two hours past midnight

I was encouraged too soon. It didn't work at all. I'm trying not to feel as downhearted as Terrael was. I think he knew how I felt, because he came to sit next to me when I'd retreated to my corner, before I started writing again, and gave me a board with a th'an marked on it in that dotted-line shape.

"It's a fire-making th'an," he said. "The fire-starting pouvra seems to be the one you're most comfortable with. This might help clear your head, and maybe you can work out how it intersects with your pouvra."

He gave me some chalk and then went back to the circle. And he was right; it does help clear my head, even though I have no hope of learning to scribe the th'an in just a few hours. So I practice with it for half an hour, and then I go back to trying to make that complicated th'an work. It's something to do when there's nothing to write, like now.

15 Coloine, half an hour later

Had to take another turn in the kathana circle, this time manifesting the binding rune in fire. That was effective, but Cederic says there's no way for them to know when or where in the kathana to use it. That frustrates me more than failure would. Cederic said, "It's progress," and then he kissed me in full view of everyone, which made me happy. He's going to solve this problem.

I have faith in him and in all our mages—no more Vorantor mages and Darssan mages, all one group with our squabbles set aside. I'm going to practice Terrael's th'an again for a bit. It's as soothing as writing, at least for short periods. Then it gets tedious, and I go back to my futile efforts at creating a new pouvra.

Another tremor. There's no way to predict when one will happen, they're still coming at irregular intervals, but they're definitely coming closer together.

15 Coloine, dawn

I can't believe it. I'm starting to feel the pouvra come together! The problem is it doesn't seem to do anything. Sovrin told me it's another binding th'an, but I think—this is just my instinct—it won't actually work unless there are specific things for it to bind. And I can't tell if it's supposed to work through my body, or around it—there's a lot about it I don't know. But Cederic closed his eyes and breathed out a long sigh of relief when I told him, so I'm accomplishing something. I'm trying not to feel too relaxed, because I haven't succeeded yet.

15 Coloine, breakfast (not that anyone's able to eat)

Something strange happened. Cederic came to sit with me for a few minutes—I'm glad he's realized his going entirely without rest helps no one—and I leaned against his shoulder and pretended the world wasn't about to end. He smells of fresh linen and, faintly, of old paper, which is one of my favorite smells, and now it's doubly so. I had Terrael's board in my lap, and Cederic picked it up and twirled it in his fingers, just for something to do, and then he stopped abruptly and held it at arm's length to look at it.

Then he swore, and leaped up, and ran out of the room before I could ask him what was wrong. He took the board with him, whether because it was important or because he forgot he was holding it, I don't know, but it left me with nothing but this book to entertain myself.

If things weren't so urgent, the way everyone stopped in mid-step when Cederic left would be funny. One of the Sais rallied them, but it's clear everyone knows if they're going to discover a kathana that works, it will be thanks to Cederic's genius, so him tearing out of here like he's being chased left everyone bereft, including me, since everyone else's leaning on him is metaphorical, and I nearly fell over when he got up. So it must be important.

Nothing else to write. I've accomplished as much as I can with the pouvra without actually taking part in the kathana. I don't dare wander over to see what the mages are doing and possibly interrupt them. I'm going to look at the painting and think about what spring will look like. It's six months away, according to my count, though I've said I don't know if Castaviran seasons match up with mine. But how could they not?

Then again, how can the desert around the Darssan be grassy plains in my world? I don't know. It all seems pointless when it's possible both plains and desert might be destroyed.

15 Coloine, twenty minutes later

We won't be destroyed. I can't believe it was sitting in Cederic's room this whole time. It seems obvious now, but I think—no, I should start at the beginning.

Cederic came racing back a few minutes ago, clutching some large papers that turned out to be our maps. He practically fell to his knees in front of me, spread them out one atop the other, and said, "There's a pattern. I didn't see it because I was so obsessed with the missing th'an—you won't see it, Sesskia, you don't know the th'an, but—come and look at this, everyone, and tell me what you see!"

It's true, I was mystified, but Terrael came forward, rotated the maps to a sideways position, and said, "It's the unlocking th'an."

"The lines are not quite perfect," Cederic said, "but even with Sesskia's information, we knew we did not know the location of all the ruins. Knowing what th'an it is lets us extrapolate the position of the remaining ones." He took my chalk and drew a th'an quickly, connecting the marks on the map and interrupting the line once so it wouldn't activate. It's an elaborate shape, and it's surprising anyone could look at those X's and see that pattern, but I think desperation makes everything look different.

"So what does it mean?" asked one of the mages.

"It means they bound the land to the kathana," Cederic said. "It explains why the ruins are all so uniform, and so small; they were built specifically for that purpose. That is why Master Peressten was unable to identify the missing parts of their kathana. The ruins are the missing parts."

He stood and brushed off his knees. "Sai Howert, take half our mages and clear the circle for a binding kathana. The rest of you, copy these marks to your boards—be accurate, but don't worry about perfection. We need to connect these ruins in a new th'an. You are looking for anything that suggests union or coming together. Master Peressten, with me, please."

He walked away without waiting for Terrael to respond. I followed him, Terrael trailing behind, to where the books of the Darssan library were piled on a couple of tables scrounged from nearby rooms.

"For this to work, we need three things," Cederic told us—well, he told Terrael, and I listened. "We need a binding kathana—"

The room stretched and contracted with another tremor. Cederic fell silent until it passed. They feel like they're lasting longer as well as coming more frequently now. "We need a binding kathana," Cederic said, "one based on the original unlocking kathana. Sesskia—"

"It's not the right one, is it?" I said, and I can't describe how discouraged I was. "The one I've been working on."

Cederic shook his head and laid his hand along my cheek. "It was not wasted effort," he said. "We still need your magic in the kathana. The binding th'an are simple; you may be able to learn them in time. Master Peressten, we also need to draw a new th'an that connects all the ruins, or as many as we can find. And we need some way to attune our kathana to the landscape, to the ruins themselves, in effect scribing th'an on them the way Sesskia draws on her board."

He drew in a deep breath, and in a lower voice said, "And I have no knowledge of how to do that. I need you to go through the books I cannot read, looking for some hint to that secret."

"Sai Aleynten," Terrael said, "that could be impossible. We've been through these books dozens of times. I've never seen anything like that."

"You saw that th'an on the map when no one else did," Cederic said. "We need to look at these books with a fresh eye. And pray what we need is not in one of those books we cannot read."

Terrael nodded. "I'll—" Another tremor. "—do my best," he said. "And I already have an idea." He began shifting books on the table, making a neat stack, because even in this nightmare he's still Terrael.

I pulled Cederic to the side, and said, "You know there's no way I can learn a new th'an in time. What can I *really* do?"

Cederic sighed. "If we cannot find a way to put your magic into this kathana, everything else we do may be for nothing. And I see no way to accomplish that. What do *you* see?"

I had to shake my head and say, "I don't know."

"Then practice pouvrin," he said, "and think, and allow me more time to consider. We still do not know what Aselfos has in mind, nor what the God-Empress might do. If it comes to it, you may be defending us against one or both of them."

"I hope it doesn't come to that," I said, and went to stand near the door. I practiced pouvrin until my eyes and my chest ached, then rested and wrote for a bit, then back to pouvrin. My fire-summoning pouvra is more effective now; I think I could encircle five people at once, and I'm steeling myself to burn flesh. My mind-moving pouvra isn't ever going to be strong enough to hurt anyone, and though I think I could drown someone by holding a globe of water around their head, that's not practical in a fight, where the person might have fifteen friends trying to kill me at the same time.

But the concealment pouvra, and the walk-through-walls one—I figured out how to turn them outward, so I can work them on another person so long as I'm touching him or her. If we weren't all so busy, I'd celebrate, but there's no time. I'm not sure how useful that will be, particularly turning someone else virtually invisible, but it's something.

Cederic and Terrael are having an intense discussion, Cederic gesturing with large swoops and Terrael shaking his head. It reminds me of the first time I saw them interact, when Terrael was trying to convince Cederic to use the aeden on me, and how much I disliked Cederic then. That seems so long ago, but really it was less than two months. Two months to go from hating someone to loving him—I think I must have been more lonely than I knew. I hope I didn't

I was going to write "I hope I didn't just attach myself to Cederic because I was desperate for love," but I feel certain it's not true. Maybe we haven't known each other very long, and maybe that means our marriage is doomed, but I don't think so. True, we still have so much to learn about each other, and I'm sure there are things I'll do wrong. I don't want to be like Mam, blaming Dad for every little thing that went wrong and for not being a good provider, even though he went out on that boat every night and brought home a good catch, then had to sell it himself because Mam was unreliable. But I feel more myself than I ever have when I'm with Cederic. I don't want the world to end just as my life is finally beginning.

Another tremor. Cederic is pointing at a book and now Terrael is nodding. They've got their boards out and they're drawing. I can't believe they found anything useful—we weren't able to bring the entire Darssan library here, so what are the odds one of those books would have the right th'an? No, more likely the two geniuses saw potential in something completely unrelated. I should be practicing, but I can't stand the tension, I have to see if they've figured it out. I don't want to disturb them, though, so all I can do is stand over here by the door

I hear someone coming. A lot of someones. Boots.

It's soldiers. Aselfos or the God-Empress, I don't know, but it can't be good. I've called out a warning and now I'm going to stand where I'm the first thing anyone entering this room sees. Putting the book away now and hoping this isn't my last record.

CHAPTER TWENTY-FIVE

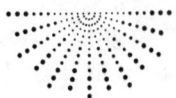

unknown, could be 15 Coloine still

Now that I've recovered from the kathana, I'm going to write everything down because, as is often the case, writing helps me stay sane when everything around me is confusion and strangeness. And then I'll figure out what to do next.

As I wrote, I went to stand where I was the first thing visible to anyone coming through the door. Soldiers entered, silent except for the sound of their boots on the fancy wooden floor. It was eerily like the way they'd made a double file in the circle chamber, just before Vorantor was killed, and I think everyone felt the same way, because the mages all drew in together, into a loose clump near the middle of the room that put them behind me. Cederic came to stand beside me, not touching me, but his presence was a comfort—not enough to dispel all my anxiety, but still a comfort.

For a few seconds more, I held out hope it was Aselfos, that I'd be able to reason with him or at least threaten him with more of the walk-through-walls pouvra. Then the God-Empress came through the door, and the hard, cruel look on her face dispelled any hope this might end well for anyone. I tried not to look as despairing as I felt and waited, because I didn't think I had any chance at tricking or manipulating her with words.

"Sesskia," the God-Empress said, "you are God's choice. Do you understand what that means?"

"No, Renatha, I don't," I said.

"Your magic is God's gift, direct from her without need for all this scribbling," the God-Empress said. "You should have been most high priestess from the beginning."

"Thank you, Renatha, it is a gift—" I began.

"Do not waste my time, Sesskia, we all know no one deserves my gifts," the God-Empress said. "And I have been especially generous with you. You are God's choice. You will stand by God's side today."

"I—all right, Renatha," I said, though I could sense Cederic going tense beside me. "How can I serve God?"

The God-Empress smiled. "We have rebellion," she said. "There are fools who have chosen to fight against God. My army is going to war, Sesskia, and you will use your magic against the enemy, you and every mage here. Bring what you need, scribblers, and we'll leave this place now."

"The convergence is upon us," Cederic said. "If we do not perform this kathana now, the world will face destruction that will make your battle irrelevant."

"Your excuses are what's irrelevant, Cederic Aleynten," the God-Empress said. "God will not allow her world to be destroyed. Do you really want to disobey God?"

"You must surely have felt the signs of the convergence," Cederic said. "We need more time."

The God-Empress turned her mad eyes on me. "You gave me everything in exchange for him," she said. "Command him. You are God's choice."

"No," I said. "And he wouldn't obey that command anyway."

I don't think anyone's said no to the God-Empress in her life. For a moment, her eyes went wide and her jaw slack. Then she said, "Take them."

I was too slow. So were the mages. Before I had time to do more than circle the God-Empress with fire, several of our mages were grabbed by soldiers and pinned against the walls or held tight with knives to their throats or hearts. One of them was Audryn.

Terrael brought his slate up and raised his stubby piece of chalk as if it were one of those sharp knives, and I shouted, "No!" though I had no idea what he intended to do with those unlikely weapons. "Let them go, Renatha," I said, making the fire blaze hotter.

"Burn me, and my soldiers kill every one of them," she said with a cruel smile. "You always were the soft one, Sesskia. How you can wield such power and still be so weak baffles me. Command them, or they die."

I felt so weak. I could have killed the God-Empress, and ended that threat, but some of our mages would have died before the rest could defend themselves—at the time I didn't know how effective that defense could be. Maybe I should have killed her. It would have changed everything.

But all those deaths...like I said, I felt weak, unable to condemn people I cared about, especially Audryn, to death. I dismissed the fire and said, "Let them go. We'll do as you ask," thinking we'd find a way out of it, that Cederic would see a solution I didn't.

Instead, he raised both his hands and began rapidly scribing th'an on the air. Several soldiers screamed and dropped their weapons, their hands turning red like the coals of a blacksmith's fire. "*Get out!*" he shouted, and I turned the fire pouvra on the rest of the soldiers while some of the mages moved and others, those holding their boards, began scrawling on them.

I set three soldiers on fire—I was too tired for more than that —and a few more soldiers shouted in pain as their skin smoked and cracked. But there were too many of them, and we were all weary from lack of sleep, and we still weren't fast enough. Two mages screamed as knives found their mark, more soldiers tackled Cederic and immobilized his hands, and still more soldiers moved to block the exit, their swords drawn. More mages went down to those blades, and the rest of us fell back, away from the carnage.

"Stop, stop!" I shouted. "If you kill them all, who will fight for you?"

"I don't need disobedient priests. God will raise up others," the God-Empress said. "Your gift tried to fight me, Sesskia. I'm not happy with your inability to control him." She turned her gaze on Cederic. "Kneel before me, Cederic Aleynten," she said, and the soldiers holding him kicked his knees so they folded, and he landed on the floor with a grunt. "No, I think you had better bow instead," she continued, and they forced him to bend until he was prostrate in front of her.

"You gave him to me, Renatha," I said. "I'm responsible for his actions. It's me you should punish."

"Sesskia—" Cederic shouted, and one of the soldiers kicked him in the face, making him cry out at the same time I did.

"I still need you, Sesskia," the God-Empress said, as if this were the most obvious thing in the world. "I don't need him." To the soldiers, she said, "Remove his hands."

"*No!*" I screamed, and stupidly threw myself at the soldiers, forgetting entirely about pouvrin. One of the men grabbed me and dragged me away, and then I did set him on fire, but he kept hold of me even as he screamed and tried to extinguish the flames. My mind-moving pouvra was too weak to force his hands open. I watched Cederic struggle as the soldiers holding him stretched out his arms, leaving his wrists bare, and another soldier drew his longsword and approached, raising it high for a powerful two-handed stroke. I wrenched myself free—

—and even as I set the man on fire, Cederic's captors flew backward into a knot of mages, knocking them all down, and he reared up, his eyes wide and panicked, and with a sweeping motion of both hands sent half a dozen soldiers to the ground.

It took me a second or two to realize he hadn't scribed th'an, that his terror had woken the magic within him and given him his own mind-moving pouvra. I had no idea it could be so powerful, though I guess he's used to being able to move much heavier things than I can with th'an, and maybe it translates. That thought came later. At the time, though, I reacted by shouting, *"Strike back!"*

The mages moved, the soldiers dropped their knives and drew their swords, the God-Empress opened her mouth to give a command, and without stopping to think I grabbed her, bore her to the ground, and worked the concealment pouvra on both of us.

I only intended to give the mages a few more seconds by keeping the God-Empress from commanding her soldiers to attack. They'd probably act on their own initiative if she didn't give the order. Instead, all the soldiers looked confused, as if they didn't know what they were doing or even why they were in the room.

That was all I had time to observe before I had to use all my strength to subdue the God-Empress. I was able to make out the outline of her face before the pouvra's compulsion for me to look elsewhere took effect, and I jammed my arm into her mouth so she couldn't shout. She ground down with her teeth, but my sleeve protected me enough that it was just a dull pain, though not an insignificant one. I pressed harder and tried to ignore it.

Gagging her with my arm left me with only one hand to fend off her attacks, but her greater height didn't give her any advantages while we were on the floor, and I both outweigh her and have experience with fighting dirty. I learned a long time ago that the only technique that matters, for someone my size, is the one that gets you away from your assailant.

So we punched and clawed and elbowed, neither of us able to see the other, and I was able to smash my forehead against her chin, which stunned her for a moment, but not as long as if I'd hit her nose, which is what I was aiming for.

She rocked, trying to roll me off her, and I got my knee up to give myself a stronger position, and that's when I realized Cederic was standing nearby, shouting my name in a way that told me he had no idea where I was. So I released the pouvra while still keeping a grip on the God-Empress, and then hands were taking her from me, and I pushed to my knees and let Cederic help me stand.

My eyes were watering because she'd managed to claw my face, just at the end, but I looked around the room and was stunned to see no soldiers left standing. Some of them had blood running from their eyes and noses and ears, and others had faces tinged blue from asphyxiation, and some lay in heaps next to the walls as if they'd been flung into them, hard. I still haven't seen mages use th'an in a fight, and I know they're useless if someone has a sword to their throats, but give them enough space and they're deadly.

"Are you all right?" Cederic said, touching my cheek; I winced away from how his touch made the wounds sting. I'm glad I didn't think, at the time, that they might have been poisoned, since the God-Empress is the kind of person who might paint her nails with poison just to have that extra weapon. I was already on edge and that would have been more strain than I needed.

"I'm fine," I said, wiping my eyes. The God-Empress stood a few feet away from me. No one was holding her—I figure a lifetime's habit of revering her as God couldn't be broken easily—but there were at least five people between her and the door, so it's not like she could go anywhere. (I thought. We all thought.) She looked awful. Her golden crown of hair was completely disordered, she had bruises forming on her chin and at the corner of her mouth where I'd gotten in a lucky punch, but she looked as self-possessed as if we were all in her pavilion and she were about to pronounce judgment.

"You've disappointed me, Sesskia," she said. "You were God's choice and you rebelled against her. You will have to die."

"We're all probably going to die thanks to you ruining the kathana," I said.

She shrugged. "I told you God won't allow that to happen," she said. She looked at Cederic, then back at me. "You don't appreciate your gift," she said. "You will watch as I peel the skin from his body, and then you will die, screaming."

She raised her hand as if to point at me, but instead she did that complicated salute she'd done at the honey day ceremony, only rapidly, and I could see amber light outlining her fingers just as Cederic said, "Th'an!" and lunged at her. It was too late. She...flattened, like dough being rolled out, going thinner and thinner until she was a mist that dissipated and was gone.

"What was that?" I said.

"I don't know," Cederic said. "It's not—"

That was when the biggest tremor we'd ever felt struck. I was in five places at once, only one of them in that room, and it hurt when I pulled back together, enough that I had to stand and breathe deeply so I wouldn't faint. Everyone around me was doing the same, leaning on each other, and I saw Terrael supporting Audryn, whose robe was bloody along the front.

Then an actual tremor sent shockwaves through the room, staggering everyone. Cederic reached out to grab my hand, and I held onto him until the room stopped trembling. Then he let me go, and said, "Clear the circle. And move quickly."

I don't think anyone needed to hear that last part. We all dragged bodies to the sides of the room, mostly soldiers, a few robed mages we didn't have time to mourn. The circle, which had been drawn in ink, was intact, but the th'an scribed in and around it were ruined. Mages dropped to their knees and scrubbed what was left of them away, while others began writing new ones, these more permanent. I stood to one side, watching, but then Terrael grabbed me and tore off my shirt before I could protest.

He began drawing on my chest and shoulders with his fat writing tool, and *then* I squeaked and batted at his hand. "Stop it," he said, and slapped my hands away. "I don't have time to explain, Sesskia, just hold still," and he kept on scribing.

I obeyed him, praying he wasn't about to remove my breast band too, but he secured my hair messily on top of my head using the clips I'd last seen Audryn wearing, then turned me around and drew on my back, th'an after th'an. The ink was cold and felt wet, as if it were trickling across my skin.

Another tremor struck, and I was in the throne room and my bedroom and the observatory and somewhere down in Colosse, where I saw people screaming, and then I was back in my body, aching everywhere as if I'd been beaten. Terrael was crouched on the floor, one hand holding himself up, the other still clutching his writing tool. I reached down and helped him stand while the earth shook. "Thanks," he said, and made a few more marks on my cheeks. "Sai Aleynten will tell you what to do, when it's time," he said. "I think it will hurt. I'm sorry."

"If it will help save the world, I think I can endure a little pain," I said, but I was starting to feel afraid, because I don't like not knowing things. I wished he'd been able to explain—though I think, now, if I'd known what was coming, I wouldn't have been able to do it.

The mages were done scribing th'an, the inert ones, in black ink rather than chalk, and there were so many of them they made a thick pattern around the black circle. They outlined two more circles, one only a few inches across, near the northwest point, the other about two feet across, centered on the south point.

Three mages were walking around the room, slapping the walls or stomping their feet. "Right here," one of them said, and the others came to sit on the floor with her, making a loose circle around a spot that didn't look special to me. Then each of them took off one shoe and tapped with the heel on the wood, as if testing for sound.

"Sesskia," Cederic said, and I turned to face him. His face was so emotionless it looked as if it had been carved of marble. "It's almost time."

"What's going to happen?" I said. My voice didn't tremble. I'm sure I looked as emotionless as he did. He was already under enough stress without seeing me burst into tears.

"The binding kathana is simple enough," he said. "And we have found a th'an that connects the ruins, as many as we can identify, in a way that will reverse what the original kathana did. We will make a correspondence between the ruins in each world so they will be drawn back together. Binding the worlds at those points will allow all the other places to merge, not only in Castavir but over all three continents and all the oceans, though any manmade constructions that overlap that are not one of the ruins will be destroyed. It is the best we can do."

"That doesn't explain why Terrael used me as a slate," I said.

Cederic looked away from me. "The ruins give shape to the th'an; they are like instructions for how the worlds are to fit together. If the ruins in each world are simply drawn back together, they will destroy each other, and the worlds will also be destroyed. So the ruins must be made to slip together, to occupy the same space at the same time. To be insubstantial just long enough for the worlds to merge completely."

"You need the walk-through-walls pouvra," I said. "That's how my magic will be part of the kathana. But I have to touch things to make them insubstantial. How am I supposed to touch all those ruins, let alone quickly enough to make a difference?"

"The th'an on your body will draw all the ruins into one place, symbolically, so what you do to one, you do to all," Cederic said.

"What if you've missed some of the ruins? Won't the kathana fail?" I said.

"The th'an connecting the ruins is what matters," he said. "So long as enough of those ruins are part of the th'an, the worlds will still come together. Any of them we miss will be destroyed, as any two overlapping structures will be. We have done our best."

"You—" Another tremor, putting me at seven places throughout Colosse and in two places I didn't recognize, and it felt like having my heart and lungs ripped out of my body to be pulled back together. "You aren't telling me everything," I said when we'd both recovered.

Cederic looked away from me again. "You will need to maintain the pouvra for almost three minutes," he said.

My face went numb. "I can't hold my breath that long," I said.

"You will have to," he said, still looking away. Now I know he was trying to keep his composure, but at the time I felt abandoned. Then he looked back at me, and said, "I cannot even touch you without ruining Master Peressten's work. I wish I had thought of that before I told him to begin."

"I understand," I said, and he leaned down and kissed me, gently. It felt so much like a farewell that tears came to my eyes, and I had to duck my head so he wouldn't see them. "Can we do it now? The kathana?" I said.

He nodded, and took my hand to lead me to sit in the larger of the th'an-described circles, with my back to the rest of the circle. I crossed my legs and rested my hands on my knees, forcing myself to breathe normally and relax so I could fill my lungs as deeply as possible when the time came.

From somewhere off to my right, the three mages began tapping a beat, then pounding it with the heels of their shoes. The wood resonated, making a hollow sound: *thump, thump, thump-thump, thump-thump, THUMP*. Mages moved past me, and I could hear their bare feet brushing the wood as they moved with the rhythm, finishing the kathana.

Then Cederic knelt in front of me, hand raised to my forehead. I didn't dare break the rhythm by speaking, and that was when I realized I hadn't told him I love him. But I think he knew what I wanted to say. The cool ink of the writing tool brushed across my forehead, once, twice, and then I sucked in a deep breath—

It felt as though I were being branded over my whole upper body, everywhere Terrael had drawn th'an. I let go my breath and screamed —I couldn't help myself, it hurt that badly. Cederic was gone. The room was gone. I was in a white void that spun so fast some of my hair came loose and whipped past my face, stinging, and I had to swallow hard to keep from throwing up.

Pale gray shapes lunged at me through the whirlwind, though none of them struck me; it was as if I were already insubstantial, though I knew I wasn't because I could breathe easily. Then a darker shape loomed up in front of me, rushing hard and fast toward me, and I sucked in a deep breath and worked the walk-through-walls pouvra just as I would have collided with it, and turned it insubstantial with me.

The th'an on my body activating had been agony. Being insubstantial while inside another object was a different kind of pain—not so much pain as the kind of discomfort you want to crawl out of your skin to get away from. It disoriented me for a few seconds as I felt my bones and my organs and my brain adjust to sharing space with something else. I hoped the discomfort would lessen as my body adjusted, but it only got worse. Soon all I could think about was getting out of there, and it took an effort of extreme willpower to remain where I was. I'd lost count of how long I'd been part of the ruin.

Then I realized when I became substantial again, I'd be a permanent part of it.

I struggled to move, trying to keep track of what was me and what was stone as I walked in what I hoped was the right direction. If there was a right direction. I needed to get out of the ruin; touching it from the outside would be enough to keep it insubstantial. I couldn't see, because I didn't have enough concentration to spare to make my eyes work.

I had to remind my body with every step that my muscles were connected to a brain that could make them move, all the while fighting the tide that threatened to make me part of the ruin. The air I'd inhaled before I did the pouvra...it wasn't like I could tell it was running out, but it was becoming more difficult to convince my body it was separate from the stone.

Then I was out, first my legs, then one arm, and I had to move more carefully so as not to lose contact with the ruin. Finally I was at a point where my palm was the only thing resting against the stone, but I could barely remember what I was doing or why I had to go on doing it. And then I went unconscious.

I woke up at some point and lay looking up at the sky. It was late afternoon (it's nearly evening now) and there were big, puffy white clouds trailing across the sky. I was probably still a little light-headed, because I lay for a while imagining shapes in the clouds: a shell, a crab missing a leg, a dragon. The th'an had disappeared from my body. My left hand hurt, and when I looked at it I discovered it was missing all the surface skin of the palm and fingers where I'd rested it against the ruin.

Oh, yes, the ruin. It's not a ruin anymore. I think the original buildings were split in half—not evenly, not down the middle like cutting a cake, but like a brick wall, jagged where it's missing bricks— and the merger put the pieces back together to look the way they had before the original disaster. Well, not perfectly. I suppose you could still call it a ruin, because large chunks are lying on the ground, but it's not nearly as destroyed as it used to be. I think you could live in it if you didn't mind the mess, though it's not much more than a couple of rooms with a roof.

I wonder why there were books there, if the buildings were only made to be part of the th'an. Just one of the many things I'd like to ask its builders, though "What the hell were you thinking?" is at the top of that list.

But it seems the worlds are one again. I don't know how much destruction has happened. I also don't know where I am. I thought, though now I realize Cederic never said this, that the kathana would take me to where I needed to be and then return me to the circle. I'm trying not to panic over the fact that it didn't, that I'm sitting here in a clearing in a forest (I forgot to say it's in a forest) next to what used to be a ruin, with no shirt and my only possessions being Audryn's hair clips and these two books I always keep on me. I'm grateful it's the end of summer, and still warm, rather than midwinter, but I have no food and no money and my stores of gratitude aren't very high.

I'm going to wait for nightfall and hope it's a clear, moonless night, so I can find my bearings by the stars—it's been a while since I've had to do that, but I still remember how. Then I'll start walking. If I'm lucky, the mages will have some way to track me down, but if not, I'll have to find a town and hope I can convince them to be friendly. Then I'll make my way to the Myrnala River and see what happened to Colosse. Cederic and the mages might stay there, or they might go back to the Darssan, depending on whether that desert wasteland is still there. Who knows how many other changes there might be? But I'll find him. I've faced worse than this and survived.

PRONUNCIATION GUIDE AND
GLOSSARY

General note: in Sesskia's language (Balaenic), long A and long O are usually written "ae" and "oe," and she writes Castaviran words as they would be spelled in Balaenic (i.e. Coell (Coll) River)

aenemica (ay-NEM-i-cah) – in Balaen, a name one uses for one's enemy to avoid referring to that person in a way that might indicate a positive or friendly relationship

Balaen (bah-LAIN) – Sesskia's home country

Castavir (CAS-tah-veer) – Empire ruled by the God-Empress Renatha Torenz; also the central country of that empire

collenna (coh-LEN-nah) – engine, either self-propelling or attached to a loenerel

Colosse (col-LOSS) – capital city of the Castaviran Empire

Darssan (DAR-san) – combination school and research organization for Castaviran mages

Endellavir (en-DELL-uh-veer) – country annexed a century ago by the Castaviran Empire

Helviran (HEL-veer-an) – country in the Castaviran Empire

kathana (ka-THAWN-ah) – ritual or spell composed of th'an

Kilios (KEY-lee-ohs) – "highest master"; a mage who has mastered all known th'an and all kathanas that can be performed by a single person

loenerel (LOH-neh-rel) – a train-like vehicle that runs on any surface, not on rails

pouvra, plural pouvrin (POW-vrah, pow-VRIN) – a form of magic requiring no words, gestures, or th'an, that is instead manifested through the mage's will

praenoma, (plural) praenomi (pray-NO-ma, pray-NO-mee)— Balaenic first name, used only by permission; reserved for the use of friends and family

Sai (sigh) – "great master"; a mage with advanced knowledge of magic

senet (SEN-et) – any wheeled vehicle without means of self-propulsion; one section of a loenerel

th'an (TH-AWN, with a glottal stop at the apostrophe) – magical pictogram or rune; may refer to a single rune or a simple combination of three or four

Venetry (VEN-uh-tree) – capital of Balaen

Viravon (VEER-uh-von) – country annexed by the Castaviran Empire, in rebellion to regain their freedom

THE BALAENIC CALENDAR
Winter:
Hantar (30 days)
Jennitar (31 days)
Teretar (30 days)
Spring:
Shelet (30 days)
Dorinet (31 days)
Auret (30 days)
Summer:
Evray (30 days)
Senessay (31 days)
Lennitay (30/31 days)
Autumn:

Coloine (30 days)

Nevrine (31 days)

Seresstine (31 days)

Cast of Characters:

Sesskia (SESS-key-ah) – Balaenic mage of ten years' standing

Cederic Aleynten (SED-er-ic ah-LEN-ten) – Kilios and leader of the Darssan mages

Terrael Peressten (ter-RAIL per-ESS-ten) – Darssan mage, genius; Sesskia's friend

Audryn Engilles (AW-drin en-GIL-is) – Darssan mage; Sesskia's friend

Sovrin Ustanz (SAW-vrin uss-TANCE) – Darssan mage; Sesskia's friend

Denril Vorantor (DEN-ril vor-AN-tor) – powerful mage and most high priest of the God-Empress

Renatha Torenz (ren-AH-tha tor-ENCE) – mad God-Empress of the Castaviran Empire

Perce Aselfos (PERSS ah-SEL-fus) – spymaster for the God-Empress

BONUS SCENES

The following scenes from Cederic's point of view were written to amuse myself. I hope you enjoy them. Dates correspond with the ones given in Sesskia's diary.

(25 Senessay)

Sleep was a long time coming. Cederic lay still in his bed, his eyes open and gazing at the darkness, and tried to order his thoughts so his body could rest, but as was happening more frequently as the convergence bore down inexorably upon them, he found them impossible to control. Plans for new kathanas that might work as part of a larger one to summon the Codex Tiurindi flashed past his unseeing eyes; administrative details presented themselves for review. A rest day had been just what they all needed, himself included, and it had been unexpectedly refreshing.

It would not have occurred to him to seek out Thalessi—Sesskia —as a companion, because she was... It surprised him that he couldn't immediately complete that sentence. She was an other-worlder, and a mage whose powers differed from his, but neither of those should disqualify her as someone he could spend an afternoon with. And she was not Sai, but she was also not a Master, someone whose rank would separate her from him—not that he thought of himself as better than those of lower rank, just...and there was another sentence he didn't know how to finish. He'd never realized how great that divide was until Denril had left and taken the other Sais with him. And he'd never realized he was lonely until this afternoon.

He gave up trying to sleep and went to the refectory looking for something hot to drink that might calm his disordered mind. He liked this time of night, actually, when everyone was sleeping and the lights were dim. The refectory stoves were off, so he used a couple of th'an to boil water for tea, then carried the cup back to his room, sipping occasionally. The hot astringency was already relaxing him.

Back in his room, he finished his drink, set the cup on his dresser, and climbed back into bed. That had been the right decision; his muscles relaxed, his eyelids closed involuntarily, and he drifted into sleep.

In his dream, he wore not the Kilios's robe, but the honey-gold satin and silk of a high priest, and in the logic of dreams, that made sense even though he had not served as priest for almost a decade. That was Denril's passion, not his, and Cederic was fairly sure it was the lure of the most high priesthood that had drawn him to Renatha Torenz's service and not the prospect of researching ways to protect the world against the convergence. His dream-self, despite wearing the priest's robe, walked the halls of the palace at Colosse instead of standing in the great amphitheater officiating in front of a crowd of thousands. This was one of those dreams in which you were looking for something, a dream where doors opened on rooms filled with more doors, and the deeper you trod in the dream, the greater the number of possibilities.

As a boy, Cederic had trained himself in lucid dreaming, so he didn't become agitated as the doors and hallways multiplied, but despite his efforts, he couldn't make his dreaming brain decide what it was looking for. So he relaxed, and wandered, enjoying his trip through memories of the palace. They were good memories, even if they were tainted by the God-Empress's presence, but there were still plenty of uncorrupted places to go, like the library.

As he thought this, one of the doors opened, and Cederic could see the shelves of the library beyond it. Feeling as if the dream had presented this as a gift to him, he entered. The dream version of the library was endless, shelves extending beyond sight ahead of him and disappearing into an invisible ceiling above. He let himself move instantly from one shelf to another, removing a book here and there even though he knew the pages would be blank. It was a pity he couldn't make the dream bring him knowledge his waking brain didn't know; he might find the solution to his problem here.

He took another step and saw a figure in the distance, little more than a black silhouette. It, too, was looking at the books on the shelves. He so rarely saw other people in his dreams that he went toward this one, and was surprised to discover that it was Sesskia, paging through a book as if it did have contents that she could read. How frustrating it must be for her to be surrounded by books in the waking world that she couldn't enjoy. It would drive him mad to be in her position. Then again, she did have all those books she could read that he couldn't; he was a little envious that she was the first to read books that hadn't been read in centuries.

Sesskia closed the book and put it on the shelf, or rather it was no longer in her hands, and turned to look at him, silent. She was wearing the clothes she'd worn that afternoon, though her feet were bare, and she looked at him with no expression, which made her look like a stranger, because she never concealed how she felt. That was one thing they didn't have in common; controlling his emotions had become such a commonplace for him that his face no longer reflected what he felt. Looking at Sesskia now, he wondered if it was worth it, that self-control he so desperately needed.

Sesskia took a few steps forward until she was so close she had to tilt her head to continue to meet his gaze with those enormous green-gray eyes surrounded by thick black lashes. Suddenly they were in the central cavern, standing at the exact center of the kathana ring, and the lights were gone, replaced by a red glow like lava boiling in cracks in the walls. As he thought this, those cracks appeared, and the ground shook and began peeling away until the two of them stood on a pinnacle surrounded by molten rock. His foot slipped, and he could feel the pull of the lava trying to carry him off solid ground.

Arms went around his waist, and Sesskia drew him close and laid her head on his shoulder. "I won't let you fall," she said—

—and he was awake, ejected from the dream by surprise and, unexpectedly, a rush of desire. He lay in the darkness and willed his heartbeat to slow. Where had that come from? She was a...a colleague, really, and might become a friend, but that had felt so intimate, as if he'd thought of her romantically instead. Which was a terrible idea. He didn't need a personal relationship now, of all times, and a casual sexual encounter was a very bad idea if they had to work together, not to mention that she didn't strike him as the kind of woman who was satisfied with that kind of thing.

And now he couldn't stop thinking about it. He dragged the pillow from behind his head and pressed it against his face. *She's your colleague, she would despise you if she knew you were thinking about her that way when she has no interest in you, and besides, this is just because you haven't had sex with anyone for over two years.* But those eyes, and that hair...he pressed harder, willing himself to fall asleep and into a less complicated dream.

He didn't sleep again all night.

(27 Senessay)

"You stayed up all night reading, didn't you," Sesskia said, closing her book and setting it back on its pile.

"What makes you think that?" Cederic said, and immediately had to stifle a yawn. He'd stayed up late reading to keep from dreaming the way he had the past two nights. The dreams all began differently, but all of them ended the same way: the pinnacle, Sesskia's arms around his waist, that low voice reassuring him.

"Because your eyes are bleary, and you keep pretending not to

314

yawn, and you're cranky as hell," she said, and promptly yawned herself.

"I find that amusing, coming from the woman who stayed up all night trying to learn the concealment pouvra," he said, and immediately regretted how snappish he sounded. Sesskia's lips thinned in a scowl, and her eyes (*those beautiful eyes*) narrowed.

"At least I accomplished something useful," she said. "All you did was exhaust yourself."

"I learned a great deal from my book, whereas *you* did not succeed in your task, or I would not currently be looking at you," he shot back.

"Too bad *you* don't have a concealment kathana, because I wish I wasn't looking at you either."

"I was not aware my presence was so objectionable to you. Perhaps you should take your lack of success elsewhere."

"Maybe I should!"

Cederic closed his lips on an angrier retort, conscious of listening ears as well as of how childish they both sounded. "This is pointless. Have your lunch, and take a nap, and let us see if we can salvage anything of this day after that."

"You'd better take a nap, too," she said. "Maybe you'll shock everyone and turn reasonable." She turned and stomped away across the chamber and disappeared down the hall.

Cederic leaned against the table, then had to make a grab for a book as he brushed against it and knocked it over. He ignored the covert stares from the Masters in the room. Probably they had never seen him so close to losing his temper before. God willing, they never would. The thought of some of the rages he'd flown into in his youth filled him with shame and embarrassment. And he'd been about to turn that on Sesskia, who....

He stood upright and walked out of the chamber with measured steps, willing himself calm. In his bedchamber, he lay down fully clothed and stared at the ceiling. He really ought to eat something, but he had no appetite. He was a little afraid to sleep, if he was going to find dream-Sesskia there, with her unchanging expression and her grip around his waist that he could feel even after he woke. Her dream-self was nothing like her real-world counterpart; the real Sesskia was fierce and intelligent, quick-witted and quick to laugh, stubbornly unwilling to let him intimidate her, passionate about learning magic and unraveling any mystery that crossed her path—

I'm falling in love with her.

He squeezed his eyes shut against that idea. Her dream-self was chimerical, and bore no resemblance to the reality of her. It was wrong, it was a little obscene, for him to let his dreaming mind's obsession with her translate into a belief that the real woman cared for him. But... it wasn't the dream he cared about, was it? That had only made him see the real Sesskia in a different light. He replayed the conversation they'd just had in his memory and groaned. He would have to apologize. He had definitely allowed his self-control to slip. *I don't want her to hate me,* he thought, and exhaustion caught up with him, and he slept.

This time, he was searching through the halls of the Darssan, through rooms he knew did not exist, searching for Sesskia so he could wake from the dream. The Darssan was empty, and as he became aware of this, he knew that it was empty because the convergence was upon them, and everyone had evacuated but him. The knowledge filled him with terror, and he ran faster, knowing in the way you do in dreams that he could only be saved from disaster if he could find Sesskia.

He came out of a hallway into the cavern, which was unexpectedly empty of everything except the inlaid gold kathana circle. Sesskia sat cross-legged near it, her head bowed and her eyes closed, with her hands resting loosely on her thighs.

Cederic approached her slowly, filled with dread, not knowing if she were alive or dead or merely asleep. He knelt before her unmoving form and discovered a brush and pot of silver ink in his hands. He dipped the brush in the ink, then hesitated, and in his moment of hesitation she raised her head, opened those beautiful eyes, and smiled at him with such tenderness that it made his hand shake. Without opening her mouth, she said, *I love you.*

Cederic felt the dream shake around him as surprise nearly jerked him out of it. With the brush, he sketched a few swift strokes of a th'an on Sesskia's forehead, and her eyes went wide with pain, and she screamed, and then he was sitting up in his bed, shaking at the intensity of the dream. His heart ached as if he really had hurt her. He was off the bed and halfway to the door before he remembered it had been a dream, Sesskia was perfectly well, and she would not want his comfort in any case, no matter how much he wanted to give it to her.

He returned to his bed and sat on its edge. He felt surprisingly rested, given how deeply he'd dreamed, but the thought of returning to the cavern to face Sesskia made him uneasy. If she knew how he'd been dreaming of her, she would be embarrassed, maybe even angry, even if he wasn't doing it on purpose.

But you welcome the dreams, he told himself, *you look forward to feeling her hold you, you lonely, desperate man.* He craved the dreams, but he now knew that he wanted even more for Sesskia to turn those remarkable eyes fondly in his direction. And that was unlikely; he wasn't repulsive, had had many relationships, many lovers, but he'd become so withdrawn in the last two years he'd forgotten how to attract a woman, let alone someone as defiantly independent as Sesskia was. *You don't need a relationship now. Time enough for that when the convergence is over.* But he couldn't convince his heart otherwise.

Eventually he realized there was no point putting it off any longer. He took a few moments to calm himself, to put on the expressionless façade that helped him remain strong for the men and women under his care, then combed and secured his hair and went to the cavern. Sesskia was already there, paging through a book rapidly in a way that told him she wasn't actually reading it. She glanced up at his approach, and that one look sent his heart beating faster. *Stop being a fool.*

After that one glance, she returned to her "reading," allowing Cederic to say, when he finally stood by her side, "I apologize for my

317

harsh words earlier. You were correct, I was tired and I allowed that to override my good judgment."

She looked at him with some surprise, then blushed a little and turned away again. "I wasn't being very polite," she said. "I shouldn't have said any of that. I'm sorry."

"I think we have both learned the value of rest," he said.

She looked his way again, and this time she smiled, and he thought his heart would leap out of his chest. *I would do almost anything to make her look at me that way always.* "We may be a little too much alike to be comfortable friends," she said.

"Are we friends, then?" he said.

"I think we must be. Only friends could say such awful things to one another and then forgive them."

"Then I hope we will find enough differences to be comfortable friends."

"Well, you're sarcastic and I'm rude, when we're irritable," she said with a grin. "Those are differences."

"And I am sensible and logical and you are not," he said, thinking, *Does she know I'm flirting with her? Would it matter if she did?*

"I am so logical," she said with a friendly scowl. "If you could read my book, you'd see all the lists I make when I'm coming to a decision."

"I accept your assertion, then, and will cast about for some other difference," he said with a tiny smile. *When did I lose the ability to smile like a normal person?*

"Our magic is different. And I did learn things I want you to know about. I don't know how useful it will be to the kathana, but maybe understanding my magic will help in some other way."

"Then I suggest we retire to one of the sitting rooms, if this will be an extended discussion, and I think it will," Cederic said. *She can't know how much I want to be alone with her. This is a logical proposal.*

They talked all afternoon, Sesskia explaining how she learned pouvrin, Cederic asking questions that led her to further explanations. Evening came, and Cederic called for dinner to be brought to them, and they ate and talked some more until both of them were yawning again. He was conscious of feeling buoyed up by the fierce pleasure of his knowledge expanding and the excitement of being with someone he was attracted to. When she finally said, "I think it's time for me to sleep, if I don't want a repeat of today's debacle," he felt disappointed at more than just the end of their discussion.

"Very wise," he said, and they both rose and left the room. "Thank you, Sesskia," Cederic said, "for your patience. I'm afraid I still don't fully understand how your magic works, but I am beginning to grasp it."

"I was actually thinking you must be brilliant to have understood it so quickly," Sesskia said. "It took me so long to work out how to make a pouvra work—I think it was nearly three years before I gained a second one."

"Then I thank you for the compliment," he said, and they parted ways. Cederic went to his room and again sat on his bed. He ought to be grateful she didn't hate him for his spiteful words, but all he could think was how much he wanted to kiss her. He flopped gracelessly back onto his bed and sighed. *Two years of celibacy, that's what this is, and she's the first woman you've seen in all that time who isn't your subordinate.*

He smiled to think of Sesskia as anyone's subordinate. No, this wasn't just enforced abstinence. He was falling in love with this woman. Even now, after spending the entire afternoon and evening with her, all he could think about was seeing her again. He began to imagine what it would be like if she were here with him in his bed, and thoroughly quashed that indulgence. He wasn't going to use her as an outlet for his sexual frustration.

He undressed for bed, then pulled the blankets up around his neck and stretched, feeling himself become sleepy almost immediately. Might she someday return his affection? If he pursued her openly, how would she respond? *You don't need this now, it will just be a distraction*, he reminded himself. But there would be a time not too far distant in which the convergence was a memory. Someday, he would be able to tell her of his feelings for her, and see how she responded. There was no reason to think she might not eventually feel the same. He carried those happy thoughts into his dream.

(31 Senessay)

"My instructions are to take your research back to Colosse," Denril said. He was smiling as if pleasantness could temper the blow he'd just dealt Cederic. "We will make better use of it than you can. You know that."

It took every ounce of willpower Cederic had gained in the last fifteen years not to attack his old friend with magic and with his hands. This was not Denril's idea. It was the mad bitch who sat on the throne at Colosse and manipulated the lives of others who had decreed it. But it was Denril's hand that was going to carry it out. "You cannot take the knowledge in our heads. We will still be able to summon the Codex Tiurindi," he said, and was satisfied at how calm he sounded.

"Possibly," Denril said. "With the help of the woman. I thought her name was Thalessi."

"Sesskia is not a name she shares with casual acquaintances," Cederic said, "and her magic is key to that kathana, yes."

"Unfortunate that the God-Empress has instructed me to bring her with me, then," Denril said, with a smug smile that said *I have beaten you, and you can't fight this.*

That was a blow he could not withstand so easily as the first. "She is not a thing you can simply carry away," he said, barely containing his fury.

"No, but she will not refuse the God-Empress's command, I think."

"I would not count on it. She has no more loyalty to this world than you have to hers."

"I have brought thirty-five mages, thirteen of them Sais, to ensure her compliance."

"That might not be enough to contain her."

Denril's smile disappeared. "They aren't to contain her," he said. "My orders are to begin killing the mages of the Darssan if she refuses. From what you wrote of her, we know she's developed an attachment to them. The God-Empress thinks she won't want to see them die when she can prevent it with a single action."

His anger vanished, leaving him cold and stunned. "Denril," he said, "how can you possibly condone this? Let alone preside over it?"

"Cederic, I have little choice in the matter." Denril said.

"No choice," Cederic said. "That is never true, and you know it. I warned you about this. I warned you not to throw in your lot with hers. She's insane, Denril, you know she is. Only a madwoman could order such a vile thing."

"Do not make such accusations, even where only I can hear," Denril said. "She is our ruler, Cederic, and she deserved to know what was coming. We will need her temporal power in the aftermath, however well we are able to contain the destruction. She has amassed an army the likes of which no one has seen since the days of the Conqueror to maintain Castavir's stability after the coming disaster.

"But the God-Empress is preparing for war against an enemy she knows she can't fight, and her paranoia is increasing. She insists that I produce results, regardless of the cost, and you and I agree on one thing: Thalessi, or whatever you call her, as an inhabitant of the shadow world, is crucial to our ability to preserve this one—that's true no matter which of our theories is correct.

"And I am *sorry*, old friend, I am truly sorry, but you must give up this mad, doomed quest. I need your help. Your skills are unparalleled; I can even admit that you're better than I am. Your continued refusal to join me *will* mean the deaths of hundreds of thousands, perhaps millions. You made a request of me. Let me extend the same to you. Help me. *Please*."

Cederic had to turn away. He couldn't bear to see how triumphant his old friend looked, so at odds with the false sorrow in his voice. He had come here not to gain understanding, but to compel Cederic to do what he'd refused to do every day for the last two years. He looked at the stones of the wall, and saw something shift, and there was Sesskia, watching them both with a horror that matched what was in Cederic's heart. That she should have witnessed this—

He pleaded with her, silently, to understand. *I cannot condemn them all to death for the sake of a principle, but it is you who will bear the burden of Denril's ultimatum,* he thought. *Forgive me, my love, my secret love, for betraying both of us.*

She nodded once, slowly, as if she'd read his thoughts—*though she would not be so calm if she had,* he thought. He turned back to look at Denril and said, "I will join you. And Sesskia will come peacefully."

"Thank you," Denril said. "And I truly am sorry for this."

"I am sorry, too," Cederic said, though he didn't say what he was sorry for.

Denril stood up from his chair and said, "I will leave you to decide how best to tell the mages. They really should be evacuated from the Darssan."

"And I suppose you have a plan for that as well," Cederic said.

"I have called for another *loenerel* to transport them to Trengia," Denril said. "From there they will be able to return to their homes."

"And forbidden the opportunity to save their world," Cederic said, expressionless again.

"You know most of them lack the skills to give us any advantage. Choose your best, and thank the others for their assistance to date."

"They were *your* best, once, Denril. Are you so completely lost to human feeling?"

"This is a hard time, and we must make hard choices," Denril said angrily. "Past time you learned that."

Cederic felt weary. Their conversation had drained him beyond his capacity for politeness. He waved his fingers dismissively, and Denril rose and left without another word. He was at least intelligent enough to know when Cederic had reached his limit. "I wish you had not heard that," he said.

"I'm sorry. I know I said I wouldn't use the pouvrin on anyone. I just...." Sesskia dismissed the concealment pouvra and came to sit in the chair next to him, not the one Denril had just vacated.

"I am not angry at your eavesdropping, Sesskia, but you do not need to be burdened with the knowledge that we are at the mercy of a mad Empress who is willing to slaughter innocents."

"Why not? It was me she wanted to coerce. I'm the one she's going to try to control. I think I have a right to know in what way I need to defend myself."

He shrugged. "You have a point," he said. "And now I must decide how to tell two hundred mages that our work is not only over, but has been a waste of time. Without implicating Denril."

"Why not implicate him? It's his fault!"

"He is the Empress's right hand in this matter. If I give them reason to murmur against him, and that murmuring gets back to her, their lives will be forfeit," Cederic said. "I will take the blame myself. I will explain that in light of new evidence, I have been convinced that our work needs to take a different direction, and that the Darssan must be closed for everyone's safety. If I am lucky, they will hate me and not Denril."

"That's not fair," she said.

The stubborn tone of her voice nearly broke his heart. She was in danger, she had to be careful not to do anything to make Denril think he needed to kill her friends, and *she* was worried about *him*. He wanted nothing more than to throw his arms around her and let her strength bear him up. "This has never been about fairness," he said. "Was it fair to pull you from your world into this one, make you a pawn in a game you never agreed to play? Denril was right, in part— this is a hard time that requires hard choices. The difference is that he believes he has the right to make those choices for everyone else. I have never agreed with him in that respect."

"Do you still believe you're right?"

"I do, and I will take with me the mages most capable of proving me correct. We will summon the Codex Tiurindi, and it will prove the truth to Denril. I only hope it will do so before it is too late."

"I'll help *you* find a solution. I don't have to be cooperative." Then her stubbornness faded as she remembered the consequences of her non-cooperation.

"You see the problem," Cederic said.

"Damn him to hell and damn your God-Empress too," she said, furiously.

Fear for her once again stabbed at his heart. "Never say that again. Never even think it. She is dangerous in ways you cannot imagine, because she is erratic and paranoid and is capable of destroying things, and people, even when that destruction hurts her cause. Your guess is correct: she wants you in Colosse so she can control you personally, and not because Denril has told her you are necessary to his work. But if she turns on you...God only knows what she might decide to do."

"I can defend myself," she said, "but I can't defend everyone around me."

"Exactly."

She sighed, but with resignation rather than despair, and it gave him hope. "How can I help *you*? Since it's clear I won't be able to help myself."

Tell me that you love me. Lend me that strength you seem to have in such limitless quantities. Give me a future to look forward to. He made himself smile, just that thin little twist of the lips that seemed all he was capable of these days, and said, "Behave as if you know nothing of this conflict. You don't have to be cheerful about it, naturally, but a desire to mitigate the coming disaster would be appropriate. Cooperate with Denril when he asks you about pouvrin. I'm glad you understood what I asked you earlier."

"Now I'm especially grateful I did," she said. "Having pouvrin he knows nothing about could save my life."

"I hope it doesn't come to that. We will not leave until that second *loenerel* arrives to transport everyone—I won't let it seem that I'm abandoning anyone. You and I will have to find a way to pursue the correct line of research without me seeming to be insubordinate. It could be dangerous."

"Because nothing about the rest of this is dangerous. What's a *loenerel*?"

"It is a device powered by th'an that can transport many people, depending on how many sections are connected to it. It will require a fairly large *loenerel* to move all the mages of the Darssan—minus the few I am to be allowed as part of my entourage," he added, unable to keep from sounding bitter. "I cannot believe Denril is so dismissive of their abilities, simply because he took many of our best mages when he left for Colosse two years ago."

"Those men and women with him, they used to belong to the Darssan?"

"Many of them, yes. Some of them were privately employed before Denril coaxed them to work for him. But enough of those mages have friends here...." They both sat silent for a moment, and he wondered if she was thinking, as he was, about what kind of people could agree to kill their friends for any reason. Perhaps the God-Empress's madness was catching.

"And there were more Sais here, once," he went on. "Seventeen of us. They all believe as Denril does." Seventeen people who had been his friends in a way the Masters could not. In a way that no one had been for years until Sesskia came along.

"So you were the only one who believed in this possibility," Sesskia said.

Cederic nodded. It still felt like betrayal. He was Kilios, he was Sai, he'd spent his entire adult life on this problem, and that mattered nothing to any of them. His weariness redoubled, and he stood, saying, "I hope for all our sakes you are as good a liar as you are a thief." He regretted it instantly. He'd meant it as a joke, but his withered sense of humor might have distorted his meaning into an insult.

But she smiled, and said, "I never thought anyone but me might find value in those skills. Are you sure you want to encourage me in my criminal ways?"

"I did not think you needed encouragement," he said, raising an eyebrow, and she laughed, a merry, carefree sound that lifted a weight from his heart. He held the door for her, said, "You should gather your things. I do not know when the *loenerel* will be here," and went to his room where he could regain his self-control enough to face the mages of the Darssan.

(3 Lennitay)

He balanced the tray in one hand and knocked on Sesskia's door with the other, then waited for her "Come in" to open it and enter.

325

She'd been lying on her bed with her face over the vent, but now she sat up and stretched a little. Her hair was tangled on one side, and he had to stifle an impulse to run his fingers through it to straighten it.

"You look unwell," he said, setting the tray on the foot of her bed.

"I feel better than I did," she said. "It's just motion sickness. I think writing is making it worse."

"I will not make the obvious suggestion that you should stop, if that is what is making you ill."

"I knew you were smart." She pulled the tray toward herself and began eating. "This tastes terrible."

"*Loenerels* are not known for their cuisine."

"Yes, but this tastes even more terrible than it should. Maybe it's the sickness." She pushed the tray toward him. "You tell me how it tastes."

He took the offered fork and speared a piece of meat, trying not to dwell on the casual intimacy of the offering. "You are correct, this tastes terrible," he said, handing the fork back. "I am sorry."

"Well, you didn't cook it. I assume." She ate a few more bites, drank some water, then pushed the tray away. "I can't bear any more, and my stomach is upset enough that it agrees with me. How much longer until Colosse?"

"A day at most." He felt incredibly awkward every time he came to her room; it was small, and there was nowhere to sit except the bed she was occupying, and he never knew what to do with his hands, so he ended up clasping them behind his back in a way he was certain made him look smug and superior. He'd had a teacher as a boy who always stood that way, a man he'd hated, and the idea of having anything common with him was repulsive. But he couldn't stay away.

He told himself he was providing a buffer between her and the others, helping her conceal her book, but the truth was that as they neared Colosse, he needed her strength more every day. At night, he lay in his own narrow bed and fought with himself. *Tell her how you feel, ask her if she might not learn to love you in return,* he thought, then, *You don't need a distraction, and you don't need an emotional attachment that the madwoman might use against you,* then, *Imagine having her with*

you every day, every night, that strength and that beauty bearing you up.
So far his sensible self was winning.

"I'm a little eager to see the palace. Audryn says there's nothing like it in the world."

"Master Engilles is correct. It is the oldest building in Colosse, at least parts of it are—the God-Emperors were all fond of adding to it."

"I'm looking forward to exploring it. What a challenge!"

There was a familiar note in her voice, the sound that said she had come upon a puzzle she couldn't wait to unravel, and it prompted Cederic to say, "You should not go wandering through the palace uninvited and unsupervised. The God-Empress has been known to take lethal offense at people abusing her gift of hospitality."

"I'm not going to get caught, Cederic," Sesskia scoffed. "Even without the pouvrin I can keep from being seen. I've been doing this for a long time—as long as you've been a mage, probably, maybe longer."

"You are not infallible, and the consequences of your failure could be fatal."

"Then I'll just have to be extremely careful." She grinned at him, that expression that never failed to catch at his heart. *Tell her. Don't tell her. Tell her.*

He sighed. "If you were a Darssan mage, I could forbid it."

"Lucky for both of us I'm not. We certainly couldn't be friends like this if I were, and just think of the knowledge you'd miss out on." The teasing look turned serious. "Believe me, Cederic, I never take unnecessary risks, and I don't anticipate exploring the palace to be important enough to mean necessary risks. Don't worry about me."

"I think that is an unreasonable request. But I will try to remember that I have faith in your abilities." He picked up the tray and went to the door. "Take care, Sesskia."

Later that night, he lay awake and thought of her. He needed to stop doing that. In Colosse, he would be observed all the time, would have to be constantly alert to ward off any attacks the God-Empress might bring against the mages, and the summoning kathana would need all his attention. Thinking of Sesskia was an indulgence he couldn't afford, but he couldn't stop himself, as if he were falling off a cliff and she was all that stood between him and the stony ground.

He fell asleep clutching that image and found himself in an old familiar dream, the first dream, in which they stood atop that precipice holding each other. But this time, she put her hand behind his head and pulled him down so she could kiss him, her lips soft against his and the very tip of her tongue flickering out to brush against his mouth. He groaned, and they were in an empty room with smooth walls and floor, and he pushed her up against the wall and felt her respond with an eager desire that matched his. Another movement, and they were both naked, though he could only feel her skin against his and not see her shape, and—

then he was awake, breathing heavily and on fire with need. He had his hand on the doorknob before he came to his senses, then had to clutch it so hard he was afraid he would crush it. *If you burst in on her like this, you'll destroy everything you've built between you.* Still breathing heavily, he returned to his bed and flung himself face-first onto it. This could not go on. He would be useless to everyone if he could not control himself.

He made himself think logically, trying to convince his body to relax and forget that horribly, beautifully realistic dream. If he told her how he felt now, she would either spurn him (the list of possible ways she might do this was far too long) or tell him she felt the same. If she spurned him, things would become awkward between them, and since they had to work together on the kathana, that could be disastrous. If she loved him...well, that would be its own distraction, but not as bad a one; the problem was that her love would give the God-Empress a handle on him. He prided himself on rationality, but he wasn't sure he could stand firm when the God-Empress was threatening to torture Sesskia if he didn't obey. Which meant that not telling her was the only sane course of action.

I will tell her when the convergence is over, he thought, then planned ways of doing so until he finally fell asleep. He didn't dream again that night.

(18 Lennitay)

Cederic sat at his usual seat in the mages' dining hall and pretended not to look for Sesskia. Like him, she always sat in the same place; him alone or with Denril, her with Master Engilles and Master Ustanz. Unlike him, she talked enthusiastically and laughed without self-consciousness, cheerful despite the precariousness of their position. It wasn't because she was stupid, or frivolous, he'd decided; she simply knew how to find joy where others—himself—could see only despair. But today her seat was empty.

He took a bite of—it was porridge, whatever had possessed him to choose that from the kitchen? He'd been preoccupied with the latest problem with the summoning kathana, something he'd been working on with the other Sais for a few days now. He must be truly caught up in working out the correct th'an not to have noticed what was put on his plate. He hadn't even noticed he was holding a bowl.

It occurred to him that he hadn't seen Sesskia much at all since she had returned from her day with the God-Empress. They'd talked about it briefly, and Sesskia had asked questions about the different color-days, and now that he thought about it, she had seemed unusually subdued, but he'd put it down to tiredness from driving around in the heat all day. Her nose had been sunburned, something that made her look younger than she was, and he'd thought about offering to relieve the pain, but healing th'an were all rather intimate, and he didn't dare cross that divide between them.

And after that brief conversation, he'd been busy with the kathana and hadn't spoken to her at all. He'd been aware of her presence, as always, but she had...she'd still been rather subdued, hadn't she? Uncharacteristically quiet. Master Peressten hadn't commented on it, when he gave his daily report on her progress with the fire th'an, but he wasn't the sort of person who easily noticed people's emotional states.

He pushed his bowl away, wrinkling his nose at it in distaste, and went to where Master Engilles and Master Ustanz sat. They sat up straighter when he approached; he'd paid attention since they'd arrived in Colosse and joined the other mages, and was chagrined to realize the Darssan mages were far more formal around him than in interacting with the other Sais, except Denril, whom they avoided, either from loyalty to him or from personal dislike, he wasn't sure. Those other Sais were capable of joking with the Masters without losing their respect, but he didn't know how to maintain discipline through anything but formality. He couldn't even imagine what it would be like to have them as friends. He wished he could, to share in their mutual affection for Sesskia. Perhaps when Master Peressten became Sai, or Kilios...but that was still years in the future. Assuming they had a future. He shook that bleak thought away.

"Excuse me," he said, "I am looking for Sesskia. Do you know where I might find her?"

The women looked at each other. Could they hear his emotions in the way he spoke? Surely not. "Sesskia wasn't well last night," Master Engilles said. "She's been having trouble sleeping the past few nights and I gave her something to help her relax. We were going to check on her after breakfast."

"I will see if there is anything I can do to help," he said. "I hope she is not ill."

"I think she's just tired from working on the kathana," Master Ustanz said. "Couldn't you arrange for her to have a rest day, or something, Sai Aleynten?"

"I think so, if it turns out she is overworked. She certainly bears a greater burden than any one of us."

"Sai Vorantor—" Master Engilles began, then closed her mouth and looked around as if she were afraid someone could hear the thoughts she could not speak.

"Sai Vorantor is very committed to this work," Cederic said, blank-faced. "He sometimes forgets the limitations of others." *Sai Vorantor cares little for anything that will not advance his personal power.*

"I'm sure he means well," Master Ustanz said, with an expression that said she didn't believe her own words.

"We all could use a rest day, Sai Aleynten," Master Engilles said with a meaningful look.

"I will ask Sai Vorantor again," Cederic said, "but we have very little time left. We must all do our utmost." He nodded at the women and left the dining hall, ascending the stairs to the Sais' wing as quickly as he could without running. Trouble sleeping—uncharacteristically sober—isolating herself—something was definitely wrong, and he would do everything in his power to fix it.

He passed a servant in the hall and wrinkled his nose at the stink of vomit coming from the rags she carried in a basket over her arm. He knocked on Sesskia's door and waited for an invitation. Silence. He opened it anyway and went into her room.

She was in bed, lying with her back to the door, curled in on herself as if in pain or misery. He could hear her slow breathing, but it was not the sound of someone who was asleep. So, pretending sleep so he would leave her alone? Did she think he was another servant? The faint smell of vomit still hung in the air; she might just be ill. He thought back over the last three days, recalled memories he hadn't realized he'd made, how despondent she'd been. She hadn't looked ill. She had looked haunted.

Making a guess, he said, "You are not asleep. And you did not tell me everything. What happened when you were with the God-Empress?"

She rolled over to look at him. Her eyes were shadowed, her nose was peeling, and she would have made a comical figure if her face hadn't been so still and miserable. "I don't want to talk about it," she said.

He wanted so badly to give her the comfort she needed. A simple embrace—that would be acceptable between friends, yes? But he knew well that once he had his arms around her, he wouldn't be able to stop at an embrace. So he went toward the bed and stopped a few feet from her. She was wearing a loose shirt with a wide neck that had slipped down over one shoulder, and he had to concentrate on her face to keep from becoming aroused at the sight. "Whatever happened is making you ill," he said quietly, "and will continue to do so as long as you allow it to fester inside you. Tell me."

She looked up at him with those beautiful, haunted eyes. "I didn't realize just how little she cares for human life," she said. "Cederic, we were always—everywhere we went, anyone we met was just a thing to her, something whose death was meaningless. That man at the eating place would have died if someone else hadn't been quick-witted enough to distract her insanity. And—" she took a deep, shuddering breath—"for all I know she decided they paid too much attention to her on a rose day and sent her soldiers back to shut those people into the building and burn it down. And the only reason she didn't kill me is that I tricked her into thinking the river could obey me."

He didn't know what to say to that. *Don't worry* was fatuous and a lie. *You're safe* was doubly so. And he couldn't assure her that all those people were safe when they both knew Renatha Torenz's mad whims meant exactly the opposite.

Sesskia lowered her head. Her hand was picking at the coverlet, twisting it around her fingers. "She killed the collenna master," she said quietly. "Her soldiers picked the woman up off the seat and just... twisted her neck. I can still hear it snapping. It wasn't even a snap, more like the pop of a knuckle cracking. She looked so surprised. She didn't even have time to be afraid. I can't stop seeing her face, except now, sometimes it's Audryn, or Terrael, and in my dreams I can't do anything but watch, as if I don't know a single pouvra."

"And you are not accustomed to helplessness," he managed.

She nodded. "And at the end," she said, "when we were back in the palace, she asked me about our progress on the summoning kathana, and I babbled something about how everyone was doing their best, and she said—it was something like "then I will allow a little more time." As if we were all working at her sufferance. And I know...I swear I'm doing my best, Cederic, but it's just not coming together and if I can't..."

She stopped, clenched her fists in her lap, and said, "Tell me I'm wrong. Tell me I'm wrong that everyone's safety depends on me."

She raised her head and looked at him with those enormous eyes, and his heart turned over in his chest. At that moment he could have killed the God-Empress and been cut down in turn by her guards and counted it no sacrifice if he could lift her burden. "You are not wrong," he said.

He reached out and pressed the tips of his first and middle fingers against the center of Sesskia's forehead and pushed just a little, saying, "Lie back." Obediently she lay back on her pillow, puzzled, and he was struck by a desire to comfort her that was so strong he had to turn away and lean on her dressing table, fighting for control. "This is not a burden you should bear, and I cannot take it from you," he said. "But I may be able to ease it."

He turned around and returned to her side and, daringly, tugged at the neck of her shirt to expose more of her throat. "This will make you sleep, and keep you from dreaming," he said, "and it may also clear your mind to make your task easier. Do not go wandering tonight, Sesskia. That is not a request."

She nodded, and the movement made her chin brush against his fingers. He had never touched her since the first day, when he caught her trying to sneak out of the Darssan, and at that time he had no interest in her except as a problem he needed to solve. *How far we've both come from that moment*, he thought, and pressed gently up on her chin so he could see her throat.

He could feel her eyes still fixed on him, but he focused on the th'an he needed and traced their outline on her skin with the tip of his forefinger. She sighed, and as he lifted his hand to her brow he saw that her eyes had already begun to close. He traced more th'an on her forehead and watched her eyelids flicker just a little, those thick black lashes settling to rest on her face like a silken fringe. Before he could stop himself, he brushed her cheek with the back of his fingers, so lightly he hoped she wouldn't notice. She smiled a little, and leaned into his touch, and then her breathing changed, and he stood there with his hand on her face, unable to move.

She was asleep, he told himself, *it didn't mean anything*, but his heart didn't want to be convinced. He removed his hand, and Sesskia rolled onto her side, tucking her hand under her cheek as if capturing his touch. It was more than he could bear. He turned and swiftly crossed the room, almost forgetting to lock the door behind him—she would be so upset to know she'd slept unprotected.

He passed Masters Engilles and Ustanz in the hallway. "Sesskia is sleeping," he told them. "She was...overcome by the pressures of trying to learn this th'an. She will wake this evening and I think she will be well."

"Thanks, Sai Aleynten," Master Ustanz said. "Is there anything we can do?"

"Continue to perform to the best of your abilities," Cederic said, "which I know are exceptional. Help Sesskia realize that we all share her burden. I believe she became overwhelmed because of the isolation she must necessarily work in."

"We'll make sure she's not alone, Sai Aleynten," Master Engilles said.

"Thank you," he said. "Shall we go to the circle chamber? I have observed your progress and I believe the Darssan mages have mastered their part of the kathana, so I think we should try to perform it in active form."

But all day, as he supervised the mages' work with the kathana, and argued politely with Denril about Sesskia's absence while wishing he had the power to simply order Denril to be sensible, he could still feel her cheek under his fingers, and began to question whether his decision to remain silent was best. How bad could it be, after all, if he declared his love for her and she didn't return his affection? She was honest and kind and considerate and wouldn't be cruel, and they were both reasonable people; they could work past any awkwardness it might create between them. *And suppose she does return my affections? I barely dare imagine it.*

He responded absently to a Sai who, by the sound of his voice, had addressed him at least once already. *Think of how she reacted when the burden of this* kathana *was laid on her,* he thought. *Imagine what kind of burden your love might be if she feels nothing for you. Stay silent, be patient, and one day, perhaps....*

He went with a servant to Sesskia's room late that afternoon, giving the woman instructions for Sesskia's care. Then he spent the rest of the evening distracted, irritable though not showing it, and ended up lying on his bed, sleepless, wondering if his th'an had helped her at all. If he shouldn't go back to her room—no, that was a terrible idea. Eventually, he fell into an uncomfortable, dreamless sleep.

(30 Lennitay-2 Coloine)

He ended up in the observatory without remembering how he'd gotten there or what he'd been thinking. It was possible he hadn't been thinking at all. His mind insisted on replaying everything in a kind of hallucinatory detail, the images sharp-edged as if he were feverish, the sounds echoing in memory. *They aren't meant to be apart*, Master Peressten said, with that pitying, embarrassed look on his face, and Denril's mocking, triumphant voice saying *I'll have some ideas for your research* as if he were a child and not Kilios and Denril's intellectual superior. Which, apparently, he wasn't.

And the whispers and glances, eyes averted when he happened to look their way. Master Engilles' tears and the white, shocked expression on Sesskia's face. That last memory filled him with more humiliation than the rest. He wanted only to be worthy in her eyes, and now he was nothing but a laughingstock, a strutting, preening fool.

He walked over to the edge of the observatory and looked down to the base far below. The bricks of the wall made an irregular pattern, and he spent some time analyzing it, because while he was thinking about that he couldn't also think about what had happened in the circle chamber. And then he couldn't stop thinking about it. He should have seen the truth. He *had* seen the truth, but he'd told himself he could find another way. He'd been condescending in his own mind toward Denril and the other Sais, pitying their blindness; he'd felt smug when Denril's letters revealed yet another failure on their part and had amused himself by devising kathanas that worked far better than theirs.

He closed his eyes and shuddered with the effort to master himself. He was in Denril's power now, Denril whose glee at seeing Cederic proved wrong so publicly revealed his deep-seated hatred of his "old friend." He would use this to tear Cederic down at every opportunity, and Cederic would be powerless to fight back because

Denril would be right: he was a proud, self-righteous fool whose skills and learning were a sham.

He heard footsteps, distantly, and closed his hands on the pillars to either side of him as if he could tear chunks from their stone. He needed to be alone, not forced to endure pity or mockery or whatever someone might feel entitled to inflict on him. He heard his name shouted, and humiliation surged through him again, because it was Sesskia's voice. He couldn't bear to see her look at him with pity in those beautiful eyes. *She might go away,* he thought, then smiled, bitterly, because if there was one thing Sesskia could be counted on to do, it was to pick away at a mystery until it fell apart and lay bare and defenseless before her.

Her boots tapped almost noiselessly up the steps, paused, then came toward him, slowly. He said, hoping to forestall her, "There are stones in a strange pattern here."

"They're a secret way into the God-Empress's treasure tower," she said.

He closed his eyes and willed himself composed. Just the sound of her voice was stripping away his composure. "I suppose I should expect you to know that," he said.

"I'm a thief," she said. It was supposed to be a joke, but he felt as if his sense of humor, such as it was, had been left behind in the circle chamber along with his dignity. He bowed his head toward the ground far, far below and prayed that she would know enough to simply leave without saying anything more.

"Terrael feels awful about...he didn't want to have to do that," Sesskia said. Her tone of voice was that of someone trying to coax a wounded animal out of its den, and it felt as if she'd cut him open and poured acid into the wound. He didn't want her pity, her of all people.

"Master Peressten is an honest man. He would not have concealed it, even for me," he said, willing her to hear his true meaning: *Go away, leave me to my suffering, you're just making this worse.*

She was silent for a long, blessed moment in which Cederic

336

thought she really had read his mind. Then she said, "What will you do?"

He replied, in a level, controlled tone, "You mean, what will I do now that it is clear that I am a fool, and that I have wasted two years of my time and that of Castavir's finest minds?"

"You're not a fool, Cederic, don't say that." Her voice was full of pity again, and he felt himself shake and had to struggle to control his anger, though he wasn't sure who he was angrier at, her for being so blithely, ignorantly cruel, or himself for letting it matter.

"Denril and the other Sais were intelligent enough to see the truth," he said. "I let my pride in my rank convince me that I could succeed where they could not. That makes me a fool. An arrogant, selfish fool."

"Don't say that," Sesskia said, "you *are* better than they are, and you made a mistake—"

The cajoling, humoring sound of her voice, as if he were a child to be cosseted, enraged him. He turned on her furiously and shouted, "What do *you* know of it? You, another of my many mistakes, snatched out of your world because of my carelessness! You simply cannot leave things alone, can you? I did not ask you to follow me. I did not ask for your patronizing sympathy, your cautious tiptoeing around the truth, and I cannot understand why you believe anything you have to say means anything to me!"

Sesskia's mouth was frozen open, caught mid-word by his torrent of anger. She clasped the front of her shirt as if she expected to find steel emerging from it. Cederic's words echoed back at him, and he felt the fury drain away, replaced with something cold and heartrending. "Sesskia," he said, "I didn't...." Didn't what? Didn't mean to lash out at the one person in all the world he never wanted to hurt?

Her face crumpled with a pain that stabbed him through the heart, and she turned and ran. "Sesskia!" he shouted, and ran after her, thinking that he could not let her leave without—he didn't know what he had to do, but he couldn't bear for her to go on looking like that. He was two paces behind her when she reached the top of the stairs, but she leapt forward and flung herself through the floor, and he was just in time to see her disappear from sight.

He stood at the top of the stairs, breathing heavily, then sank to the floor and buried his face in his hands. *My love, my love, come back, I didn't mean it, I cannot bear this alone.* All his reasons for not telling her he loved her seemed unimportant now. She would never, never forgive him for what he'd said, and any chance he might have had of seeing those beautiful eyes turn lovingly in his direction was gone.

He pushed himself to his feet and walked down the stairs and along the hall to his room, where he got as far as the awful blue rug in the center of the floor before collapsing to his knees and shuddering so hard he thought he might break apart. *I cannot lose control,* he thought disjointedly, *or I will lose myself entirely,* and he shook with the effort of controlling himself against the emotions that threatened to overwhelm him.

When he came to himself again, night had fallen, and he was stiff and aching from kneeling on the floor for however long it had been. He breathed, rhythmically, with his hands resting on his thighs, and finally he could rise and stretch out his legs and let the blood flow freely through them again. Then he went to the window and looked out over the palace roofs. Sesskia was out there somewhere, hurt and miserable and hating him, and he shuddered again before pushing the thought aside. No sense dwelling on what he'd lost. Even though he'd lost everything.

He began undressing for sleep, though he was sure he'd just lie awake for hours. In the morning, he would leave Colosse—no, he couldn't afford to indulge his humiliation. He would humble himself before Denril, ignore the whispers and the laughs and the pity, and bend whatever skill he had toward helping save what little of this world they could. It would be his penance for hurting the woman he loved, having to be in her presence and endure her anger or wounded feelings or whatever reaction she would justifiably have toward him.

He dropped his robe to the ground and kicked it away. He didn't deserve it, what it represented. He didn't deserve any consideration, not respect nor forgiveness... He sighed, and went to pick it up and hang it properly, but stopped before he could do more than remove the hanger from the wardrobe rail. He didn't deserve Sesskia's forgiveness, but he craved it so desperately that it burned inside him. If he were going to humble himself before anyone, it should be her.

He dressed quickly and went to her room, knocked on the door and waited for an invitation. There was no light coming from beneath the door, and after only a brief hesitation he scrawled th'an on it to make a window through which he could look. The room was empty. He wiped away the th'an and drew more of them around the lock. They glowed faintly green, then vanished, and it clicked open. He slipped inside her room and locked the door behind him, then lit a few lamps with more th'an and looked around. She would see the light burning, would use the see-through pouvra to investigate, so if he stood *here...*

Cederic arranged himself in the right place and prepared to wait. It was an intrusion, yes, and she would no doubt hate him more, but he was starting to feel desperate for an ending, even one in which she rejected his apology and told him never to speak to her again. He stood with his back to the door as if he could look through the curtains at the palace.

She always left her curtains closed. She'd said something jokingly about being spied on, joking because they were more than a hundred feet in the air in the Sais' wing, but there had been a seriousness beneath her words that made Cederic's heart ache for her, for the suspicion and distrust in which she'd lived her life. He had wanted to be someone she could trust, someone she didn't have to hide from, and instead he'd turned on her. He closed his eyes and bowed his head briefly. He didn't deserve her forgiveness. He'd hurt her and now he was imposing himself on her. He was an arrogant, thoughtless fool.

He'd decided to wait five more minutes and then leave when he heard the door open and close, almost noiselessly. If he weren't always so completely aware of her presence, he'd never be able to hear her approach. She took a few steps toward him, then said, "What are you doing here?"

"Wondering if there is any point in asking your forgiveness," he said, honestly. He ought to turn around and face her, but his hands were shaking again, and if he looked at her, he would lose control entirely.

"You think you deserve forgiveness?" Sesskia said. She sounded angry, not hurt, and that made it a little easier, because he might not deserve forgiveness, but he certainly deserved anger.

"I think we need forgiveness most when we do not deserve it," he said. He took a deep breath, and added, "I said things I deeply regret and I am—I cannot express how sorry I am." He winced. He didn't sound sorry. He sounded as if he were telling her some banal detail of how his day had gone. Was he completely incapable of expressing human feeling? What had he done to himself over the last two years, that he was so unable to admit to failure?

"Sorry you've made a mistake? Or sorry you haven't been able to correct this one?" Sesskia's jab stung him into bowing his head. The mistake had been in thinking this was a good idea. "I don't know why you care about my forgiveness," she said, "since nothing I say means anything—"

It was more than he could bear. "Sesskia, *no*," he said, turning to face her, startling her into silence. He felt as if she'd torn him open again, revealing his every secret, all his hidden desires. "You mean *everything* to me," he said, "and I beg you to forgive my hasty words, because I cannot forgive myself for saying them."

He waited for her to shout accusations at him, to throw more bitter words his way, so he was utterly unprepared for her to instead cross the few paces between them and put her arms around him, laying her head on his shoulder and pulling him close. He put his own arms around her waist in reflex, too stunned for anything else, then madly thought *Don't let her change her mind* and clung tightly to her so she wouldn't leave him, though she didn't seem inclined to move. If anything, she tightened her grip around his shoulders, and the smell of her hair and the feel of her body against his threatened to send him once again spiraling out of control. He shuddered, and she turned her head and whispered, "I won't let you fall."

It was so unexpected, the old dream coming true, that he expected to feel the sharp pinnacle beneath his feet. She was strong, and unwavering, definitely no dream, so he held onto her while grief and humiliation and pain and anger raged through him, and let her bear him up as he fought for control, to remain Cederic and not some creature mastered by his passions. He wondered, as he held her, what had motivated her, pity or compassion or, if he were truly blessed, love, and realized he didn't care which of the three it was just so long as she held him close. *You will endure*, he told himself, and knew it was true; he had a duty to this world, and that was more important than Cederic Aleynten's pride.

Finally, he felt himself calm enough to be rational again, and became conscious of Sesskia's strong, unwavering presence. *She will not lie to me*, he thought, and said, "Tell me you love me." It was not an order, but a plea.

She shifted her weight, and her fingers trailed along the base of his neck. "I love you," she said. "And not because you told me to say it. I love you."

He breathed out a long, thin sigh of relief. "Tell me I am not useless and a failure," he said.

"You could never be useless, and you are not a failure."

"Tell me I still have something to offer this world."

She let out a low chuckle. "Vorantor's an ass. You may have to save the world over his objections."

He laughed, and was surprised to realize that he couldn't remember the last time he'd done it. "Denril hates me," he said. "I tried to believe otherwise, but the summoning kathana almost failed because he tried to take too great a role, hoping to make himself look powerful in the God-Empress's eyes, hoping to lessen me. I had to fight him to keep it under control. Then I humiliated him by creating that shield kathana as easily as breathing, something he knows he could never do."

"Inventing a kathana on the fly, or breathing?" Sesskia said. "Because I know he used to be your friend, but I personally would be just as happy if he forgot how to breathe."

Cederic laughed again, harder this time, and it relaxed a tension he hadn't even realized was in his chest. He loosened his grip on Sesskia enough that he could look at her, and his heart ached with joy to see the way she smiled at him, those beautiful eyes shining with happiness. *She truly loves me*, he thought with amazement. "I cannot wish Denril dead," he said, "though I wish I did not have to walk back into that circle chamber today and submit to his patronizing scorn. I have been too proud, Sesskia, and now I will have to pay for it."

She smiled, and shook her head. "You still know more about magic than anyone else," she said, "and everyone knows it, and this will pass, and you'll make Vorantor's kathana work better than he ever could. And we'll save the world."

That dispelled much of his good humor. "Part of it, anyway," he said, feeling bitterness and humiliation rise up in him again. Sesskia made a little noise, part impatience, part sympathy, and took his face in her hands to draw him down so she could kiss him.

Her lips were warm against his, warm and soft and tender, and all his bad feeling melted away as they kissed, slowly, letting everything else fall away, even his amazement at the turn the night had taken. She slipped her fingers across his cheeks to follow his hairline, then down to rest on the front of his robe, and he found himself kissing her more intensely, drawing her closer.

Then she slid her hands inside his robe, touching his chest and his shoulders, and he lost track of everything except removing her shirt and her trousers and her underclothes and helping her do the same for him until there was nothing but her skin against his, silky-smooth and warm. He took half a step back so he could look at her, the curves of her hips and her breasts glowing in the low light, and she ducked her head a little, and he thought she blushed.

He started to tell her how beautiful she was, how he'd gone so many weeks wishing this could happen, when she said, "I've never done this before."

He gave her a look of total astonishment, then mentally kicked himself when she ducked her head again, lower this time as if she couldn't bear to meet his gaze. *Yes, let's make this beautiful, wonderful woman feel insecure and self-conscious when she's standing naked in front of you.* "Never?" he said, then kicked himself again.

"No," she said.

She still wouldn't look at him, so he put his fingers under her chin and raised her head to kiss her, threading the fingers of his other hand through her hair to cup the back of her head. "Are you ashamed of that?" he said.

She shook her head a little. "Afraid of being awkward and terrible," she said.

He kissed her again. "You could never be awkward and terrible," he said, "and I promise to show you the truth of that."

He was gentle with her, taking pleasure as much in her reactions as in his own. It felt a little like the first time for him as well, because of all the lovers he'd had over the years, Sesskia was the first woman he had loved so intensely, body and soul. Her initial shyness—and when had she ever been shy with him?—soon passed, leaving her so responsive to his touch that he had trouble going slowly, he wanted so much to lose himself in her. Then she gasped, and arched her back, and the look of astonishment on her face pushed him over the edge and made him forget everything except his joy at the two of them becoming one.

As he came back to himself, he found, to his horror, that she was crying. "No, Sesskia, love, did I hurt you?" he exclaimed. "I thought— I'm so sorry, I didn't know—"

She shook her head, and smiled at him through her tears. "I've never felt like that before," she said, "well, obviously not, but I mean —I have never felt so loved in my entire life, and I don't know how... this is how it came out. I don't know why. It was just too big a feeling for anything else."

He kissed her cheeks, kissed away the tears, and said with a smile, "Then I think we should do that again, and see if we cannot bring you to laughter instead of tears."

Later, he lay with her tucked into the curve of his arm and marveled at the miracle that was her love for him. He had been stupid to think he should wait to tell her that he loved her until after the convergence was over and the results, whatever they might be, had fallen out. He felt at peace for the first time in weeks. No, years. The reality of her strength bearing him up was so much better than dreams.

"I wonder what Aselfos has planned," Sesskia said, mostly to herself.

He smiled. "I would ask where that came from," he said, looking down at the top of her head, "but I have learned that it is better for me not to know the paths your mind takes at times."

She shifted so she could see his face. "It was a tortuous path," she admitted. "It's just that I don't like not knowing what's coming. And I don't know how to find out more."

The idea of her coming face to face with one of the God-Empress's soldiers, or Aselfos himself, during her nightly wanderings sent a chill through him, and he tightened his arm around her as if that would protect her. "Your safety has been uppermost in my thoughts since we arrived here," he said. "The God-Empress's interest in you is dangerous, and your nighttime wanderings put you at risk of drawing her wrath, should she learn where you have been and what you have seen."

"I'm at risk every time she summons me," Sesskia said. "And I also don't like that Vorantor has a secret plan we don't know about. I think I should investigate it."

He sighed. "Is there any point to me forbidding it?" he said.

"None," Sesskia said with a grin. "And don't think you can get away with threatening to withhold sexual favors, because I know you won't be able to stick to that threat."

She poked him in the stomach, and he took hold of her hand before she could do it a second time. The mischievous light in her beautiful eyes sent desire rushing through him again. "I would never dream of doing that," he murmured, "when I could entice you—" he kissed her, his lips lingering on hers—"to do what I want—" he moved to kiss her throat, then her shoulder—"by *promising* sexual favors instead." She laughed with delight, and he found himself incapable of saying anything else.

He ended up lying beneath her, both of them breathing heavily from exertion, and he closed his eyes and put his arms around her. "I had no idea," he said, "when I woke this morning that this is how my day would end, humiliated by my former friend and then lying together with you in your bed. It seems unreal, except that you are so wonderfully tangible."

"As are you," Sesskia said, rolling over to nestle against him once more. He turned out the light, and they lay like that, not speaking, in the quiet darkness. The feel of her body against his, so content and peaceful, filled him with joy once more. That he might give anyone that kind of happiness had never occurred to him; he'd been so consumed with this oncoming disaster for so long that he'd forgotten there was anything else to life. And yet there she was, relaxing in a way that told him she was settling in to sleep, trusting him enough to leave herself defenseless before him. That she intended to spend the night with him, to wake as one with him.

Loves me, and wants to marry me, he thought. It wasn't something they'd discussed, and he was a little surprised at her directness, at the way she'd assumed he wanted the same thing. Which he did. *I want her to be my wife,* he thought, *I don't want to wait any longer to be joined with her,* and cast about for something he could say to accept her proposal, wordless as it was. Finally, he said in a low voice, "I dream about you, you know. About this. I have dreamed of you so many times. You have been my foundation, even though you did not know it. My foundation, and my surety in the dark times." It was the best he could do at an explanation of everything he felt for her.

She said nothing. He knew she wasn't asleep, and he began to feel nervous. *Dreaming about her when she felt nothing for you, that sounds almost predatory,* he told himself, *she might take offense, she might be appalled. Please let her hear those words the way I meant them.*

She shifted a little bit. "When I was sixteen," she said in a quiet voice to match his, "I worked at one of the Thalessian fisheries. There are a lot

345

of them, but this one wasn't one of the big ones—it doesn't matter, that's not the point. There was...one of the workers. He was maybe twice my age, full beard, walked with a bit of a limp. He used to watch me while I worked. I hated it, but there was nothing I could do to stop him, and since he never did anything but watch, I learned to just ignore him."

She took a deep breath. "And then one day I was walking home and he came out of nowhere, grabbed me and shoved me into one of these alleys behind the fishery. He...he choked me, held me down while he tore my trousers and undershorts down around my ankles. I was trying to scream, but I could hardly breathe, and he was so much bigger than me. He'd unbuttoned his trousers and forced my legs apart, and I was still trying to scream even though I knew no one would come to help me, and that did something to me, unlocked something inside me.

"I worked my first pouvra, the fire pouvra, on him, and I think my desperation made it burn hotter—I've certainly never been able to repeat it. He burned from the inside...he went black, like a lump of coal, with red lines like fire crisscrossing his skin, and then he was nothing but ash and bone."

She shifted in the darkness as if she'd raised her head to look at him. "I was so overwhelmed I just lay there half-naked in the alley, shaking and crying, covered in ash, because I'd nearly been raped and I'd killed a man and I'd done it with magic, and even with all of that I knew I would never stop learning magic, because it was all I had in the world."

She went silent then, but it was a silence that held the promise of more words, and Cederic waited for her to decide what those words would be. Finally, she said, "I've never told that story to anyone before, Cederic. I've never even written it down. But what you said... I've never meant so much to anyone before, except maybe my Dad, years ago before he died, and I wanted you to know how much you mean to me."

He drew her closer to him, stroked her hair, with his heart so full he felt unable to speak. Finally he said, "If that is what it takes to make a mage in your world, I am surprised that there are any of you."

"There have to be others," Sesskia said, "and I doubt most of them have been nearly raped. But there are other terrors that can make you fight for your life, or for your identity."

"True." He brought his hand up to trace the line of her jaw, gently. "My instinct is to protect you from all harm," he said. "But that instinct is wrong. You would not be who you are if you were not willing to risk yourself. Even so—allow me a little fear on your behalf, please."

"It makes me feel loved, that you want to protect me, and even more loved that you know you can't," she said, and turned her face a little to kiss his hand before reaching up to take it in hers. "I love you," she said.

"I love you," he replied, and they lay like that, not speaking, until Sesskia's breathing changed and he knew she was asleep. He breathed out, slowly, and closed his eyes. They would spend the night together, and wake as one, husband and wife—

—except he couldn't, could he? Thanks to the God-Empress's insanity, their love for each other was a weapon she could use to force one or both of them to do whatever she wanted. He couldn't walk out of Sesskia's bedroom in the morning where any of the Sais could see him and spread the word that the Kilios had given a hostage to fortune.

He squeezed his eyes shut and mentally cursed the madwoman, thoroughly and at length. Then he eased himself away from Sesskia, called up a soft amber light, and began to dress. He looked at her once more before he left her room, his heart aching, then quietly went back to his own room and lay on his bed fully clothed. He was too tense to sleep. He practiced some old familiar relaxation exercises to no effect; his mind kept bringing up the image of Sesskia's face, peacefully sleeping. Who knew what she might think when she woke alone?

Finally, after what felt like hours, he couldn't bear it any longer. He got up and went back to her room, thinking he could at least leave her a message, and remembered she couldn't read his language just as he arrived at her door and saw light shining beneath it. He knocked, and entered without waiting for an invitation. "I'm sorry, but it's not safe for me to be seen loitering outside your door," he said.

Sesskia looked up at him. Her face was tense and unhappy. "You thought I'd left," he said.

"Because you left," she pointed out.

He came to take her hand. "No one can know what we are to each other," he said. "If the God-Empress finds out, she will use or threaten one or both of us to try to control the other. So I could not be seen coming out of your room this morning. I shouldn't even be here now, but I went back to my room and lay awake in my cold bed, cursing the God-Empress for keeping me from you when you should have woken to find me next to you." She smiled at him, and his heart lifted. "So I had to come now," he continued, "so you would not misunderstand me. I would have stayed, if not for that danger, you understand?"

She smiled more broadly, and nodded, and he felt a little dizzy, realizing the step they'd taken. Actually spending the night together was a technicality as far as he was concerned; in his heart, they were married. She was his wife. Denril's scorn was nothing beside that.

He kissed her, and left the room before he could become distracted by her body, still naked with the coverlet wrapped around her loosely so the shape of her breasts and her legs were visible. Sleep was out of the question. He would go to the circle chamber to study Denril's work, and see what he could make of it. Yes, he'd been proud, and it had led him to blindness with regard to the research the two of them had done together, but he was still Kilios, and he might yet see possibilities Denril had overlooked. And he wasn't alone anymore. Who knew what he and Sesskia might accomplish together? Maybe she was right, and they'd save the world after all.

Denril, you persist in being sloppy, he thought as he surveyed the walls where his "old friend's" work was written. Cederic would not make the mistake of disregarding Denril's work out of pride again, but it wasn't pride that made him irritated with the lack of organization displayed on the boards. He found his slate and some blank papers and started putting everything in order, defining th'an combinations and linking them to the conclusions Denril had formed. At least he hadn't made any mistakes that Cederic could see, despite the disorder, though he'd repeated himself once or twice and had misused a couple of th'an in a way that unnecessarily complicated the kathana.

The conclusion was obvious: the worlds were coming together unstoppably, and Denril's plan was to create pockets of isolation centered on Colosse that would be...shielded was probably the best word, though it was far more complicated than that, necessarily complicated. It would save their country, most of it, and obliterate civilization almost everywhere else, but it was the best they could do. It made Cederic ill to think of it.

He stepped back when he finished reorganizing Denril's work and scanned the wall. There were a few pieces he hadn't been able to integrate, and his first thought was to ignore them. *No more pride*, he told himself, and examined them more closely. Just because he couldn't immediately see a use for those facts didn't mean they didn't have a purpose, even though it seemed Denril didn't know what to do with them either.

They reminded him of the failed summoning kathana that had brought Sesskia to Castavir, which made him smile in memory of how she'd looked when he left her an hour ago. He would need to figure out a way for them to be together secretly; being unable to share her bed at all would be torture. He closed his eyes tightly and willed himself to focus again on the th'an.

When he opened his eyes, the pattern fell into place. He caught his breath in astonishment, stepped back a few paces, and looked at it once more. In that first, failed kathana, they'd inadvertently defined Sesskia's world rather than the reality that the Codex Tiurindi occupied, and all those loose pieces...extra pieces...

Cederic tore away the pages he'd been writing on and began again. Missing pieces, that's what Master Peressten had said, but they couldn't simply be missing, they would have left...call them holes, they would have left holes in *this* world. Places for those missing pieces to fit into. The worlds weren't trying to obliterate each other, they were trying to *meld*.

He set his slate down on a table and rubbed his eyes, then looked at the rest of Denril's research. He'd come so close to the truth—only a few adjustments would make everything clear. Cederic went to rub out an incorrect hypothesis, but stopped before his sleeve touched the wall. No. Denril didn't understand this, or he would have seen what Cederic just had. And Cederic knew Denril well; the man was as proud in his own way as Cederic, though his pride was tied closely to his need for adulation. He would resist any changes Cederic suggested, would insist on using his kathana, and the worlds would be destroyed.

If I do not take charge, he thought, *it will mean the deaths of hundreds of thousands, perhaps millions.* That was not pride, but plain fact. Pride had been telling himself that because he was Kilios he was the superior man; honesty was knowing that being Kilios meant being the superior mage, something objective, something measurable. There was no more time for him to pretend to be Denril Vorantor's subordinate. He would have to take control while still letting Denril believe he had power, and that would be a very fine line on which to dance. But he remembered Sesskia, and the love that was in her eyes when she looked at him, and he felt his confidence returning. She was his foundation, and from that foundation he could do anything.

He scrawled a pair of th'an on the slate that flashed the time at him. Nearly six o'clock, when the mages would be waking, so he had very little time. He ran out of the circle chamber and bounded up the stairs to the Darssan mages' wing. He needed an ally. He needed Master Peressten and the Codex Tiurindi. *Or rather,* he thought, amused, *I need what it does not say.*

***

He sat wearily on the edge of his bed, too tired to remove his sandals. He couldn't remember when he'd last slept—more than a day ago, and he was starting to feel the effects. He wasn't twenty anymore, able to remain alert and awake for forty-eight hours at a time. But it had all been worth it.

Master Peressten had done his job well, once Cederic had gotten him to stop apologizing for his role in Cederic's temporary downfall. He had looked incredibly guilty when Cederic caught him sneaking back to his room, and Cederic had taken a look at the doors and drawn the astonishing conclusion that he and Master Peressten were both happy newlyweds that morning. He sensed Sesskia's hand in bringing her two friends together; Cederic had thought Master Peressten and Master Engilles would never overcome their fears that their respective loves were unrequited. But he concealed his smile so as not to embarrass the young man, who had understood immediately why Cederic was asking him to lie about the contents of the Codex, or at least some of its contents.

Then everything had played out as he'd intended. It had been very enjoyable to see Denril scramble to maintain his control over the mages, more enjoyable to see his awareness of what Cederic had done and his impotent fury at being outmaneuvered. Since Cederic was obeying the letter of his oath, Denril had no way to challenge him except by breaking his, and Cederic had left the room at the end of the day knowing that the mages' allegiance was his now. He couldn't take it for granted, of course, and he would have to work hard to maintain that control, but he felt strong now in a way he hadn't when he was still operating on pride and arrogance.

That part had been easy. What had been hard was spending the day in Sesskia's presence and maintaining the friendly but distant attitude to her he'd perfected in the early days when he was falling in love with her and needed to conceal it. She, for her part, treated him with the same casual friendliness she always had, though once he caught her looking at him and saw her blush, just a little, before looking away. They shouldn't have to hide, they should be celebrating, publicly, the way Master Peressten and Master Engilles were, congratulated by their friends over a raucous midday meal. Cederic couldn't even think of a way to spend the night with his wife.

He leaned wearily over to remove his sandals, feeling exhaustion seep into his joints and muscles. He could at least go to Sesskia's room and bid her good night; that was a habit everyone was aware of, not something that would give either of them away. He eyed his sandals. He shouldn't have removed them, and now it seemed like an impossibility to put them back on. He lay back on his bed and sighed with pleasure. He would rest just for a minute, then visit Sesskia. Maybe she had come up with a plan his tired brain had overlooked. He blinked, closed his eyes, and slid into sleep.

He had strange dreams in which he was manipulated like a puppet and forced to remove his robe, one creaking joint at a time, and then he was sailing through clouds that made slopes he slid down the way he'd sledded down the hills behind his parents' house during winter as a child, and bouncing from peak to peak of the clouds, except the snow was black and pebbly and then he was swimming through it like a dog, paddling with his hands. It all seemed so real that he was disoriented when he woke, and then startled to discover that he wasn't alone in his bed. He jerked in surprise, and Sesskia lifted her head blearily and rolled over to face him. "Is it morning?" she said.

Panic at first made him unable to speak, filling his mind with images of the God-Empress dragging them both away to be tortured, probably in front of one another. He was about to say *This wasn't worth the risk* when another memory surfaced, Sesskia dropping like a stone through the floor of the Sais' wing, Sesskia standing concealed while he and Denril talked, and he laughed at himself and put his arms around her. "I wasn't thinking very clearly last night, was I?" he said.

"You were not, but I think you had a good excuse, what with everything that happened," Sesskia said. Then she scowled at him, an expression whose impact was blunted somewhat by her laughing eyes, and added, "And you should be ashamed of yourself, taking advantage of an ignorant otherworlder who had to find out she was *married* from someone else."

Cederic closed his eyes and groaned. He'd made a huge mistake. Of course Sesskia had no idea of Castaviran marriage customs. Probably spending the night with a man meant nothing in Balaen. She must have been furious that he'd made what to her seemed like a unilateral decision. He opened his eyes. She didn't look furious. She looked mischievous again, that expression that made him want nothing more than to tear the clothes from her body and make her cry out in pleasure. "I take it you decided to forgive me, since you are here now," he said.

She grinned at him, and ran her fingers over his chest—hadn't he been clothed when he fell asleep? "I decided you were worth being married to," she said, and he pulled her close to kiss her and discovered she wasn't wearing anything either. How convenient.

ABOUT THE AUTHOR

Melissa McShane is the author of many fantasy novels, including *Burning Bright, The Book of Secrets,* and *Servant of the Crown.* She lives in the shelter of the mountains out West with her husband, four children and a niece, and three very needy cats. She wrote reviews and critical essays for many years before turning to fiction, which is much more fun than anyone ought to be allowed to have. You can visit her at her website **www.melissamcshanewrites.com** for more information on other books and upcoming releases.

For news, new release announcements, and other fun stuff, sign up for Melissa's newsletter **here.**

If you enjoyed this book, please consider leaving a review at your favorite online retailer or on Goodreads.

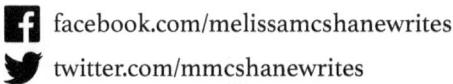 facebook.com/melissamcshanewrites
twitter.com/mmcshanewrites

www.ingramcontent.com/pod-product-compliance
Lightning Source LLC
Chambersburg PA
CBHW070154260626
47160CB00002B/338